THEO STEREN CHAMPLAIN:

A QUEST OF ONE

L.W. Cipriani Jr.

ISBN: 978-1-7342282-0-5

This book is dedicated to my darling wife, Cindy. She believed in me even when I did not believe in myself. Cindy inspired me to carry out my dreams of writing this book. She patiently stuck with me every step of the way.

She inspired my ideas with our deep conversations and painstakingly edited my mistakes. She is one of the brightest people I have ever met and I am blessed to have her in my life.

Table of Contents

Theo Steren Champlain:

A QUEST OF ONE

CHAPTER 0: The Beginning - Thousands Of Trillions Of Years Ago

B efore the beginning of the universe, there was a Void. Living in this Void were nine powerful and magnificent entities who sat on mighty thrones. They came together in a council and decided to make all of creation. However, they hit an impasse in choosing which among them should be king.

Then Atomos, who knew he was the strongest and wisest of them all, suggested a contest of powers to see who could come up with the mightiest creation. This was to demonstrate who was the most worthy of being chief among them. He suggested that the victor should forever wear a diadem of Godhood with the engraving "UKSCOGSM: King of the Gods and the God of the Gods." UKSCOGSM in their language is a designation demanding the utmost respect and reverence for the bearer's authority. Some of the other entities did not understand what was meant by the term 'God' as it was unheard of before creation.

Atomos explained that the term 'God' referred to a supreme being that created a living universe and is in turn recognized by all as being vastly superior. Because they had not created anything yet, there was nothing to be the Gods over. The participants of the contest would earn the title of God because, in the process of obtaining the prize, they would have created something. The term 'King' referred to being a leader and essentially they would be responsible for dictating the direction of this innovative endeavor.

All of the other entities nodded in approval at this suggestion. Atomos also proposed that to solidify the title of the King of the Gods and the God of the Gods, each of them should put one-ninth of their power into the diadem so as to make the leader more powerful than any one of them. This would ensure that the King's will was always enforced.

The other entities agreed, for this seemed very fair in all of their minds. They quickly set to work at devising their creations.

At the proper time (I am using 'time' loosely because the concept of time had not been created yet) when they were all ready to present their creations, the entities began *The Contest of the Nine.*

The first to present her creation was Archituria. Her thick, waist-length, dark brown hair fluttered as she flew up above the other entities. Her dark brown eyes flashed in great concentration as she used the utmost of her powers to create a massive glowing sun. It was the brightest and hottest there ever will be. Her arms were outstretched, supporting the weight of the sun on her shoulders. The sun got bigger and brighter and in so doing, the attractive Archituria held on to it and grew with it. She supported it on her shoulders like a proud parent not willing to let their child take flight on their own. Finally, she allowed the first sun of creation to be free from her embrace and it sat there in the midst of the congregation of the yet untitled Gods.

Archituria was muscular and feminine at the same time, a sort of tomboy as the term did not come into existence as yet. The scorching heat did not have any effect, for it was a mere plaything to her. With the sun shining upon her face with soft unburnt olive skin, she turned to her audience and said, "I have ignited a light in this void to shine bright for all eternity." The other entities marveled at this formation because the sun shone mightily upon them, warming them intensely.

Next, the beautiful Cosmica rose up and as she did so the tresses of her knee-length hair, a deeper black than the deepest recesses of space, flowed and billowed behind her. She reached within herself, mustering all her might and formed a black hole of the darkest matter. The hole was so powerful that it sucked in the sun's rays reaching the entities. Her green eyes flashed with satisfaction as they shone from a round face as beautiful and deadly as her creation.

She stood there, arms akimbo, her skirt fluttering in the vortex of the black hole, but she seemed unmoved by the suction. The pull of the hole tugged at her shirt as well, making it cling to her

CHAPTER 0

strong shoulders. Her caramel skin and lean physique were magnified as she exuded pride in beholding her outstanding handiwork. She authoritatively said, "This brought balance to the sun because there can be no light to shine if there is no darkness to drive away." This too was marveled at by the audience. It was going to be a tough decision indeed.

The craggy Technon followed after her and crafted intricate, metal and flesh men to view the light and fear the darkness. Now, he was the least attractive of the entities, being a bit lanky and not as chiseled faced. Even his muscles were not as defined as the other males and even some of the females. Nonetheless, everyone marveled that such an erudite entity could construct such tiny, wonderful beings. He ran his left hand through his greyish black hair, his soft hazel eyes observing his fragile creations in his right hand. "My comrades, you have produced such wonderful things, should we not have designed beings to enjoy them?" All of the past and future participants of the contest nodded in approval.

Then the mesmerizing Galaxyia stood up and as she did so, her golden body length hair followed her to the middle of the congregation of the entities. Her blue eyes burned with passion and her lips parted with an emotional shout, "All that is in my heart come forth!"

She fashioned a galaxy made up of billowing gases, bright stars, roving comets, orderly solar systems, and beautiful planets. She grew larger as the galaxy formed and eventually surpassed planets themselves. Her long sexy legs lightly walked between the solar systems and as she did so, she trailed her slender red-tipped feminine fingers over her masterpieces.

Examining what she had made, the other entities marveled at her contribution to The Contest of the Nine. This creation joined the ranks of the other creations as grandiloquent. Each planet was more beautiful than the next but their beauty could not compare to Galaxyia, from whose heart the conception was spawned. "Many aspects must be present to compare the beauty of anything. One thing alone cannot make up perfection, but all parts working in harmony," she said. All the entities surely thought she was the winner however, there were still more participants left to present their ideas.

CHAPTER 0

Next went Anthraxis, who poured all his powers into fashioning a great and wicked looking weapon. It was capable of slashing the other contestants' creations into pieces. In addition, he made armor embossed with the ancient language of the nine. In the center of his chest plate was an emblem that showed the mighty sword of War cleaving a galaxy in half. His wicked-looking helmet imitated a bull with bladed horns. The full armor had been made with the blackest dark matter and the reddest metal mixed in agony and destruction.

"The role of lead entity is open and what better way to show might than create something that is capable of defeating the mightiest constructions!" said Anthraxis. His brown muscular arms wielded the great weapon. His dark eyes flashed with passion as he presented the instrument of conquest. He proudly displayed the armor, a defense against anything in all creation. All the other participants, after careful examination, agreed that this was a contest of might and that his weapon and armor were powerful indeed.

Caddeussus stepped forward and with all his essence, produced crystal flowers from his supremely defined chest. His light blue eyes sparkled as he implanted them in all of the other entities' creations. They came alive and sang and worshiped the entities, filling the air with their praises. Everyone marveled at Caddeussus and his entry into the Contest. He nodded his head towards the council and as he did so, blond locks of hair fell in his face. "If you have no consciousness to enjoy the things made, then what good is everything that will ever be created?" This inspired everyone because it was a wise and prudent saying and the other beings nodded their heads in approval.

The strikingly handsome Detrimentus raised his mighty hand and all the other entities' eyes were upon him. He voraciously sucked out the life from the creations of the other participants. It formed the reddest ruby ball possible which swirled with the agony of all that was alive. Standing straight and stoic, he was beyond the epitome of physical perfection with muscles in places that mere mortals could not fathom, if and when they were created. His face contained a solidly chiseled chin and penetrating dark green eyes. His appearance was topped off with thick dark shoulder-length hair and a goatee complete with a ringmaster mustache.

"If there is no end to your existence, then there are no reasons to enjoy the life that you have been given. Therefore I have created death so that all would be grateful for living," he said quietly. This creation moved the other entities because this too made perfect sense in the contest of power for the role of king.

Subsequently, the passionate Heddonna stepped up into the middle of the gathering. Her buttocks length, fiery red hair swirled around her as she gathered power. She passionately spoke into existence, an enormous book. It had a solid *Foreverum* cover embossed with intricate carvings only the original nine entities understood. Foreverum was a metal and stone amalgamate that changed color in the light. It was the strongest substance in the yet uncreated universe. The pages were made of the heaviest crystals, filled with written words penned with brimstone ink. It chronicled the ongoing Contest of the Nine. A pure silver bookmark held the page.

Heddonna's purple eyes flashed and burned with fire as she cradled the book in her hands. She gently passed it around to them, as if it were a newborn baby. All the entities read it as they desired. "This will be a record of events from before the beginning to after the end, keeping our actions alive for the living universe!" she said. All the contest participants agreed and marveled at the importance of her creation.

Finally, all looked to Atomos, who had been sitting in deep thought while this contest among powerful entities was going on. He honestly said, "Well done everyone. Indeed, all of you have proven your great skills. It is now my turn." He stood up and walked with a slow and deliberate stride into the middle of the other beings. He took a deep breath, thrust out his hands and moved back the void with a mighty push of his powerful muscles. Dexterous as a spider with a web, he weaved the walls of the universe with dark matter coated with time and folded over with space.

Next, clasping his hands together, he produced a big bang from his fingertips that was far greater than anything ever seen. The bang radiated across the cleared space, forming everything that was to come. It expanded and reached across time and space to form universes and multiverses. In fact, the blast was so powerful that even today the universe is still expanding.

However, everything stood lifeless. Every atom, molecule and electron stood in their positions. Every single microbe stood still in every corner of the universe not making energy or swimming. The animals, plants and insects stood where they were called into existence. The innumerable birds that were formed on numerous planets were suspended in mid-air. The newly formed waters that held a myriad of fish also stood still. There was not one ion of water moving from its place.

Lava, the lifeblood of planets, did not flow. The clouds of some planets did not drift across the newly formed expanses of skies. The dust storms and raging winds on faraway planets did not sway or blow. No solar winds could be felt. No solar flares or coronal ejections from countless suns occurred. Nothing moved. No galaxy rotated. No black hole swallowed any light particle. Not a breath was heard or felt anywhere and in anything. There was no time because, like all other things, it did not move. There was no life in anything.

Then the great being Atomos raised a mighty right palm to his mouth and inhaled a deep power-filled breath. A breath unlike any other in the entire history of breathing: going from the top of his head to the bottom of his soul. Atomos stopped and let out that breath into his palm. The breath of life coagulated in his hand like a lump of liquid mercury, mixed with supercooled gases, mingled with silicone gel. After he exhaled the last breath from his lungs, Atomos looked around at the other entities. Everyone watched in fascination as he raised his hand and spoke in a mighty voice as deep as the deepest depths of space: "LIVE, MY UNIVERSE!"

The breath of life radiated throughout the universe in an instant. Everything from one end of the universe to the other moved. Atoms moved. Cells moved. Winds blew. Planets rotated in their orbits. Suns shone upon their solar systems. Photons lighted those solar systems. Animals took in the breath of life. Fishes swam. Water moved and trickled. Everything was alive.

Time began to move forward by the nanoseconds. The present became the past as life moved on. When anything and everything moved, they made billions and trillions of multiverses, giving rise to infinite possibilities. Every scenario that could have occurred did happen. Anything that was probable became possible. In the first nanosecond, the past was created along with futures and presents. Time also became self-aware, existing in some parts of the multiverses and not in the rest. *Infinity was also created.* Infinite lives, infinite multiverses, infinite possibilities, all created from that single action.

"Behold, I give you the multiverse and all within. Everything in existence formed by my hand," said Atomos.

All the other entities stood in awe of the creation of the Universe. Atomos' creation encompassed and surpassed all the other beings' accomplishments. They had created impressive things but this design of Atomos was far beyond their wildest imaginations.

All eight beings reverently genuflected before Atomos and hailed him as UKSCOGSM: the King of the Gods and the God of the Gods. The enigma known as *Free Will* was born into existence, from the unparalleled unison that stemmed from the decision to crown Atomos. It would radiate throughout the universe as time unfolded and the will of the entities became apparent. The entities took the diadem of Godhood and placed it upon the head of Atomos. They used their power and engraved the crown. With the title and power given, Atomos stood up and spoke before the council of the entities:

"Behold the multiverse that has won the contest. Behold the diadem of Godhood that you all have willingly placed upon my head. At this moment I decree that all of us have transitioned from entities and have become Gods!" spoke Atomos with pride and joy. There issued a unanimous cheer from his fellow Gods.

Atomos continued, "My fellow Gods, I give you dominion over the universe to do what is decided. All circumstances and their possible outcomes shall be known to us. In addition, I give you the powers to exist in the pasts, presents and futures. Your omniscience and omnipotence shall be eternal."

Atomos continued his speech filled with the adoration coming from the new Gods:

"I am the space between the subatomic particles. I steer their course and dictate their reaction. All the bonds that hold them to one another forming materials, they do at my will. I organize and put into place every living and nonliving particle that was in existence, is in existence, or that will ever be in existence.

The heavens are held up by my will. The Seas bow humbly before me. Each raindrop is fashioned according to my will. Every grain of sand I have called by name and set upon the seashore and in the oceans. There is nothing made that is hidden from my eyes and from my mind. The planets march at my command upon the paths I set for them. They cannot stray unless I wish it. The suns get their power from the palm of my hand. With burning zeal, they carry out my commands. Asteroids are my minions, attacking what I will, sparing whom I wish. I inhabit the space between the planets. They dance for my pleasure, acting according to the role which I have given them.

The universe unfolds like a map before me and everything genuflects before my might. I have set the boundaries of the universe and created them to keep out the Void. I am the universe's architect, cartographer, builder and destroyer. I have created good and made evil without discrimination. Time has no meaning before me, yet it yields to my will. All creation is slave to it, save those that I decree to be outside of time.

My will is the law of the universe, my whim the reality of space and time. All live from the pith of my existence. I am before the beginning of the beginning and will be after the end of the end. I am UKSCOGSM Atomos, the King of the Gods and the God of the Gods." Atomos looked around at each of the Gods and none challenged his authority. He then continued:

"You all have created from your hearts. Now, I will use what you have fashioned to make the perfect roles for you to play in our universe.

Caddeussus I charge you to be the God of Life because you showed that life is essential for enjoying creation. Every creature that is alive, I will give you power upon that life.

Detrimentus I charge you with being the God of Death, so you shall take control of what life gives you. Therefore everything in existence will be balanced betwixt life and death. For both are needed to define the other.

Galaxyia, I will charge you with being the Goddess of Love and Beauty, because your galaxy was full of beauty and planetary attraction that work in unison to achieve perfection.

CHAPTER 0

Cosmica, it is my determination that you be the Goddess of Chaos. You created a black hole that sucks the light out of existence and spreads darkness. This too is subjected to the balance of my universe. Reaching into the lives of all, you both shall exert your influences over whom you will.

Archituria, you created light to brighten the way, therefore I charge you with being the Goddess of the Architecture of Civilizations. You will oversee the rise and fall of Empires throughout the ages, in all of the multiverses.

Anthraxis, since you created a weapon that could cleave a galaxy, I deem you God of War. I put you in charge of conflict and destruction, but I must warn you, do not turn your weapon to the Gods.

Technon you were very wise in inventing creations that could enjoy our works, therefore I make you the God of Technology. Use your discretion and your intellect to make advancements and give them out when the time is right.

Lastly, Heddonna, I will make you the Goddess of Knowledge, because you have chronicled the deeds of the Gods. So shall you be responsible for recording all the information in the universe, of all that was, is and ever will come to pass. Record well, so that all may enjoy the fruits of your labor.

You all must work in unison and exert your power through all of creation in order to have balance in the universe. My fellow Gods, keep in mind that we must influence all but not interfere. In so doing, we will see the outcomes of everything in the universe as it should be."

All the Gods wholeheartedly agreed with Atomos, each one of them knowing that they had made the right choice in bowing to him and making him UKSCOGSM.

Atomos raised his hand and out of nothingness came nine *Temple Planets* that gathered up the thrones of the newly appointed Gods. The size of each of the temple planets was a trillion times the size of the earth's sun. Each temple planet was its own palace that catered to the liking of each of the Gods. Each palace was even more grandiose than the last. Foreverum formed the foundations of the homes of the Gods. There were even more precious metals and stones that embossed the walls and punctuated the features of all of the uniquely designed temple planets. The architecture was far beyond any that all creation could come up with, even if everything pooled their ideas together.

Atomos' throne and temple planet stood in the middle of all the others, a place for them to convene and to make decisions that had to be made. The thrones on the temple planets were in the exact center of the universe.

"All of us shall have a planetary dwelling that is worthy of our Godhood and a temple to carry out the duties of our offices as Gods," said Atomos smiling as he showed the new Gods their gifts. He continued his discourse.

"Consequently, the creations that we, my fellow Gods, have produced to show our might, I deem them *The Contest of the Nine*. I propose that they be kept on display in my temple planet. They will serve as a testament to our powers and the decisions that we have made here.

Now my fellow Gods, heed this decree for it is my will. I will do well by all of you because you have willingly elected me. I shall see to it that all our interests are in my heart from now until all of eternity. I bid all of you to go forth and see the works that I have made. Examine them and touch them. Look at the intricacies of them and ponder on the beauty of them. But above all, I would like you to look into your hearts and minds to see the rightness of what we have done here today. I myself shall inspect your temple planets and make sure everything is as it should be, for your benefit and glory. When we are done we shall convene to talk about the minute details of this creative endeavor. We shall outlay the ground rules for our newfound roles as Gods," said Atomos.

The newly appointed God of Life cheered Atomos on and said, "You are truly the wisest among us and very generous. I speak for all of us in saying that it should be done." All of the other Gods were spellbound at Atomos' speech for they foresaw that he would be a fine King of the Gods.

Consequently, the eight Gods swelling with the excitement of their newly appointed offices went forth and started examining all of creation without delay, just as Atomos commanded.

However, Atomos sat for some time on his mighty throne in the middle of the temple planet that resided in the heart of the newly created universe. He felt the present and future life of everything that there is and ever will be. He knew where each of the molecules in every cell was, and where they would go. He knew who would make what, and when the idea is supposed to take root. He knew just what particles they would breathe in and which would not be used. He could see the decisions that were made and what courses would lead to what outcome.

He envisioned all of the impacts that a single solitary soul would have on the future of others. He saw the rise of ideas and the fall of empires. He saw what some will go through and what others would lose. Atomos being a God saw all and foresaw all. He knows all and knew everything.

His heart welled up with feelings for his new creation, which he produced from the depths of his soul. Everything came from him, everything had a piece of him, from the largest planet to the smallest molecule and tinier. *He loved his creation and that love he bore, spread through the universe and encompassed it and ran through it.*

CHAPTER 1: Theo Steren Champlain

T *heo Steren Champlain* woke up in bed with his lovely dark-brown-haired wife, Catherine, curled up in his arms. His middle name was supposed to be Steven but there was a typo in his birth certificate and he never bothered to rectify that minor inconvenience. It would have taken up too much of his already limited time.

He quickly reached over to turn off the alarm that signaled the start of a new day. He turned his head and smelled his wife's hair, which always smelled like apples. She stirred, knowing that they had to get up but, both she and Theo lazily lay in bed.

Five minutes later, both of them heard the downstairs television turn on to an annoying Saturday morning cartoon. Their six-year-old daughter Katie was watching television as she always did before her parents got up on the weekend.

Both of them completed their morning toiletries almost half asleep. As his wife got out of her nightclothes and into her home clothes, he gazed at her wonderful body and shoulder-length hair as it fell around her face.

He came up behind her as she was reaching for a bra and shirt and hugged his wife, a big squeezing hug and kissed her on the nape of her neck. She smiled breathily and continued to dress. When she finished, she turned around and gave her husband a delicate kiss on the lips and put her hands around his neck.

"Would you like peanut butter pancakes or chocolate chip pancakes for breakfast?"

"I would like peanut butter, please. I'm thinking of doing a veggie omelet. You interested?" said Theo stealing another kiss.

"That sounds perfect. Let's go see what our little Katie cat is up to" Catherine said turning to go.

Catherine's parents were picking Katie up to spend the day with them. That was great because Theo had to work the ten to seven shift that day and Catherine was trying to finish her online class.

Theo worked in a department store that had it all: electronics, hardware, grocery, furniture, appliances, clothes, and home essentials. He was the deputy inter-department manager, a special position that was created just for him. He had all the power, all the responsibilities, all of the hassles and none of the pay. Theo didn't take the manager position because it would mean more hours and more pay, but less time with his wife and daughter. They were the most important thing to him in the world.

Luckily, he had four condominiums that he owned and rented three of them out to pay for the house. The fourth condo was being fixed up by him and his friend John, whenever they had time. John was an old college buddy that he had known for half his life. His labor was cheaper than professional tile guys but equally efficient. The house that he and Catherine bought when they got married was almost paid off, so that was good.

Theo worshiped the ground Catherine walked on ever since they met in college. He never in his wildest dreams thought that a woman of her caliber would ever go out with him, let alone marry him. Catherine gave him the most amazing gift in his life, his daughter Katie. Theo was happy with his in-laws. They were cool and easy to get along with.

During the preparation of breakfast, Theo spied a single lonely piece of his wife's famous apple caramel cheesecake, just sitting dejectedly in a plastic container in the fridge. Apparently, it was waiting patiently to be consumed by an overzealous connoisseur of fine pastries. Theo decided that he was going to save that fine piece of goodness for when he came home later. Some things are worth the wait.

"Are you ready for your big day out with grandma and grandpa my little Katie cat?" said Theo as the three of them sat at the breakfast table.

"Yes, daddy! We're going to the science museum and then we're going to get pizza at the place where they have all the games, and then after that, to see the new movie. I hope I have room for the popcorn! We'll go shopping at the shopping center maybe for clothes and toys. I hope grandma and grandpa packed a lot of money because everything might cost a lot of money!" Katie said excitedly in the innocence of childhood. She was a bright girl and shared her parents' enthusiasm for experiencing new things.

"Wow baby, that's a long list of things. I couldn't remember all of that," smiled Catherine, looking like a field of flowers on a hilltop, freshly sprinkled with dew and illuminated with the first rays of the morning sun.

"Daddy, mommy, what do you get when you cross a border collie with a watermelon?" giggled Katie as she tried her best to suppress laughter long enough to tell the joke.

"I don't know honey," said Theo.

Catherine widened her eyes and looked at Theo and Katie and with a theatrical show of shoulder shrugging, said, "Beats me, Katie. That must be some dog!"

"A melon collie dog (melancholy)!" Katie said bursting out laughing and pointing at her parents.

"Baby, do you know what melancholy means?" asked Catherine.

"Yes," Katie smiled, "It means when you're a little sad, like when you want more ice cream but there isn't anymore and then you feel melancholy. It is different than feeling a big sad like when grandma went to the hospital, and I was sad because she had a booboo she got."

"I taught her that," Theo announced, "You're a bright girl."

"Just like her father. Theo, my parents are really going to enjoy today. They are going to spoil her big time. Let's just hope she doesn't come home with a P-U-P-P-Y just yet," supposed Catherine.

"A PUPPY!" Katie excitedly squeaked, "I know what that spells mommy!"

"No puppy, or kitty, or hamster, or pony, not till you're older, okay. Remember what happened last time. Katie, it's a lot of time and care that goes into having a pet." said Theo as he sipped the last of his coffee.

The doorbell rang as Theo, Catherine and Katie were washing up the dishes. Katie spied her grandparents as she ran and looked through the living room window. She opened the door.

CHAPTER 1

Catherine's parents filed into the living room and dished out hugs and kisses to all that stood in their way.

"Hello pumpkin, how are you today? You ready for a big day of fun?" said grandpa as he knelt to look Katie in the eye. As he did so both his knees popped like burning brush from a bonfire.

His wife, 'grandma' to Katie, smiled and said, "Don't worry his knees are younger than Katie so we'll be fine."

Everyone small talked for a little and then soon realized it was time to go their separate ways. Theo had to go to work, Katie and her grandparents to their fun day of activities and Catherine to her online course. Theo kissed his wife as he left for work, wishing he was on his way home before he even got into the truck. As Catherine closed the door and looked at her husband driving away to work, she glanced at the time and saw it was nine-thirty in the morning, just enough time to shower and get ready for her guest.

John Duboise knocked on the door of Catherine's house at precisely ten o'clock. He had known Theo and Catherine since college and was now their next-door neighbor. John was a member of the neighborhood watch group and often seen hosting parties during the various holidays throughout the year. John was a lean, blond, six-foot-six wall of abs and muscles with short hair and a constant five o'clock shadow.

Catherine opened the door in a white and blue flowered sundress that flowed an inch past her knees. Every time she walked, the dress flayed and swirled around her trim waist and fecund hips revealing shapely legs and calves.

"Come on in John. I wanted to see you for so long." She smiled as he came in and gave her a kiss on the cheek. "Have you eaten?"

"I have," replied John, "but I'm hungry for something else...."

John kissed Catherine full on the lips with a deep passionate kiss that showed how hungry he was for her intimate attentions. Catherine let out a sigh of passion as John finished kissing her. The sundress, whose purity and beauty were accentuated by the delicateness of Catherine Champlain, was now thrown aside carelessly on the love seat. It bore witness to Catherine being

CHAPTER 1

passionately defiled by a ravenous lover upon the living room floor.

CHAPTER 2: The Adventures Of Brentt Williams, Present Day

T he burly twin bouncers were as big as the double doors they were guarding. They were big chinned, square-jawed, no-nonsense kind of bouncers that probably did time in the slammer. The type who wouldn't let their mom inside the establishment even if she owned it, it was her birthday, and she tipped each of them a grand of cold hard cash, sprinkled with hugs and kisses. The hoodlums that they were filtering formed a line to get into the seedy joint. They were all booze and drug-filled ruffians that could have possibly been the bouncers' cellmates. All looked like they would mug you at the sight of a dollar and a pack of minty chewing gum. The shady characters jostled each other under the scrutinizing gaze of the bouncer twins.

Good thing two patrons in the aforementioned line brought some class to the congregation of rabble-rousers. One of them was a surprisingly well-groomed, dark yellow golden retriever. He stood next to a man that looked like he belonged on the cover of a fireman's calendar. Of course, no fireman is complete without a signature mustache and his was looking borderline faux. Both the dog and the man looked out of place, like a bride wearing a wedding dress to a pool party.

Detective Brentt Williams was well shaven (not the whiskers though), muscular and definitely not a criminal. He wore a colorful knitted wool sweater that looked like something a druggie sheep with a hangover barfed up. His grandma happened to pick up the wool and knit it for him. The jeans looked ok, except for the wallet chain thing which went out of style in the 1700s. Well, at least the heavy-duty hiking boots would fend off any attacker if they tried to yank his chain. Brentt and the dog, whose name was Henry (who names their dog that?) were there for the underground dogfighting championships. They both came up to the bouncers.

"What the heck are you doing here with *this* dog?"

"We are here to fight sir," said Brentt very solemnly.

"Your dog looks like he belongs in a hat and sunglasses, on a sofa watching his owners have tea and crumpets while talking about the shenanigans of the wives of somewhere."

"That's a good word. Nice to see the educational system is doing ok."

"Look, buddy, you get your bad Christmas sweater butt out of here and take this furry sack of crap with you!" yelled one of the bouncer twins.

"My dog can fight. In fact, I taught him a move called Eight Ballbreaker. Do you want to see it?"

"Look Shit head, don't make me laugh. Get out……"

"Henry, Eight Ball Breaker!" Brentt interrupted.

Before the bouncer finished his sentence, a change came over Henry and he turned from too scared of his own shadow, into a snarling hound of destruction. Henry lunged at the bouncer, head butting him in the midsection. As the twin doubled down in surprise, Henry pushed up on his hind legs and caught the twin under his chin with the top of his head. The twin fell down, legs apart and stunned. Henry went for the "ball" part in Eight Ballbreaker but stopped short of masticating the bouncer's chew toys.

"I need you to let me through the door before my dog turns your rooster into a cat," said Brentt.

"Ok. Ok, let him through. The cages are to the left. See the cage master. He'll hook you up with the fights," whimpered the bouncer, ready to pee himself.

"Thank you Mister Bouncer. You have been very helpful. Henry, give the man a kiss."

On command, the dog changed from hell hound to docile again and removed his face from the bouncer's balls. He wagged his tail and waited for the quivering bouncer to sit up. Henry went forward, turned on the slobber faucets and lovingly licked the bouncer all over his face. A crowd, who had been privy to the

CHAPTER 2

scene, most of whom didn't care what happened to the bouncer's "bouncing balls", looked on in amusement. A few hired escorts for the bouncer's romantic night out laughed out loud and pointed at the bouncer.

Brentt looked at the scene before him, which made him sick to his stomach. Loads of people geared up to watch trained dogs rip each other apart. In the corner of the cage was a veterinarian, who looked like he only showed up the first week of college and never bothered to go back to school. He was injecting a dog about to fight, with something, probably steroids.

The dog looked like he tried out for Mr. Olympia but they turned him down because he was a dog. The other dog that he was fighting looked equally as terrifying but with one distinction, he was a poodle with a bad Mohawk haircut. Brentt didn't blame the dog for taking his anger at the bad haircut out on someone.

He had to move quickly to get to the security cameras. He needed the footage so that all of the people here could get arrested for participating in such illegal activities. After weeks of investigations and midnight stakeouts, he was finally going to take down these criminals.

Brentt was with the force for thirty years, too long for some, but to him, it seemed like he joined just yesterday. He liked what he did, no-nonsense, no bull, a lot of balls, and a whole lot of heart. He was a good guy who caught bad guys and kept the innocent guys safe.

His parents had been killed in front of him and his three adopted sisters. The bad guys killed them with weapons that he would never forget. The weapons were special daggers that shot lightning, which were supplied by The Immortal Count. He knew the smell of his parents' killers. He could never forget it, like the stench of death only more putrid. He prayed for strength to overcome the attackers, but none of his prayers were heard. He was not strong enough to fend off the attackers and he had held that regret ever since.

After the hooligans scurried away from the fight, he and his sisters met the cold lifeless bodies of their parents on the floorboards of the room. All three curled up in the arms of the dead loved ones that would never hug again. His parents were scientists, cutting edge and full of ideas that would change the world.

"The chaps that installed these cameras were not very neat," he said to Henry the dog as if expecting an answer. The dog looked up and wagged his tail as any ordinary dog would. He followed the cables to a door marked 'No Entry'. The bad guys would take videos and pictures of all who attended, to blackmail some of their clients later if necessary. For example, a sleazy politician with a couple of high priced hookers, watching an illegal dogfight, snorting some illicit drugs or smoking banned cigars.

A guard, who was an employee of *Rent a Henchman Enterprises,* sat in front of the doorway that he needed to go through. He brandished a gun that looked illegal. He was engrossed in watching funny cat videos on his twelve-inch tablet.

"Excuse me old chap I'm looking for the latrine because I need to relieve myself like a MoFo," said Brentt in a deep tough-guy voice.

"What the hell did you say?" asked the confused guard who looked up from his funny cat video.

"I need to take my trouser snake out for a walk. Hey is that a funny cat video? Oh man, I love those!" Brentt said as he leaned in to see the video.

"Yeah, this is pretty funny. Look at this…"

The guard did not have a chance to finish the sentence. Brentt karate-chopped him on the back of his neck like they do in the movies. He slumped back into the chair and Brentt posed the guard to look like he was sleeping.

The tablet was real nice and looked expensive. The case was incredible too. Brentt decided to look through the tablet: phone numbers of bad guys, hookers, probably girlfriends, some games. "Well nothing of educational value here, but I'm sure it will come in handy later," he said to himself. Being real careful, he disabled the location and factory reset the device. He now had a birthday gift for his sister. (It's not bad stealing from bad guys, well not in Brentt's mind anyways.)

He decided to look through the guard's wallet which he found in his front left pocket. Michael Jones: driver's license, library

CHAPTER 2

card, grocery club card, a bulk item grocery club card, electronics store credit card, clothing store credit card, hardware store credit card, university id card, lingerie store discount card (say what?), and three thousand dollars. Can someone say Christmas fund! He grabbed the keys and opened the door.

The room was filled with electronics of all sorts. Monitors that showed every inch of the outside and hard drives that recorded everything. But even with cameras everywhere, somehow they neglected to put a camera in front of the door to the most important room in the building.

Brentt commanded Henry to keep watch outside while he rummaged through the room. He quickly put some device that the precinct had given him to upload the goings-on of the illegal operation to the headquarters of the police. In doing so, the reinforcement could roll in at the correct time which is at the end of it all. The guys back at headquarters should be seeing this now. Brentt got on his cell:

"Hey Chief squared, are you all getting this? I mean this event has every big shot in the city."

"Nice work. I knew I could let you, an undercover cop, go in alone without any backup and you could do what the others couldn't. Do you want me to send backup or should I wait for you to tear the place up and send reinforcements through traffic and construction? They would be delayed until the last possible minute." said Chief squared.

"Send them in now. I'm not feeling a hundred percent. I'll see if I can disrupt any fights in the meantime," replied detective Brentt Williams.

Maxx Chief was the chief of police for the district. It seemed weird to call him Chief Chief so everyone agreed that Chief squared was a better idea. He was a former navy seal that got transferred to black ops then to delta force. The reason he got transferred so much was that he was so good at what he did, but he couldn't tell you because it was top secret. He held five doctorates including hematology, forensic pathology, criminal justice, computer forensics, and law. If that was not enough, he had a bachelor's in liberal studies. Chief had a wife that was as pedigreed as Chief squared and even more tough. She had a 9th-degree black belt in martial arts. Chief squared had only a 5th-degree black belt.

Brentt exited the 'control center' of the complex and headed outside toward the fighting cages. But before he left, he picked up a random box of beef jerky that happened to be the unfinished dinner of whosoever was manning the control room. It just might come in handy.

"Come, Henry, let's go stop some bad guys," said Brentt, not really waiting for an answer in the form of a tail wag.

The fight between the two dogs from earlier was just beginning, he had to act fast. Brentt quickly made his way down the main thoroughfare to the fighting cage as he tore open the beef jerky. He determinedly plowed through the crowds, not caring if he threw the wrappers on the floor. He'd pick it up on the way back.

Scores of rich big wigs clad with their expensive finery sat in anticipation, waiting on the dog that they bet on to win the fight. He had two handfuls of jerky by the time he reached the cage and threw both handfuls in different directions. Both dogs were stunned and stopped fighting at the appearance of jerky in their match. They went for it. The referee looked stunned and so did everyone else in the abandoned warehouse that served as the arena for this savagery.

Nearest Brentt, a huge 32 cubic foot refrigerator of a man, courtesy of 'Rent a Henchman Enterprises', prepared to attack him and Henry. The henchman tried to pull off a right-hand punch that had all the flair of a fighting video game but encountered an epic fail worthy of a viral video. The bruiser would have taken Brentt's head off, had it not been for Henry getting tangled in his legs.

In addition, he would have fallen upon the undercover cop, had not Brentt's great sense of proprioception kick into maximum overdrive. Mid fall, the bruiser was turned and fell flat on his back upon the steps leading to the octagon with the detective landing on him. That knocked the wind out of the giant henchman, but for good measure, Brentt kneed him in the balls. He thought he felt three testicles but Brentt could have been mistaken.

The audience, now in full blood lust frenzy, wanted a show of savagery. They started chanting, "Fight! Fight! Fight," and were determined to get their money's worth. Three more employees of 'Rent a Henchman' pulled up to the scene. They had guns, but no one pulled their weapons out of fear in hitting the clientele. All three rushed at Brentt in their cheaply made bad guy suits and tried to dog-pile him. Brentt threw punches left, right and center, tossing in a few kicks. He was a ninth degree black belt in over a dozen martial arts but really in the heat of the moment, he just focused on not getting his butt kicked.

One guy with a very long goatee and smelled of overpowering cologne, managed to get him in a face-to-face bear hug, pinning his arms to the side. Brentt did what he could, a big bite to the neck. The cologne tasted bad as he drew blood and the burly man staggered back.

Henry was nowhere near to be seen. In fact, he had run off to the cage to stop his fellow canines from fighting, unbeknownst to Brentt. Henry encountered some opposition on the way to the cages in the form of the referee and two handlers. They were quickly dispatched by some head butts to the groins and bites to their calves. Henry barked some orders to the combatants in the ring who were busy chewing their jerky. They looked down at the well-groomed Henry who was about three quarters their size. One could see the amusement in their eyes as they wondered why this noob was giving veteran dogfighters commands.

These dogs were so tough that if they wanted to sleep in their owners' beds, the owners took the dog house, outside. So tough that playing with a full-grown tiger was like playing with a kitten to them. Henry did not back down, he let out a growl/roar that sounded like a lion and a wolf had a child, and he was from that union.

In fact, the frenzied audience that had turned into a bloodthirsty mob, stopped. All of the henchmen that had gone to henchmen school, stopped. All of the dogs that were restless in cages, stopped. Brentt Williams, who was in mid punch to a man's pockmarked face, stopped. They all stopped what they were doing when they heard the unearthly sound coming from

CHAPTER 2

Henry and looked in the ring. The well-groomed dark yellow golden retriever wagged a long fluffy tail in response.

In the seconds of stillness that followed Henry's animal kingdom defying roar, about a hundred policemen burst into the building. They shouted orders and barricaded the exits so that none of the patrons of the illegal dogfighting championships could leave.

Last to arrive on the scene and looking to make a grand entrance was police chief, Maxximillian Chief. He had thrown both of the double steel doors open and knocked out a poor brigand that was trying to escape. An overhead light flickered above him and bathed his six-foot, six-inch frame, which was clad in a standard-issue tan trench coat and black shoes. He towered over the fallen bad guys like an angel that doubled as a demon. He looked like a denizen of justice come to exact his will upon the scores of loathsome rabble that were now bent to his pleasure.

He took off his matching tan fedora ringed with a pink bow that his long-dead daughter had given him. Piercing brown eyes gazed at the scene before him as he ran his hand through the thick black and gray stubble that had taken up residence on his square jaw.

"Damn, this is going to be a lot of paperwork. Well, this doesn't look as bad as last month though," he stated as a matter of fact, in a rare accent. "Brentt Williams, where the hell are you?" he yelled.

Brentt, who released the pockmarked scumbag he was in the middle of punching yelled, "Over here!" However, before he could get another word in, the scumbag brandished a knife, one that looked like the man had owned it since he was a little kid. He courageously stabbed Brentt in his abdomen. You have to commend the guy for not going down without a fight.

As it turned out Brentt's deskmate, Brenda Nga Ling, shot the man dead in his tracks before he could inflict more damage upon her friend. She was by his side as he collapsed upon some panicking older lady wearing what looked like a stupidly expensive dress. His blood dripped on the fabric that cost more than he made in a year, as she wiggled under him. Brenda, who tried to pick up Brentt as best she could, encouraged him to get up. Brentt, thankful for the assist, gained a second wind and forced himself up. Brenda mumbled a quick, insincere apology to the woman and left with the injured cop.

"Brentt, let's go get you checked out and patched up my tall, dark, sexy and bloody man," said Brenda as she put Brentt's arm around her to help him to steady himself.

She really liked him but never had the guts to tell him how she felt. She had dropped clues before, but Brentt was so dense he never got it. Nonetheless, she would follow Brentt anywhere, to hell and back if need be.

The activities that followed were regular police stuff, all presided by Maxx Chief. Names, numbers, reports, searches, seizures, animal cops coming in to take the animals to the vet, expensive lawyers speed-dialed on expensive phones and all the like. Those who needed ambulances were loaded into them by paramedics, photos of the crime scene were taken, and all the other stuff that comes with the territory.

Brentt would not be taken to a hospital, but to a special doctor that had served him well in the past with other injuries. He was Doctor Francisco Mendellsohnn. As Brenda drove him to their destination, he lost consciousness and slipped into a well-deserved dream world.

CHAPTER 3: The Inspection Of The Universe Trillions Of Years Ago

Trillions of years ago, all the Gods, except Atomos, went to visit the planets of the universe to make sure everything was in order. The Gods were walking along the beach of a planet located in Orion's belt as it is called today. It teemed with life and was sustained with the combined efforts of all the Gods. The blue of the waters was as clear as crystal, complete with dolphins jumping for show. The clouds lazily hung in the blue sky and formed different shapes. They occasionally blocked the infant sun that shyly observed the Gods as they walked along the beach. The sands got between the celestial toes of the gorgeous Goddesses who walked barefoot. Each sand particle counted itself lucky to touch their naked feet.

Galaxyia was sporting a yellow sundress that showed off her bare arms and dropped below her knees. Technon had no problem soaking up the radiance that came from her golden hair as he walked alongside her. Galaxyia's bright blue eyes did not match the color of any of the blues on the planet.

Cosmica, similarly clad in a dress of black and white stripes, looked elegant and beautiful. She too had no shoes on.

Heddonna, with her fiery red hair in a ponytail, walked in front of the group. She held her longer purple floral print dress up as she climbed a high rock that overlooked the ocean in all its pristine glory.

Meanwhile, Anthraxis, who lagged behind, fantasized about what his temple planet had to offer.

Suddenly, Caddeussus, Detrimentus and Archituria, rose up from the ocean. All three of them looked like mountains

CHAPTER 3

emerging from the sea. As they walked towards the shore, the shirtless figures of Caddeussus and Detrimentus could be seen shrinking. Archituria decided that she was going to fly. She shrunk herself and flew towards the others on the shore. She was clad in a wetsuit that did not in the least hide her muscular legs. Water glistened upon her abs as she heated herself up and changed into an orange sundress, following suit to the other Goddesses.

"We checked the bottom of the ocean. Everything looks great so far," said Archituria.

Anthraxis picked up a conch along the beach and said, "I think this creation is fragile and weak. Why is it taking up space and more importantly wasting our time?"

"It is fragile because it was made that way by Atomos. Just like the birds were made to soar and the fishes to swim. They were made to do the things that they do, as part of a bigger picture," said Archituria.

"Perhaps Anthraxis, you might like to go play with the dinosaurs. They are very friendly," joked, Cosmica. Her long black hair was in a bun and she decided to let it down at that moment.

Caddeussus and Detrimentus had just come on the shore to be with their fellow Gods. They too, whisked the water from their bodies away in the blink of an eye. Caddeussus then went over to Technon who was examining a sand dollar. "The intricacy of the shell is extraordinary," he said.

"Yes. Atomos did an excellent job with the details and the craftsmanship. Absolutely, perfect. Look at the way the shell protects the creature."

"What use is this tree to me? What use is all of this to anyone?" asked Anthraxis. He placed a hand on a nearby coconut tree and foresaw that its trunk would be made into spears that would be used in wars. "We should make mighty creations that fight for pleasure and conquer in their spare time."

"What use is creating if they only fight and die? Is it not enough that there are beauty and peace in this world with the occasional scuffle for mating rights between animals?" said Technon.

CHAPTER 3

Anthraxis grew taller and more menacing as he got in Technon's face, "It was a little confrontation that got us in the situation of electing a King of the Gods in the first place. Fights start with disagreements, and disagreements start with differences of opinions."

"It is when those differences of opinions are not tolerated, then it leads the way to discord and escalates into violence," stated Galaxyia.

Caddeussus put his hand on Anthraxis' shoulder, "Come on, we have more work to do. There's still some more of creation to inspect. Hey Technon, didn't you say that we had two more planets to check before we had to convene at the center of the universe with UKSCOGSM Atomos?"

"Yes, Caddeussus. One is a volcanic planet and the other is an ice planet. There is a little moon with no life orbiting the volcanic planet as well," said Technon.

"Of course I will record our findings, while you guys do the dirty work. I am going to stay here and enjoy the beach a little bit longer," offered Heddonna as she created a mighty throne and desk from the very sands underfoot. She multiplied herself and soon a couple thousand gorgeous Heddonna's stunned the male Gods. They quickly teleported to the last two planets in question and began their examination. A couple of other Heddonna's stayed behind to keep the others company.

"I think this mountain and valley coming up is the last place we need to examine before we're done here. Oh, by the way, there are giant beasts here like scorpions, ants, cockroaches, and spiders. So be on the lookout. We don't want to ruin any ecological balances," stated Detrimentus. "Let's split up to cover more ground. Who wants to go with whom?"

"I'll go with Technon," said Archituria.

"I got Caddeussus," said Galaxyia happily as she grabbed the God of Life's arm.

"I guess I'll go with Detrimentus," offered Cosmica. Detrimentus felt a little dejected because he wanted to go with Galaxyia, however, he did not let it show on his face. He was grateful that he was still in the company of a beautiful Goddess.

CHAPTER 3

He did not want to pair up with Anthraxis and listen to his whining.

"That leaves Heddonna and Anthraxis," stated Detrimentus.

"I'll take my chances with Archituria and Technon. Anthraxis is a big boy, he could take care of himself" stated Heddonna as she flirtatiously grabbed Technon's arm and pulled him away.

"Okay. You ladies need to protect little ole Technon over there from the big bad spiders," Anthraxis teased in a baby voice.

Heddonna, Technon and Archituria headed down towards the green, lush valley in the shadow of the mountain. The twin suns were at midday and the mountain stood in the middle of the two great balls of blue fire. The picturesque serenity was captivating. The freshness of creation still hung in the air like when you buy a new car and the smell lingers for days or even weeks.

The Gods parted ways and examined the last parts of the planet. Everything was in pristine order, as it should be because Atomos made everything perfect. When the inspection finished, they decided to move on to the ice and the volcanic planets.

"We'll inspect both of the planets at once. Besides Heddonna's already started," said Caddeussus as he multiplied himself a million times over. "Half of us go for the ice planet and half for the volcanic planet."

The six other Gods thought that was a great idea and followed suit. The inspection of the last two remaining planets in the galaxy was complete. The Gods congregated above the remote moon, a planetoid located between the two opposing planets at the far edge of the galaxy. It was barren and the coldness of the rock could be felt by the Gods. Each of them knew everything that was happening on the planetoid. All of the molecules and dust particles that composed the craggy rock wasteland were read like a book. Nothing of supreme importance was there, just minerals and rocks locked in an orbit between the volcanic and ice planets.

It happened that a pod of Korsol fish was in the process of mating at the equator on the ice planet. Korsol fishes are 100 feet

long and 60 feet wide at the largest fin span. They look like black
sharks with a white stripe going down the middle of their lateral
sides. They have rows of stubby teeth for grinding and a very
long tongue for scavenging off the seafloor. Two mid-sized arms
with four sharp claws punctuated this bizarre-looking creature.

"Even at the dawn of creation there is a difference of
opinions," spoke Anthraxis deep in thought as he looked down at
the planet, so full of life.

"What do you mean?" asked a puzzled Caddeussus.

"The fish down there are jostling for mating rights. It seems
to mirror our own action, in choosing who was to be leader of
the Gods," answered Anthraxis.

"How is that even comparable? They are just insignificant fish
and we are mighty Gods," stated Archituria succinctly.

"The differences of opinions are the same. It is why we
created what we did before the beginning," Anthraxis pressed,
"Unfortunately, your disconnectedness from the fish proves that
you are not as vested in this creation just like the rest of us."

"Why do you say that?" asked Heddonna as she focused on
Anthraxis.

"When you forged your book, did it come from your heart?"
asked Anthraxis.

"Yes, I poured my soul into it. We all poured our being into
our creations," answered Heddonna.

"What has this to do with anything Anthraxis?" queried
Caddeussus.

"The point of that endeavor was to pick a leader to guide us in
crafting a living universe to be Gods over. However, Atomos
went ahead and forged the universe on his own. You are not
supremely interested in things that you did not create, are you?"
inquired Anthraxis.

"He created something that surpassed all of ours and it won
him the right to be crowned. I admit that we ought to have had
more input into things. I personally do not feel as close to these
creations as I should." offered Galaxyia speaking up.

"Nonetheless, the embodiment of the universe stands in the
temple planet of Atomos along with the other Contest of the
Nine. We all willingly chose him as king. We know what

happened before the beginning because we all were there," chided Cosmica.

"Before the beginning, we were all equals and now after the beginning, we are subjects to a master," hissed Anthraxis.

"That is what a leader is. You have to lead followers," Technon jumped in.

"He led us, no deceived us, into giving him our powers as well," stated Anthraxis, waiting a little to let that revelation sink in.

"I don't think Atomos would do that. I feel it," advocated Detrimentus.

"I don't believe it either," supported Technon.

"Do you all hear yourselves? Atomos is nine times more powerful than all of us with that diadem on. This does not concern you? He tricked us by already creating the universe. Then he tries to make us feel important with the bribes of our temple planets," emphasized Anthraxis.

"He does make a valid point. We were our own beings before and now we have titles. We are the Gods of something or the other. You need to classify the work of running a universe, but I also see the need for more input from the others as well. That equality went out the proverbial window when we put that crown on his head," supposed Caddeussus.

"Thank you, someone, who sees the direction I am going. My first point is that he created all of this." Anthraxis waved his hand at the newborn universe that came into existence by the will of Atomos. "Second, he tricked us into giving him our powers. What he made was just an amalgamation of our ideas," argued Anthraxis.

"Were those fishes your ideas? How about the trees that we saw or the sand dollars? Not your ideas, if anything they were closest to Technon's," piped Archituria.

"Thanks, I appreciate that," Technon said as he nodded to the brown-haired Goddess. Turning to Anthraxis, "Maybe Atomos wanted to show that if we pooled our creations, something great could happen. Look at this universe."

"You think this universe is great? Look at everything: they are in opposition to one another. From the galaxies to the planets:

from the animals to the very tiniest atoms: all in opposition. Just like the fishes that this conversation started with and even with us, before the beginning," implored Anthraxis.

All of the Gods had seen the universe because they had just finished examining it and found that it was very good. However, it was very good for the wrong reasons. They had no input in building this masterful creation. It was the work of one being alone, with them as supplementary help. Deep in their hearts, there was some truth to the story. They could not deny the exquisite nature of the universe's craftsmanship but they wondered about the integrity of the maker himself.

"Everything is in conflict. If you look all around, the planets are pulling and pushing one another. Just like the atoms and molecules that the planets are made of, they are in opposition. Look at a solar system, a sun to surpass all the others with its gravitational pull and planets fighting to hold on to their little moons. These things show imbalance just as there is an imbalance among the ranks of the Gods. Black holes, which are newly formed, will eventually amalgamate everything in their paths, warping space and time to fit their will. They are in the midst of most galaxies, ready to feed.

So much destruction of life and for no purpose other than it is predetermined. I invite you all to look at the futures of everything in the universe. Everything dictated by the will of Atomos," coaxed Anthraxis.

"Yes, I see some beautiful planets being destroyed in the distant futures. Some civilizations that have created beautiful cities and wonders, lost to destruction. Innocent children, gone before they reach adulthood. I know you can see beautiful paradises vaporized by disasters and cute animals destroyed in fiery deaths. Plants blooming in fields as far as the eye can see, destroyed in an instant. So much loss of creation, so randomly and to what end?

However, even though we cannot read the mind of Atomos and the minds of each other, the futures of the universes are there for all of us to control. We all can see our part in the universal picture even until the end. In every system created,

CHAPTER 3

there must be someone to lead. Atomos set that example for us to follow," said Galaxyia, innocently.

"Why destroy something that you create?" queried Caddeussus.

"We can see the futures of everything. What is the purpose of that destruction? What does Atomos plan? The predetermination of things for no purpose other than to take up time and space? Even though I am the God of War, I do not condone needless destruction!" asserted Anthraxis.

"Why does he see the need to destroy altogether? It is to appreciate what has been taken away just as life and death, beauty and unsightliness. However, I do see the point of not creating if only to destroy," Cosmica hesitantly offered.

"That would possibly negate our positions if everything were equal." supplemented Heddonna.

"What is your plan then...if you had been chosen as king?" asked Technon cautiously.

"Not king, just a guide for us. Everything would stay as it should be, not in conflict but in harmony for our pleasure. There would be no destruction and cataclysms with lives lost, without a higher purpose. Nothing would be predetermined pointlessly. We would be equals in the universe and not subjects and master," spoke the God of War, as he rode the attentions of the other Gods.

"Everything has a purpose now," said Caddeussus sternly.

"Everything would answer to us. Do you think that the Korsol fish down there know we are up here? No, they are too busy fighting to mate with each other. They don't say 'what is Technon up to today?' or 'how does Galaxyia look?'. NO. What is on their minds? They are thinking of mating. Do you think criminals think about their victims? No, just what they can get. Do you think a volcano or earthquake care about their victims?

Even though Atomos predetermined everything, what use is making a decision if it is already determined for you, in any multiverse? All the potential, destructive freedom that Atomos has allowed, would not occur if I had led us as equals in this endeavor." stated Anthraxis vehemently.

CHAPTER 3

"I feel that what is to be done with this creation is that they have to do what they were designed to do. Atomos has predetermined what they should do, their courses are set. Yes, they have some choice but ultimately the parameters have been given to what they could do.

Take for instance the invention of the automobile. It is used to transport people to and from places. That is what it was built to do. People have lived in their cars. People have blown up their cars. People have killed people with their cars. That freedom has parameters. The car was built to do something specific and even though it has the freedom to do other things, it does what it was made to do," argued Caddeussus.

"What you are saying is that a car cannot be anything more than a car? What about an ambulance? It saves lives. Does that apply to people too? The choices made in the universe will lead to a predetermined outcome, but the person making the decision does not know that. Everything not knowing the outcome, but we Gods do. That is why we are here and the creations are there," spoke Heddonna very passionately.

"There cannot be equals on a project that requires a leader. Someone must make the calls," rebuffed Technon. "That's what being a God is, predetermining things so that the outcome is as it should be."

"What about choices that aren't made by anyone, but are imposed by us. Tell that to all the people that will lose loved ones in the future for no reason. Tell that to the cities that have been wiped out in the future. There are galaxies that have not grown to capacity but, are all doomed before they even existed. What do you tell a mother whose child is born dead? How do you tell a 4-year-old girl, who has a life-threatening disease, that she will not live to see her sixth birthday?" glared Anthraxis.

"I admit that you have some great philosophical claims, Anthraxis. However, if we build something and don't know the outcome then we are not as powerful as we thought. Things have to be predetermined so that we are in control. You are arguing that having constructed a plan for everything, negated freedom of choice. However, that is what a plan is in the first place," rebutted Detrimentus.

CHAPTER 3

"How can there be freedom of choice when everything was prearranged even before the creation of the things that have to make those future choices? I do not agree to it," said Anthraxis, now turning to Technon, getting in his face. "The funny thing is that, as I said before, conflict existed even before there was King of the Gods. That's how we got a King in the first place. Who is to say that Atomos did not predetermine that too? He's a crafty one."

"Do you mean that he should not have been King of the Gods? What about freedom of choice? We all chose the King of the Gods. We all chose Atomos as UKSCOGSM," Cosmica frankly stated.

"There was no treachery involved in us choosing the King. We did that of our own volition," argued Heddonna, now exasperated with this conversation.

"Do not go any further with your treasonous talk Anthraxis. Atomos is wise but he is also just" Technon raised his voice in a stern warning. "Your treasonous talk of Atomos is out of place. We are inspecting creation and you have to know your place. Atomos will hear about this travesty at the council meeting," Technon seethed as he pointed a finger at Anthraxis.

The other Gods felt that the situation was getting tense and stepped closer to intervene if needed.

"Ok guys. That's enough! Anthraxis, Technon, we'll let Atomos sort this out," shouted Caddeussus.

"That was something. Apparently, all of us are not used to having a leader, because we were all just recently equals before the creation of this universe. That being said, we all did agree to follow the King of the Gods no matter who it was. Yes, we all see that there will be destruction and chaos and disorder in the future, but we have to trust Atomos. Are we not Gods that know what was, what is, and what will be?" Heddonna spoke thoughtfully.

Detrimentus, Galaxyia, Cosmica, and Caddeussus grasped the chiseled arms and muscled chest of Anthraxis and parted him from Technon. Heddonna and Archituria held the God of Technology back. There was a collective sigh of relief as the situation seemed to fizzle out. Anthraxis wrenched himself free from the grips of the others. He stepped back from the group and glared at each one.

"Before I leave you imbeciles, when we were choosing a King, Atomos himself suggested the diadem of Godhood! I am going to my temple planet. At least there I am in the company of like-minded individuals, namely me!" said Anthraxis with a sarcastic snort. He then spirited himself away from the bunch, leaving all of them speechless.

Finally, after a few minutes of silence, Heddonna spoke up and broke the awkwardness of the situation, "I don't really think there's a time we have to be at the Temple of Atomos."

"I will go to tell Atomos of the incident nonetheless. He must be made aware," stated Technon.

"I would like to go with you, Technon. I want to see the outcome of this interesting situation," supposed Archituria.

"Yes, as do I. I just feel sad that the newness of creation has to be marred by doubts about the creator," said Heddonna

"Hey we still have this rock to look at!" exclaimed Galaxyia.

"I've looked over it from here. Give it a once over if you want. Anthraxis is a mood killer in the worst way. But I do have to give him points for a good argument. He has made some valid claims," stated Detrimentus.

"I think we should all go to our temple planets and relax for a few. That will calm our minds," suggested Cosmica. Everyone agreed that this was a great idea and teleported to their temple planets.

All except Caddeussus, who stood there, in the cold depths of space, as he thoughtfully, overlooked the planetoid.

The God of Life was pondering about what Anthraxis said before he left. About how Atomos created the universe without the other Gods' input. Caddeussus suspected that to be true. This universe was created and everything followed the will of Atomos. Why would he do that? Anthraxis was also right in inferring that conflict was an inevitable part of this universe. A difference of opinions is what started The Contest of the Nine. Before creation, all of the Gods were equal. In fact, they were powerful beings and not really Gods of anything. He mechanically flew to the barren planetoid and landed in the depths of a gorge.

Was this what the King of the Gods had planned? Atomos, what were you thinking? All these lives lost and made, for what purpose? He walked around the wasteland feeling every moving particle that made up this area. Each molecule and atom had no motion before the breath of life was breathed into them by Atomos. Deep in thought he walked, looking at everything but not really seeing.

Suddenly, he mashed something gooey and blackish gray, like putty that had some oil on it. How did he not see this thing underfoot? Caddeussus picked it up and rolled it around in his fingers. He could foresee no future or past for the thing in front of him. There was no multiverse version of this goop. He did not see the atoms moving in it, nor the makeup of the thing. There was no knowledge of the thing before him.

He examined the place and found more of the unknown gray putty. In addition, he spied some marks where something had dragged itself. Had this thing been alive? He followed the tracks to a hole that lay under a massive stone. The big boulder, rich with iron and minerals, weighed about a hundred tons. It blocked an entrance to a cave. He moved it without breaking a sweat.

The normally seventy-foot tall God had to shrink himself to six feet in order to slide into the cavern. There was no light so he quickly made a sun ball and held it in his hand. He saw that the cavern had pieces of the gray putty strewn about the cave and it lead deeper into the cavern. He followed the slope to a gooey pool of the substance and looked at it. He could sense nothing from the pool. It was as if it never existed. Summoning a flower from his chest, he gently laid it in the grayish putty and stepped back.

CHAPTER 4: Theo Came Home To A Very Bad Day, Present Day

Theo Steren Champlain was very good at his job, but it was the ultimate conundrum because he abhorred it. He started out bright-eyed and bushy-tailed. His ears were filled with promises of rewards for hard work but that led to letdowns galore. No matter what he did, it was always an uphill battle. Everything had to be hard-fought. In every job that he did, Theo made it his business to know it all. But for all his knowledge. there came the time when he knew that he wasn't going anywhere.

Like any other day, he was busy doing menial tasks that needed to be done. Some of the other employees were slackers when it came to their work. Theo, however, had a family to provide for and that drove him to be his best. He often felt mentally and physically drained.

At this moment, he happened to be in the grocery section of the store and was making sure the temperatures on the meat cases were nominal. An average Jane mom came up to him and nonchalantly asked:

"Excuse me, sir?"

"Hi miss, how can I help you?"

"What's the difference between pork ribs and beef ribs? I'm having a BBQ on Sunday and I can't decide which one."

Theo stunned at the question took a minute to process the answer.

"Well miss, they're two different colors. The pork back ribs are a brown and pinkish color and the beef back ribs are more red and white in color. Both taste great and come from two tasty animals. Now any BBQ needs variety and having both could make you a great hit with your guests. In fact, I would suggest

CHAPTER 4

you throw in some BBQ chicken as well to make it an even better party."

"That sounds very good. How much do I get?"

"How many people are coming? Are they big eaters? I figure about two beef ribs, one chicken leg quarter, plus about four pork ribs per person and you got a total. Oh, don't forget the leftovers. I recommend some hickory-smoked BBQ sauce for the beef, some tangy BBQ sauce for the chicken, and mesquite seasoning for the pork. That'll be some great eating. What time should I be over?"

"You are very helpful," Jane mom giggled, "thank you."

"No problem. Have a nice day," Theo said as he walked away. He continued to check the aisles for anything out of place and if customers needed help. His manager, Benjamin Doyle accosted him:

"Hey, Theo, I need to speak to you right now. It's very important."

"Ok boss, what's up? Anything I can help you with?"

"We don't have enough hours to go around, Theo. I 'm going to have to send you home early. You're ... well expendable for now. You get paid a lot, so not having you here is burning less money. You know how it is; businesses are cutting back and hiring fewer people. Don't worry, you're too valuable to let go, just too expensive to have around all the time."

"Ok. I guess I'll head home then. Two o'clock now, just in time for lunch. See you tomorrow Doyle." Theo replied. Doyle sadly waved him off.

Imprisoned in the cold dark abyss of the 32 cubic foot, luxury refrigerator, sat the overpriced but hardy plastic container that confined the lonely apple caramel cheesecake slice. It was segregated from the other inmates. The slice, doomed to a commuted sentence of consumption by Theo, did not try to escape. The apple caramel slice passed the time in silence, only interrupted by the occasional defrost cycle motors. Suddenly, without warning, the fridge doors opened and light bathed the contents of the cold prison.

The apple caramel cheesecake that was hidden behind a few containers of leftover food, found itself being dragged to the executioner's block before its time, by an unknown hand that was not Theo's. Abruptly the fridge doors closed and the inmates of the refrigerator were once again doomed to a cold, dark dungeon awaiting their time of extermination. The delicious slice was laid on a plate and put into the microwave to heat up for 30 seconds, just right for the taking.

John was completely naked in Theo's kitchen, leaning against the dark brown wood paneling of the cupboards, waiting for the slice to heat up. He and Catherine had begun their clandestine activities in the living room and then barely made it to the bedroom. John got hungry and went for the thing that looked the best in the fridge: the apple caramel cheesecake. While the comestible was being heated, John thought about Catherine and their lovemaking. Surprisingly, he did not feel guilty that he cheated with Catherine on Theo. He was a nice guy, but not good enough for Catherine. John hated not openly having her. The cheesecake was ready.

John came into the bedroom carrying the cheesecake and reclined on Theo's bed. He was fully satisfied not only by their recent rendezvous but also by the gooey goodness that was the apple caramel cheesecake. It was about two o'clock when he put the plate by the bedside, the caramel stains and crumbs, the only reminder that any slice had ever existed.

Theo thought of calling Catherine but he didn't want to disturb her in case she was in the middle of an online test. He knew how important it was for her to complete the online Psychology degree. It was what Catherine wanted and he would support her always. Catherine was investing in their family's future and so was he. That's why he'd bought fixer-upper condominiums.

CHAPTER 4

It took Theo twenty minutes to reach home without traffic. The ride in the truck home was a smooth one, owing to the vehicle having a powerful engine and excellent shocks. He knew that companies started cutting people's hours first and then laying them off after. He hoped his family would be okay. He and Catherine always were on the same page and stuck together.

Theo pulled the car into the driveway instead of the garage because he might be going out for food if Catherine decided she wanted something. Theo went through the front door and noiselessly closed it.

He had oiled the doors so that when he had to work the early shifts he would not wake his wife and daughter. He looked in the downstairs office, which was to the left of the front door and did not see Catherine. He figured she must be upstairs in the room. He climbed up the stairs and went to his room where he met the door ajar. He pushed it open.

Catherine was naked and cuddling with John. John looked stunned at the sight of Theo staring at them. Catherine was equally startled to see Theo.

A number of thoughts ran through Theo's mind as he struggled to make sense of what was before him. His first instinct was to start throwing punches, but that would not have undone the things that were done to his wife. Secondly, he might go to jail, but he would still have the satisfaction of kicking some butt. However, he could not be with his daughter if he was in jail. So, Theo had to put away his emotions and keep as calm as he could in this situation.

He stood in stunned silence, taking deep breaths, trying to fight down the rage swelling up inside him. He was hurt and confused at the same time.

"Theo, please, I can explain. Actually, I can't, but please!" pleaded Catherine. John made no move to put clothes on. Catherine got off the bed and stood at the foot of it. Tears welled up in her eyes, "Please."

"I ...ahh....we" John was trying to talk. Theo paid him no attention.

"Stop, all of you. I'm going to get a piece of apple caramel cheesecake that I had set aside for dinner and then I will come back to figure out what is going on. Right now this is too messed up to deal with." Theo waved them off and went into the fridge to get the apple caramel cheesecake but it was not there.

It had escaped execution by his hands and stomach. While Theo had gone to find the desert, the occupants in the room were trying to decide what to do next. Catherine was still naked at the foot of the bed, tears streaming down her cheeks. Theo stormed back in the room and came face to face with Catherine. His eyes wildly looked for the dessert and found its decaying remnants on the plate, left there by the perpetrator.

"Theo, look at me," Catherine said as she grabbed his face and looked in his eyes, "Theo, please, I didn't mean to hurt you, please don't."

"Don't what? How long Catherine, how long? Why?" Theo said breathlessly.

Catherine took her hands from his face and looked down either in shame or disbelief, "Six years. I have been seeing him behind your back for six years."

John suddenly entered into the conversation, "Yeah I've been with her for six years. Every single day you leave for work I come over."

"John, enough," piped Catherine.

"You've been seeing him during our whole marriage? Why would you do that? I love you. I was a good husband. We were happy. Did you eat my apple caramel cheesecake?" fumed Theo.

"I did," said John.

"You're a monster! You stole my marriage! All these years have gone down the drain. You desecrated my wife. I trusted you, John, I trusted you. You're my child's godparent for heaven's sake! But I can't believe that you took my god damn piece of apple caramel cheesecake! It's not enough for you to take my life away. You ate my dessert!!!"

"Dude, you're more upset about some stupid cake than me with your wife?" John broke in.

"Why do this Catherine, why?" Theo seethed and queried, "Why did you marry me if only to cheat for six years, Catherine?"

"You're a good man. You were not as wild and fast as some of the other guys that I'm used to dating. That was what drew me to you. You took the time to get to know the real me instead of getting in my pants. You gave me all your attention instead of ditching me to go out with friends and party. In your own words, you worshiped the ground I walked on and I liked that. When we got engaged, the reality of being married set in and that's when I knew I had a good man, but I didn't know how to commit to being a good wife. I guess I wanted the stability of a husband but at the same time keep the assurance of being able to do my own thing."

Theo felt stifled as his world was collapsing in front of him. The love he had for his wife turned off like a light switch in his heart. Tears of anger doused the burning fire that he had felt for his wife. The memories that both of them had made through the years came rushing back to him like a tsunami in his mind, carrying with it all the emotions that accompanied each event. He stood there as the voices of the adulterers John and Catherine were drowned in a sea of emotions that Theo was floating in. Theo snapped back to the situation.

"I needed some excitement in my life. I needed to get away from being the mommy or the good wife. I love you but, it's just that the physical attraction went away over time. With John, I got it back. Honey, we can work this out, we can get help."

"You're not getting her she's mine. She's been mine for the last six years. I don't know what she sees in you. I don't even know why she married you. You're a nice enough guy but she's too good for you," held John.

"We're beyond help. The minute you said six years it was over. I'm going to get my stuff and move out. You can have everything else. I don't care. Tomorrow I'm going to the doctor and get tested for every STD and STI known to man. Then I'm going to change my mailing address. I'm going to shut down our joint bank account. Oh yeah, you'll have to see about Katie. Explain to her what happened. I don't know how she'll handle this. I don't need to fight for you. I lost the fight before we even got married. I'm getting a divorce," Theo solemnly said, turning to leave.

He went to the garage to find the sixty-gallon wheeled totes that he'd gotten at a variety store. He had bought them for storing holiday decorations. They were going to hold his belongings when he moved out. When he carried the tote upstairs, Catherine was all dressed but John was still naked. Theo's demeanor was unflappable in the face of such brazen defiance.

He continued to remove clothes from the drawers and then put the gaming consoles between the clothes for padding. He then went to his walk-in closet and started pulling things down and stuffing them into the tote. When one was full, he filled another one. He piled in the blue rays from downstairs, all collectors, all his, in the totes and padded them with a sleeping bag. Soon tote after tote was filled with all of his belongings.

Meanwhile, Catherine had gone downstairs to watch Theo gather his things in silence. Catherine sat motionless on the couch, the weight of the situation bearing upon her shoulders like a ton of bricks.

Theo put all of the totes downstairs and with the rage that swelled up inside, he hoisted all of the heavy containers into his truck. Catherine watched in muteness. She studied all of Theo's movements carefully and contritely, but no inkling of regret was portrayed in Theo's demeanor. He finished packing in two hours.

Angry, he stood motionless in the archway of the front door. "Damn, I forgot my cell charger." He went upstairs to get it and found John still reclining on the bed, naked.

"I am taking everything from you, Theo. Whatever I haven't taken yet, I'll get," John said laughing. Theo did not give him a second glance.

Theo expertly reconnoitered the upstairs and then slowly walked down the stairs, knowing full well that this was his last time inside of this house. He then walked around downstairs making sure he did not miss anything. He stopped in front of Catherine and stared down at her. She had missed a few buttons when she hastily got dressed, "Thank you for giving me a daughter. When we both had time to think after a few days, we'll have to do the inevitable."

It was about seven o'clock when Theo finished unloading his things from the truck and into the two-bedroom condo that he owned. Lugging the totes with his things up the stairs wasn't as

CHAPTER 4

heavy as the heart in his chest. There was no furniture except for a fridge, stove and a microwave. He sat there, in the dark, with his back against the wall and cried until no more tears could come.

CHAPTER 5: The Adventures At Dinner

The air was warmer than he had anticipated, but he knew that by the end of the night it would get colder. Martin Luther was glad for the extra-large sackcloth robe that kept him a little hot on his evening stroll to his hosts' house. It would keep him warm on the stroll back in the wee hours of the morning.

The aging footman, Haggins, let him through the ornate wrought iron gate that held the path to the magnificent mansion. Actually, it looked more like a castle that was straight out of a creepy horror film, complete with surprisingly well-manicured grounds.

About ten horses were grazing to his right and most of them were facing away from him. They casually took a pause from their evening meal of grass and more grass to look at him. The monk felt uneasy by the mischievous looks the horses gave him. They should be familiar with him by now. He had been coming here for the past five years. He wasn't an animal person. The animals he did get along with were usually on his dinner plate. He was also amiable with his cat, Pawper. The cat was out most of the time, so that was a win-win situation.

He stopped to look at the beautiful mares and stallions then all of a sudden, he knew why they had devious smiles on their faces. All ten horses had farted in his direction. It stunk really bad. A wind from nowhere blew the stench away and thwarted the plans of the fiendish horses. The man grabbed for the marble rosary that hung around his neck and passionately offered up a prayer to the Almighty for that small miracle. He also prayed for the horses' souls, though not as fervently as he should have.

He was a monk that had dedicated his life in service to God and the church. His mentor had given him the Rosary that he clutched passionately. He completed the walk to the stairs leading to the imposing front door of the castle-looking mansion.

CHAPTER 5

Martin stood at the foot of the stairs trying to decide if the figure standing guard upon the door looked like either a really ugly angel or a really pretty demon. He couldn't tell after all these years and he did not have the courage to ask his friend what it was. His friend had carved the door himself. He had put a lot of time, effort and love into the woodwork. Martin did not want to hurt his friend's feelings.

He could smell the succulent lamb, the warm bread and the freshly baked cake from just beyond the door. He raised a hairy arm to knock on the door but the occupant, somehow clairvoyant, opened it before he touched the wood.

Brentt Williams' dad, Dr. Henry Williams, was a man of great scientific prowess in an age where religion was god and it looked upon science as the devil. That age was 1495 A.D. He was truly a renaissance man before the word was even invented and before the renaissance had ever begun. He knew much about astronomy, biology, anatomy and physics, albeit in the age where the scientific disciplines were in their infancy. His wife Flora Smith Williams was very prominent in the ladies' circle with her cosmetics and fashion line.

However, behind closed doors, she and her husband discussed scientific and theological issues that no noble-born lady would be caught dead discussing. Henry Williams thought his wife should have a doctorate because she was so smart. Actually, she showed more proficiency than most of the men who were doctors themselves. Their circle of friends both liked them and envied them because of their great love for one another and their love for their son, Brentt Williams.

Bertha Fossway, Agness Clairmont and Lynne Lyons, all fourteen years of age, had come to live with the Williams about two years ago. They had become quite fond of the family. Brentt's parents had taught them the science of things. Henry and Flora had learned that the three girls were extremely intelligent, especially in math and science. They were smarter than most of their cohorts.

However, they had been told that they had to hold their tongues because it might make others feel bad. Brentt was equally as gifted and all of them got along well in the family residence.

CHAPTER 5

A common sight at the Williams house was that of a humble monk named Martin. Every so often he would come over for dinner from his monastery. However, this evening was to be inspirational.

"Martin, how are you? It's good to see you," asked Dr. Henry Williams as his guest came through the doorway.

"Very good, my friend, I can smell your food from outside."

"Yes, Flora is a very good cook. She comes up with the most amazing recipes."

"I have something that I need you to see, some of my research that I was telling you about. I have an incomplete copy here and I would like you to review it. It is very sensitive and if found by the wrong people, it could be ...," said the monk very cautiously.

"As always, dinner first then everything else afterward," soothed Dr. Henry Williams.

"Lately, I've been seeing shadows around every corner. Hearing footsteps at every door and seeing imaginary enemies in everything. I thought that even your horses were plotting against me tonight."

"Martin, my horses don't like me most of the time. When I dangle a carrot in front of them, they acquiesce begrudgingly," said Dr. Henry Williams, jokingly.

Debora Smith, Flora's mom, was setting the table in preparation for the feast that she and her daughter had prepared. She had come to visit Flora and Henry for a few days. She got along great with her son in law and beamed with happiness for her daughter.

"Come on gentlemen, time for dinner!" announced Flora excitedly.

Her thick shoulder-length blond hair was tied back in a ponytail. Her bright blue eyes shone with love and adoration for her family. She beamed with pride at the preparation of a fantastic meal. She loved to see her family eat and enjoy themselves. She herself maintained a very shapely figure because she practiced ancient Indian yoga techniques. Her circle of friends did not know of her practices and she liked to keep it that way.

CHAPTER 5

She was glad that her curious mind had found a soulmate in Henry. He challenged her mentally and supported her emotionally, not to mention he was a handsome gentleman. When he first found out about her Indian Yoga texts, he was surprised, but he came around and now they practice every day together. There were other more erotic texts that they read. They passionately practiced those as well.

Dinner was excellent and eaten in silence as Dr. Henry Williams preferred it. He believed his wife's food should be thoroughly enjoyed and not supplanted by commonplace speech.

The night's menu consisted of roasted lamb exquisitely seasoned with garlic, black pepper, salt, and oregano. Additionally, some onions, carrots, celery and potatoes were also roasted and drizzled with the drippings from the lamb. Freshly baked bread, sprinkled with finely grated cheese, gave off an irresistible aroma.

The beverages served with dinner were equally as exquisite. Water from the coolest, cleanest mountain spring Martin had ever drunk from, wet his pallet. Expertly pressed and filtered apple juice, lovingly hand-picked from the well-tended gardens, tasted refreshing. Lastly, fresh milk precisely chilled by putting it in the river in a sealed wineskin rounded off the drinks.

During dinner, all of the Williams and their guest lusted after the centerpiece of sweet goodness sitting in the middle of the dining room table. It was a gift from Flora Smith Williams. A carrot cake that looked fit for a king and his court, the crowning jewel of the night. Freshly baked and topped with angelic cream cheese frosting, it seemed devilishly decadent. The cake was made more sinful by adding shaved Bavarian chocolate on top. After dinner, when all of the gastric longings were satiated and all of the thirstiness quenched, then the talks about the day's activities commenced. Brentt and his cohorts were sent upstairs to do lessons while the grown-ups talked.

"Doctor, have a look at this. It is my findings, all 65 Thesis. But I feel I might find more. I've worked diligently on them. The supplementary discourse is incomplete because I still have more research to do. However, I do want your expert opinion on them."

CHAPTER 5

Dr. Henry Williams took some time to read through them. The monk watched the expressions on his face but did not interrupt. The Doctor studied the manuscript intently as he read them. Each word and sentence sunk into the Doctor's astute mind. When he was done he put the manuscript down and leaned back in his chair.

Flora, who was busy wiping up the counter and putting away the last of the dinner plates, sat down next to her husband. She took the manuscript from her husband and began reading it. Dr. Henry Williams turned to his friend, Martin.

"Martin, are you sure about this?" asked Dr. Henry Williams.

"I am sure my friend. I need to do what God tells me. It's what's right. I have to post it for all to see. I have found my truth." said Martin.

"The church will not like this. I don't have any issue with it, but this could be very dangerous."

"You and I both see what is going on, supposed men of God doing the devil's work. You and I are both the same, trying to make the world better. Don't you as a scientist seek to find the truth?"

"The scientific research that Flora and I do is not to discount or discredit the existence of God, but rather to prove that everything made had a designer and a maker. The church doesn't see it that way though. They see us as trying to undermine their authority," replied Dr. Henry Williams.

"You are on grounds that they know nothing about. I am using the same text that they should all be familiar with, the same from which I derived my thesis."

"About two years ago, the parents of these three girls Bertha, Agness and Lynne, were jailed for their dissident speech. They were part of a group that spoke against the crooked ways of the appointed governing officials. Sadly, we do not know when they will get out. How do you tell teenagers that? We took them in because their parents were close friends. We are their guardians now. Unfortunately, that is our truth. We all have to be careful," stated Flora sadly, looking up from the reading material.

CHAPTER 5

"I feel we've gotten lucky so far because of our status in the upper echelons of society. However, sooner or later we need to move from here," said Dr. Henry Williams.

"Where will you take your family? Your whole life is here," said the monk.

"I've been hearing about a lost continent that some traders have found. *Amerigo Vespucci*, I believe his name might be, was an explorer that found a new world. The word is that others have verified this new world as well. We could go there and be free to discover all that needs discovering," said Dr. Henry Williams hopefully.

"It will be dangerous my friends. But I fear the greatest of God's creation is the most dangerous of all of them. The evil that men do to each other is abhorrent. For people like us, that deem life precious, it seems that there is no hope. The church is everywhere," said the humble monk rising from the table.

"It seems at times the thin line between those that do God's will and those who serve the devil is all but erased," spoke Flora Williams solemnly.

"Time to go already Martin?" asked Dr. Henry Williams.

"Yes. I have a lot of praying to do tonight. For I must do what heaven commands and continue searching the scriptures for more proof that the church is straying from the truth," stated Martin determinedly.

The Williams saw the monk out and wished him God speed. They all knew that it could get dangerous, but all of them had the hope for a better tomorrow. Dr. Henry and his wife Flora went upstairs to the teenagers' bedrooms and brought them downstairs.

"Now everyone, it is time to take your medicine. This is to help you get big and strong like your fathers," said Flora soothingly.

"My daddy was really fat! Am I going to be fat like my daddy?" asked dark brown haired Bertha.

"No. No. This will help you to be strong and live a long time," said Dr. Henry Williams.

"I hope I get to be pretty like my mommy!" exclaimed curly blond-haired Lynne.

CHAPTER 5

"I'm sure you will honey, just like your mother," smiled Flora sweetly.

"When will we see our parents and go back home? I miss my farm," asked Agness.

"Agness honey, I don't know. The courts are very crowded and it takes time to hear out the case," answered Flora.

The three girls gulped down the bluish-green liquid. Brentt gulped down a brownish one. Disgust plainly showed on their faces but they knew that they were going to get a piece of chocolate afterward. It was a routine that they followed every two days as prescribed by Dr. Henry Williams. They were tucked in and kissed goodnight in their separate rooms, except Brentt, who was taken downstairs by his father.

"Flora, I have to meet with the sisters for a little bit. I just have this nagging feeling in the back of my head. I don't know what it is. Stay here, I'll be back shortly," said Dr. Henry Williams.

"Ok, but hurry back. I too feel that something's not right," spoke Flora softly as she placed her hands on his shoulders and gazed into Dr. Henry Williams' one brown eye and one hazel eye.

"I'm going to take Brentt. He's been training with them and it's about time he's initiated. Besides, he's a big strapping lad and very mature for his age."

"To me, he'll always be my baby. They're all my babies," cooed Flora who had become fond of her friends' children.

Dr. Henry Williams and Brentt stepped out of the warm coziness of the house and the chill of the night air hit them like a horse and carriage. Good thing Flora knows how to sew properly because their coats were well made.

The walk wasn't that far, about half an hour away. Both walked in silence. Dr. Henry Williams pondered about his family and their welfare as he mechanically put one foot in front of the other. Brentt, Bertha, Agness and Lynne were his life now and he did all that he could to ensure that they had a long and happy one.

Pretty soon he saw the spire that marked the finish line for their destination, St Agatha's Convent. It was a convent that was famed for doing the Lord's work with the poor and needy. They

CHAPTER 5

ministered to the sick and elderly and preached the word to any that needed to hear it.

He called at the gate and a middle-aged woman answered. In the torchlight, he could hear that the woman sounded older than she looked.

"Do you seek the Lord, my child?" she asked in a surprisingly pleasant voice.

"I wish to know the Lord. Because to know the Lord is to find the Lord," said Dr. Henry Williams solemnly.

"Come in my child and you will know the Lord. For the knowledge of the Lord is our life," chorused the middle-aged woman at the gate.

The small, wrought iron gate swung open without a creak, which Dr. Henry Williams did not expect. However, if you wanted to make secret visits late at night, then the gates should not make a sound. The nun with the torch flashed a smile.

"Greetings to you, Dr. Henry Williams, peace and knowledge go with you," she said in a lowered voice as he stepped through. "Welcome young Brentt Williams. Good to see you again. And might I add, I am happy you are still interested in the knowledge of the Lord," she added, smiling.

"Peace and knowledge be with you too, sister Valetta. I see that you are wearing a new habit. Also, your prayer beads are looking well-polished," joked Dr. Henry Williams.

"Flattery might get you somewhere that you may not want your wife to know about," she kidded back. "Follow me, please." The nun turned and led her guests into the nunnery. This was the secret stronghold of *the Sisters of The Black Habit*.

The Sisters of the Black Habit were an offshoot of the secret society called the *Legacy of the Ascended Knowledge of the Nine (LAKN9)*. Their roots spanned millennia and involved a host of diverse cultures. They served the Nine Gods and kept a record of their teachings that were passed down from time immemorial. Their ranks were subdivided into those that followed a particular deity, such as the *Sisters of the Ascended Knowledge of Heddonna* or SAKH for short. There were also the *Brothers of the Ascended Knowledge of Technon* or the acronym *BAKT*. They were a very powerful and elite organization that helped the world and kept dark forces at bay.

The structure looked like an old building on the outside, but it had the grandiloquence of a palace on the inside. The vaulted ceilings rose high into the night, canopied with ornate chandeliers holding crystal mirrors that magnified the lighting. Finely crafted woodworks bejeweled the walls and depicted scenes from imagined lives of past saints and sinners alike. The souls of artists poured out on the canvas of the ornate Bastille in the forms of paintings and sculptures.

Yes, it was a cathedral, church, nunnery, Bastille, and convent all in one. The premier group of nuns that did the Lord's work for the church, diligently, unquestioningly and wholeheartedly, enjoyed the benefits that the hierarchies had to offer. However, the hallowed halls of the place of worship were not the destination of the illustrious Dr. Henry Williams. It was under it.

Just like in the churches of the Plaza de Armas in Cusco, the good stuff is always buried below the finery and decadence. Sister Valetta took a key that was long and jagged, completely encrusted with rust and decay, out from the folds of her robes. She put it into the surprisingly well-oiled lock of the door. This door too opened without any hesitation or groans. A gust of cold air mixed with sweet aromas passed over the two onlookers.

"The incense that we burn is to remember the saints buried here," said sister Valetta to no one in particular, just in case the wrong person was listening. They stepped through. The heavy-looking door that was light on its hinges, closed shut behind them. The Nun, the Doctor, and Brentt Williams were left in flickering lamplight, as they had been so many times before.

A muted television was the first thing Brentt saw when he woke up. The next thing that he saw was the pretty face of Brenda Nga Ling as she brushed back strands of shoulder-length black hair with dark brown highlights. Her big brown anime eyes peered into Brentt's as she leaned over him.

CHAPTER 5

"Thank God you're okay. Dr. Mendellsohnn patched you up pretty good. By the way, you slept for very long. He might have accidentally given you elephant tranquilizer," Brenda said smiling.

"It does feel like I've been asleep for a while. How long was I out?" Brentt queried.

"You have been out for a day. You have a hardy constitution. In fact, your belly fat absorbed most of the knife wound," chimed in Dr. Francisco Mendellsohnn, of course kidding at the belly fat part.

They were at the medical offices of the extremely cutting edge doctor. He was more pedigreed than even Maxximillian Chief, possessing six doctorates and six masters. His laboratory was state of the art, equipped with the latest and best machines, medicines, tests, vaccines, and gizmos you could find on the planet except for a secret government facility.

Next to Brenda, Brentt could see Bertha, Agness and Lynne all crowding around the bed. They looked very refreshing in their floral print dresses which apparently they had acquired on a girls' trip to the mall.

Red-haired Agness had on a white dress with red rose print on it and she accessorized with a medium thickness red belt with a gold buckle. The color choices really accentuated her body.

Bertha had on a black and white striped sundress. She had on flip flops that had a medium sole and preferred her dress on the longer side. The black and white dress had a slimming effect on her, even though she and Agness had the same body type.

Lynne sported a navy blue sundress that stopped short of her knees. Her long, toned calves were accentuated by blue pumps with gold embossments. A blue choker with a silver ringed onyx rounded off the attire.

They stood in stark contrast to the blue jeans, random college shirt and yoga class sneakers that Brenda wore.

Henry was there too. He wagged his tail so hard that he could not walk properly. When Brentt acknowledged him, Henry moved his head up and down as if to bark, but was too excited to do so.

"Hello ladies, how are you?" Brentt asked cheerily.

CHAPTER 5

"We're okay. You gave us a shock Binky (Bertha, Agness and Lynne called Brentt by that name ever since he had accidentally pounded his thumb with a hammer and they had caught him sucking it. It still annoyed him but it made him feel better because it was a term of special endearment.) You should really stop doing dangerous work like that," said red-haired Agness as she came closer and put her hand in Brentt's hand.

"She's right. You got hurt last month as well. I'm afraid that one of these days, it may not end so well," said Bertha with passion in her brown eyes. She leaned in for a half hug.

"Brentt, I got some clothes for you to change if needed. I also brought some toiletries for you as well. If it's okay with the doctor, we can keep you company for a little while. If there is anything you need, just let me know," Lynne calmly spoke as she showed him the things that she had brought.

"Did you happen to find a nice big tablet in a pretty snazzy case when they put me in the ambulance?" asked Brentt Williams.

"I did. It looks pretty sweet," piped up Brenda.

"Thanks. Give it to Bertha please." Turning to Bertha, he said, "See, I told you I was going to get you a nice tablet. I'll need all the rest I can get because you can bet that Maxx Chief is going to be here. He may be grumbling about a lot of paperwork," laughed Brentt Williams.

"Speaking of the Chief, he busted quite a few celebrities. Lots of high priced lawyers were called in. This could get really ugly. Unfortunately in cases like these, the bad guys with good defense lawyers and loads of money win the day. I foresee them getting a slap on the wrist or less," said Brenda sadly, sitting down on the chair next to the bed.

"Actually, a few of the celebrities accosted us," stated Lynne. "Of course we turned them down because of our workload. We have that slumlord case that we're working on and there are illegal immigrants and human trafficking thrown in the mix as well."

"I have to get going. I've been here for a long time and I've got to go home, shower and try to get some rest," said Brenda as she leaned in for a big but gentle hug. The hug lasted longer than usual. All of the ladies said goodbye to one another and as

CHAPTER 5

Brenda walked out the door, she patted Henry on the head. The dog wagged his tail in appreciation. She looked back and closed the door shaking her head. She had her chance to tell her feelings to Brentt. However, she had too many spectators. Brenda would have to make another opportunity later.

Lynne took the vacated chair. Agness and Bertha went to the window to see Brenda walk to the parking lot from the fifth story of the medical center. Lynne leaned over and checked Brentt's vitals on the machine.

Brentt saw what she was doing and said, "I have been alive for a while. I'll be around for a lot longer."

"I know, but we can't lose you. You are very important to us," smiled Lynne.

"Alright everyone, keep him in good spirits. He's already on his way to a good recovery. There was not much blood loss and you are already healing. I feel ashamed to call myself a doctor with you as my patient Brentt. I hardly had to do a thing. Your overall healing abilities are unlike anything that I have ever seen," said Mendellsohnn.

"Yes doctor, we are unlike anyone that you have ever come across," Lynne reassured.

"I'll give you some good pain medication. Ladies, please make sure he takes it on time because you know how forgetful our friend can be. Let us hope that it is not because of his advanced age," advised Dr. Mendellsohnn before he left the room.

"Brenda likes you," said Lynne calmly, looking deeply into Brentt's eyes.

"I know but I don't think it will work out. I don't think she would have a problem with an older man. However, I might be too old for her," smiled Brentt.

"You were tossing and turning as you slept. Did you have a nightmare?" asked Bertha.

"I did have a dream. I dreamt about my initiation into the Sisters of the Black Habit and the LAKN9," said Brentt solemnly. Just then Henry started whining.

"Aye ladies, I got to go make me own Irish ale. It better be quick or else the lot of you might be treated to dealing with some

CHAPTER 5

inedible chocolate leprechauns," said Henry, the dark yellow golden retriever with a tail wag.

CHAPTER 6: The Talks About Deceptions

The temple planet of Atomos was located in the dead center of infinite multiverses. The largest planetary body in the entire cosmos, it housed a higher representation of every single lifeform ever born into existence. From the tiniest bacteria to the largest dinosaur, to great trees and mountains, everything that was out in the universe was on this planet, under the watchful eye of Atomos.

The planet was as meticulously detailed as its creator. There was a place for everything and everything was in its place. Lifeforms that needed an acidic environment nestled peacefully next to frigid landscapes that held their own flora and fauna. Volcanic sceneries that were home to Lava people were situated next to tropical landscapes that held the prettiest of flowers and the rarest of birds. Oceans hid marvelous underwater creatures that surfaced from the depths of one's imaginations. They swam alongside goldfishes, seals, dolphins and Korsol. Each environment was separated from the other by the will of Atomos.

While the other Gods were inspecting the rest of the universes, he leisurely walked among all life present within his planet. There were innumerable lifeforms all living in harmony in the presence of the mighty King of the Gods. That was quite a sight for any onlooker and so much more for those dwelling on the planet.

Everything in the multiverse on one planet, how is that possible? Space separates everything. When space is taken away, life can fit into a smaller area.

The crowning achievement on his planet was the temple that housed The Contest of the Nine, the first creations of the Gods before the beginning. Each artifact was placed upon a magnificent foreverum pedestal that told its story. Foreverum was a material that never rusted, broke, or diminished in its

CHAPTER 6

beauty and luster. Each artifact was aligned so that directly above it, was the temple planet of the God that formed the mighty creation. These were the most powerful objects in existence.

Standing amongst The Contest of the Nine, Atomos looked upon them with pride and joy. He had something special planned for the other Gods, something that involved all of their inputs. Something that would change the way the universe opened before them. *They were going to create Athlogoss Drones and decide the rules for all of creation to follow.*

Technon, Heddonna, and Archituria had teleported themselves to the great temple planet of Atomos. Even though they could see every part of the universe, they could not invade the privacy of the other Gods by looking into their temple planets. They were in awe of their surroundings, as they beheld the magnificence that Atomos had made for himself.

"This is amazing… All of the things in the universe are here…. Yet it feels as though I have learned a whole universe of knowledge in a split second," gasped Heddonna.

The other two Gods were as amazed and hungrily soaked up the new information that flooded their minds.

"Yes, it is quite awe-inspiring," said a voice as thunderous as the crashing waves on the seashore, yet gentle with a little wind.

The trio of Gods turned at the voice of Atomos coming from behind them. He was smiling at them in a loving and inviting way. "Welcome to my temple planet, where everything in the entire universe that was ever made or will be made, resides," he said as he spread his arms out and showcased his creation.

"This is so amazing..," Archituria managed to stammer out, her head still flooding with new knowledge from the planet.

"This is utterly remarkable, UKSCOGSM Atomos. Thank you for the temple planets that you have so generously given us. My planet exceeded all expectations and I'm sure the others did as well," said Technon, as he genuflected before Atomos. The other Goddesses nodded in silent agreement and followed suit bowing until they got permission to rise.

"I am glad you like it. It wasn't easy finding the right designs for you. We've had our existence before the beginning, so I had to put a lot of thought into what each of you might like," Atomos said, smiling broadly.

"We just finished certifying the universe. Everything looks absolutely incredible!" offered Heddonna.

"I trust you all have seen what must be seen?" asked Atomos.

"We have. However, Anthraxis was not satisfied with the outcome. He made some treasonous talk and this worries us," stated Technon hesitantly.

"This could upset the balance of the universe even while it is just an infant," added Heddonna as she looked at Technon.

"I see. Tell me of what has transpired as we walk to The Contest of the Nine," said Atomos as he turned to go.

The God of War, Anthraxis, was at ease on his newly made temple planet. Contrary to popular belief, it was not a war-torn planet. There was no destruction, no dead bodies were strewn everywhere and decay was not written all over the landscape.

In fact, it was quite the opposite. The temple planet of Anthraxis was pristine and orderly, as the planet of a dictator should be. Everything had a purpose and everyone had a position. They all worked together to serve the God of War. He had to admit, the old fart Atomos did a great job with decorating. Everything was as Anthraxis wanted it, congested and elegant.

There were over the top designs, but they weren't too cheesy. His planet showcased every design motif from all across the universe that would befit an iron-fisted ruler. Furniture from across the cosmos, picked from different times and gleaned from different cultures, dotted the floors of his magnificent palace. Each had a different story to tell as it related to some battle or another that hadn't happened yet. Glass tiles had aerial views of faraway planets and distant stars. They moved as he walked on them to simulate him strolling through the stars in the sky.

There were paintings which hung upon the walls of his palace, held in place by nooses. The artists that poured out their souls upon the canvas showcased the struggles within their hearts. In fact, there were a series of paintings by the same artist but from different universes, which were displayed side by side on the dark marble walls. The contrast was extraordinary because it took one minuscule act that would define the outcome of a whole artist's career.

Anthraxis liked how the painter, *Jacques Von Blutdruckt Gemacht*, used oils and acrylic to capture what was deep in his soul. He used tenebrous and chiaroscuro styles to convey his feelings of looming dread. His paintings really spoke to the God of War. In addition, Gemacht had not limited himself to one style but branched out in other areas such as aerial view and divisionism.

Elsewhere on the walls of the temple planet, there was a life-sized picture of Zeus fighting one of the hundred handed giants on Mount Olympus. Anthraxis' eyes scrolled the walls further and he came upon the picture of Cain slaying Abel. It was wrought with hate and jealousy and exuded a feeling of sadness and fear.

The next painting took up two massive rooms. It was a depiction of a battle in heaven where angels were fighting each other. One side was for eternal devotion and the other side for a revolution against the Creator. It was an unending cycle. Even in the newness of creations, there was a need for violence.

All of the Gods exist in the past, present and future. Therefore if there is a painting hanging up on the walls from and artist that is not born yet, it is because that painting is supposed to be painted.

Anthraxis walked slowly through his halls of weapons. They contained weapons from every time and every planet and from every civilization that would be in existence. He was amused at the primitive arrows, spears and shards of obsidians that lifeforms used in battle. He saw that further down the halls, were weapons capable of destroying planets and even killing suns. How have the creations come so far that they feel they can destroy the things that the Gods have made! They feel as though they have reached the pinnacle of existence, but they are wrong. There is more than they can ever know in the universe.

He sat heavily upon his throne, not caring if he was dirty from exploring the universe. He and his fellow Gods were making sure

CHAPTER 6

everything was good for Atomos. He had been his own master before the contest to see who would be King of the Gods. He was not used to the role of, subject. He was not used to bowing or answering to anyone but himself. 'This throne is really comfortable' thought Anthraxis as he sat. The throne was crafted from four of the deadliest vehicles in existence:

One of his armrests was made out of a massive tank, lovingly called The Metallurgist's Hand. It had a strong magnetic field that superheated the attracted metals and repurposed them into explosive materials. At the right time, the explosion would rain down molten shrapnel upon the unlucky victims. The tank showcased the savagery of the inhabitants of planet Zyster. They wrestled for everything and on every occasion. You wanted food, you wrestled for it. You wanted a date, you wrestled for it. You wanted votes, you had to wrestle each of the other candidates for them. They were hulking brutes and both the males and females had similar musculature. The twelve-foot tall beings had a myriad of skin colors and a squared face made complete with a combative disposition.

The other armrest was a space vessel that served as a ferry for passengers and doubled as a transport for soldiers. This was a deadly planet killer if there ever was one, named The Laboratory. The Ghrits civilization scouted the planet which they were going to invade and captured a representative from all of the different life forms that they needed to defeat. They experimented upon them and created a toxin that killed them instantly. The ship of theirs came into the atmosphere and released the toxin upon the hapless planet.

All of the passengers and soldiers watched as the entire planet died. They released the antidote into the air and took over the planet as if nothing happened. They had a slender build with an eight-foot-tall frame. Their oversized heads were a little disproportioned for their bodies but hid an excellent brain capable of such horrific feats.

The Planet Ravager spaceship made up the backrest of Anthraxis' throne. It was a piece of engineering that truly deserved to be there. It was the brainchild of planet Hycol. There was a split in the planet in which the more civilized inhabitants were called Hycolians and the less civilized were called Hycolites. They differed in their methods to run the planet. However, they came together and created this wicked contraption. The ship was made of Hycolium, which was the second hardest and most durable material in the universe, next to foreverum.

The Hycol race had claws on their fingers. They were about ten feet tall, with a cat's tail and the body of a bull. Their hair was like a lion's mane and covered most of their bodies. Their face looked like apes and the more evolved Hycolians had an even more homo sapient look to them. The Hycolites lived on the ground, while the Hycolians inhabited great floating cities. Each of the inhabitants of the planet could fly a ship by the time they learned to walk. They were expert pilots and navigators and traversed the toughest terrains and the farthest reaches of space.

The ship in question not only shot down opponents but rammed through them. The ships were so well built that they rammed through an entire planet and emerged unscathed. That won them the right to be where they are, the backrest for the God of War's throne.

The Bauge race was definitely an inventive race when it came to genocide. They believed in using everything and wasted nothing. That principle guided their deadliest invention, the Elemental Missile Array. The missile array was dropped upon the intended planet by a portal whilst the Bauge was in a far orbit. The missile array fired automatically at different points upon the planet encasing it in a field. As more missiles fired, everything on the entire planet turned to the basic elements in the universe. The Bauge would send in freight ships that collected all of the materials and brought them back to their home planet. They were the ultimate recyclers of the universe and their invention was used as the footrest for Anthraxis.

The giant metallic throne also had a little something extra to make it comfortable: a quilt that was specially designed by Atomos. It was made from the pelts of a million teddy bears and provided comfort and warmth for Anthraxis. The two hundred foot tall figure of Anthraxis said to himself, "Well done Atomos, well done old fool," as he reclined upon the massive throne.

CHAPTER 6

The other Gods did not understand him and he did not care to explain himself to them. They were not worth the effort. He knew he was right when he had told the others what Atomos had done. However, they were blinded by the magnificence of the universe and their own temple planets. Anthraxis heard some shuffling behind him and knew instantly who it came from. He rose slowly from the throne and turned to greet his courtesans.

They were the most beautiful life forms from all across the universe. They were made up of different materials such as water, air, fire, stone, metal, magma, flesh, and other more exotic materials. All of them wore armors of the finest material from their homeworld. Every so often, the armors transformed into different armors from different eras, right on their bodies. War broke out in a big smile because he had spied them when he glanced at his temple planet before going out into the universe. Now he had more time to get to know them. Atomos was using the pleasures of the flesh to bribe fealty from Anthraxis.

Actually 'God of War' was a title that was given by the King of the Gods to Anthraxis' displeasure. Anthraxis was no one's fool. He would take what was given and enjoy it very well indeed. His loyalty would, however, reside with himself and himself alone.

He turned to a very demure looking courtesan from the planet *Droflelix*. It was a planet that had seventy-five percent of its surface covered in deep pink, very viscous water. It also sported the highest mountain in the galaxy, with the tops reaching past the upper atmosphere of the planet.

She was a soft bubble gum pink with four arms and three legs which were webbed. Her four eyes were big and bright and carried extra lenses so she could have them open underwater. There were twin dorsal fins on her back, which she could expertly use to swim in an underwater ballet, for her people's enjoyment. She had a small mouth with even teeth, just right for eating vegetation and seaweed.

Her armor consisted of the exoskeleton of a giant crab that had been gutted and dried in the sun. The Droflelix clans would paint scary faces on the chest plates to ward off any enemies.

CHAPTER 6

There were some warriors that used the giant crab claws in combat as well.

There were about ten billion courtesans present in his palace at this particular time, but there were trillions more around his temple planet.

He looked at her and around at all of the other courtesans clad in their various armors and immediately multiplied himself a billion-fold. The giant Anthraxis that sat upon the throne raised his left hand and said in a thunderous voice, "I shall hunt and slay the *Leviathan* and the *Behemoth* and then we shall barbeque their flesh and feast until the moon is at its highest!"

The giant Anthraxis got up and strode to a very deep and wide pit that was in the back yard of his palace, covered with a protective barrier. All of his courtesans and embodiments followed him, screaming his name.

The God of War disrobed and stripped bare to a metallic chainmail loincloth. The giant muscled mountains of his arms and shoulders flexed and churned, their power surpassing that of the mightiest earthquake. Great sinews moved in his powerful calves and legs with veins and arteries flowing like the Nile River through his muscles. Deep valleys carved on his abdomen, made even the Grand Canyon look minuscule. He removed the protective barrier with a wave of a hand and called forth the two great beasts that would be their dinner.

The Leviathan was a great scaly beast that had metallic, black as night spikes running along its back and down its four tails. The tails were ten times its body length and as dexterous as anything one could imagine. Four massive legs had powerful razor-sharp metal claws that gripped with the might of a sun holding planets in place. Six giant dragon wings flapped and moved, creating hurricane-like winds that swept across the crowd of onlookers.

All of the embodiments of Anthraxis stepped in front of his courtesans and shielded them from the terrible onslaught. Eight heads reared their ugly faces and cried a deadly and deafening roar that sent chills down the spine of the entire planet. However, the fearless Anthraxis stood resolute against his dinner. Sharp rows of venom coated teeth, as large as the two hundred foot tall God of War, lined the creature's eight gaping maws. Red

CHAPTER 6

and brimming with hate and unbridled destruction, eighty eyes looked on at the one who would dare defy this monstrous creature. But there was more to come, for there was a teammate to this potential meal.

The Behemoth rose from the pit where it was spawned. This two-legged creature unfolded itself from a fetal position, an offspring of the planet just like the Leviathan. It had two long arms that overflowed with muscles and power. Muscles ran down his back, legs, abs, and torso in such quantities, that any onlooker would have a hard time comprehending how this creature could ever be flexible and agile. His head was pocked with millions of eyes that saw everything and relayed information to the ganglion located at intervals in his body. In addition, ampules on his skin sensed the electromagnetic impulses of his opponent so that the Behemoth knew when and where his opponent was at any given time.

Both he and the Leviathan were about the same size. Both were so big that the two hundred foot tall Anthraxis could fit in their mouths for a single swallow.

A battle of this proportion would become a regular occurrence on Anthraxis' temple planet. It gave him an opportunity to quench his thirst for battle and to feed his courtesans at the same time. During the night, the beasts were regrown in the womb of the planet and birthed for the next day's festivities. Atomos had read the cravings of the God of War correctly, Anthraxis had to give him that much.

While the giant Anthraxis got ready to enter the pit and catch dinner, another of his embodiments turned to the droflelix he had shielded from the hurricane-like winds. The bubble gum pink of her arm was so smooth and silky that it ignited a fire in Anthraxis' veins, far different than the battle with the beasts. He smiled at her and cooed, "You look very delicious. I'm going to…"

"Yes they do look very fun indeed," said Atomos as he appeared in the middle of Anthraxis' consortium with a sonic boom. All the courtesans, all the embodiments of Anthraxis and the two great beasts stopped what they were doing and looked at the King of the Gods and the God of the Gods.

CHAPTER 6

Anthraxis amalgamated himself into one embodiment and bowed the way an opponent does to another before a karate match. It was quick and haphazardly, which communicated that both he and Atomos were equals.

"I am very glad to see that you are enjoying my creations Anthraxis, God of War," spoke Atomos solemnly as he looked around at the courtesans. "Please leave us for a few moments, I have to chide my fellow God," he said as he waved a mighty hand and teleported all of the courtesans to another part of the planet. "You, great beasts, please go back into the pit. You shall resume your match after I have spoken to Anthraxis," commanded Atomos. The two great beasts did as they were told and the barrier was placed back over the pit. "Anthraxis, come let us walk to your palace."

Anthraxis looked dejected at being blocked by the God of the Gods, but that little discomfort may have paved the way for the things ahead. There was silence between them for a few minutes as they made their way to the palace. Atomos studied the face of Anthraxis, searching for an unseen sign of guilt, like a little dog that did something wrong, but nonchalantly looks away when caught.

"Your fellow Gods told me of a conversation that you had with them. It seems that you disapprove of my methods. They said your talk was treasonous and disrespectful. Tell me your version of it," said mighty Atomos, sitting down on Anthraxis' throne that had a quilt made of teddy bear pelt.

"It is as they said it is. They are gullible but they are not liars," spoke Anthraxis as he ran a hand across one of his sofas.

"Are not my creations great? Did you not examine everything in the expanse of the cosmos and find that everything was very good? Did I not win the contest to see who would be king? This creation was made before I became UKSCOGSM Atomos. Complete with multiverses. After all, did I not make your temple planet far beyond the wildest dreams of a God?" inquired Atomos.

CHAPTER 6

"Yes. We examined everything and there was no imperfection, except struggles everywhere and between everything. Yes. You won the contest but there is nothing left for us to make because all is made. Yes. The temple planets are beyond expectations but they feel like bribery for loyalty. Why make life to kill it off? What is there to gain by doing this?" the God of War shot back at Atomos.

"Struggles determine who we are and where we go. Did not The Contest of the Nine determine where each God's place was, before the beginning of the beginning? You need to destroy before you build. Did I not move back the void and clear a space for the universe? You need to turn your back on things in order to move forward.

Did I not start time so that we may move back and forth in time? You need to become a leader before you lead. Did I not construct the creation that would give me the right to be crowned King of the Gods and God of the Gods? We give life and we take life. That is the way it is," spoke Atomos authoritatively as he got up and went up to the God of War. "I have no need to bribe you because this is what you would have made yourself. I merely saved you the trouble of doing it."

Anthraxis nodded in agreement. What other choice did he have?

"I know it's a very hard adjustment having a king and even more so, to follow rules. However, there must be order. My rule must be unimpeded by your nonchalant ideas. The next time we have a contest, if we do," spoke Atomos sternly as he went face to face with Anthraxis, *"Don't bring a letter opener to a universe making contest."*

"Am I to expect any punishment for talking ill about you?" asked Anthraxis tentatively.

"I will confine you to your temple planet for one million years. You will have no influence on the outside world. You may have the other Gods visit you though, which I'm sure they will. Don't worry if the sentence is long, you should have plenty of things and beings here to occupy your time," Atomos rolled his eyes in the direction of the teleported courtesans, "Your sentence will be in effect after we have finished the project I had planned.

CHAPTER 6

I will see you at my temple planet in about a week," Atomos pronounced his judgment upon the God of War.

He vanished with a sonic boom and in his place, the courtesans were returned to their original locations. Anthraxis unflustered, picked up from where he left off before the interruption by Atomos.

Caddeussus landed on the temple planet of Anthraxis just after Atomos had left. His experiences on the planetoid would remain a secret for the time being. He knew what he had to do.

He arrived in the middle of a full-blown gladiatorial party, officiated by Anthraxis and attended by a billion of his incarnations and courtesans. They were intently watching their God fighting two monsters to the death. At the arrival of Caddeussus, Anthraxis did not suspend his actions but summoned an embodiment to greet the God of Life. He led him away from the festivities, but not out of earshot of the shrieks of pleasure coming from billions of beings.

"What happened with Atomos?" Caddeussus got right to the point, speaking over the cheering.

"He confined me to my temple planet for a million years. He said that his will must be respected," spoke Anthraxis, as he looked at his fellow God. Just then his two hundred foot embodiment launched an uppercut at the Behemoth.

"Did you tell him that he made all without us?" asked Caddeussus, restless.

"I did, and the old fart gave me some crap about being a leader, you have to lead," he said exasperated.

Caddeussus looked into the future a million years from now and saw a bright beautiful planet that Galaxyia had taken a special interest in. The planet was vibrant and flowing with beauty and life. Rahab was untouched by the ideas of war and destruction but it had the influences of all the other Gods upon it.

In fact, the whole futures of civilizations in the universe had shifted, because of Anthraxis' confinement to his temple planet. This situation could be used to prove a point and further show that Atomos was incapable of leading. He had broken his own ruling, right out of the starting gate of creation.

"I feel that is an unfair punishment. It is too long and hard. The universe was just created," Caddeussus empathized with Anthraxis.

"It's ok. I think it's a mountain of Korsol crap anyways. I'll look on the bright side, at least I get to be lazy for a million years," Anthraxis spoke sullen and dejected.

"Anthraxis, you know of the planet Rahab?" asked Caddeussus.

"Yes, I do. I see that it is a gem of a planet, untouched by my hand. The time will come when I will assert my will upon that world," Anthraxis said, distracted by his embodiments.

"You have to destroy that planet because it should feel your influence. You have to make the planet Rahab feel the hand of War," suggested Caddeussus.

"What about Galaxyia?"

"She's a hearty Goddess, she can take it. If Atomos wants to destroy things already predetermined, so be it. Give him what he wants," the God of Life said as he turned to go.

"Why... why are you suggesting this?" Anthraxis asked unnerved.

"The universe started with Atomos deceiving us. You brought that to my attention. Now he wants to punish you for speaking the truth! Don't stand there and take it," suggested Caddeussus as he spoke with his back to Anthraxis.

"Yes. I may be nonchalant now, but the day will come when I will take my rightful place in the universe and all will tremble before me!"

Caddeussus turned and encouraged the God of War, "That's the spirit. You have to nip this in the bud before things get out of hand. I for one do not like Atomos' deceitfulness."

"I'll see you soon then. Meanwhile, I have a lot of courtesans to attend to."

Caddeussus disappeared as quickly as he came, like a light rain on a sunny day, where the drops had evaporated before they hit the hot asphalt, however you knew that it rained.

CHAPTER 7: Everybody Tries To Explain Some Things

Theo sat up from the sofa in his condominium, very tired. While he stretched, loud cracks and pops were heard from different parts of his body. He got up from the sofa and stopped short. Where did this sofa come from? It was dark brown, extra plush, and had reclining seats. He did not remember moving it from the house.

He looked around and the whole living room was furnished. A three-piece sofa set, an ultra-high-definition, 3D television was mounted on the wall, and a three-tiered wood and tempered glass television stand completed the living room furnishings. There was even a picture of lilies hanging on the wall.

Blu-Rays were neatly arranged in alphabetical order, housed in a uniquely designed wood and glass bookcase. Even his 3D Blu-Ray player was plugged in and ready to go.

Theo scratched his head in disbelief. He quickly went to the next room. There stood a grand eight-person marble top dining set, complete with a candelabra centerpiece. He examined the set more closely and realized that this was a very expensive piece of furniture. 'Where the hell did this come from? I just left Catherine yesterday afternoon.'

Catherine, just the thought of her name was like a dagger being driven into his testicles. He looked to his right and hanging on the wall, was a larger than life painting by some great artist, depicting bathing nudes. Theo looked stunned at the giant picture and wondered where it came from and who put it there.

Suddenly, the sound of dishes moving pulled his attention away from Catherine, the mysterious dining table and the oversized painting. It was coming from the kitchen, a few feet away. Sneaking on all fours like a big 180-pound house cat, he crept to the entrance of the kitchen and peeked around the corner.

There was a curvaceous woman present in the kitchen. Her chestnut, thigh-length hair hung in a ponytail as she stood in front of the stove. She was making pancakes and eggs. She stared at Theo, apparently having heard him.

"Hello Theo, how are you today?" she asked with a non-toothed smile. "Did you sleep well on the sofa? I know that people can sleep just about anywhere. Some examples are in drains, on couches, in cars, at church, and at funerals," said the bombshell, which he did not recognize.

Theo felt embarrassed and croaked, "I'm very good thank you. I did have a very good rest. What are you doing?" He stood up and looked at her apprehensively.

"I'm making you breakfast, silly! Go ahead and do your morning toiletries. Breakfast will be ready in 5.82 minutes," offered the long-haired woman, as she started cutting some onions already on a cutting board. Theo noticed she did not look at what she was cutting.

"No. I mean, what are you doing in my condominium? Don't misunderstand me, while I'm grateful for having such a beautiful lady in my kitchen making me breakfast, who are you?" he asked reluctantly, as he came closer.

"I am an *Artificially Intelligent Robotic Entity*. My name is Asheley. Did you have a bout of amnesia? Should I call for medical attention? I have access to all of the medical information in the entire world," replied the woman as she inched closer to the surprised and somewhat turned on Theo.

She put a warm hand on his body and felt for any temperature fluctuations and his heart rate. As she did so, Theo had a chance to inspect her. He saw that she looked very faux but moved in a natural human way. What is she doing here? He looked into her big, brown, glassy eyes surrounded by thick, long eyelashes, framed by perfectly formed orbitals. Her jawline was soft and delicate, ending in thick juicy lips that broke into a perfectly symmetrical smile. She demurely brushed back a strand of realistic-looking hair that was placed behind masterfully crafted ears.

CHAPTER 7

He could feel no breath coming from her. It was a little creepy, but it did not detract from the beauty of this creation in front of him. What's more, she was cooking for him on the day after he left his wife!

"Your heart rate is a little elevated, but your temperature is fine," she said, letting her hand linger a little longer on his heart. "If you like, I can hum musical tunes to soothe you?"

"No. I'm good thank you," he said as he hesitantly put a hand on her bare forearm. He was surprised at how realistic she felt. "I didn't know that I had such an esteemed guest in my house."

"You built me yesterday, showed me around and said to take care of your household needs," replied Asheley. "I have the whole compendium of human knowledge inside me, thanks to the internet. I can do anything that you desire," she said with a smile.

"I will take breakfast, thank you," he said submissively and went away to the bathroom. Perhaps after breakfast, he might be able to sort this interesting situation out.

Before leaving, he took one final glance at his unusual guest. She was dressed in three-quarter blue jeans and a mid-cut top. Actually, she looked exactly how his ex-wife would have dressed.

He looked in the master and guest bedrooms and as before, there was very exquisite furniture in the rooms, which should not be there. Theo stood in the hallway that separated the two rooms and tried to figure out what to do.

"Excuse me, Asheley…"

"Yes," she replied.

"Did you help me set up the furniture in the condominium?"

"No. The abode was furnished when I became aware of myself," she supposed, looking at the eggs she was frying. "Why do you ask? Does something need adjusting?"

"No. I feel out of sorts. I'll be back shortly."

He examined the master bathroom and noticed that his toiletries were neatly put away in their respective areas. The tiling in the master bathroom was done. He knew that it was not done when he got here last night.

There was a spacious shower with six shower heads coming from the three walls. Glass tiles had the backdrop of a rainforest embedded inside them. When the occupant took a shower, it felt as though they were in a rainforest. The light-brown marble tiles on the bathroom floor looked great and Theo bent down to give them a closer inspection.

"The grout is the same height as the tiles, just how I do them. No one else does them that way. But who could have done this?" he said to no one in particular. He immediately went to do number one. The master bathroom door was open but he did not care.

He washed his hands with blue liquid soap that he did not remember putting there. He stopped to look at a jar of sweet-smelling soaps that were shaped like seashells. He still had no idea who placed them there. His toothbrush was right there in a holder, lovingly put there by some unseen hand that was not his. He sluggishly brushed his teeth.

He went into the bedroom and studied the new furniture that was not his, but somehow was in his condo. The bed was a twenty-four-inch thick memory foam mattress on a twelve-inch base, which measured eight feet by eight feet. The frame was made out of a high-density wood called Schinopsis Balansae. Four eight-foot-tall, intricately carved posts overshadowed the frame. The head and footboards were made of dark marble that had finely sewn leather padding.

The nightstands were equally as gorgeous and held marble lamps that matched the bed. He found secret drawers that held no answers as to how this luxurious ensemble got in his house. He looked at himself in the mirror of the dresser. He was disheveled and a five o'clock shadow had gone from shadow to full-on solar eclipse on his face.

He did not see any of the bins that he had brought from Catherine's house. Theo assumed that they had been put away and opened the top right drawer. He was not really shocked to find underwear neatly folded, just as he would have folded them. He looked in the top left dresser drawer and pulled out some panties and bras, no doubt belonging to his guest that he did not remember building.

"I need something to drink," Theo said out loud, exasperated at not finding the answers in his own home.

CHAPTER 7

He strode to the fridge to get water out of the water dispenser. Just out of curiosity, he pulled it open and it was packed with food. The good stuff, the kind of food you would find in the fridge of a bachelor who could cook.

He looked at his house guest with one eye as he drank the water. She obviously did not need food, so where the hell did this food come from? Robots couldn't just walk into the store and buy a basket of food, now could they?

Sitting at the breakfast nook in the corner of the kitchen, he devoured a hearty breakfast. It consisted of a steak and vegetable omelet, pancakes, chicken sausage, hash browns, and orange juice. His guest was standing in front of him unaware of her awkwardness, so he offered her a seat at the table.

"Hmm, this tastes exquisite. Wow, Asheley, you can really cook!"

"Yes," she nodded. "Thank you. This is the first meal that I have made. I took the recipe from several sources and amalgamated them into the dish you are consuming. I can see from the look on your face and by referencing human facial expressions from movies, television series, books, and magazines, that you are satisfied with the result," offered Asheley.

"Thank you, this is delicious," Theo agreed happily putting food in his mouth.

Making small talk, he looked up from his plate and said, "So what are your interests or hobbies?"

"I'm interested in everything," replied Asheley.

"That's a generalized answer isn't it?"

"I don't think so. Humans form opinions based on what they are exposed to. However, they are not exposed to everything. Therefore they have a limited view of what they enjoy. I have been exposed to everything and consequently, can make an informed decision of my likes and dislikes. Everything is likable in some way, that is why I like them, because of the potential for the enjoyment of everything in the world," theorized Asheley.

"Well said. That is a very unique view of the world that I would imagine an Artificially Intelligent Robotic Entity would express." asserted Theo, now fully intrigued by the direction this was going.

CHAPTER 7

"Of course, I am always interested in what you have to say, not just because you created me to interact with you, but because of the potential to develop friendships," replied Asheley smiling.

"What do you know of me?"

"Well, your driver's license is DL123456. You were born...," started Asheley.

"Not facts or figures that you can find online. About me, what am I all about?"

"I don't think I know any of that. Please tell me."

"My wife Catherine was seeing my best friend for six years. I am looking to get a divorce. My family was what I was all about and now that's falling away before my eyes. I am here because I moved out of our house yesterday evening. I guess that's when I made or met you."

"Divorce is a document stating that two people do not have any more marital ties. Usually, it is accompanied by a settlement. You cannot be too happy about that? Do you still love your wife?" asked Asheley very intrigued or showing something close to it.

"I still love her but I also hate her. I have to be civilized to her for the sake of my daughter."

"You hate and love her at the same time. The closest thing I can use to comprehend that feeling is the example of a rose, beautiful, but it also possesses thorns that can hurt you. Is that an accurate description?" offered the AIRE.

"Yes, that is very good. Since my wife hurt me, I don't know what to do. My family was the world to me," Theo sadly said.

"I am here for you. I will never hurt you, at least not intentionally. Besides, I can be your family. There are many examples of humans with no blood ties becoming attached to one another, creating an extended family. Is that why you made me because I am here to replace your family?" smiled Asheley, quizzically.

"Why does an artist create a painting? Why does an author write a book? Or why do people make movies? Some do because they can, others do it to tell a story, and yet others do it to get out of their boring real lives and live in a world that they can control. I am glad that you are here. I look forward to us being friends,"

CHAPTER 7

said Theo smiling broadly as he ate the last mouthful of food on his plate.

She nodded and smiled at a job well done of making her first breakfast. "Thank you, I would like to see where our interactions take us as well!"

"What can you tell me about rapid divorces?" said Theo crinkling his eyebrows.

"They are uncontested divorces which are very quick and easy. The number one rated firm that does those types of divorces, is the law office of Clairmont, Fossway and Lyons" suggested Asheley.

"Hold on a second, I'm going to get a tablet so we can see what this is about. I hope that I remember where I put it," said Theo, getting up. As he did so, Asheley got up and took the dishes to the sink and started to wash them.

"It is located in the second left drawer of your computer desk. I charged it for you last night. Actually, I was looking around the house memorizing where things were, just for this type of occasion," smiled Asheley.

The tablet was where Asheley said it would be. He brought the tablet into the kitchen as Asheley finished washing the dishes. Being near such a beautiful woman turned him on and he had to control himself.

The process of divorce in itself was sad and disheartening. Theo had looked up a lot of things on the internet before, but this is the one subject that he'd hoped not to research. After some promising results, he made a quick phone call to the law firm, to make an appointment. As he hung up, Asheley looked at him extremely excited and innocent.

"How did it go? Actually, I am just asking as a courtesy because I heard everything. Shall I set a reminder of the appointment for you?" she asked.

"Normally you don't listen in on people's conversation, but since you did, probably don't bring it up before they do, okay?" he gently told her. "I'm going to call Catherine and get things in motion," he reluctantly said, as he politely excused himself.

"Good luck," Asheley said with a hint of emotion as he walked to the bedroom.

CHAPTER 7

John picked up the phone.

"Hello, is Catherine there?"

"Why yes, she is. Let me get her. We just finished making love in the shower and she is drying her hair." John moved his face from the receiver and yelled to Catherine so that Theo could still hear his voice, "Catherine honey, it's your husband. My former best friend... the man whose wife I've been seeing for the past six years." He came back on the phone, "Here's your wife Theo. Don't take up too much time. We're about to have brunch at the *Worldwide House of Breakfast Foods*," John said, his voice seething with malice and dripping with sarcasm.

"Hello?" Catherine's lovely, angelic voice came from sweet lips.

"Hi. I've been looking for information about uncontested divorces. I think on Monday we should go and see about that. My terms are these: you get the house and get Katie for the week and I keep my condos and get Katie on the weekends. We split the joint account funds. How about it?" asked Theo, who showed no hint of emotion.

"Boy, you don't play around. Right down to business, as usual."

Theo still waited for an answer.

"Yeah, that sounds good." Catherine looked and saw that John had gone downstairs. "That's one of the reasons I love you. You throw all your emotions into it. At the same time, you don't let things faze you. You just move on. Theo, there are times when you cannot keep things bottled up inside because eventually, they will come out. When you were packing yesterday, you were unflappable, so composed that I was worried that there was nothing left of the love that we had for each other."

There was only soft breathing on the other end of the line. "The time for that has gone. See you Monday morning at ten o'clock, in the law office of Clairmont, Fossway, and Lyons," Theo said as he hung up. He had hung up the future that he had planned with Catherine.

Theo was sitting in front of his laptop by the desk in his bedroom. Someone that was not him had taken the time to set it up. In fact, there were some new things there that he had not seen before but still would have wanted anyway. He decided to look at his credit card bills online, to see if there were any binge charges on them. It came up empty. He then decided to look for any receipts for the things in his house. That investigation came up empty as well.

He needed a refreshing shower because of all the strange things going on. He checked on the AIRE in the kitchen. She had just put away the dishes when he announced that he was going to bathe.

"I know what bathing is, but I actually have never seen a human do it. May I watch?" she asked.

"You are waterproof right? You can join me," said Theo with a mischievous smile on his face. The way he saw it, Catherine had her fun, so he might as well have his. Asheley followed Theo to the shower and took off her clothes. Needless to say, Theo was physically excited.

"Theo, Catherine engaged in intercourse with someone who wasn't her husband, which is something that you were very hurt by. She did you wrong. However, on the eve of your divorce from her, you hope to engage in some intimate activities with someone else. That is exactly the same thing. Is that what you would like to remember about your marriage?"

He stopped short and drew back for a minute, looking at the pretty AIRE in front of him.

'Theo, that's not you. You do the right thing because it's what you do. One more day is not going to hurt,' he thought.

She was stuck with him now, this AIRE, and it was his duty to show her the ways of the world and to figure out how she got here in the first place. He was letting his hate of Catherine and all of the pleasure that she had suffered at the hands of John, cloud his judgment. *The eye for an eye mentality was never a good idea in any circumstance.*

"You are beautiful and attractive Asheley. However, I do want to get divorced knowing that I have never wronged Catherine in any way."

'Perhaps after the divorce, they would continue from where they left off,' thought Theo as he reluctantly stepped into the shower by himself.

CHAPTER 7

When Theo hung up, Catherine did not put the cell phone down immediately. She held it near her ear for about a minute, feeling a combination of fear and shock. Taking a deep breath, she had relived the whole of yesterday in that one moment of inhalation. Her life would change drastically. No more sneaking around, no more lying, no more Theo. She sat heavily upon the bed.

Theo was a good man, very considerate and genuine. He loved their daughter; she was the world to him. Her eyes fell upon a picture of both of them during Christmas in Times Square. They seemed so happy then. The happiness was genuine. Though the smile was big, she had been hiding a bigger secret. She sat listlessly and looked around the room remembering that time. She reminisced about their college days, the past that had shaped their future.

She had always been attracted to John. He was a beautiful, manly supermodel. Unlike Theo, who was nice-looking, John was a muscular, rich bad boy that always got what he wanted. He wanted Catherine. They somehow became friends with Theo. Theo was the odd man out most of the time. He seemed to not mind. She and John were always in and out of a relationship with each other. The day it really broke off was on their anniversary, when she came home and caught John in bed with someone else. That was what drove her into Theo's arms.

She found being with Theo so different and exhilarating. Catherine was always an independent woman and she found her independence in jeopardy when Theo proposed. He had written a sixteen-page paper on why she should marry him. It was the sweetest thing that John never did for her. During their courtship, she and Theo had slowly rekindled their friendship with John. Theo did not know Catherine had rekindled something else. Even on their wedding day, she was with John. It was passionate and thrilling, which satisfied her and inflamed her at the same time.

From then on, John slept with her. John. Always, all of the time, she was too exhausted for Theo. Catherine had a surprise

CHAPTER 7

for Theo and her parents, Mr. and Mrs. Jansen. She was going to share with everyone that she was pregnant. John did not know. It could be either John's or Theo's.

John came into the room. He was making sure that Katie was getting ready for breakfast with Catherine's parents.

"You ok, honey?" he asked sweetly.

"Yeah...," she said flatly.

"You don't sound ok. Did Theo say something to piss you off?" he said with a hint of interrogation.

"Theo's going through with the divorce. Tomorrow we are going to see a lawyer and get it over with. I've never seen him so resolute before. Besides, my parents are expecting to see Theo and me today," she somberly stated as she put her hands on her knees.

"We'll just tell them that we are a couple now. That will be the end of that. No more sneaking around. I want your parents to treat me like their son now, not just the nice man across the road," John passionately said.

"No, not yet!" Catherine blurted, "Not now."

"Then when? You can't keep me in hiding forever. What are you afraid of? It's been six years. Go get dressed. Wear something pretty," John said as he got up and went into the walk-in closet to get dressed.

Catherine's mom did not look 65, she looked about 40. Her long, black hair, spotted with some silvery ones, was tied back in a ponytail. Even though she was older, she looked superbly fit and still looked amazingly beautiful. Mrs. Jansen had a meaty, five-foot, ten-inch frame that exuded vibrancy. One could definitely see where Catherine got her good looks from.

Mr. Jansen, on the other hand, was a rugged mountain of a man, standing at six-feet, six inches tall. Also 65, he looked in his forties and could have outrun guys in their twenties in an ironman contest. His new knees had something to do with it too. He had completely shaved his head, which was wholly grooved. A phrenologist would have had a field day with his head, if Mr. Jansen let him near it, which was very unlikely.

CHAPTER 7

"Hi, grandma and grandpa! I can't believe we're going to have pancakes two days in a row. I must be really special!" cheered Katie as she hugged her grandparents.

"Yes you are Katie cat," said Mrs. Jansen as she smoothed Katie's hair.

Mr. Jansen looked up and saw John coming down the stairs with Catherine.

"Oh don't you look so handsome. Such great attire...," giggled Mrs. Jansen.

Catherine's parents had known of the past between John, Theo, and Catherine. They both thought that John was a stuck up brat while he was dating their daughter and were secretly glad that John was not with Catherine anymore.

Catherine looked positively heavenly in dark-blue stretch jeans, accentuated by a dark-brown leather belt with a gold belt buckle. Her attire was topped off with a black cardigan showing a mild neckline that just gave a hint of cleavage, but not enough to be inappropriate in front of your parents.

"Mom and dad, it's great to see you. Are you guys ready to eat? Theo won't be joining us today, he had to work," she lied.

"No. No. No! Katie honey, go watch some cartoons in the living room. We have a few minutes before we go," said John quietly.

"What's the meaning of this, John?" asked Mr. Jansen sternly with a hint of puzzlement.

John turned to Catherine, "I can't hide it anymore." He turned to, who he hoped his future in-laws would be. "Catherine and I have been seeing each other for six years. Yes, we've been doing so behind Theo's back. Now he knows and they are getting a divorce tomorrow."

Catherine stood motionless, except for her lower lip quivering as if to say something, but the words couldn't come out. She looked at her parents but did not see them. You could see the tears welling up inside her eyes, a sign of indecision that the rich, bad boy, musclebound, meathead, John, did not notice.

Mr. and Mrs. Jansen looked at each other in total disbelief. They were married for forty years and their daughter had fallen

CHAPTER 7

far short of that benchmark, now with the divorce looming overhead.

"Are you kidding me? Cathy honey, is this true? What's going on?" her mother stammered to put words into cohesive sentences.

"Yes." Catherine looked down at the floor. "Yes, it's true. I've been seeing John. I…" She continued to look down at the floor in submission. "Theo's a great guy and I still love him but I was still in love with John as well."

The Jansen's little girl looked up from the floor with tears of passion. "See John and me, we have this chemistry that is so overwhelming. It's just that I knew he was a bad boy, with the drinking, gambling and the trips to strip bars. I figured that I could change him when we got together. But I couldn't and his wild nature just made me want him even more, like forbidden fruit," she sighed a great big sigh. "Theo, he was sweet and nice and kind. I love him too."

"Just not enough," Mr. Jansen said sternly, "Just not enough. Theo doesn't go gallivanting all over the place. He doesn't come home drunk or has strange phone numbers written on parts of his body. Honey, you came to us with these things. That's one of the reasons you dumped John in the first place. I helped you pick up the pieces as did Theo. What does Theo have to say?"

"He just left yesterday. We are going to get an uncontested divorce tomorrow. I don't think he's coming back. There's something else," Catherine said. Everyone waited for the next sentence, no one offering up a question as to what it might be. John looked at her in surprise. Her parents looked at her in bewilderment.

"I am eight weeks pregnant," announced Catherine.

The mountain of a man that was Mr. Jansen cascaded in an avalanche on the sofa. He was followed by the meaty mother of Catherine, Mrs. Jansen. Both needed a minute to process the news. John was thunderstruck as well. He looked like Theo had given him an uppercut that he rightly deserved. He grabbed Catherine by the shoulders and hugged her in a teddy bear hug. There was an obvious question in the room but everyone was too shocked to mouth the words.

CHAPTER 7

"Is it mine?" asked John, finally breaking the silence found on the polar ice caps.

Mr. Jansen, who sometimes substituted for a Himalayan mountain, felt the overwhelming urge to punch John Duboise.

The law offices of Clairmont, Fossway, and Lyons were in the heart of Costa Mesa. It was a posh, ten-story office building that shared its space with a state of the art laboratory belonging to the Francisco Mendellsohnn Medical Group. Theo was about twenty minutes early and Catherine had not arrived yet. The pretty assistant, who looked like a part-time college student took his name and had him fill out some paperwork.

The door to the lawyer's conference room was open and he saw a tall, brown-haired woman, who had on a black business suit with a skirt reaching just past her knees. She was arranging some papers on the table as if for a presentation of some kind. She looked up and noticed Theo staring at her. Not startled by this action, she gave him a warm smile and he noticed that she had doe eyes that were soft and kind. She went back to what she was doing with a smile.

Just then, a similarly attired tall, blond-haired woman walked through the main door of the building. She threw a glance at Theo that said 'I'm way out of your league' as she walked through the office to the conference room. The blond was just as tall as the brown-haired lady but not as thick. Her eyes looked sharp and astute as she hugged the other woman in the conference room.

Things got a little weird last night, with the whole not knowing who furnished your house and having an AIRE hanging around. He was thankful that Asheley made a delicious breakfast for him though. He had called in to tell work that he was not coming and when they asked the reason, he said flatly "to get a divorce."

He went back to filling out the rudimentary paperwork. He looked up and saw that the other party for the divorce had just walked through the door. John had accompanied Catherine. They

CHAPTER 7

had also brought along Katie, which was going to complicate things. Sadness welled up inside him and he knew that this encounter would be heart-wrenching.

Catherine looked radiant and professional, in a navy blue pants suit. However, beneath that layer of wild beauty was a cold-hearted gorgon that had petrified Theo's beating heart with her debauchery and lies.

"Daddy!" Katie ran to her father, the man that had taken care of her for the past six years. The man, that pulled her out of her mother's womb. The man that personally fixed up her nursery and eventually turned it into her bedroom. The man that bought all of _The Adventures Of The Binky Animal Babies_ books so he could read to his daughter (Don't worry, I am working on those too!).

"Katie," he hugged his daughter as he slid off the chair and knelt down, "How good to see you!"

"You didn't come to breakfast with us on Sunday," she said frowning.

"I know, I had some things to do," he said looking at Catherine.

"Hi Theo, how are you?" she managed to calmly say.

"I'm okay. Just a little surreal," he also calmly said.

"I'm going to sit over here. If you need me, I'll be close," said John as he kissed Catherine from behind on her cheek. He smiled a cocky one-sided smile and snorted in Theo's direction.

"Daddy, can you guess how many pancakes I ate? I also had lots of syrup and orange juice too!"

"How many did you eat?" said Theo, the soon to be divorced man smiling at his daughter.

"I had three big chocolate chip pancakes. How come you didn't come with us? Why is the neighbor kissing mommy? Why did he sleep in your bed? Did his bed break so you let him use yours?" she innocently asked.

"Did you tell her?" he asked Catherine in a whisper as he hugged Katie.

Catherine, who was looking at the heartwarming scene before her, was having second thoughts about this whole scenario. In addition, she was undecided about telling Theo that she was pregnant. Sadly she shook her head, unable to get out the words.

Finally, she mouthed, with those delicious looking lips of hers that had expertly applied purplish lipstick, "No, I did not know how to tell her."

"The bed did not break and the neighbor is kissing mommy because... Honey, remember when you got the teddy bear *Mr. Wuggles*?" Theo started.

"Uh-huh," said Katie looking down.

"Remember that you loved him so much that you said you would marry him?" Theo looked at Catherine then continued.

Katie nodded.

"Then we said that you couldn't marry him because he's a doll. But then when we got you *The Ticklish Doll That Poops and Laughs*, you didn't play with Mr. Wuggles a lot, right?"

Katie nodded. She knew something was coming.

The sharp-eyed lawyers stopped their paper filings and stood very conspicuously at the doorway of the conference room. They were looking on at the heartwarming scene unfolding in their offices.

"Then you loved the new doll more than you loved the old Mr. Wuggles and you even let the Ticklish Doll That Poops and Laughs sleep in your bed. But then you gave Mr. Wuggles to your friend from school because she moved away to a different school and you wanted her to remember you. Mr. Wuggles would always remember you and love you just as you would remember him and love him. But he's in a new house right?" continued Theo, tears trying to escape his eyes but he was doing his best to keep them on lockdown.

"Yes, I remember" Katie mumbled.

"I am like Mr. Wuggles because I am going to live in a different house. But you'll get to see me every week. Mommy got a new husband now, but that does not mean that I did not stop being your daddy. Besides, I have to go and live in my smaller house that I'm fixing up."

"Why? We have room at our house for you to stay. You could stay in my room."

"I need to stay at my little house because if I don't, then ghosts might want to move in. You know how ghosts like to live in empty houses right?"

CHAPTER 7

"Yeah, I do. You're not afraid of them?"

"No. Daddies are not supposed to be afraid of anything. Because that's what daddies do," Theo said with a sigh of relief. He looked at Catherine who had her hands to her face and also breathed a sigh of relief.

Even John looked slightly impressed, which Theo did not really care about.

Agness Clairmont was not at the proceedings in the lawyers' office that day. She kept Brentt Williams company while his wounds healed.

Bertha Fossway and Lynne Lyons motioned the participants into the conference room. Waiting there for them was a pile of neatly stacked papers on the light oak, rectangular table. Catherine and Theo took seats on opposite sides of the table. John just barely rushed in before the door shut.

"Hello and welcome everyone. I hope both of you are well. I'm not seeing any other lawyers in here so that means either that they are very late or are not necessary. In my experience, these things usually start off cordially and end up very heated and violent. So, we do have cameras to capture what goes on in here in case we have to call the police," Lynne stated as she looked at her guests for compliance.

As the lawyer spoke, John put up a beefy arm around the back of Catherine's chair and glared at Theo.

"Ok. Why are we all here?" asked Bertha.

"Thanks for having us here," said Theo shakily, "I am here to get an uncontested divorce from my wife. The reason: that she has been seeing the man next to her for six years."

"I see. Do you have any terms that you need to put forward?" asked Lynne.

"She gets the house and I keep my condos. I get Katie every weekend and Catherine gets her during the week. We split the joint account evenly," offered Theo.

"Do you have any objections or any counter terms?" solicited Bertha.

Catherine sat in a daze as she stared blankly at the pile of papers before her. "I don't think that..." she hesitated, "we should not have rushed into this so soon."

CHAPTER 7

John looked at her in surprise, "What?"

Catherine looked Theo in the eyes, "Theo we just broke up Saturday and today is Monday. Yeah, you caught me with John, but I think that we need to think about this…"

"Cat, honey what are you saying!" blurted out John.

"John shut up for once in your life you big sack of cow poop," Theo finally said with an imposing air of authority. "I have had just about enough of you. Let her speak and shut the hell up, meathead."

John looked surprised and wondered where this bag of balls came from out of Theo. He sat down and let the proceedings go on, but glowered with his arm still around Catherine's chair.

"Ok guys. Easy, let's not get too hyper here. It's the opening minutes. We just started things off," soothed Lynne as she turned to Theo. Bertha took the words right out of her mouth.

"Wait a minute, you decided on a divorce two days ago? Usually, these things take weeks to hash out before the couple even begins to call lawyers. Usually, this is preceded by marriage counseling and therapy. Needless to say, we're still getting paid for this. What's going on?"

"Look, therapy is out of the question. How is this going to even work? I'm pretty sure she's not going to give up John. She has been sleeping with this guy for the past six years. Are all of us going to sit in the counselor's office and do what? Talk about how we could get a bigger bed, and who gets her on what day?

I love my daughter and yes I still love Catherine but, I cannot do this," fired Theo at everyone in the room. He wasn't done yet, he still had some ammo left and aimed at Catherine. "Catherine, what were you thinking? Then why marry me at all? Was I that bad of a husband, that I drove you into the arms of this guy instead?"

Catherine felt the eyes of everyone in the room watching her like she was in a stadium before a huge game, waiting to sing the national anthem but couldn't remember the words. She finally managed to croak, "I love both of you, Theo. You're nice and kind and a great father to Katie. You do romantic things and write beautiful poems for me. We go on awesome vacations and have wonderful times.

CHAPTER 7

But John, he's a wild stallion that you want to tame but, it's ok if you don't because that's who he is, which makes me love him even more. He's a burly supermodel of a man. He has the physical passion and with you, it's the emotional passion. You know John and I have a history together."

"You also know we had a future together. Who do you want to be with?" asked Theo.

John looked interested in this question as well.

"I don't know…" Catherine replied like a little kid being asked if they told a lie.

"Cat, I don't understand why you went ahead and married this idiot, even after we had relations on your wedding day in the limo ride over to the church. Why?" demanded John.

"Wait… Do you mean that you cheated on our wedding day? You have to be kidding me!" Theo blurted out trembling with fear and shock. "Dare I say it…. Is Katie even my biological daughter?"

"I don't know… I," Catherine feebly tried to reply.

"Quite frankly, this divorce is happening, right? Because you," said Lynne as she looked at Theo, "look like you don't want a daily rotation and you," she shifted her pointer finger to John, "look like you don't like this guy at all."

"Yeah, that's it," said Theo in a monotone voice, "I have a pen. Let's do this and stop wasting my time."

The lawyers pulled out the necessary papers from the pile and distributed them to the soon to be divorced couple. Theo felt the weight of the pen in his fingertips. It became hard to scribble his name as he read and reread the fine print. The friction of the pen against the paper's surface felt almost overpowering.

His mind was bent upon having a divorce but his heart and body were organizing a revolution. He looked over and saw that Catherine was in a struggle of her own. *There was a war within and both sides were losing everything they were fighting for.*

John had gotten up and was looking out the window, either oblivious of the ensuing struggle going on inside Catherine's mind, or not really caring about it.

The two lawyers watched silently as the clients very hesitantly filled out the forms that would change their lives forever. When

CHAPTER 7

they were done, Bertha gathered up the paperwork and put them in a folder to process. She went through the door to the outer office and the door started to slowly shut in super slow motion, on the final moments of the marriage of Theo Steren Champlain and Catherine Jansen Champlain.

CHAPTER 8: Family Under Attack

They came swiftly in the dead of night, descending stealthily upon the mansion. Haggins was slain where he sat. His throat slit from ear to ear as he took a nap in the gatehouse of the mansion. As a ritual, the brigands marked the sign of the ankh upon his chest, a symbol of immortality.

The cold, crisp air did little to slow their progress. They used darkness as a cover as they flashed around lanterns that sliced and diced through the chilly night.

There were eight of them, a cohesive unit that had done this so many times before. Countless midnight excursions cataloged upon their resumes. Dressed in clothes that seemed unfamiliar to the occupants of the house, they entered, announcing their arrival.

Even the figure standing guard upon the door to the abode couldn't block the miscreants from entering. The door was kicked down violently. The soles of their feet stepped all over the face on the door.

Their very presence defiled the pristine house filled with lovingly crafted furniture, period wallpaper, exquisite paintings, and passionately manicured floors. The stench of mischief replaced the sweet-smelling aroma of fresh-cut flowers, lingering hot cookies, and expertly baked bread. This house wasn't their house but the intruders paraded in like it was theirs.

They wielded weapons that were as sharp as the minds of the residents in the house. Small, easily handled weapons which were not something you want to be pointed at you. The little dagger had a large secret. It shot electricity at the intended victim.

The intruding team decided to send in just two people as if the occupants of the house were not worth the time and effort of the other six marauders. They guarded the other entryways into the mansion.

CHAPTER 8

They came through the front door, thinly beamed lanterns flashing and special daggers pointing, ready for... Well Debora Smith, who was on her way from the kitchen, did not want to find out. She had come downstairs for water but soon regretted that decision. Flora Williams' mom had decided to stay by her daughter that evening. That was very bad timing indeed.

"Hello is anyone there? We have come for the Williams family. The Immortal Count commands that you appear before him. First, we need some information," said a middle-aged man in a monk's robe. He said it while sporting a smile that bordered upon lecherous.

His partner, a younger man with a skull and crossbones medallion around his neck, stood behind him and placed a wicked-looking device upon the end table. It messed up a perfectly placed doily in the process. The *pear of anguish* was a torture apparatus that forced open the jaw of any who was unfortunate to have it used upon them. The skull and crossbones on the man's medallion looked like a foreboding sigil that signaled his dastardly intentions.

Debora's skirt ruffled softly as she quickly dove behind the sofa, the fastest she'd moved in decades. Her body strained to silence her breath so she would not give away her position. Fear gripped her as she dared not move. She worried about her daughter and the kids upstairs, wondering what they were doing at this moment.

"Shush... did you hear some rustling?" asked Middle-Aged Man as he turned to Skull and Crossbones. "We know someone is there. Come out and do not resist. What the Count commands, so it shall come to pass. He is allowing you an audience. What he does after, is up to your behavior now."

"Yeah, I think it came from over there," Skull and Crossbones said as he motioned to the sofa.

Skull and Crossbones proceeded to climb on the clean sofa and make himself ridiculously comfortable. He shone the light around to see if there was any evidence of the individual that they knew was there.

The place that Flora had sat many a day and watched Brentt, Bertha, Agness and Lynne play was now sat upon by strangers.

CHAPTER 8

The place where Flora and her husband talked, the place where they had kissed, was now defiled by ruffians. The sofa that had been a part of the family's personal life was now desecrated by this knave who thinks he has the right to stand up on the couch, their couch, the Williams' family couch.

They got right to the point, these brigands and burglars, who invaded their personal space. Coaxing the residents to come out, using deception to accomplish what they needed to do.

"We have to look around. They might be upstairs or in one of the adjoining rooms," said Middle-Aged Man who proceeded to pick up a rocking chair and toss it in the darkness.

Skull and Crossbones held up the *pear of anguish*, again moving it around him as if burning incense. It was perfectly polished and he looked forward to using it. They shone their lanterns around the room, to the absolute horror of Debora.

The two men stepped quietly looking for their quarry, both deep in thought, possibly conjuring up ways to torture and harass their frightened prey.

She raised her head to look over the sofa, a futile attempt in such darkness. It came inches away from the beam of Skull and Crossbones' lantern. She strained to stifle a gasp but Skull and Crossbones heard it and looked over his right shoulder.

"I just heard a breath and the hair on my arms is standing up," he whispered as he grabbed for the wicked-looking knife next to him.

"Are you sure? Flora Williams, we have some questions for you and your family. Come quietly and you may, for the right price, have clemency," said Middle-Aged Man, pausing as if she'd give him an answer to his question.

"The Count wants no harm to come to them yet. He said to bring them to him alive and intact," chided Skull and Crossbones.

'Oh my goodness they don't know I'm not Flora,' Debora thought. 'They know who my son-in-law and daughter are. Why us? What did we do to deserve being hunted like this in the middle of the night?' she wondered as she ducked back down and hugged the ground.

Suddenly a miracle happened. Her hand fell upon a little toy jack that one of her grandkids' friends had apparently lost.

CHAPTER 8

Debora looked out from behind the sofa and knew the doorway to the stairs was on the other side of the room. Quickly and inaccurately, she threw the jack away from her hiding spot. It landed next to Middle-Aged Man, who felt it fall on the hardwood floor.

"Hey, something landed next to me!" Middle-Aged Man exclaimed as he brightened his lantern to see what the object was. While he was intently examining it, Skull and Crossbones came over to check it out as well.

Now was Debora's chance to slip away, hopefully unnoticed. She crept slowly and stealthily, making her body blend into the darkness. She had about 6 feet to go when they scanned the room with their lanterns. 'It's now or never,' she thought. She leaped up and just as she dashed through the doorway, the beam of the intruders fell where she had been moments before.

"There! Did you see that?" exclaimed Middle-Aged Man as he nonchalantly walked to the door and examined it.

"Yes, I did. Somebody just passed through here. I saw the door move a little," stated Skull and Crossbones. He pushed open the door further and heard hurried footsteps going up the stairs with an almost muted gasp of "kids".

Both Middle-Aged man and Skull and Crossbones walked determinedly up the stairs with paced strides. Skull and Crossbones led the way. Both had their special daggers in hand and relished the opportunity to use them.

Elsewhere, in the master bedroom, Dr. Henry Williams heard the commotion downstairs and had seen unfamiliar lanterns shining upon his front lawn. His first thought was for the safety of the kids, into whose rooms he ran. He burst into Bertha's room, roused her and they both went to Agness' room. They awoke the sleeping princess whose dreams of talking furry animals at a tea party, were cut short.

"Hush. Don't talk. Be very quiet. We're going to get Lynne," whispered Dr. Williams as he lightly patted his charges. Agness rubbed her eyes groggily and sat up. Sleep was fighting her as she was picked up in his strong arms and pulled close to his six-foot, six-inch frame. "I'll protect you both with my life," he softly whispered.

CHAPTER 8

He led them out of the room and towards Brentt's bedroom. He heard talking downstairs, which meant that they were in the house already. He walked softly and quickly so the old floorboards wouldn't creak. It was only about 10 feet to Brentt's bedroom, but it felt like ten miles. He opened the door to his son's room and saw no one in the bed.

Dr. Henry Williams heard the sound of light footsteps behind him and in one swift move, turned and put the kids behind him as he faced the potential threat. It was Flora, with Lynne by her side. He breathed a sigh of relief as he hugged his wife and Lynne.

"I don't know where Brentt is," said Henry worriedly to his wife.

Unbeknownst to them, Brentt had gone to check on his grandma. His room was next to hers and he had heard the old woman coughing in the middle of the night. He had overheard his dad telling his grandma that she was sick and needed some rest. He had heard something about a lung infection during his eavesdropping. He had knocked softly on the door and found no answer, so he peeked inside. The sheets were moved as if the occupant had gotten out of bed and gone somewhere.

The mansion had a back staircase to the kitchen and Brentt decided to go downstairs for a drink. The house had running water by means of an Archimedes pump which pulled the water from the nearby stream and ran it through the house. In fact, most rooms had a small pump, which when the crank handle was turned a few times, pulled the water up through the piping, straight to your destination.

He was on the landing of the second grand staircase that overlooked the living room. He saw them, two marauders that had a lantern that shone precise beams of light. They also had wicked looking daggers that were attached to something else. He was above the living room and luckily they did not see him. He quickly dropped down and lay on the floor, looking and waiting. In the dim darkness, he saw his grandma hiding behind the sofa.

CHAPTER 8

He could make her out, but the bad guys could not. He hoped that it stayed that way.

Brentt could see well in the dark, thanks to his medicine that his dad and mom gave to him and his friends. Actually, his family could do lots of things that most people could not do. They were smarter, stronger, moved faster, healed better and had enhanced vision, and hearing. Essentially, they were *hyper human*. In addition, they had the prestigious pleasure of learning secret knowledge from their father and his associates at The Sisters of the Black Habit. They were a clandestine society of warrior assassin nuns, who took great pride in their ascended knowledge of the universe.

Grandma was in trouble and he needed to do something fast. Brentt saw when she threw the toy away from her position and the two strangers went for it. While they were examining the jack, it gave her time to escape through the door that was ajar. Brentt saw them head after her and that was his time to strike.

He leaped from the banister and landed like a cat on the hardwood floors, making a noise that mimicked the footsteps of the assailants. He noiselessly crept to the doorway and peeked around the corner. Luckily the house had long staircases because they were halfway up by the time he got there. He would take the middle-aged man out first, making it look like an accident.

Brentt woke up in his bed and found that it was very chilly. He drew the covers up around his neck that was pulsing with so much life. He thought about what Bertha and Lynne were doing now. They were probably still asleep, but Agness loved to get up early and make breakfast for everyone.

They had all been friends since they were teenagers and had come to live in the Williams' home when all of their parents got sent to jail for dissident speech against the government. After some time, the news of their parents' accidental deaths in jail devastated the children. From then on, Henry and Flora Williams took care of Bertha, Agness, and Lynne like their own. They had

CHAPTER 8

given them a long life. Actually, longer than everyone that they knew.

He headed to the bathroom and shut the door. Brentt brushed his teeth in the double sink and wasted no time getting in a morning shower. His towel hung loosely around his waist as he headed into the walk-in closet to get clothes for the morning.

"What is that scratching sound?" Brentt asked himself, as he stood up and walked to the source of the sound, which was the bedroom door. He pulled it open to find his dark yellow golden retriever standing there, looking straight into his crotch.

"Aye, I don't need to see your Hangus and McKracken so early in the mornin. That's a sight to make the top of the morning turn into a bottom of the evening. Breakfast is ready compliments of Agness, the sneakiest woman on the moors. She thinks me a four-footed errand boy. She bamboozled me with a piece of chewy bacon from the breakfast she be serving," said the dog.

"Henry, thanks for letting me know," Brentt said to his trusty, furry sidekick.

"Yuck and phooey. You humans look really nasty naked, with all these body parts hanging around and jiggling," exclaimed the dark yellow golden retriever.

Just then, Lynne came out of her room looking as fresh as the crystal clear waters of a soft waterfall tumbling down rocks and meandering into a lazy stream.

"Give me a few minutes so I could get dressed," Brentt smiled as he closed the door and did exactly that.

Agness loved to cook. She loved to try new recipes for her family. They always worked out well. She had gotten up earlier than Brentt, Bertha, and Lynne to start the day off meditating and cooking. She was making a fabulous breakfast of turkey bacon, scrambled eggs, waffles, hash browns, and of course, the coffee of the day from South Africa.

She was a lawyer like her friends; however, she did not enjoy it as much as they did. All of the Williams family members had lots of doctorates and degrees. Well, they had time on their hands to complete them, not to mention the brainpower.

CHAPTER 8

Most people might think that having a cockney talking dark yellow golden retriever was crazy, but it was normal in their household. It had been three months since Brentt had been stabbed and Henry was by his side every day, making sure he was recuperating as per the doctor's orders. Dr. Mendellsohnn knew about the talking dog and about the history of the Williams family. Actually, they went way back.

Brentt's house was big, like ten bedrooms, ten bathrooms, four kitchens and eight garages big. It was situated on ten acres of land that had the peace and quiet that you needed when you have a big family secret to hide and plenty of talking animals that you needed to keep hidden. It also had a two-bedroom guest house, just in case there were any visitors but that rarely happened, if ever.

Their neighbors were even more reclusive than they were. Their house was situated on a two hundred acre piece of land that had pine trees encircling the whole perimeter of the house. They had met their neighbors a few times, but even then it was a few times too many because they creeped out even the Williams.

Agness remembered meeting someone named Raechellee from next door and asked about her name to which she replied, "I was named that, so I don't worry about it." She hurried off before they could ask any more questions. In the long run, it was for the best. You don't ask about my life and I don't know about yours.

Brentt, Lynne and Bertha came downstairs, wide-eyed and excited for the delicious breakfast that Agness had lovingly prepared for them. Brentt hugged Agness tightly and planted a sloppy kiss on her waiting cheek.

"Breakfast looks great, as always. Did you sleep well last night?" he complimented and asked her.

"Thanks, I did. Let's have breakfast and then you guys have to get ready to go to work. I'm staying home because I have to be here when the delivery guys get here with the TV," she giggled, making fun of them for going to work.

While Agness was washing up the dishes, after everyone had left, she called to Henry, who was in the living room enjoying the morning news. "Henry, make sure that the other Binky Animal Babies are up so I can give them their breakfast please."

"You bet your last dollar in my overcoat I will!" exclaimed Henry as he bounded to the basement where the other animals were sleeping.

The basement looked like a zoo turned into an animal common room, but each of the animals was part of the Williams' household, just like the humans:

Iigglloo, a three-foot-long chameleon iguana hybrid, was sleeping soundly with his cage door open.

Bunnie, a ten-pound dwarf rabbit, slept in her cubby. She was gray on the lower half of her body with white toes. She had white fur on her top half but had gray ears and cheeks. She had the lightest blue eyes.

Boobie Woobie was a twenty-pound white cat with black fur over his face and on the tip of his tail. He lazily lay on the old sofa that occupied the room.

Squiggles, a half-pound, light brown hamster, snuggled in the woodchips of his cage.

Boberta, a four-pound, black, brown and white mottled guinea pig, snored a little in her cubby.

MacGraw, the rainbow-colored Macaw, slept peacefully on his mahogany perch.

Henry entered the room. Like a good furry alarm clock, he woke all the sleeping critters from their dreams about whatever sleeping animals dream about.

"Chow time, guys! Come on, get up sleepy tails!" he said with a tail wag.

CHAPTER 9: More Gods

I t came to pass that the newly appointed Gods assembled in the temple planet of Atomos, which was situated in the exact center of all of the multiverses. Each of the thrones that the Gods sat upon was overlooked by The Contest of the Nine. Atomos sat in the middle of them but faced each of them, so that the other eight Gods could talk face to face with him and not feel left out. They had just finished examining the multiverse and had come back at the request of the King of the Gods and the God of the Gods.

"Hello everyone, how are my fellow Gods doing?" he asked with a jovial air.

"Very good, thank you," replied Galaxyia, excited at the first official meeting of the Gods in the entire history of the universe.

"How did you all find my multiverse? Was it not beyond your wildest imaginations?" asked Atomos.

"It was perfection and beyond," answered the God of Life, Caddeussus.

"Everything is structured perfectly and is a sight to behold. Thank you for the opportunity to examine all of creation," commented Archituria as she nodded.

"The order and organization of the galaxies are impressive. They are in such a way as to allow different environs. The creatures are perfectly attuned to their surroundings. I like the bunnies. They are cute," Galaxyia smiled demurely.

"Thank you. I was going for cute and cuddly," answered Atomos.

"The molecules and atoms are a technical marvel. It's amazing that the same building blocks can be used for creatures that are cute and cuddly and for those that are not," joked Technon nodding to Galaxyia.

"Yes, those building blocks are great, aren't they Technon? Did you see how they interlock and twist?" Archituria pointed out excitedly.

CHAPTER 9

"I was looking at how the positioning affects…" Technon continued but was interrupted by Atomos.

"I am glad that you like them. How about you, Goddess of Knowledge, do you find that you have enough knowledge to fill that book of yours?"

"Atomos, King of the Gods and God of the Gods, I did find lots of knowledge. It is exhilarating. I will need a Library," beamed Heddonna.

"We will work on that," replied Atomos.

"The life flowing in the multiverse, I feel, almost negates my position, Atomos. It seems a waste to take away any life," surmised the God of Death, Detrimentus.

"Yes, my fellow Gods, that brings me to why you are all here. I have three things that need to be done. I need all of your inputs because:

We are going to create beings called *Athlogoss Drones* which means 'the ones whose actions convey the will of the nine'. We shall give them gifts that have a part of our powers so they would spread knowledge of us through the ages.

We are going to decide the rules and regulations of the behavior of the Gods toward the whole of creation and the role that creation should play towards the Gods.

We will implement a system of reward and punishment for the entire multiverse. This will encourage all its inhabitants to always strive to do better and reach a higher state of spiritual well-being."

All the other Gods looked around at each other, trying to comprehend the magnitude of what would be discussed and done in this gathering. They were finally going to get their say in creation.

CHAPTER 10: Theo After The Divorce

After signing the divorce papers and driving from the lawyers' office, Theo came home with a mission; to find out how the AIRE was made and how she got here. He started by questioning her and by trying to figure out what made her function. He performed experiments that tested Asheley's ability and saw what her intellect was like. Theo got nowhere with finding answers. He could not get to the bottom of this mystery. Eventually, the strangeness of having an Artificially Intelligent Robotic Entity in his condo subsided and he began a physical relationship with her.

Three months had passed since Theo's divorce and it was as good as a newly divorced person can have, especially when you have a condominium and an AIRE. Asheley had really grown on him and her sense of emotions had skyrocketed. She understood more of the human psyche, the ways of the world, and grasped human inter-connectivity with each passing day. She understood that there were good and bad people in the world and that they should always strive for good.

She developed a unique sense of being and it was truly amazing to see her flourish. He felt closer to her and comforted in knowing that she would be there for him, always. It was different being around something or someone that knew everything in the world, but yet in their eyes, you were the world to them.

He introduced Asheley to Catherine and Katie one evening when he had to pick Katie up for her weekend with him. John was usually upstairs when he came by. Catherine was surprised that Theo scored a unique woman like Asheley, who looked faux but seemed nice enough to be around. Great! Asheley passed the test of human interaction with flying colors.

"How are you doing, Theo?" asked Catherine softly.

CHAPTER 10

"I'm holding up. Are you doing okay?" replied Theo.

"John and Katie are getting used to each other. My parents have been over every day since the divorce. They are playing relationship police. Where did you meet her? She seems very plastic surgery oriented."

"I met Asheley at my condominium complex. She and I hit it off very well. She's a great cook."

"Oh, that's nice. I'm glad you found someone. I am a little jealous it was so soon," she said as she put a hand on his shoulder.

"All I want is for you to be happy. I wish it was with me. However, if you are happy with John, then I am happy that you are," Theo said as he put his hand on her hand, that was on his shoulder.

"Theo, I am twenty weeks pregnant. I was holding off on telling you because of everything that happened. However, I can't hide it anymore."

Theo felt the urge to remove his hand from hers but he did not. He loved the touch of Catherine, no matter how small the contact was. He needed her touch now, even though she gave him the bad news that pained him. Her touch was still comforting.

"I am happy for you. You are a good woman and a good mom. Katie will make a great big sister. Dare I ask about...?"

"Not till after the baby is born," Catherine commented, finishing Theo's train of thought.

They stood in silence, hand in hand.

"Feelings aren't like a light switch. I know that you pretend they are. I know you feel the same way I do. Do you think we made a mistake?"

"Right now, I don't know what to think. Asheley is wonderful and I don't want to spoil that."

They reluctantly parted ways. Each was thinking about what the other said and each not wanting to make a tough decision tougher.

Theo and Catherine dragged their feet on the DNA test for Katie, not wanting to know the truth or give up the thing that

CHAPTER 10

bound them together. John pressed for the issue to be resolved but Catherine would have none of it.

Halloween time was just around the corner and Theo was going to take Katie out to get her costume. Asheley was in the car suggesting types of candy she can get, along with all of the nutrition information for each one. Katie agreed that they sounded very delicious and couldn't wait to try them all.

"Daddy, what do you think I should dress up as?" she innocently asked.

"I don't know. I'm sure there are lots of things you could be. Like a princess, or a policewoman, or a firefighter, or a robot, or a ballerina, lots of possibilities," he said concentrating on finding a parking spot near the store.

"May I dress up for Halloween as well Theo?" asked Asheley.

"Sure. We will pick out something for you too!" he happily suggested.

"Actually, there's a new dolly that I want and she has a big house. She also has cars and everything that you need to give a dolly a good life. It's the *Ultimate Dolly Good Life Play Set* that I saw on TV," suggested Katie.

"So do you want that as well as a new costume? What about candy?" asked Theo thinking how much this doll is going to cost him.

"All of it, if I can please," she said looking up at her father and smiling.

Asheley gave a big smile too, "Katie, that's a great idea. We can play with the dolly together!"

They walked into the store and Theo realized that Asheley might set off the store alarm but thankfully she did not. They looked around a bit, picking up some stuff that they needed for the weekend ahead. They stopped at the costume aisle and looked through hundreds of costumes, but it seemed like Katie was not into any of them. He led her to the toy aisle and let her loose. She happily looked at everything, trying to decide which toy to get for herself.

While she decided, Theo looked at the other shoppers that were in the area; Jane moms that may or may not be single, all dateable now that he was free. In hindsight, how was he going to explain a robot woman living in his house? He'll just play it by ear and see what happens. He might want to get out there and date. There were plenty of opportunities to do so with the apps and stuff, but his heart was not in it, just not yet. He was still picking up the pieces.

He knew that this transition from married to single was hard on him, but it must be especially hard on Katie, having to adjust to a new dad in the house.

"Katie cat, did you find anything?" Theo asked when she did not get the toy she was looking for.

"They don't have it...," she said sadly.

"Theo, I have settled upon this outfit. What do you think?" asked Asheley as she held up an adult fairy costume.

"I think it's perfect," replied Theo flagging down an employee.

"Excuse me; do you have The Ultimate Dolly Good Life Play Set?"

The employee, who was a middle-aged man that looked very haggard and overly exhausted, answered as cheerily as he could, "No sir, we are all sold out at the moment. It would be at least a month till we get another shipment. This toy is the hottest thing on the market right now."

"Do you know if other stores would have it?"

"I don't know but I am hearing from other customers that everywhere is sold out."

Theo thanked the man, gathered Katie and went to the checkout line. He explained to her that the store was sold out, but gave her hope in the fact that they were going on a treasure hunt to find the toy. Asheley began searching her database for any stores that might have it. Her suggestions came in handy. However, the next six stores were out of stock of the toy as well.

A dejected Katie sat in the car on the way to Theo's condo. In an effort to cheer her up, he bought fast food from a drive-through. It was good and she nibbled away on the hungry man fries, almost eating out the whole bag before they got home. It was very late by the time she had been given a bath and her storybook was read to her. Asheley happily made all the sounds in the background for added effect.

CHAPTER 10

While Theo was fixing the covers around her, she asked, "I want it to be the way it used to be with you, mommy and me. Why can't it be like that?"

Looking down and trying to find the answer he smiled, "Look on the bright side, instead of one daddy, now you have two!" After bidding goodnight to his daughter, Theo went to his room and closed to door with a sigh. Asheley was sitting on the bed and saw the sadness in his eyes. "Are you okay?" she inquired.

"I know that not having her mom and dad together is hard on Katie."

"I have ascertained that there are different levels of sadness. Like when you are rooting for a team and they do not win the game, you feel sad. Another example is when you do not get that job that you applied for, or the raise that you were looking forward to. I know that another, more extreme form of sadness, is when someone close to you dies, which is grief. No doubt a divorce falls into that category as well. Am I right?"

"Yes, there are different levels of sadness however; people deal with them in different ways. Kids are not as emotionally matured as adults, so special care has to be taken to consider their needs, especially in a broken relationship. I am glad that you are getting along with Katie. I see that she has grown fond of you. I'm tired. Sometimes all of this is very stressful." Theo said sitting next to her on the bed.

Asheley excitedly got up and grabbed his clothes and a towel for him to bathe with. "We'll take a bath then relax" she proposed. Theo promptly did as she ordered.

Theo descended into a deep satiated sleep alongside Asheley, who apparently had a sleep mode as well. He did not dream about Catherine, or about beating up John, but he did dream about the doll and accessories that he could not get for his daughter Katie. The doll came alive in his mind, peeking at him from the edge of the bed.

He woke up a little past seven in the morning, just as a scream issued from Katie's room. He quickly got dressed and Asheley was right behind him. They sprang to Katie's room, down the hall. When he opened the door, there on the floor, displayed like in a toy store window, was The Ultimate Dolly Good Life Play

Set. It was out of the box and in pristine condition, arranged on a play mat of fake grass. His daughter was standing in front of the playset, as excited as he was shocked to see it.

The day before Thanksgiving was excruciatingly long. The kind of day that seemed like it had extra hours when you really didn't want it. That day, in a sense, did have extra hours. Theo willingly agreed to pick up 4 extra hours at work. Work, which had been a very scarce commodity as of late, was like gold for a struggling part-timer.

"Theo, looks like you're a good worker with loads of experience and a people person too. You'll go far in this company. We just have to figure out where to put you." That was what his boss assured him ten years ago. 'Not much upward movement there,' Theo thought. Well, he couldn't complain because work was work and bills needed to be paid. Could he be the same bright-eyed and bushy-tailed worker that he used to be? Well, he would act the part like he always did.

On this particular day, all the customers at the department store seemed to look, sound and want the same thing. Monotonous trips to load supplies into people's cars seemed to dominate his day. Mundane duties such as cleanup in aisle 2 for a bottle of drain cleaner that someone carelessly cast aside wasted twenty minutes of his action-packed life.

The dreary art of stocking goods in the back was completed with almost perfect mindless accuracy. Yes, mindless accuracy. This coming from Theo's brilliant and open mind, zealously hungry for knowledge of the unknown and beyond. A library was his nirvana, a science expo his Shangri la, the hordes of documentaries on television from Aliens to Zebras was his transcendence into ecstasy.

"Mom, I'm going to see my boyfriend, Tyler, in the hospital today. The doctor said that he had a hairline fracture in his shoulder that he got when he was skateboarding. So I don't think he could walk for a few months. But I don't understand how a fracture in your head could affect your walking. I mean unless you hit your head pretty hard.

But I need to figure some stuff out. I mean why did the doctor use a cast on his shoulder when he had a hairline fracture that clearly points to his head?" A thirty-something blond woman, who looked like a ridiculously tall, gorgeous supermodel spoke to her cell phone. She pressed the button on her keys to pop the trunk on her brand spanking new ultra-high-end SUV. "My sixty-year-old husband gave it to me last week for my birthday," she smiled to Theo.

"It looks great," Theo replied.

The barbeque grill she bought was a behemoth and Theo did not relish the chance to wrestle with this great beast. Using his Herculean strength, Theo hoisted the Titan substitute into the voluminous trunk. The trunk was so big that he heard an echo. 'Damn, this looks bigger than my condominium,' Theo thought. After saying goodnight he turned back to the store wondering how some people had all the luck.

His mind wandered to his ex-wife and daughter but was interrupted by the soft sliding of the glass doors of the store. 'Man, Stanley really polishes that thing at least 5 times a day. I don't think I see him doing anything else,' thought Theo. Two more hours of menial tasks that ranged from "what wattage bulbs should we get" to "how long should my dryer cord be," bombarded his remaining time at work.

There was a respite in between the bombarding when he helped a happy couple pick out some paint for their new home. Theo remembered when he was a happy couple. However, the fresh scars of a sutured broken heart still pained and he quickly derailed that train of thought.

Finally, it was time to go home to Asheley. He texted her earlier that day to let her know don't bother with dinner, he was going to pick something up. He knew exactly where he wanted, no needed, to go for dinner. His mind was set on a nondescript burger place that had the one thing with which his famished soul could be satiated. Theo's mouth watered at the vision of a mushroom and Swiss burger with all the fixings, house special sauce, a large box of hungry man curly fries, chicken nuggets, mozzarella sticks that were crispy on the outside and oh so gooey in the middle. An ice-cold soft drink rounded off the menu. That would all be his in a few minutes.

Theo had the dessert at home; divine apple caramel cheesecake. It was absolute decadence, lovingly made for him by the vivacious Asheley. She insisted that it be a special present from her alone because she knew Theo loved it. She had never struck out when it came to cooking. She could recreate recipes just perfectly.

It was very fortunate for him that this nondescript burger place and his work were streets over from where he lived. The time ordering in the burger place was not fast enough. His walk home was brisker tonight than most nights, well because he had hot food in his hand and he was very hungry.

Theo went inside his elegantly furnished condo and set the food down on the foyer table. He then took off his shoes and went to the kitchen with his meal and set it on the counter. Usually, Asheley met him at the door. "Where is she? Darn, I didn't realize I drank out the soda," he mumbled to himself. "Maybe she's in the room," he continued to mumble. Theo turned around to go to the bedroom to change his clothes but stopped in his tracks.

There before him, stood a robed figure in black that was a head taller than him. Two soft pops could be heard in between the beats of his heart as every molecule in his body stopped, frozen in fear. Theo looked down and saw two deep, blood-red stains on his shirt. "Hmm...I wonder why there isn't more blood." He sank to the kitchen floor gasping for air as his assailant moved closer.

His heart, or what was left of it after his wife broke it, was trying to claw its way out of his chest. The room was fading and turning as if he was seeing some type of slide show. Surprisingly, Theo was not in that much pain. His lifeblood slipped away, staining the floor and his sweaty clothes. He couldn't kneel up anymore and lay down on the bare tiled floor facing the counter and his dinner.

The smell of blood, burgers, chicken nuggets and fries filled his nose, creating a repulsive aroma. The unknown assailant grabbed his dinner, with all its succulent glory just waiting to be ravenously devoured, and left. Theo Steren Champlain could not hold on to his meager life after seeing the pilferage of his hard-earned dinner. He let go and slipped into blackness.

Asheley kept herself occupied every day by watching the news, surfing the web and looking at funny cat videos. She usually used the tablet, the computer, or herself as she perused the internet looking at the things people post online, from the funny, to the why, to the insane. She loved to cook and her programming had amalgamated all of the recipes, from all the chefs in the world, to give Theo a culinary orgasm from the well-lit and organized kitchen of his condominium.

Asheley had a good idea when Theo usually got home and tonight was no exception. He had texted her on the phone he had gotten for her, to let her know he was picking up his dinner. Immediately, she did the calculations in her magnificently crafted brain and figured out the minimum and maximum estimated time of his arrival at home.

Theo had allowed her to venture outside because she had reached a level of maturity in interacting with people. Most people could not tell that she was an artificial being. They just thought she had lots of plastic surgery. Asheley would run errands and go to the grocery and she could even drive. She had attained a driver's license, but how, Theo could not figure out for the life of him.

She was in the living room watching the news, when to her surprise, an emotion that she had come to learn, she heard someone at the door. Asheley got up and very spryly looked through the peephole to see who it might be. Even though the AIRE was six-feet, two-inches tall and weighed two-hundred and fifty pounds, she carried herself like the wind. Looking through the peephole, Asheley could see someone fiddling with the lock on the door to the apartment. It was not Theo and if it's not Theo, then it could be a robber.

CHAPTER 10

This person was extremely tall and wore a hoodie with dark glasses and a bandanna over the lower half of their face. Theo had always told her that it was paramount to keep herself out of trouble because there might be people that do not understand her. She immediately turned off the television which already was low and went to the master bedroom shower that looked like a rainforest. Asheley used a mechanism that even Theo did not know of; cloaking, to blend in with the shower tiles.

She heard the burglar come into the condo and shut the door quietly; her sensors picking up the intruder's vibrations even in the shower of the master bathroom. The brigand crept through the house to make sure that no one was home and eventually came into the bathroom. The shower door was ajar and the thief slowly opened it and saw no one, however, the AIRE in the shower saw the perpetrator.

The intruder quickly turned and went to sit on the bed, checking a watch for the time. The person was tall, much taller than the six-foot AIRE. There was bulk behind the baggy clothes of the individual as if they had purposely filled in their clothes with padding to hide prominent areas of their bodies, namely a shapely chest or a backside. The intruder walked around the room as nervous as a new singer before a performance on a show.

There seemed to be hesitation in the intruder's footsteps and even hesitation in the act that was about to be committed. The intruder glanced at the gun and shook their head in indecision. The intruder got up and came to the big mirror in front of the sink and looked into it through dark shades.

The AIRE, through the partially open shower door, could see the intruder psyching themselves up for the deed about to be committed. The watch on the intruder's hand said it all. Asheley knew Theo was due home in ten minutes. The criminal walked to the bed, laid back and spread out as if they owned it. She did not know what to do. Theo had told her to not harm anyone and she could not do so for his sake.

Asheley closed her eyes and hoped for everything to be okay. Soon, the would-be assailant got up and hid in the next room as the AIRE heard Theo walk through the doorway. She heard the rustle of the bag of food in his hand. She heard the work boots of his coming off. She heard him walking into the kitchen. She heard him mumble about finishing his drink. She heard the two soft pops of a weapon go off. She heard a slump to the floor. She heard the rustle of the bag of food. She heard the front door close quietly. Asheley heard nothing else after that.

Asheley jumped out of the shower and within milliseconds was standing over Theo, who was lying near death on the kitchen floor. She dropped to her knees, trying to stop the bleeding with all the medical knowledge of the world at her fingertips. Asheley frantically grabbed a knife and slit her finger open. She then put it next to the open wound on Theo's chest. *Red, viscous, Nano Machine Filled Molecular Fluid* poured into the limp body of Theo.

"I will try to use my internal Nanobots to close the gash and stop the bleeding. Normally they check for any internal system malfunctions inside me, but this time they'll be doing it for Theo. I am seeing a rupture in the aortal artery. Working on repairing it right now. I'll also try to see if I can soak up the blood that has spilled out and purify it. Then I'll introduce it back into his body. I'll have to get emergency services," exclaimed Asheley as she grabbed Theo's cell phone and called the emergency operator.

"I'd like to report a shooting. You better hurry, he's seriously injured," she said surprisingly collected.

"What happened? How bad is it? Is the victim conscious?"

"He's been shot through the aortal artery. He lost consciousness and a lot of blood but I'm a doctor and am doing all I can to save him. Looks like a home invasion," said Asheley focusing on saving Theo's life. "The address is 123 Canyon Road, Condo number 1A."

"You're in luck. Someone else had called for emergency services at that same residence. An ambulance and a police unit are very close by. Please remain on the phone with me," relayed the dispatcher.

She hung up the phone. She began the process of shifting the bullets away from Theo's heart and repaired the pericardium and the aortal artery. The Nanomachines, quadrillions and quadrillions of them, all worked simultaneously to fix the bleeding heart of Theo, as the AIRE studied the results in her internal logs. She heard the ambulance and saw the lights and was still kneeling by the limp body of Theo as the paramedics put him on a stretcher and took him outside.

The Artificially Intelligent Robotic Entity, Asheley, which knew everything in the whole world, found out what it felt like to not know anything that was about to happen to her friend, lover, and creator, Theo Steren Champlain.

She sat at a corner table by a coffee house located inside a bookstore, with a bag of delicious smelling food. It contained a big juicy mushroom and Swiss cheeseburger with house special barbeque sauce, large hungry man spicy fries, crispy chicken nuggets and fried mozzarella sticks, crispy on the outside and deliciously gooey on the inside. The food was steaming hot as if recently bought, but it was a few hours old and it was someone else's. That someone else was probably near death, which made the food taste even better in her mind.

She looked every bit as expensive and as high maintenance as the ultra-luxurious SUV she drove. There, at that table, by that coffee house, in that bookstore, she looked out of place. A woman like her belonged in every man's dreams. She seemed formed from every man's desire and stepped straight out from an artist's rendering of beauty and perfection.

Her beauty was like a sunset at the beach on a cool summer's evening. Her looks were as refreshing as the view from a mountaintop that overlooks the fertile, verdant valley and a winding, life-giving river below. The light of a full moon peeking from behind the silver clouds could hardly describe the mystery surrounding her.

In fact, if all three of these scenarios were to have a celestial daughter, it would be her, in all of her cosmic transcending beauty. She was at least a head taller than most men and sporting a well-proportioned figure. Her hair cascaded in a luxurious torrent of blond velvet. The deep blue of her eyes burned like sapphires in a jewelry store's glass case, whilst her long dark ethereal lashes struggled to put out their fire every time she

CHAPTER 10

blinked. A face as bright and radiant as a glowing star punctuated her figure. Her beauty was so awe-inspiring, so overwhelming, that one couldn't help but grovel before her.

She took in the aroma of the bag of food before her. She then, with surgical precision, slit the bag in two and formed a place-mat in which all the contents lay. Her long fingers with blood red-tipped nails gripped the burger before her. The gorgeous blond goddess bit into the food with feral vigor and ravenously ripped the meat apart with her sharp star-like teeth. Savoring the juices of the meal, her eyes rolled in satisfaction.

One would think that she would devour the meal instantaneously, but she did the opposite; savoring the food in front of her. No one saw her. No one looked in her direction. No one marveled at her radiant, overpowering, legendary beauty. It was impossible to imagine that a beautiful goddess looking woman like this escaped the attention of everyone around her.

After her meal, she leaned back and said to herself, "This tastes good and it's ok once in a while, but I want to make sure that he eats like a king. After all, he's got to keep up his strength for what's ahead."

The blond goddess got up and dumped the trash in the wastebasket. She walked out of the bookstore on those long, sexy legs that ended in hiking boots and looked across the street towards the hospital. Staring up at a particular floor and looking hard at the room that held a special guest, Raechellee then turned and headed towards the flower shop next door.

CHAPTER 11: Brentt Williams At Work

B rentt drove to work in his dark grey muscle car that had all the bells and whistles, which a man like himself would be proud of. He snapped on the radio while he sat in traffic. The Chief was still doing paperwork from the bust three months ago, but everything turned out all right.

There was a crappy, cookie-cutter song on the radio that spouted something about women, money, cars, and power; not his style. He turned off the radio, wishing there was a volume setting lower than off. He had been around long enough to learn to play a myriad of musical instruments and have a plethora of doctorates, plus a whole lot of knowledge about other stuff that....

Someone just ran a red light in front of him, barely missing cross traffic. He quickly turned on his police lights and gave chase. It was a red minivan with a blond occupant inside, who was not on her cell phone or otherwise distracted.

"Come in dispatch, this is officer Brentt Williams," he called on his radio.

"Hello, officer Williams, what seems to be the problem?"

"I am clocking in early today because I am on the tail of a traffic violation. They ran a red light. It looks like she is pulling over in a deserted parking lot, near some buildings. Hopefully, it's a routine traffic stop and nothing else," he supposed.

He got out of the car and checked himself for his handcuffs, two pairs of them. However, his sidearm was in the trunk. He cautiously walked up to the minivan and stopped at the window.

Sitting before him was an attractive blond about thirty-something years of age that had on a low cut top and yoga pants. She smiled sweetly as she said, "Hello, officer, what seems to be the problem?"

CHAPTER 11

"Are you aware that you just ran a red light?" he asked in a gentle way.

"Yes, I did run the red light. I was in a hurry to get home," she spoke in a valley girl accent.

"Most people who run red lights are usually in a hurry. Let me see your license and registration please," he said in a cordial tone.

"My name is Jenny. Here it is," she reached up in her visor as she spoke, "anything else that you might be interested in seeing?" The blond suggestively ran her hand down her throat.

"Miss Jenny, I don't think that's a good idea," said Brentt already knowing where this was going, having seen it tons of times before.

"I am just scratching my neck while you check on my credentials," she said pouting.

"Now listen, Jenny, I'm pretty sure that it's against the law to flirt with a police officer. I don't know which law you're breaking at the moment, but it's there somewhere," Brentt said, blushing a little.

"I'm nursing my first child and I'm 22 weeks pregnant with my second one," Jenny said very innocently.

"Jenny, that's great," replied Brentt, trying to keep on task.

"Look, I was speeding home to see if my boyfriend was sleeping with his mom's best friend. I have proof of it on my security camera that I can access through my phone, but I want the satisfaction of catching them in the act. So, is there any way I can get out of this ticket?" she asked as she moved her hand lower down her tight, fit pregnant body.

"I have to uphold the law. So Jenny…"

"Everyone hands up! Now! This is a stick-up and I'm taking all your cash," said an unknown voice that both Brentt and Jenny looked alarmed at hearing.

In front of them, was a tall man with nondescript features that looked vaguely familiar. He was holding a gun that was pointed at the police officer and the traffic violator.

"Everyone, hands up. You, lady, get out of the car! No sudden moves, fake mustache, crotch face! Come on, move!" he said as he came closer.

CHAPTER 11

Jenny got out of the minivan. Brentt's hands remained up. Great, he had his weapon in the trunk.

"Easy. Relax. No one needs to get hurt here. I am a police officer and of course, you know what you are doing is wrong," Brentt spoke calmly to the brigand.

"Really, I did not realize that! What's going on with her?"

"I stopped her for speeding through a red light and I was going to write her a ticket," explained the detective.

"He wanted a bribe for not giving me the ticket. I didn't have any cash on me so I figured I could show him some..." explained Jenny untruthfully.

"That's a lie, lady. I did no such thing! How could you do that?" exclaimed Brentt, looking at her in shock.

"Really! A dirty cop! This is my lucky day. Looks like I'm the hero and the villain today. Let's see those goods lady," the man demanded.

"Wait, I know you. At the illegal dogfighting ring, you were the guy who was standing guard at the control center," Brentt recalled, as everything was flooding back to him.

"Yes, that's right. I was paid a pretty penny too. Just make sure that no one goes in or out of that room. That's what the guys at Rent a Henchman Enterprises told me to do," he said as he came closer brandishing the gun in Brentt's face. "You look like the fella that bopped me over the head. You haven't seen my tablet around, have you? I killed my grandma for it. It has special meaning for me, my first murder."

"EEHH, you are heartless! That's the most horrible thing I've ever heard. You monster!" cried Jenny, terrified.

"Hey what did I say?" he screamed at Jenny.

"Look, why would I want your stupid tablet, I've got a two-in-one laptop at home!" lied Brentt Williams, knowing full well he gave it to Bertha.

"Come closer if you want!" Jenny seductively suggested. She then proceeded to rub her body slowly and deliberately as if in an effort to mesmerize the crook. He came closer, reaching out a hand to grab the seemingly innocent Jenny with his dirty fingers.

Brentt Williams, taking advantage of the man's distraction, overpowered him in a lightning move and had the cuffs on him before Jenny could recover from the siesta. The subdued man lay there, with the police officer on top of him. Brentt read the crook his rights. He then pulled him up and put the crook in the back seat of the unmarked police car.

Before Brentt Williams closed the door, the crook shouted, "You corrupt cop, I saw you with her. She said you wanted a bribe. What are you going to do to get out of that?"

"Shut up, idiot," snapped Brentt Williams as he closed the car door.

"I guess there is no ticket for me today since I saved your life," suggested Jenny, as she flashed a beautiful grin.

"No, you did not save my life. You lied about me. Why would you do that?" he quietly said.

"I got the robber to trust me, didn't I?" she defended herself.

"You broke the law. However, I must say, that was quick thinking," he pointed out, giggling a little.

"Thanks. So we are even now, aren't we?" she defended again, smiling.

"You have to come to the station to make a report. I need you as a witness," he asked politely.

"I am afraid that's not possible. I have to get home to my cheating boyfriend," she explained as she turned to go.

"I won't ask again. Come with me to file a report and you can go home after and deal with your boyfriend. I'll come with you, if necessary. I don't mind."

"You'd do that? Well, you did see me do a naughty dance, but no thanks," she turned to go.

Brentt Williams quickly and smoothly slipped the cuffs on her before she even knew what was happening. He was behind her and smelled her perfume, which was like the expensive one Lynne wore at home.

"You like handcuffs. Hmm, that's kinky. I don't mind that," she purred as he walked her to the car.

"I'm sorry. I will help you with your boyfriend but we need to get this guy to the precinct. You heard how bad he is," explained Brentt gently. He put her in the back seat next to the criminal.

"My baby, please get my baby, James. He's in the back seat," she pleaded.

CHAPTER 11

"There is a baby too? Okay, I'll get him," said Brentt.

He looked in the backseat of the red minivan and sure enough, he found the little guy sleeping. He had slept through the whole ordeal. He also took the keys from the ignition and locked the car for Jenny. She seemed nice, a little messed up, but nice. It was a shame that a nice girl like that had to be cheated on by what sounded like a crappy boyfriend.

"Okay everyone, move over," Brentt said as he put the baby, who probably won't remember his first ride in an unmarked police car, in the back seat with the others. He drove them to the police station.

- -

The door to the office of Maxximillian Chief was shut. It was a good thing that it was soundproof, because anyone passing by would have heard a tirade of bad words coming out from the mouth of the six-foot-six police chief. It had glass in front of it though and all of the officers could see the verbal beating that was being administered to their colleague, Brentt Williams.

The chief took off his hat and paced the floor like a hungry tiger that just had his fat juicy antelope taken away. The Chief was pissed, however, Brentt was the only one in the precinct that he talked to this way because they went way back, like in Brentt's way back.

"Brentt Williams, you brought a baby in the back of an unmarked cop car? What were you thinking? This dumbass says that you were asking for a bribe from the woman?" said the police chief in an accent.

"No. The woman was lying to the crook about me asking for a bribe. It was a routine traffic stop until we got interrupted by this Michael Jones fellow. He saw what was happening and took it the wrong way," defended Brentt, "He tried to rob us."

"He said she was being very seductive," argued Chief squared, holding a surprisingly blank face.

"Yes. Because she was getting his attention," explained Brentt.

"Okay, are you dropping the traffic violation charges?"

CHAPTER 11

"Yes, no charges. But this guy is getting the book because he pulled a gun on a police officer and a civilian. I can't see how they let this guy get away after he was at the scene of the illegal dogfighting bust," persuaded the police officer.

"He fell through the cracks in the system. We'll get him this time. Alright, that's settled. We'll let the officers in booking deal with the small stuff. I've got another assignment for you to deal with.

Some guy named Theo Steren Champlain got shot in his condo. There are two emergency calls about the incident, one from an untraceable number and the other from the victim's cell phone. But here's the kicker, when the paramedics got there, he was unconscious and the girlfriend was there. She said it was a home invasion. She was hiding in the shower. The place was dusted for prints and the only ones found were that of his daughter, his and the girl," explained the chief.

"Forensics did not find anything?" asked Brentt, intrigued.

"They did not find anything of value. He got divorced three months ago. I think it is suspicious he has a girlfriend already."

"He probably has a jealous ex-wife," surmised Brentt.

"Get down to the hospital and see what's up. Talk to the girlfriend and the ex," ordered the Chief.

"Sure. I THINK IT'S GOING TO RAIN TODAY, I FEEL IT IN MY GUT!" remarked Brentt as he pulled out his cell phone and put it on the Chief's desk.

The Chief did the same and took out a plastic container from the side drawer of his desk and put both phones in it. The Chief then walked over to the old, never used microwave and put both phones into it and shut the door. The microwave acted as a cage that inhibited any signals from leaving the phone, as well as any signals being communicated to the phone. Essentially it cut off any ability to use the phone as a listening tool when clandestine conversations needed to be had. He then walked over to the glass office door and pulled the blinds down. When he sat back down, he leaned back in the plush leather manager's chair and listened intently to what Brentt had to say.

"In China, there was a discovery of a giant Gadha or mace that is breaking all the rules of science and archaeology. I think the mysterious *Immortal Count* might be after it. This seems to be right up his alley. It looks like it is a very powerful *Gift of the Nine* that was given from the Gods to their Athlogoss Drones. I heard from the Asia branch of the Sisters of the Black Habit that it would arrive at the Grand Museum in California, just in time for the New Year's Day parade."

"What the hell does this thing do?" asked Maxximillian Chief in bewilderment.

"Well according to the research in the *Legacy of The Ascended Knowledge of The Nine* (LAKN9) database, whomever or whatever gets hit by this mace feels the wrath of what essentially is a nuclear blast. However, the wielder is protected by a shield. Oh and it weighs about fifty tons," explained Brentt.

"Should we call in *SAKH Porast* and her crew of fighters? After all, she can feel into the future," suggested the Chief. Sister Porast was the head sister for the Sisters of the Ascended Knowledge of Heddonna or SAKH. The pseudonym was a title given to the operative to identify which branch of the LAKN9 they belonged to.

"No. The news gets worse. Some members of *The Animal Kingdoom* have been spotted in California," added Brentt.

"Those guys are a deadly bunch of hoodlums if I ever did see one! Those eight guys and eight women can take on the powers of any animal in the world. What are we going to do? Who do you have in mind to back us up?" exclaimed Maxx Chief.

"I'm calling in the *Assassin Priests* and *Warrior Rabbis* to help us out. They're a good group and tough as anything the Count could throw at us. They are Kung Fu Mages, which means that along with martial arts, they could throw down if it comes to magic on magic. They'll give us the support we need. Their leaders *Jacob Ocaj* and his wife *Jezebelle Dorcas* are two really powerful badasses that pack a punch. I'm also going to see if I can bring a little surprise to the party," suggested Brentt.

"Let's hope it doesn't come to that... What about the *Triple Magician*?" asked Maxx Chief.

"Last time he did not get the *Emerald Tablets* and I'm betting he's looking for a rematch. What he doesn't know is that there are 300 tablets that have various texts on them, all made from various minerals and precious stones. Luckily we have the complete set, locked away and being studied as we speak."

"Great, looks like we got lots to look forward to," exclaimed the Chief.

"We are done here. I'll keep you posted on any new developments. There is one thing I have to do before I start on this new case."

Brentt came out of the office with the file on the case he was just given, but he had to finish what he said he would do first. Jenny had to go back to get her car and then go confront her boyfriend.

"Jenny, looks like you're done here. Let's go get your car and see that no-good boyfriend of yours," smiled Brentt.

"You'd really do that for me? Thank you." She hugged him in excitement.

He nodded his head and she hastily ran off to get the baby, who was still sleeping through it all. They drove back to get her car and then went to her boyfriend's mom's house. (He is not really important to the story so I'll just call him BF). She went into the house and Brentt stayed outside on the porch. The baby was with him.

"I caught you, son of a gun! I have you on the cameras sleeping with your mom's best friend! Don't you lie to me, here it is right here!" she screamed.

"No! It was an accident. I was drunk and she took advantage of me. I didn't know what I was doing," BF defended himself against video evidence.

"She's your mom's friend. She's a hundred years older than you!"

"Look, okay it was a one-time thing. I didn't mean anything by it. Look, honey, we have a baby together and one on the way. We both work and I wanted to blow off some steam..." he defended himself with futile excuses.

"I've caught you cheating many times and always took you back. I thought when we had a baby that this would all change, but I was wrong," she cried, a cry of desperation and dejection as her world came crashing down.

CHAPTER 11

"No I…" he tried to say but as it turned out the friend of the mom came out wearing only a bathrobe that was loosely tied, having just been woken up by the sound of the argument. BF's mom was 60 and the friend was 50, but she looked like a leathery 80.

"I saw both of you doing it on the couch in the living room. I am leaving. I need to go pack my things. I had enough of your lies and we'll hammer out the custody battle later," she said through more tears.

"I want to see my son …" BF said knowing that there was nothing more he could say.

Jenny started packing her things in several suitcases she had put away. The next thing Brentt knew, a five-month pregnant woman was coming out of the door with suitcases. He helped her because that was what he did. She was crying all the while and the boyfriend stood there speechless and actionless.

"Who the hell are you?" asked BF in surprise.

"I'm the policeman that escorted her here. I also saw her do a seductive dance to distract a robber while I arrested him, but that's something different." He smiled and went to the car window as Jenny put James, her belongings and herself in the vehicle. She rolled down the window when Brentt tapped on it and asked, "Where will you go?"

She started crying anew and replied, "I don't know. I don't know. I don't know."

"Give me a moment, I might have a place," he said as he called Agness at home to let her know they would be having company for lunch.

Needless to say, Brentt bringing home a pregnant woman and her baby was the sweetest thing but also the dumbest thing he could do, considering the fact that he had talking animals and a big family secret to hide. He was a sucker for people in need and the Williams family would act the part as they always did.

Agness received her house guest very hospitably and soon showed her to the two-bedroom and two-bath, completely furnished guest house which was not connected to the main house. She gave her some time before a late lunch to get settled in, while she talked to Brentt.

CHAPTER 11

"You brought home a pregnant lady whom you arrested and her baby?" exclaimed Agness.

"Actually, I had her in cuffs and the baby in the backseat with her. Oh and there was a very bad guy who tried to rob us there as well," he explained.

"How did he try to rob her? Wait, he tried to rob both of you?" she asked still confused.

"Well I had stopped her for speeding and we got interrupted by the same guy from the illegal dogfighting. He decided to rob both of us while I was giving her a ticket," he continued.

"Did you see her..." Agness was interrupted by a knock on the door; the new guest had arrived early for the late lunch. Bertha had let her in and was making chit chat with her, while Lynne was peek-a-booing the baby.

"Everyone, I have to go to work. I'm sorry I cannot stay longer but duty calls," detective Williams explained. The police detective excused himself from the company of the beautiful women.

Jenny was in tears at the kindness the Williams family was showing her and couldn't express her gratitude enough. Brentt smiled as he walked to his car. He was glad that he could help one more person and make the world a better place.

CHAPTER 12: The Freedom Of Anthraxis

The million-year confinement of Anthraxis was almost up and his influence upon the universe was at hand. There were civilizations that had flourished across the expanse that was the universe. However, the reign of peace was soon coming to an end, for the God of War wanted vengeance for his unfair punishment.

Atomos called together all the Gods to meet and discuss the progression of the universe thus far. They met in the palatial temple planet of Atomos to conduct their business.

Caddeussus pulled aside Technon and whispered, "Anthraxis must be pissed off about his confinement. We have to keep an eye on him. I fear he may do something foolhardy. I know he will go after the planet Rahab."

"We know that he has his part to play in the future of things, but you are right. He may seek vengeance for his confinement," whispered back Technon.

"He has a dislike for you and couldn't care less about anyone else. However, involving the others might fuel an already flaming fire," suggested Caddeussus.

In the middle of the congregation of the Gods was the great throne of the King of the Gods and God of the Gods. The throne was infused with power that emanated from two planet-sized spheres that stood at the back of it. All the Gods stood in awe of the display until Atomos bade them sit. Each God sat on the thrones which had been present before time as they listened to Atomos:

"My fellow Gods, I hope that you have enjoyed the universe that we have created. All of it looks very good and pleasing to the eyes and heart. The life forms, planets, and galaxies look incredible. Each of you, my fellow Gods, are fulfilling your part perfectly and without err. I would also like to welcome back

CHAPTER 12

Anthraxis from his vacation on his temple planet. I hope you got lots of rest and relaxation?" Atomos inquired raising an eyebrow.

"Hail UKSCOGSM Atomos, my dread lord, sovereign master, and the King of the Gods and God of the Gods. I have an issue with the creation of certain things," said Anthraxis.

"Speak God of War, for it is your right to be heard in this council of Gods."

"Some of the creations lack my influence upon them. Particularly the planet Rahab in the Milky Way galaxy, the one situated between Mars and Jupiter. If Galaxyia does not let me get close to exert any influence on the inhabitants there, I cannot fulfill my duty to you, Atomos and the universe."

"I have to ask you if this is true because even though a God is omnipotent, omniscient and omnipresent, a God cannot know what another God has in their heart and mind. Galaxyia is this true what Anthraxis is saying?" asked Atomos.

"King of the Gods Atomos, this is true. Rahab is a great and wonderful planet that has many inhabitants of advanced technology and culture. Its beauty is a wonder to behold and I am very proud of it. I do not want the God of War, Anthraxis, to mar and destroy it."

"Am I right in assuming that you have seen the futures of this planet written in the multiverses?" asked Atomos.

"I have, UKSCOGSM Atomos. I have seen that the inhabitants get too haughty and destroy themselves in the quest to be godlike. However, I have also seen the future in which Anthraxis gets to the planet. It is destroyed much more quickly than if they were left to their own devices. I, as the planet Rahab's mother, could not allow either to happen."

"Galaxyia, since you have interfered and not influenced, the future of the planet has shifted. I will allow the planet to be partially destroyed by Anthraxis to bring balance to the universe."

"I shall go swiftly and carry out your word, my King," interjected Anthraxis.

All the Gods stood up except Atomos. A tear was rolling down Galaxyia's eye as they all teleported in unison across the vastness of space, to the planet in question. They were all ready to deal with the situation.

CHAPTER 12

Atomos sat for a minute on his mighty throne in the middle of the planet that resided in the heart of the created universe. He felt the present and future life of everything that there ever was and will be. Suddenly, the King of the Gods felt something. The kind of feeling you get when you have to check for your wallet after you get out of a taxi. The weight of the diadem on his head felt heavier than when he first put it on. He couldn't shake that feeling and he could not let it be. Atomos rose from his mighty throne and contemplated a minute.

Power crackled around him as he moved and surveyed the planets that he had made for his fellow Gods. Not being able to see in them, because he respected their privacy, he looked past them into the vastness of space and across the universe. He looked in all directions and in all the multiverses. He could not help but beam a smug smile at a job well done. However, Atomos knew there was something else that seemed unfinished. It nagged at his soul and frustrated him that he could not determine what was out of place.

"I am going to inspect the walls of the universe," he said to himself out loud and with a sonic boom that rang through his temple planet, he disappeared.

The Gods were at the planet Rahab dealing with the situation that was getting frighteningly worse. Atomos was somewhere at the edges of the universe looking for a needle in a universal haystack. Everyone was preoccupied and no one expected something to occur at the most sacred place in the universe, the temple planet of Atomos.

A shadowy figure teleported in front of The Contest of the Nine located in the center of the temple planet, next to the mighty throne of Atomos. This being had no counterpart anywhere in the vastness of space. The being was not noticed by any of the Gods, nor felt by them. It was as if it did not exist. There were no alternate realities of the being or any pasts, presents, or futures. Nothing that even hinted it existed. The figure was about six feet tall but grew in stature to a magnificent

CHAPTER 12

seventy feet. It stood in front of The Contest of the Nine. It split itself into ten beings. Each took their stance in front of one of the creations of the Gods. The last one was left to watch over the others.

The Contest of the Nine stood on pedestals of Foreverum, the metal of the Gods. The power that emanated from them was extraordinarily destructive and awesome at the same time. They held the essence and a part of the power of the Gods. Each of them had put their heart and soul into making a creation that would have given them a shot to be crowned King. They were beyond magnificent, beyond the comprehension of mortals and beyond the reach of anything in the universe.

The nine figures stretched forth their hands to take hold of the things created before the beginning. The power that crackled around The Contest of the Nine leaped to the waiting fingers of the shadowy figures. It fed them, it rejuvenated them and it empowered them. The power changed them. The power almost killed them, twisting them in agony and burning them from the inside out. The objects seemed like they would never run out of energy and in fact, they could not.

The shadowy figures endured the excruciating process for as long as they could. If the figure watching the others had not intervened, there would be nine dead shadowy figures and one last guy to carry out the bodies. They couldn't take the intense power of these sacred objects, because they were not strong enough.

However, they did not go away empty-handed for The Contest of the Nine gave them more power than they had, to begin with. The nine figures now supercharged, amalgamated themselves with the tenth, into one being again. It disappeared as quickly and as quietly as it came, leaving no trace in the past, present or future that it was ever there.

All the Gods had grown to planet size and stayed unseen by the inhabitants of the lush world, who had no idea what was coming. The God of War raised his mighty hand and curled it into a fist. Before he could bring it down upon the planet, Galaxyia got in front of him and implored him, "Please be gentle." Anthraxis gave Galaxyia a horrific, powerful shove and she fell back into the planet Jupiter, her elbow digging into the planet. Anger and frustration surged through her, flowing from her elbow into the planet. When she got up, a hurricane began to stir and build itself upon the giant planet, an eternal reminder of that fateful moment.

Anthraxis brought his Godly fist down upon the planet, instantly turning half of it into a wasteland. Death and destruction were everywhere. The blood of the planet splattered upon the Gods, who all looked on. All the souls of the dead were taken up by Detrimentus, making him stronger.

The God of War's blood lust, not only fueled by the destruction of half the planet, but by the shoving of Galaxyia, went in for another punch. Technon held back Anthraxis' right fist as he was going to strike. Heddonna blocked Anthraxis' left hand before he could bring that beefy denizen of death down again.

"Atomos said partially and not completely. You don't need to do this again," warned Technon. "You dare tell me, weakling, how to do my duty, while you play with live-action figures of whatever creation you're tinkering with? I am the God of War and I will rend you to pieces and throw your parts across time and space," Anthraxis said acidly. "You wench, let go of me before I have to deal with you too!" he spat at Heddonna, who drew back in surprise.

He wrenched off Technon's grip, which was surprisingly firm and went for the throat of the God of Technology. The speed of the move, which was about half the speed of light, sent sonic booms across the emptiness of space. Technon had the wherewithal to throw a heavy-handed jab at Anthraxis' face. This stunned the God and he slightly loosened his grip.

Technon teleported a solar system away, but Anthraxis was also quick and got him in a surprise chokehold from behind. Technon acted quickly and split himself so that the second Technon poked fingers in Anthraxis' eyes, digging deep into the retinas of his assailant. Then the Technon that was in the

CHAPTER 12

chokehold threw everything he had into a left uppercut that sent Anthraxis reeling into a planet.

The planet was torn asunder and the inhabitants were soon debris scattered across the ensuing battlefield. The other Gods went quickly into action however, the God of War anticipated their movements and sent ten more of his embodiments to stave off the others. Three Gods of War stared down Caddeussus and three stood in Detrimentus' way. The other four blocked Archituria, Heddonna, Cosmica, and Galaxyia.

Heddonna, showing no signs of backing down, was ready to square off with Anthraxis and would have trounced him if not for the intervention of Caddeussus.

"Heddonna, don't get involved. If there are damages, you don't want to answer to Atomos. We tried to stop them, but they have to hash this out," stated the God of Life as he crossed his arms over his chest. Heddonna reluctantly stopped her advance on Anthraxis, knowing deep inside that this was a disagreement that could be costly.

They looked on as two Anthraxis squared off against two Technons. Anthraxis went in for a right cross but Technon sidestepped it leftwards and rammed a left into his ribcage. Technon used his right hand to block Anthraxis' right hand, in case he came back with an elbow. Technon coiled War's right hand in the crux of his elbow and continued pounding on his ribs a few more times. He had done this so that the God of War could not punch him straight on.

The other Anthraxis and Technon were about a planet away doing battle as well. Technon pushed Anthraxis off and flew to the other Technon that was in a bear hug from the other embodiment of the God of War. Technon pulled on the other Technon's feet so that he slipped from under War's grasp. However, Technon used himself as a weapon and swung a blow to the God of War's face. He flew into a moon that disintegrated upon impact. The other Anthraxis came to the rescue.

Punches and dodges ensued, as two Technons went toe to toe with Anthraxis. The other Anthraxis came up from behind one of the Technons and kneed him in the back. It sent him stumbling forward and then the attacker grabbed the God of

CHAPTER 12

Technology by the arm. He spun him around in a magnificent whirlwind that created a giant hurricane in the middle of the solar system. Anthraxis threw Technon at the sun in a quick calculated move. The God of Technology hit the surface at an alarming speed, which caused a coronal mass ejection that ate up two nearby planets closest to the impact point. Anthraxis thought he was going to come out of the other side, but the sun bubbled and hissed and the molten figure of Technon could be seen rising up from the surface.

Anthraxis cast a giant shadow upon the sun as the God of Technology looked at the God of War from the surface. Just then Anthraxis knew why he was staring, for, above him, a portal opened. From the core of the sun, a torrent of super-heated material in excess of 15 million degrees Kelvin, drenched Anthraxis, encasing him in flames. That move caused the other Technon and Anthraxis to pause momentarily and witness this awesome sight. The Technon that was on the sun flew straight towards Anthraxis and as he did so, the unthinkable happened.

The blow came before anyone had time to react. An embodiment of Anthraxis appeared with the Galaxy Cleaver Blade that was built before the beginning of the universe. He had taken it from the temple of Atomos and was now intent to use it upon the hapless Technon. The swing from the serrated blade came swiftly, like lightning at a billion times the speed of light. The slice almost cut the God of Technology in two from his shoulder to his hip. It knocked him backward sending him and a slicing energy wave, off into the distant universe.

The recoil made a blast wave that forced all the Gods to block their faces. The blast wave spread and destroyed the newly created Milky Way galaxy, in less time than the blink of an eye. The Korsol pod never got to finish their mating. Trillions of newborn animals never got to taste the sweet nectar of life. All of the streams, lakes, and oceans that were so clear and calm like glass, were shattered. The hundreds of billions of trees that shaded millions of planets and housed a myriad of birds were destroyed.

On one planet, there stood a mountain whose summit surpassed the atmosphere and reached the stars. It was the planet

CHAPTER 12

Droflelix, whose plea did not do it any good. Magma, the lifeblood of the planets, floating in the cold depths of space, solidified and broke apart again. Part of the adjoining galaxy was damaged as well. Bits of planetary debris floated around the stunned Gods, all no larger than a baseball. The planets around them, once teeming with life which they had inspected only a million years ago, now gone in an instant. Time ripples reverberated around them as space itself buckled at the mighty, Godly swing.

The God of Death could feel the souls of the dead giving him more power. Archituria could feel the ideas of everything in the galaxy vaporize into nothing. All the beauty, that was and could have been in the galaxy, now annihilated by the Galaxy Cleaver. Galaxyia cried because she never foresaw this universal cataclysm could be perpetrated by one of her cohorts.

The ten Gods of War that were barring the way of the other Gods disappeared. The Anthraxis' that were wrestling with the other embodiments of Technon, vanished as well. In their place was the lone form of Anthraxis who held the Galaxy Cleaver Blade.

Everyone was stunned for a second but quickly moved in to rectify the situation. The God of Life sped after Technon and at times he had to teleport himself forward. The God of Death bear-hugged the God of War from behind as Cosmica and Galaxyia grabbed each of Anthraxis' arms and tried to wrest the giant blade from his hands. Archituria went for his legs as Heddonna quickly and cautiously pulled the blade, dripping wet with the blood of a freshly created galaxy, from the muscled hands of the God of War.

Technon could stop time. In fact, he had figured out how to do it when time was first created. Before creation, there was no time, so there was nothing to stop and the ability to stop time did not really come into play. However, after time was created and that first inkling of time went forward, the ability to control time became apparent to the God of Technology. He had seen the blow that the God of War delivered to his embodiment and it was not pretty.

All of the other Gods were in slow motion, as he walked between them and around them. He was invisible so they could not see him. He was also outside of time so that they could not know that he was there. He looked at the others trying to take away the Galaxy Cleaver from Anthraxis. He had to admit that the great and mighty weapon was viciously balanced.

He immediately had a plan, a weapon that would put this hulking brute in his place once and for all. He disliked that Galaxyia's planet got destroyed and wanted to help her, but things got out of hand. He was grateful for Heddonna's help with initially holding back Anthraxis. Sure, he was not as good looking as Detrimentus and Caddeussus and not as burly as Anthraxis, but nonetheless, he was as strong as they were, perhaps stronger. He put a time bubble around his fellow Gods so that he could work without interruption.

He got to work on his creation by multiplying himself a billion-fold. Next, he set out to gather the remnants of the galaxy that was just disintegrated by the God of War's weapon. This was an easy task because he called each atom, molecule, particle of dust, piece of debris and dead bodies from the depths of space and amalgamated them into one huge ball of stuff. He was after all, a God and all of the atoms in the universe had to listen to him, as well as the other eight. This was quite a sight to behold; a galaxy's worth of material like the different colors of a child's modeling clay set, haphazardly stuck together.

The other Gods did not notice the machinations of Technon as he sorted out the particles of the shattered galaxy. These are for the housing of the unit. Leptons, protons, electrons, and quarks were for the ammo. Like a tailor sewing pieces of fabric together, Technon lovingly condensed the atoms and molecules, making the materials that formed the weapon. The spaces between the protons, neutrons, and electrons getting smaller and finally, all of the subatomic particles were touching each other. Technically this is called dark matter, which is found in black holes and pretty much the whole universe. Essentially, the gravity around a black hole is so strong that it condenses matter and does not allow light to escape.

The svelte black body of the weapon was as large as twenty-four suns. A billion Technons watched their creation take shape, as each of them worked on a facet of the great weapon. Sure he could have made it instantly, but the satisfaction of knowing the job is well-done lies in each little detail and placing every molecule just right. The gaping maw that had a *Lawrellion* (10^{300}) particle accelerators, were checked and rechecked for their calibration, ready to blast any opponent.

The individual accelerators used the opposing charges of all atoms in the whole galaxy and accelerated them through a rail system. It focused them at a single point for discharge in a 'bullet' the size of Saturn, just before exiting the chamber. The result was a spectacular weapon the God of Technology lovingly named *The God Breaker Cannon*.

He spray painted it with red paint for good measure. The red graffiti writing that was thirty thousand miles tall added a little flare to the most powerful weapon in the entire universe. As an added bonus, Technon created a *gravity box,* which holds the opponent in place by using gravity as an impediment. Best of all, it could not miss because if the person moves away, or manages to break free, it tracks their soul print. The God of War, Anthraxis, was in the weapon's crosshairs and it wanted blood.

The cannon was completed and the next phase was to put it into motion. Technon unfroze time but still hid the weapon from the others. He noticed Caddeussus went after his body. He'd have to thank him later for that service. He looked on as his fellow Gods had disarmed the God of War, waiting for the right time to strike. Using The Contest of the Nine from the temple planet of Atomos was a low blow even for him. The others gingerly released the now docile Anthraxis, as Heddonna backed away with the Galaxy Cleaver Blade. All of them kept their eyes on Anthraxis and no one paid any attention to Technon stealthily moving above them.

"You guys might want to move back," Technon stated solemnly as he stood with a confident grin on his face.

CHAPTER 12

All of the Gods looked up in unison at Technon. They noticed that just behind him was an awesome weapon that brought fear to Anthraxis' face and mixed reactions from everyone else. Technon quickly used all of his embodiments to pull Detrimentus, Galaxyia, Cosmica, Archituria, and Heddonna out of the way. In the process, Heddonna loosened her grip on the Galaxy Cleaver and Anthraxis took that opportunity to steal it from her. The Gods now overwhelmed by the embodiments of Technon, looked on in utter horror at the events unfolding before them a second time.

"Anthraxis, I am also a God like you and I demand that you respect me. I will not tolerate this behavior anymore. Here's a taste of The God Breaker Cannon," shouted Technon as he primed the weapon.

The energy that it gave off was the equivalent of all the enthalpic energy of the entire Milky Way galaxy. The other Gods stood in awe of the technological creation. Anthraxis was mesmerized by the sheer size and power of the weapon. The God of Technology decided that this was a good time to deploy the gravity box.

Heddonna looked into the face of one of Technon's embodiments that held her back and he looked back at her, into those ridiculously fabulous purple eyes. Both of them were lost in a moment, but then he said, "You know it will continue like this if I don't stand up. Don't worry; we know he'll be okay." Technon smiled at her and looked at the weapon that had taken aim upon Anthraxis.

The gravity box was deployed and it entrapped the God of War in its hold. The gravity was so strong that he could not escape. The Galaxy Cleaver Blade was immobilized as well and lay limp in the God's hands. Anthraxis looked up at the impending danger and could not summon any embodiments to save him. It was impossible to do so with the box constraining him. His fear was evident as he was shocked by the might of The God Breaker Cannon.

CHAPTER 13: The Shock Of His Afterlife

Theo Steren Champlain felt light as a feather. In fact, he was lighter than a feather, weightless and free... and *dead*. He felt an overwhelming peace of mind flow over him, like nothing he'd ever felt before. Not like a paid off the car peace, not a paid off the house peace, not even like winning tons of money peace, it was an I don't have a body any more peace of mind.

He saw the AIRE as he floated past her, with her fingers pointed at his chest, furiously trying to close the gap that had opened in his heart. She had closed the gap in his heart left by Catherine three months ago and the fact that she was trying to help him now, warmed his bleeding heart.

He looked down at his body. He wasn't a bad looking guy now that he thought about it, but now was not the time for admiring himself. He couldn't believe that his body weighed down such tranquility and freedom. He couldn't believe that his body restricted his soul so much, like a prison that trapped the real you inside yourself. He had read about these things before in books and magazines and even seen some shows about it on television, but he did not think that he would have had a near-death experience himself.

The abnormally bright light at the end of the tunnel seemed light-years away, but he could see it as if it was next to him. He was flying towards it. He looked around at his environment which wasn't really much, except absolute pitch blackness. Actually, it was darker than that. Not the kind of darkness where there is the absence of light, but the kind where there is a presence of darkness. The kind of darkness you can actually feel sticking to you.

So this is what lots of people describe when they die, Theo thought to himself. This was the greatest adventure he never wanted to go on. Finally getting to know all of the answers to all

CHAPTER 13

the questions, but he may not get to tell the fantastic tale because it's a one-way trip. Does he even want to go back? His ex-wife cheated on him, his daughter may not be his, John betrayed him, he got killed and his food stolen.

Those negative thoughts slowly got pushed away as he looked upon that bright light in the distance. Calmness peeked through the door of his heart and burst in like a worried mother, catching hold of him, cradling him, flooding him with the hope of a new adventure in an unknown destination. Calmness invited its friend, peace and together they cheered Theo up. They lifted his spirits to such heights that he vehemently had to reach the light to make it worthwhile. Theo must have been in flight for what felt like hours or days. In fact, it felt like an eternity. Time didn't really have any meaning there.

Suddenly he started to speed up as he went towards the light. The illumination was so bright now that he had to keep his hands in front of his eyes. He kept speeding up, faster than any speed that had been reached on earth. The light was unbearably bright now and he had to keep his eyes closed, but even then he had to put his hands over his eyes as well. 'This is it,' he said to himself. Theo Steren Champlain entered the light.

Theo was in the most vividly colorful forest he had ever seen. It was filled with an unimaginable plethora of hues and shades of green that lay siege to his eyes at any given moment. The trees that towered mightily above him looked like nothing on earth and were taller than the tallest skyscrapers. Leaves of all shapes and sizes hung from their branches, full and robust. The flowers that carpeted the landscape were truly adorned more spectacularly than King Solomon's robes. They displayed colors that were more rich and bountiful than he could put a name to. The sky was cloudless and the sun shining, but the weather was perfection itself, not too hot, not too cold, but absolutely heavenly.

Theo breathed in a gigantic breath that filled his spirit with such an aromatic scent that his mind could not comprehend the smells. That breath truly took his breath away. The crisp air, so fresh and clean, invigorated him and invited him to take in more succulent aromatic goodness. Peace, joy, and love overwhelmed

CHAPTER 13

him as tears welled up inside. This is the most beautiful place he had never imagined and he did not want to leave. Theo walked forward unafraid of what lay ahead, confident that before him was bliss. The trees seemed to make an archway for him as if to salute him on his way.

Around the bend, he came across some people in white robes. They were all standing around, seemingly enjoying each other's company. However, he noticed no one was talking, no gesticulating, nothing of any kind. He moved in for a closer look.

All of a sudden, he noticed incredible winged angels moving around them. They were about 8 feet tall with a beautiful and majestic appearance. Their faces radiated sweetness and gentleness. All of them had two great wings that looked as strong and forceful as the wings of an eagle. Beautiful heads of silky hair and long robes rustled every time their sandaled feet just barely glided across the green grass carpet. They looked busy ministering to families and friends.

He walked forward to get a closer look and perhaps to meet one of them. Just then he heard a cacophonic blast of voices in his head, which stunned him for a minute. He overheard a lady angel's voice in his head saying, "Mr. Jones is over by that tree on the other side. Shall I take you to him?" Theo smiled with contentment, quickly forgetting the voices for a minute. The lady angel's voice was so breathtaking and so unimaginably melodious, that it seemed like his ears were having a party.

That is, until he heard an equally symphonic male voice behind him, "Hi can I help you?"

Theo turned around to see who the owner of that voice was. The male angel looked like he was straight out of a designer clothing catalog, but very kind and radiant. He stood about 15ft tall. He was holding what looked like a stone tablet, but it shimmered like a blue sapphire.

"Hi, I'm Uriel. How can I help you Mr..." he inquired, as he knelt down to observe Theo.

His lips were not moving. Only his eyes shifted when he looked at Theo and then down at the tablet and back again. It seemed like the angel spoke directly to Theo's mind, reading it like a newspaper article. Right then someone came home and switched on all the lights in Theo's brain. Telepathic communication, that's why he had heard all the voices in his head. This was the coolest thing ever!

"My name is Theo Steren Champlain. I just got here," Theo said without moving his lips.

"I know. Overwhelming isn't it? Just give me one moment. Let me pull you up."

"Where am I? I feel that this is surreal."

"Yes, it is. I'm sorry Mr. Champlain I'm not finding you here. Do me a favor and put your hand on the tablet for me. Thanks."

"Ok sure, is it reading my fingerprints or something?"

"No, it's actually reading your *soul print*. Well, because your body is back where you came from."

"What exactly is my soul print?" Theo asked.

"Your soul print is what identifies you to the universe. For every individual, no matter what body they take on, the soul print is always the same."

"What body they take on? Do you mean like reincarnation? But I thought that kind of thing doesn't exist?"

"It's kind of lengthy to explain right now. Let me put it to you this way. Sometimes there are people who are on the fence with their deeds, so they get another chance. Sort of like probation. Hmm… Looks like I'm not finding you here. Let me try the bad people book."

"Are ghosts reincarnated? I mean after people die, sometimes they stick around?" asked Theo, trying to get some answers.

"Well, not everyone is reincarnated because you have ghosts and other entities still in a different plane of existence. They stay there until a decision could be made about them. Yes, some of them are there for hundreds of years, but it is because there are special mitigating circumstances that have to be taken into account.

Some kids who are reincarnated are purposely allowed to know who they were previously because it fits into the grand scheme of things. In fact, some of them choose who they want their parents to be! However, every time someone is reincarnated, it's not always as a human and it is not always on earth. There have been cases of humans being reincarnated on different planets and aliens being reincarnated as humans, animals as humans and humans as animals.

There are trillions of beings out there and to recycle souls, gives each being a different perspective on life. Remember, everything was created at the beginning of the universe. There is a finite amount of soul prints out there. The key is to remember that every one of the souls out there is different and the *Universal Management Board* knows that," explained the angel.

"Who are they? Does this cycle move on forever or is there an end to it?" asked Theo, pushing for more.

The angel had taken out another equally impressive stone tablet from an invisible pocket while he was entertaining Theo's question. This one was a fiery ruby red and looked a lot heftier than the blue.

"The Universal Management Board makes the decisions. There is an end to the cycle, but first, you have to look at heaven and hell as a break room from life in general. If you were bad, then you go to hell and you get a break from living. Then you resume life. Some people were in heaven before and then they go back down because they have more work to do. Let me see if I can water it down for you to understand.

Most people, after they have a near-death experience, do not want to go back to earth. Would you leave eternal bliss? Like if you step into a break room at work and some people are having lunch but others are on a break. They are there for different periods of time and for different reasons," the angel spoke looking around.

"No, I don't want to leave here! I don't have anything to live for!" exclaimed Theo.

"Yes, you do. Every soul is important, no matter how unimportant the life of the soul might seem. Everything is connected. Everything influences everything else. You could be a universe away and you are affected by the atoms that are in the middle of a dying star. Such are the ways of the universe.

Everyone here has had their fleshly bodies thrown off so that their souls are unimpeded by constraints. They have an ascended awareness of things in the universe that is allowed by the Universal Management Board. They don't have total omniscience, but just enough to whet their appetite. *The main goal is about ascending and being better than you were. Some people catch on faster than others,*" Uriel continued.

Theo stood motionless, soaking up the information, thinking about the things that he learned from this being.

"Can I have you put your hand here, please? Just one more time, Theo."

"Okay sure. If that's what I think it is, I really hope I'm not in there."

"Not in there either. Looks like I'm going to have to check all the other religious databases. Let me get the other tablet here."

Uriel yet again pulled out an even bigger tablet than the previous two. This tablet was made out of a cobalt stone, which was as black as the void which he had just crossed to get to this place.

"Uriel, can you please tell me what's going on?"

"Ok, Mr. Champlain. I'm not finding you in the good book or the bad book. I thought maybe you might be in the wrong religious place so I need to check the other records. Really and truly we have never, ever, ever had a mistake like this happen since time began. I need you to put your hand here on the tablet one more time, please. Thank you very much for your patience. I'm looking through all the other religions for your soul print."

"All the other religions are in there? Even Scientology and atheism too?"

"You better believe it. We are very thorough around here Mr. Champlain. Let's see here, no record of you found anywhere in all the other religions. That is odd. I'm going to have to tell the logistics division about this."

"No record??? I have a driver's license, a passport, a bookstore card, a credit card, a grocery club card, and a library card. You have to have something! *Please, you have to find me! Please, you have to find me!* I've never been a very religious person, but I do know that there is something else out there, something greater than the universe. I can't have died and not be on the list for heaven. I just can't!" urged Theo.

"I am not finding anything. Give me one moment. I am going to have to hand this over to a different department." The angel put the tablets back into his invisible pockets and clasped his hands in silent prayer.

Theo could not understand the words because it was in some language he had never heard before. He couldn't understand what was going on. Suddenly a good experience was going downhill.

"Mr. Champlain, I have called security for you and they will be taking it from here. They will send you back to where you came from and we'll see you in three days. The head office will definitely have some investigative work to do. Nice meeting you. Good luck."

"Umm… this isn't an electronics store that I can just come back in after a few days!!! This is life and death!!!"

The lightning stuck just behind Theo. He felt the electricity go through his body and turned just as the thunder from the strike reached his ears. *Theo got the shock of his afterlife.* There before him, stood sixteen of the burliest looking seraphim angels he had never hoped to see. Each ten-foot-tall angel had six wings of tough leathery hide. A pair covered their head, feet and the last two were flayed out in a defensive posture against him.

Their squad looked like a mixture of men and women, with both sexes wearing brazen armor that looked like it was straight out of an apocalyptic videogame. High plated armor with spikes clothed their wide shoulders, making them even more imposing. All of them brandished ridiculously large, unholy looking swords that should never have been in the hands of an angel from heaven.

One of the angels stepped forward, removing the wings from his face, revealing a Texas ranged style squared jaw. His blond hair was tied back in an 'I mean business' ponytail. He had a mad bull expression on his face. He brandished a long katana and broadsword hybrid which was on fire and pointed it at Theo. The fifteen-foot long sword looked wicked, like it did not belong in heaven, wicked.

"Easy fellas, there's some mix up here. They can't find my paperwork and I just don't want any trouble."

CHAPTER 13

"Be gone!!!" the seraphim with the sword telepathically yelled with such ferocity, it sounded like an earthquake rattling the foundations of his brain and soul.

Theo Steren Champlain opened his mouth to scream, but was run through with the long fiery sword. His weak hands gripped the massive blade in futility to try to stop it from going deeper. Instead, it seared his palms and cut his fingers. It was not just a quick stab, but the angel delivered a slow deliberate thrust through his mid-section. It was almost lovingly administered by the heavenly security guard.

Even though his body was back on earth, he felt every inch of pain in his soul. Fifteen feet of unbelievably thick, scorching metal penetrated his innards and came out his back. All the while, the smell of burning flesh permeated his nostrils. The uninvited guest to heaven, feeling every inch of the blade as it scraped the insides of his soul, struggled from the assault. Theo Steren Champlain slipped into the blackness again.

CHAPTER 14: My Puppy And The Monk Are Gone

F rank Lin Shao relaxed in his hospital bed and thought about last night's meditation. His dad was a former monk who started to train as a young child. He passed on the secrets of his training to Frank Lin. His dad also left the life of a monk to raise a family. Frank Lin's dad believed that it was good to find self-worth, meditate on things and lead an aesthetic lifestyle. He also believed that you needed to experience life as well.

That's when he met Frank Lin's mom. She had a quiet elegance that made people like her. Both his parents were from different worlds, but they shared the talent to run a business well. They founded a series of restaurants that served genuine monastic food. People really enjoyed their food and it made Frank Lin's family billionaires.

Frank Lin became a trust fund baby. He was focused on school and left college with four doctorates including Computer Science, Religious Studies, Egyptology and Biological Science. He enjoyed art, so he obtained a major in the subject. Nevertheless, Frank Lin felt directionless after college. Not knowing what he wanted to do, he decided he was going to find the answers traveling the world.

Frank Lin ended up with a research group in China working on restoring the Great Wall. They were in a very mountainous and inaccessible area that had been untouched by man for thousands of years. They came across some erosion at the base of the wall. There had been heavy rains and it washed away some of the mud and debris that had covered a stone slab, which looked suspiciously like a door. It had intricate carvings that were written in ancient Sanskrit. He loosely translated it to mean: *"Here lie the weapons of the Gods. They are buried in plain sight for them to see. Ready for the time when the battle begins anew."*

CHAPTER 14

He could not do any excavations within the wall because it was a World Heritage Site. This was an important discovery and he quickly tried to go through the necessary paperwork and people. He needed to probe deeper into this strange mystery.

They plead their case for months and finally got a chance to excavate the area, while under the supervision of a World Heritage Site official. He found hundreds of weapons made of titanium. They found bows and arrows, swords, knives, and many others.

There were some other gigantic weapons made of materials that no one could identify. Some of the sizes were too fantastic to be wielded by any human. There was a thirteen-foot long sword made of black metal with red embossments in a strange language. It seemed to have other weapons inside it but the item needed further study.

Also among them was a giant *Gadha*, or mace with a spherical head and a long shaft. It was the crowning jewel of the discoveries. It was 20 feet long and eight feet at the greatest diameter of the sphere, embossed with carvings and writings that were in ancient Sanskrit. It came in at a whopping fifty tons.

Frank Lin knew from his studies that ancient deities carried weapons of this size. He even visited the statues of them all over East Asia, but he knew in his heart this one was different. It was made up of metal that did not exist on the periodic table. It did not show any signs of rust, there was no weathering on the item and no rough edges on the sphere. Even though the caked-on dirt was carbon-dated at ten thousand years old, the Gadha looked like it was ten minutes old. This item should not have existed.

The foundation of the wall appeared to be older than the reported age of the weapons. Frank Lin supposed the Great Wall was built on a pre-existing trail. It made sense to build a wall where people passed. Why did it double as a tomb for the great weapons? The two instances where such a massive amount of weapons and objects were buried were if the person needed it in the afterlife or it was in hiding from somebody. But there were no remains nearby so this could not have been a tomb. Were the weapons hidden for a purpose? Did the builders of the wall expect the owners of the weapons to come back? According to the inscription, they did. Who were the owners of the weapons? Why bury the weapons? Why not just take them with you? Why keep them here?

There were so many questions and Frank Lin felt like he needed to answer them all. The wall protected the provinces of China and nobody would think to look under a wall for weapons to defend or attack with. 'In the long run', thought Frank Lin, 'this was a good hiding spot'.

Amidst the flurry of researchers and archaeologists that were examining and extracting the artifacts, Frank Lin collapsed. His friends quickly called his family and they airlifted him out to the hospital. Unfortunately for Frank Lin, it turned out to be a brain tumor. The news devastated him so much that he lost the will to live. His dad told Frank Lin to not give up because your mind is the greatest thing in the world and beyond. When his parents took him to the States to get treated, he resolved to get some answers. He had made a discovery that could possibly change the world. However he might not live long enough to enjoy the feeling and that, turned his world upside down.

His parents had a big surprise for him. They managed to get the giant Gadha and some other artifacts on loan from the Chinese Archaeology Society and it was en-route to the Grand museum in California for the New Year. They told him he had two months to get better because they wanted him as the guest of honor along with dignitaries, renowned researchers, and scholars. He was excited and determined to do so, not for his parents but for himself.

The greatest thing that Frank Lin learned from his dad was also the most puzzling - how to get to the Akashic records library. The Akashic records library was a mystical plane that contained all the information in the universe, wherein any question could be answered. No one knew where it came from or who built it. Nonetheless, you must go there with a purpose. That's exactly what Frank Lin did last night during his meditations. He asked the Akashic records library if he was going to die of a brain tumor. The answer he got back was startling:

CHAPTER 14

'Find the one who is not found.
The found must first be lost.
Be unable to put your hands on what is mislaid.
The unwritten must be read.
The unthinkable must be conceived.
The unknown must be acknowledged.
The impossible must come to pass.
I have trans-versed many dimensions.
I have defeated immortals in combat.
I have been to the edge of the universe and beyond.
I am a man among men, a man among kings and a man among the Gods.'

Frank Lin went a second time and got the same answer. Feeling frustrated, he focused himself and obtained the same answer for the third time. While he sat and contemplated, a nurse informed him that the doctors were ready to do his MRI. He went with her, still mulling over the turn of events. As he was going out the door, Frank Lin heard tossing and turning.

There was a man in a hospital bed across from him. The curtains were closed but you could still hear his pain. He moaned in his sleep. It seemed the man was having a nightmare that crawled out from under the boogeyman's bed. Frank Lin heard the man cry out, "Please you have to find me!" He stopped and listened, not believing his ears, "Please you have to find me!" Frank Lin figured this could be too much of a coincidence. No way could the Library be talking about some guy in a hospital bed. He'd have to go back to the Akashic records library and find some answers. Maybe he might ask about the man in the bed as well.

Theo was awake but not really up. His mind was racing on the events of his dream even before his eyes blinked open. Theo woke up to a very leathery skinned nurse bending over his hospital bed. She smiled and welcomed him back to the land of the living with a good pat on the shoulder. Behind her was Asheley, with a huge smile on her face as well.

"Theo, I'm so glad you're okay. I was so worried about the outcome of the crime against you. I am sorry I couldn't do more."

"I am very lucky to be alive. Thanks to you. Where were you during all of this?"

"I saw the intruder come in and I hid in the shower. I was so conflicted. I knew the person might harm you, but I did not want to do anyone any harm. I was for the first time in my short life, in an impossible situation. Please forgive me."

"Do you realize that this situation exponentially grew your feelings? You're feeling all of these emotions and that is the most amazing thing that could happen. Well, me being alive is wonderful too!" exclaimed Theo.

"I would not have anyone if I lost you. I have to protect you at any cost. I won't leave your side." Asheley said resolutely.

Just then an older nurse came into the room making her rounds. She checked if the other patients were okay. She pulled up to Theo's bed and looked at the charts.

"You were dead for an hour. Luckily we were able to bring you back," she smiled. She left the room, and in her place there came the sunshine of his life, his little girl Katie.

"Hi daddy, are you ok? Mommy told me that you got a big booboo and had to go to the hospital," she said with a bright-eyed smile.

"Thanks for coming to see me, my little Katie cat," Theo replied, smiling.

"Hello Asheley!" shouted Katie as she ran to hug Asheley.

"Hey, kitten cat. Are you enjoying your new dolls?" asked Asheley.

"I enjoy it more when we play with them. Mommy doesn't play with the dollhouse like you."

Just then her mom, Catherine, walked in. John was hovering by the door.

"Hello Catherine," Theo said.

CHAPTER 14

"Katie baby, go wait outside, okay," Catherine said as she tenderly kissed her little girl. She then came over to the bedside and faced Theo squarely.

Theo looked away, fighting down his overpowering emotions.

"Asheley used your cell to call me. I came as quickly as I could. I saw when they tried to bring you back to life. I couldn't let you go without telling you this," she sighed as if she had trouble breathing. Catherine held his hand. Asheley looked on and held Theo's other hand as if in defiance to Catherine and in defense of her territory.

Catherine's hands were soft to the touch, possibly from all of the moisturizers that she used. She was always using them, every time she washed dishes or bathed. Her hands always smelled of moisturizers. Her hands were strong as well. She worked out and kept every part of her body fit. She was the perfect balance between feminine and strong. Not only was her body strong but she had a strong will and a sharp mind. Once she put her mind to something, nothing dissuaded her from that direction.

There was a lot of Catherine inside Katie, an independent spirit that wanted to soar. Theo looked into those deep brown eyes that he had looked into during their dates, during their wedding ceremony, and during their divorce. Now her eyes looked as bright, as deep, and as beautiful as they looked so many times before.

"What is it? Why did you have to bring, him." Theo asked icily.

"Theo, I need you to say your goodbyes to Katie." She openly tried to fight back tears but it was a fight that she was not winning. "The test results for Katie came back and she's... she's not yours. She's John's." The tears flowed. They ran like a river that had overflowed its banks during the rainy season.

"No. No." Theo breathed, as he tried to hold on to the little life left inside him. Now his life was being turned upside down again. "No, please this can't be happening now," he cried trying to fight back tears, but he was unsuccessful as well.

"You're a good man, Theo. You really are. Maybe, you were just too good for a woman like me. I just couldn't believe that I could get a great man like you in my life. I fell back into old habits."

"Send Katie in, please. She's the best thing that's ever happened to me," he said drying his eyes with a hand that had several IV's sticking out of it.

Asheley looked on and felt saddened at the sight of Theo crying. She wished she could do more for him. However, with the realization that he was about to lose his little girl, there was little she could do even with all the knowledge in the world at her fingertips.

Katie came into the room. Her mom hoisted her up on the side of the bed where she stared into, as far as she knew, her dad's eyes.

"Katie, do you remember that puppy we found wandering the streets?"

Katie nodded.

"Remember how we took the puppy home and bathed him and fed him and put him in the bed to sleep in?"

"Yes, daddy."

"Remember how we called the puppy's owner and they took two weeks to come and get him?"

Katie nodded.

"Remember how you really loved that puppy and how the puppy really loved you. Then when the owner came, the puppy loved the owner too?"

"Uh Huh," said Katie.

"Remember how you felt when the puppy left? You were sad and confused and you didn't want the puppy to go. The puppy had to go because it was the owner's?"

Katie nodded again.

"You're my puppy, but you belong to someone else. I took care of you for six years. Now your real owner, John, is here to get you. Do you understand? I can't be your daddy anymore."

"You're not my daddy anymore?" she cried.

"Don't worry Katie, honey. The puppy will always remember us. Like you will always remember the puppy, right? You will remember me and I will remember you," cried Theo as he hugged his daughter for the last time.

CHAPTER 14

"Yes, daddy," she cried.

John took Katie up. Both of them walked out of the hospital room doorway and never looked back. Catherine was, for the first time in her entire life, crying not just a wail from the bottom of her heart, but a cry that was the result of her soul being destroyed. A monster wave of regret swept over her as she had watched the powerful and moving scene that just unfolded before her.

"Theo, I'm sorry. You are a good man and I will always cherish the memories that we have made together," Catherine, the once love of his life, said through a waterfall of tears.

She ran out of the room, wondering if she made a mistake. Theo's love-scarred heart still ached for her, but he knew that it was finished.

Asheley held on to Theo's hand, the one with the IV's sticking out of it, while he wept for his family that had just left him alone. Visiting hours were nearly over and Asheley had to leave. She promised that she would be back with some supplies for him. She also promised that she would look after him.

After she left, Theo closed his eyes and heaved a great big sigh. He essentially had little growing up, gained a lot of love and comfort with his wife and child, and lost everything, almost died, and essentially got kicked out of the afterlife because of paperwork issues.

Suddenly, he opened his eyes as a long beeping sound erupted from the bed on the other side of the room. Just beyond the curtain, he saw, believe it or not, a Tibetan monk. Some words were coming out of his mouth, but the funny thing was that the heart rate monitor hooked up to the monk, registered no heartbeat. Nurses quickly filed in and within an instant, the monk's vitals were back to normal. Scratching their heads in disbelief, they left the room but decided to be more vigilant in case they were needed again.

Theo was in a daze. He was trying to wrap his head around what happened in the afterlife and pondered the whole scenario with his family just now.

The monk's heart machine went off again. Nurses and doctors filed in and immediately went to work on the monk but

CHAPTER 14

he revived instantaneously. An older doctor resigned to get to the bottom of this, ordered two nurses to take the patient to another bed. It happened to be right next to Theo.

A lanky male nurse mumbled, "Excuse me," and pulled the curtain around him so that he was completely cut off from the world. Theo Steren Champlain had no choice but to sleep off the events that shattered his world.

Theo didn't know how long he'd been sleeping. He was sure that he had night terrors and screamed. His sleep was troublesome, but at one point he felt and smelled the presence of someone beside him. He looked over and was thankful that a thoughtful nurse had placed a clock with the date and time beside his bed. Alongside the clock, was a breakfast that comprised of hash browns, a vegetable omelet, a bagel with strawberry cream cheese on it, turkey bacon, and pulpy orange juice. This was definitely not typical hospital food.

The nurse had also placed a bouquet of flowers next to the bed that looked like a rainforest barfed into the vase. They looked expensive. The kind of expensive that you wish you hadn't spent the money on. Theo was thankful for it though, it brightened his day and the smell was very aromatic. He was also thankful that a gracious someone had pulled the curtains open, so he didn't feel so alone anymore. A female orderly walked into the room pushing a lady in a wheelchair.

"Hello" Theo piped up.

"Good morning. How are you feeling today?" she asked in a cordial southern drawl.

"I'm okay for now. I don't even feel the wounds. Are these for me?"

"Yes, they are. Your wife insisted that she bring you a big meal to keep you well fed. She also brought the flowers to cheer you up. She seems like a good woman. She sat there with you for a bit while you slept," she said as she helped the wheelchair-bound lady onto the bed and tucked her in.

CHAPTER 14

"Wow, I wasn't expecting Asheley to come back so soon," replied Theo in disbelief.

"Um... the lady I spoke to said her name was Raechellee. Maybe it might have been your girlfriend?" said the confused orderly.

"My wife left me and I don't have a girlfriend by the name of Raechellee. However, I'm still thankful for the food and the roses."

"Well honey, someone took a lot of trouble to bring you these. I'd say that's a very good road to recovery."

"Thanks. Do you know what happened to the monk? I know he was having some trouble the other night."

"You mean the Tibetan guy? Oh, he's in the MRI room with the doctors. They're scanning him again. He gave us quite a scare the other night."

"Oh! Good. He's okay."

"Well you have a good day now and do enjoy that breakfast!" said the orderly as she exited the room, "I've got some more rounds to make."

Theo got up and went to the bathroom. He was actually not in as much pain as he should be and that surprised him. There on the shelf of the hospital bathroom, he found a bag with a note on it that read, 'Theo, my darling, here are some toiletries for you. I made you a hearty breakfast as well. Do eat it before it gets cold. I didn't know which flowers you wanted so I got one of each! See you soon! Raechellee.' Theo wondered who this mystery woman was as he dug into the bag and pulled out toothpaste and a toothbrush.

The dream of the events in heaven looked and felt so real he wondered what it meant. The searing pain of the fiery sword felt agonizingly unforgettable. Being curious, he looked at the wounds under the bandages, being careful not to unloose them. There were two sutured bullet holes and a long gash that looked like it went through his body and came out the back. He turned around and examined the exit wound in the mirror. It left a scar on his body right where the angel ran him through.

"Oh my God," he gasped in horror as the scar stood out like a garden gnome on a slab of concrete.

CHAPTER 14

He put the bandages back on and stood there, not knowing what to think. He wondered how Asheley was doing, what she must be going through. She had shown remarkable strides in emotions the other night when he first woke up. He would have to help her cope with those emotions, as she was helping him cope with his problems. He wondered what Katie and Catherine were going through. Who the hell was this Raechellee?

Feeling refreshed after his daily toilet routine, Theo turned his attention to the delicious breakfast before him. As he ate the succulent and lovingly prepared food that filled his famished body, he reflected upon the events of last night. He lay back down and soon began to feel drowsy. Theo Steren Champlain fell into a deep sleep.

CHAPTER 15: Brentt Williams Talks To Theo

The man that lay in the hospital bed before him was one-hundred and eighty pounds of pure pathetic, complete with a heaping side of over middle-aged. Making it a meal deal, add a helping of, 'I had the living life kicked out of me by everyone that I ever knew'.

His features looked very craggy and he was once good looking. However, years of hard work and general life took their toll upon him. Any woman who risked going out with him needed a few dozen beers. They also needed a 'yes' answer to the question 'are you the last man on earth?' before making the biggest mistake of their life and ruining their future. She might want to make sure he answered the question truthfully because he seemed like the kind of man that would lie about it. He looked very leathery and could have doubled for a football. The man was a fifty-year-old that smoked two hundred years-worth of cigarettes.

"Hi, I'm detective Brentt Williams. Are you Theo Steren Champlain?" asked detective Williams.

"No. I'm somebody else. My wife shacked up with her friend's son and I tried to kill myself. Could I be locked away for attempted murder on me?" he asked.

The detective did the math but he did not want to take the test right now. "Sir, you might be locked away for it, possibly in a mental health institute. Good luck with everything." The detective turned to leave but another occupant in the room spoke to him.

"I'm Theo, detective Williams," said a younger man with short, slightly greying hair and kind eyes. Despite being shot, he had a cordial attitude and looked relatively fit for his age. He had no six-pack abs but a kept a value pack stomach.

CHAPTER 15

"Hello, Mr. Theo Steren Champlain. I am detective Brentt Williams with the police department. I believe that you were shot. What can you tell me about that night?" asked the detective, getting straight to the point.

"Well, I came home after work with some food. When I went into the kitchen, someone shot me. They were really tall and very chubby but they wore shades and a bandanna over their face and a hoodie," offered Theo.

"How tall and what time?"

"The person was maybe six-foot, eight or possibly seven-feet tall. About nine o'clock at night, you can check my work. I am a full-time inter-department manager at the *Everything Department Store,*" said Theo.

"I will verify that. Do you know anyone that may want to kill you?" asked Brentt, raising an eyebrow.

"Nobody that I know of. I did see the person take my food though," answered Theo.

"They took your food?" exclaimed Brentt, as he noted that in his standard-issue police note pad.

Theo nodded, "A mushroom and Swiss burger with all the fixings, house special sauce, a large box of hungry man curly fries, chicken nuggets, mozzarella sticks, and a finished soda."

"I'll make sure and put out an APB for that," the detective said flatly.

"Thanks!" Theo managed to get out.

"There was a call from an unidentified number detailing the emergency at your house. Then a few minutes later, there was another call to emergency with the same details, coming from your phone. Paramedics said that your girlfriend was with you when they arrived. Was that so?" asked Brentt in full interrogation mode.

"She called the ambulance. But, you mean, there was another report made?"

"Yes. Did you see the intruder...umm... Asheley is it?" asked the detective.

"I am Theo's girlfriend. I did see the intruder," she said succinctly.

"Tell me what happened," the detective said flatly.

CHAPTER 15

"I was watching the news when I heard the door jiggle. It was not time for Theo to arrive, so I went to the peephole to see who it was. It looked like someone I did not recognize so I hid in the shower to evade detection. They broke in and scouted the house. Next, they sprawled out on the bed as if it were their own abode. I was so terrified that I could not move. I heard Theo get shot. It was the darkest moment of my life."

Theo looked at Asheley and felt sorry for her. Why did her life have to be marred by violence and trauma?

"Then, they did not see you in the shower? Tell me how long have you been with Mr. Champlain?" inquired Brentt Williams, now, even more skeptical.

"Three months, since his divorce. That's not important though. I love Theo and I don't know who would shoot him. I guess you could talk to his ex-wife and her boyfriend," suggested Asheley.

"That's a good idea. What is her name?" asked the detective as he rolled his eyes and wrote on the standard-issue notepad.

"My ex-wife's name is Catherine and she lives at 5015 Palm Avenue. We got divorced three months ago after six years of marriage," said Theo.

"Your ex-wife is with her boyfriend?" asked Brentt, now leaning closer to Theo. "Tell me about them. Was it a very bitter divorce? Did any of them threaten you, or did you threaten them? Was there an altercation between you guys?"

"Not bitter. It was a real quick divorce. No altercation. I just got up and left when I found out what was going on," answered Theo.

"Are you absolutely sure? That does not sound like typical behavior," the detective said skeptically.

"Positive. It would have been a waste of time to do so and besides, I had my daughter to think about. Well, I don't anymore though, because she turned out to not be mine." Theo looked dejected after speaking that fact out loud.

The detective took a minute to process that bit of information. "Were you followed after work? Do you have any enemies at work? Are there any coworkers that dislike you?"

CHAPTER 15

"Not at all. It was late at night when I walked home. I would have noticed someone following me. I get along with everyone at work. No one hates me as far as I can tell," surmised Theo.

"Any surveillance cameras around that could have picked up anything?" continued the detective.

"No, it is a safe neighborhood, so I did not put any up. Actually, I don't think the other tenants have any cameras as well. At least, any that I noticed," suggested Theo.

"Okay. We'll be on the lookout for any suspicious characters that are somewhere between six-foot, eight and seven-feet tall. And let's hope they don't have any food for hostages," the detective remarked sarcastically. "I might give your ex-wife a visit. See if I can find something there. In the meantime, keep yourself free for any more questions."

"Thank you, detective. I appreciate it," said Theo to the detective who had already turned to leave.

The detective stopped and spoke with his back to Theo, "I need you to think really hard Theo Steren Champlain and think really long. I need you to come clean if there is anything you have to get off your chest. I am a detective and it's my job to detect even the slightest detail." And with that, detective Brentt Williams walked out of the hospital room.

Theo sank back into the hospital bed and looked at his other roommates. Carl was drifting off to sleep, his hands heavily bandaged from an attempt to kill himself. The detective had mistaken him for Theo when he first walked in. The next occupant in the room was a thirty-year-old Tibetan monk, which was laying peacefully about ten feet away from him. His eyes snapped open as the detective left and he looked Theo straight in the eyes. "I think I had a dream about you," he said frankly.

Detective Brentt Williams walked out the door and Theo breathed a sigh of relief. The monk's, hopefully, non-ominous words could be heard over Theo's sigh. "I think I had a dream about you." Theo looked over at the monk in surprise and exclaimed, "Excuse me!"

CHAPTER 15

"Theo, isn't it? I heard you scream out in your dreams. They sounded pretty horrible. Forgive me, where are my manners. I'm Frank Lin Shao, a monk, nice to meet you," he said.

"It's okay. I'm Theo Steren Champlain. Now that you mention it, I did happen to see you having some difficulty the other day as well. The doctors were really working on you. What are you in for?"

"Oh, I saw what you did there, making our hospital stay look like we're cellmates. Good one. I have a brain tumor, very malignant and in a very hard to reach area. I was off working on restoring the Great Wall of China when I made a discovery that would shock the historical world. Then my world came crashing down. What's your deal?" the monk said, reminiscing about his discovery and the events that followed.

"My wife of six years was cheating on me. My best friend was sleeping with my wife. I got divorced three months ago. I was shot just as I came home from work and my fast food stolen. I found out my daughter was not mine on my death bed. So yeah, that's about it for me. I guess, we both had our worlds turned upside down," said Theo as he stared off into a daze, then snapped back into reality.

"I'm sorry to hear that," the monk feigned interest. He wanted to help him but he had some ulterior motives to do so. "Your dream, tell me about it. It sounded like you were telling someone 'you had to find me'. Do you remember it?" inquired the monk, getting straight to his agenda.

"Aren't you supposed to be cooped up somewhere chanting something, for like your whole life?" asked Theo, a little uneasy about letting on about his dream.

"Most monks do that, but I find with trying to be good and reaching enlightenment, it is important to spread the word and to teach others about it. *Besides, for me, being on a good path means helping people get on the right path*," said Frank Lin Shao.

Theo realized that there was no harm in telling the monk his dream. He would have never met this guy in his whole life if it had not been for the incident.

"I remember I was in heaven and it was the most beautiful place that I've ever seen. There were people and angels there. I

CHAPTER 15

felt right at home. This angel came up to me and asked me to check in by putting my hand on a tablet to scan my soul print. It was weird because he was talking about reincarnation. The next thing I knew, he couldn't find me anywhere. Not in the good book, the bad book or the other religions' book. I did not know what to do. He called security and kicked me out of heaven," Theo put his right hand upon the bandages that covered his wounds and looked down at them.

"Wow! Them not finding you in heaven! That is some serious stuff! I was going to use a stinky expletive for stuff, but my swearing box is pretty full right now. Did they give a reason? Like, you know... hmm, we don't have your address on file or something?" suggested Frank Lin, also puzzled.

"No. They just said it had never ever happened before in history. So, you said you had a dream about me? Was it the kind of dream, like for humanity in general or was it specifically about me? Perhaps, you subconsciously heard my nightmare and dreamt about it?" suggested Theo.

"I am a monk and I am privy to certain things that are very hard for ordinary people to achieve. I meditate for long hours, can control pain, and channel nerve force. I can do that because I was taught how to do it and I've had lots of practice. I had a dream about you because I needed to find you. The *Akashic Records Library* told me to find you," explained Frank Lin, as he braced for the 'huh, what are you talking about crazy person?' part of the conversation.

"The Ash-kash-ic library, what is that? Is that in heaven or something?" queried Theo, now intrigued.

"The Akashic Records Library is all the knowledge in the universe, in one place. It is on an astral plane that requires mediation to get there. It is a vast and imposing place that can be overwhelming, but you need to go there with a specific question that you want to be answered," explained the monk, grateful that he still had the attention of Theo. Usually, at this point in most of his conversations, the other person tries to get away. It was somewhat unfair because Theo was bedridden.

"Wait! A place that has all the answers! Answers to life's biggest mysteries and everything else!" exclaimed Theo.

CHAPTER 15

"Yes. When I went there to find out if I was going to die of brain cancer, it gave me this answer: The found must first be lost. Be unable to put your hands on what is mislaid. The unwritten must be read. The unthinkable must be conceived.

There were other lines, but when you yelled out in your dreams about somebody finding you, it struck me that you might be the one I was looking for. I went back for confirmation and I came back with this: *To the records send the sword that ends in the shock of his afterlife.* I was hoping you could tell me what that means," explained Frank Lin.

"It can't be. I was run through with a fiery, fifteen-foot sword. I could still smell my flesh burning as the giant blade tore through me. I have the scar from that encounter. Why would you need to find me?" said Theo, realizing that this conversation just went to a whole new level.

"Let me tell you what you need to know. The universe has given me my answer and I have been charged with helping you find yours. Hopefully, in doing so, we both might find what we seek," spoke Frank Lin Shao, the Tibetan monk.

"Okay, I am listening," replied Theo.

"The secret of the universe is a secret that the universe itself tells us. It knows we are adrift in the sea of life and death. We are adrift in the seas of space and time. We are without an anchor and without a rudder. We are directionless, without a compass and maps to our destinations. We feel frustrated at times and helpless at other times because we lack the knowledge of what we need. The Akashic Records Library lies at the crossroads of knowledge and emotions.

Emotions are with us every day. They guide us and sometimes control us. You interact with people through emotions. You make decisions through emotions, whether they are good or bad decisions. Almost all are fueled by emotions. Sometimes emotion can be a curse if it cannot be controlled. Sometimes it could be a boon if is kept in check. Most people do not find that balance all the time. Some people appear to have that balance, but deep inside, there is chaotic unrest. Emotions drive the world and the world is driven by emotions."

CHAPTER 15

"Are you saying that I should try to balance how I feel? I don't think that is possible for me," said Theo quizzically.

"There is something that we can use to transcend emotion. Something that comes before it and is not part of it. Something that is the mediation between the world and the emotional being that is inside us. It is so universal that it exists without us and is different things to different people. It governs us. Everyone uses it. Everyone has it. Everyone wants more of it. It is the precursor to emotions and it determines our emotions.

Knowledge governs the universe. First, knowledge has to be gained in order to emote about it. Knowledge and emotions go hand in hand, but one carries the other, one dictates to the other, one skews the other. The key is to find the balance. That balance, at the crossroads of knowledge and emotion, is where you will find the way. After you have found the way, you must set your destination. Put your mind on the path to the seemingly impossible, but very accessible."

"How do I gain the knowledge and control my feelings about it, so that I can find the crossroads to the Records Library?" asked Theo.

"Meditate and focus your thoughts on what you want. Force out everything from your mind, no matter what the subject. Free yourself from the bonds of the mundane. Let your soul ascend higher than you have ever been. Be one with the universe. Feel the universe. Take the light of its knowledge into you and find your answer inside of you. Because you are part of the universe, part of it resides in you. You are accessing the part of the universe that is for you."

"Frank Lin, that sounds incredible. Do you think I can do it? Is it that simple? Are we really one with the universe?" asked Theo.

"It does sound incredible, but anyone can do it. I believe you can do it. I will help you get to the Akashic Records Library. Theo, you have to put away the disdain for your ex-wife. Get rid of the anger and the hate that you have for your friend that betrayed you.

Everything inside you determines outside success. You want to succeed. Use those emotions as your fuel. Let it strengthen your resolve to do what must be done. But when the time comes, channel it. Make it so that the emotions that you have to shed and the knowledge you have to shed them become a part of the answer. That is the way to find what you are looking for.

You will not find the answer to your question, but the answer to your question will find you. This is the universe giving you what you need to know. Sometimes, the answer is one that we may not want to hear. I know, because I've had that experience so many times before. This is from the universe, so I don't believe you can argue about it.

It is arbitrary. The will of the universe is unchallenged and irrevocable. It is indiscriminate to rank, class, financial status or power. It is unemotional, impassive, unflappable, and dispassionate. Ponder it, ingrain it into your essence and exude it. The answer that you receive is the answer that is and will be, forever."

Theo watched as the monk closed his eyes and breathed a sigh of relief. The sermon that Frank Lin just gave Theo, really hit home. Theo felt that he was a changed man because of it. There was a spark in Theo's eyes that was not there for a long time. He felt like there was hope after all and the monk had given him a taste of purpose.

Outside the door of the hospital room, detective Brentt Williams leaned against the wall, with his arms folded across his chest. He was out of view and within earshot of the whole conversation. The monk's line of training was similar to his own. Brentt himself had gone to the Akashic Records many times before. 'This was a very interesting day so far', he thought to himself.

CHAPTER 16: Atomos At The Edge

Atomos inspected the farthest reaches of the cosmos. He knew what was going on everywhere, but wanted to see for himself the sturdiness of the walls of the universe.

At the moment, he was planet-sized and drifted along the walls, examining them. The walls were crafted with dark matter, coated with time and folded over with space. 'Very strong indeed,' he thought to himself.

He came across an abnormal gap in the universal wall that was the size of an elephant. Oozing from the gap, a black, viscous substance dripped onto a chunk of rock that was about a half a mile square. It was almost as if the ooze was holding the asteroid in place.

Atomos shrunk himself and stepped onto the rocky terrain to take a closer look. Sunlight was barely reaching this corner, so he created a miniature sun to illuminate the way. He placed it above his head. He used his powers to contain the ooze with his right hand and blocked the entrance to the universe with a force field from his left.

He went closer to examine the sticky substance that was straining against the force shield. Atomos could see the past, present and future multiverses of anything, but as for this substance, he could not see any trace of it.

"How quickly you forget me," said many deep, monstrous voices in unison through the thick blackness of space.

"You speak. Tell me friends, who are you?" asked Atomos hesitantly, unbecoming for the King of the Gods.

"I was before the beginning as were all of you."

"Before the beginning, were the nine and we lived in the Void," replied Atomos.

"Yes. I am the Void. *I am nothing and I am everything.*"

CHAPTER 16

"How is that possible? There was nothing," asked Atomos, startled.

"Your frivolous bickering amongst yourselves drew my fascination. I was an unknown witness to The Contest of the Nine. When all nine universal dimensions were created, I was condensed into this form you see before you. I inhabit the space between the universal dimensions."

"What do you mean by nine universal dimensions?"

"Each dimension has a different King of the Gods. A different UKSCOGSM."

"Is that so? That is very interesting. It looks like the decision to crown the King of the Gods and the God of the Gods was more far-reaching than any of us thought. What may I do for you?" It was more a statement than a question from Atomos.

"I will take everything and leave nothing. My essence shall overtake and spread through this universe and others. I will have all back to me."

"You mean take over everything? Why? We are working to create a happy system. Could we not find a place for you to belong?"

The voice of the Void took on a different tone, more menacing and foreboding than it already sounded.

"I existed before the light. For before the light there was darkness. I existed before the darkness. For before the darkness there was nothing. Darkness is not just the absence of light but the presence of darkness. In the Void, there is both and neither. The energy you put into both determines if you are for the light or part of the darkness. Both belong to the Void because the Void is before all and will be after all. All need both understand the difference, yet when there is none, there is no difference.

When I take away all, there is nothing. I am casting my shadow across the multiverse and there is no light or darkness that can drive it away. You Gods think that you control the light and that you transcend the darkness. Even in the highest zenith of the sun, there is still shadow. You think that you are beyond good and evil. You Gods made it. It is inside of you. But I surround you. You live inside the Void.

CHAPTER 16

When you decided to create the universe, you created the universe out of me. The different dimensions are my children. The universe that is the dark matter is me. I want to take back my multiverse. I will infuse in all. I will permeate through all. I will exude from all. I will have all back to me."

Atomos knew there was no reasoning with such an entity. "I will push you back and wall you in. You shall not harm any of my creations!" With a mighty heave, he pushed the Void back through the hole from whence it came. The tendrils of gelatinous dark matter broke through the shield and wrapped themselves around the miniature sun that hovered above Atomos. He shot lightning a trillion times more powerful than the wildest thunderstorms in the universe.

Instantaneously, he materialized himself in a quadrillion places, to battle the vicious foe. A thousand more Atomos' had stepped through the hole in the wall. All of them shielded the entrance so that not one drop of Void could get through.

The other side of the wall was beyond black. So black, you could not see with your mind's eye. That did not stop the God of the Gods. In fact, it made him more resolute. All the Atomos' let out a blast wave in all directions, beating back their foe.

Atomos was fueled by the will to protect his universe and by the power of the diadem of godhood. He fought back this foe with all his might. In the midst of the frenzy, the Atomos furthest from the rest spotted something strange, something different. The fight was over in about three hours, with the Void being beaten back.

A wearied Atomos climbed through the hole in the universal wall. "Let all the holes in the universe be closed to the Void and its treachery. Everything in this universe is under the protection of my will. The will of the King of the Gods and the God of the Gods!" exclaimed Atomos. He used his waning energy to inflict his will upon the universe and close up the dark matter coated with time and folded over with space.

He sat upon the asteroid that still floated in the emptiness of the dimly lit corner of the universe. Atomos was out of breath and covered with cuts and bruises. He felt on his head to see if his diadem was there. Most of it was, however a piece of it was broken off during the battle. He decided not to say anything to the rest of the Gods about this new development, confident that this dark foe was defeated.

Atomos sat there on the chunk of rock at the outer edges of the universe and closed his eyes, feeling for everything that was in existence. He felt the present and future lives of everything that there ever was and will be. However, the universe seemed emptier than it usually was, like a great sadness had fallen upon all of creation. The futures of trillions of beings just disappeared before his eyes and existed no more. The paths of the molecules and atoms that they consisted of, moved on different paths than those he had set forth. Atomos being a God saw all and foresaw all. He knows all and knew everything. Right now, he knew he was missing the Milky Way Galaxy.

- -

Technon hit the wall of the universe with momentum, unlike anything you can ever imagine. He bounced off the wall and floated in space. The energy that had followed him all the way from the incident and continued through his limp body, struck the wall of the universe. The barrier that Atomos had lovingly crafted had been breached by the God of War's blade. A big gaping hole spewed out slimy sludge, which cast aside the God of Technology's body from before it.

Caddeussus got there in time to see Technon's body float listlessly in space. It was a dark corner, where the light from the nearby sun was being periodically blocked out by floating bits of what had been a comet. Technon had sideswiped it.

Caddeussus multiplied himself into three individuals and supported his fellow God with two of them. He then teleported Technon away from the breach in the walls but left his third embodiment. As he turned to go, he heard a soft voice, "Caddeussus."

- -

The God Breaker Cannon was about to fire at an 'about to poop my pants Anthraxis'. Just then, a sonic boom, unlike any ever heard in the entire vacuum of space, resounded in the ears of the Gods and the universe itself.

Atomos had arrived. He stole the show. He had assumed a form so colossal, that he held The God Breaker Cannon in his hand. The cannon was as large as twenty-four suns, whose bullets were the size of Saturn and whose name was in graffiti thirty thousand miles tall.

"What is going on here? Where the hell is my Milky Way Galaxy?" His voice boomed with such force, that all the Gods struggled to keep their composure.

All the Technons scattered like cockroaches but eventually amalgamated themselves into one embodiment. Technon, Heddonna, Archituria, Galaxyia, Cosmica, and Detrimentus stood trembling before the powerful embodiment of Atomos. He held The God Breaker Cannon in his right hand and a restricted Anthraxis in his left. Caddeussus was nowhere to be seen.

Atomos had no experience to deal with this dilemma and he was at a loss of how to proceed. Coupled with the fact of what just happened before he got here, there was no good outcome for this.

"Everyone, I need all of you to stop what you are doing and give me your full attention!" Atomos yelled in a booming voice that reverberated across the universe. All of creation shook and everything stopped what they were doing. Planets stopped in their tracks. Light stopped illuminating planets. Waves stopped mid-break from crashing against the shores. Air molecules stopped moving. Blood cells stopped being pumped. Hearts stopped beating. Everything in the entirety of creation just stopped what they were doing and focused on the words of the King of the Gods and the God of the Gods.

The two embodiments of The God of Life had returned from the edge of the universe with the now conscious body of Technon in tow. They looked at the giant figure of Atomos and marveled at the situation. 'This guy is nine times more powerful than us', they thought to themselves, as they looked on. After amalgamating into one, Caddeussus let Technon go and he rejoined his other form. Caddeussus did not give Atomos his full attention but reserved some of his attention for inward reflection.

CHAPTER 16

Atomos continued, "You Gods have proven your inadequacy at overseeing the universe. When left to your own devices, instead of protecting it, you have destroyed it. From now on, the Athlogoss Drones will be conducting the majority of the business on behalf of the Gods. Return to your temple planets! All of you are condemned to stay on your temple planets for the rest of eternity until I decide to amend your punishment!"

CHAPTER 17: In The Kitchen With The Ladies

Raechellee stood in front of the sink, washing up a frying pan. Some water splashed on her very tight, white U.S.A. shirt. She had just sautéed some garlic, onions, and bell peppers of various colors. It was for a salad that she was preparing. The leafy greens were already washed and cut. The eggs were mashed and seasoned. The croutons and fried Chinese noodles were ready to share. When Raechellee was about to mix everything up, she heard the oven buzzer go off, in the larger, main kitchen.

"I got it," said an attractive young lady, who had risen from the couch in the entertainment room. With the remote in her hand, she stopped the movie that she was watching. The young woman, whose midnight-black hair was in a bun, went to the main kitchen. She grabbed two potholders, bent over and took out a delicious three-cheese lasagna from the oven.

"It's done. I'm putting the breadsticks in now," she said, doing exactly that.

"Thanks, Alexyia. The salad is ready. How are you doing over there, Elainney?" asked Raechellee. She looked over at the breakfast nook. It was located in the smaller kitchen. Her friend Elainney was putting shaved white chocolate on an apple caramel cheesecake.

"Looks good," said Elainney.

"I'm almost done with the mozzarella sticks you guys," said a tall, red-haired woman in front of a deep fryer in the main kitchen.

All three ladies congregated by the red-haired beauty whose, name was Aerica. There had not been an assembly of beauty like this since the gathering of the goddesses before time. Even in the mundane setting of the kitchen, all four of these young women's beauty transcended their environment.

CHAPTER 17

Alexyia's emerald-green eyes sparked as she smelled the aroma of the freshly prepared food. Her long, luxurious eyelashes accentuated her high cheekbones. She was quiet and spoke softly. She was the passionate and loyal one in the group. She loved to write poetry and songs. Often, she wrote about romance and the beauty of life. She knew she was as gorgeous as the northern lights on a crisp November night in Alaska. She was as mysterious as the mermaids in the sea. All who saw her thought she was breathtaking. Unlike the others though, she didn't flaunt it.

Elainney wore a tight-fitting shirt from some college that she never went to and supplemented it with sweat pants. Her brown eyes were big and soft. She had high cheekbones and a million-dollar starry smile to top off her appearance. Her thick, dark brown, waist-length hair was pulled back in a ponytail, as it rested over one shoulder. She was the friendly and vivacious one in the group. She kept active and exercised regularly. However, she ate what she wanted, when she wanted and stuck to no particular diet.

There was a refreshing air about her. Similar to the feeling you get when you're on a cruise, in the middle of the ocean, watching the sunrise in the morning. Her loyalty was deep and passionate like the ocean. Her temper, however, was exactly like the sea, calm one moment and torrid the next. She was quite different than her friends, but they all got along extremely well and complemented each other effectively.

Raechellee was a vibrant and loving young woman with thick, body-length blond hair. She had a robust, voluptuous figure that exuded confidence and vitality. She was smart and cunning. She was adept at solving problems and always paid attention to details. She loved to eat and could put away food with the best of them. Her temperament was positive and her outlook on life, inspirational to anyone around her. She loved to live and she loved her friends.

She was beautiful, like a walk on the beach in the moonlight. She was as majestic as watching a glacier in a fjord about to calf. The blue and green in the ice, mesmerizing, just like her eyes. Nature was showcased in an event that seemed larger than life.

CHAPTER 17

Raechellee saw herself as larger than life and had the character to back it up.

Aerica took out the mozzarella sticks. Her dark red, buttock-length hair was also in a ponytail. Her purple eyes looked like nothing that planet earth had to offer. When she talked to someone, her gaze rested on them until she finished speaking. Most of the time, the one being spoken to, was unable to look away. The uniqueness of her eyes always got her what she wanted, not that she took advantage of that.

She was the motherly type of the group. She always thought about others and always gave good advice. She loved to cook and kept everyone well fed. She was a 'renaissance woman' that knew everything about anything. Her dimpled chin, round face, and perfect teeth broke out in a smile.

"I still cannot believe we found him!" Aerica said elatedly.

"I can't believe it either. After all this time, he is within our reach. My sources in heaven did confirm that he was never found in any of the tablets," conveyed Alexyia.

"I knew it before any of you. I could tell when I saw him at the store. His aura and life, just jumped out at me," replied Raechellee.

"Who is going to drop the food for Theo? I'm sure he probably will be starved when he wakes up," Aerica asked, looking at the finished food.

"I did put a powerful sleeping potion and healing remedy in his breakfast before you took it to him this morning," said Elainney.

"I think I should, well since I dropped breakfast," said Raechellee.

"Um…you almost killed him too!" remarked Alexyia, "I think it should be my turn now."

"Shooting him was the hardest thing I ever had to do in my entire life. Look, we agreed that it was the only way to make sure that he is who we are looking for. Besides, I signed my name to a note I put with his breakfast. If somebody else shows up, then it might confuse him," said Raechellee.

"How did you get past that Asheley character? She seems like an annoyance to our plans," commented Aerica.

CHAPTER 17

"Well, she did not go for the food that I put for her. I can't believe she went for twelve hours without eating or moving from the hospital room. It was as if the nurses did not mind she was there. I ultimately had to put an electric field around her to disrupt her nervous system. That caused her to fall asleep," said Raechellee.

"I wonder who she is?" asked Elainney.

"I don't know for sure, but we don't want to attract any more attention to ourselves," cautioned Aerica.

"What if Theo heals too quickly? What if the monk does not do what he's supposed to do?" asked Alexyia.

"Don't worry about that. I charmed the doctors. I also made sure the monk was in the same room as he was. I did the paperwork while I sat with Theo for a few minutes." Raechellee said smiling.

"I'm just so excited to see him again. It's been so long and we've all been through a lot," replied Aerica.

"My heart aches for him and my body pains to hold him close," Alexyia said as she hugged herself.

"I know all of us are anxious to explain everything to him, however, we need to do this in steps. Did our father tell the monk what to do?" asked Elainney.

"Yes. I spoke to father about it. He said the monk went three times and got the same answer," replied Raechellee.

"The monk will help Theo get to the Akashic records library. We will meet him there with our father. Then all of us can explain the situation to Theo and show him our powers. Our father might be able to bring up bits and pieces of the past for him to see. We have to do it that way so that if Theo accidentally uses his powers, he won't hurt anyone on Earth and we won't hurt him," said Aerica.

"Why couldn't we show him the truth through telepathic communication?" asked Elainney.

"Father said that since he has not transcended into his true being yet, it would not be a good idea. I know we all would be gentle, but we could potentially destroy him if he is not in an altered state," Raechellee said sadly.

CHAPTER 17

"I can't believe we're this close to Theo. I mean, we have been searching for him since... He changed all of us that day. I would follow him anywhere and do anything for him. I love him more than life itself," exclaimed Alexyia.

"I hope the others are successful in finding what they need to. I want them to be back in time for all of us to meet Theo," said Aerica.

All of the ladies stood around in the main kitchen. They anxiously wanted to explain everything to Theo and hold nothing back. However, they had to sit still for a little while longer so that the monk could show Theo the way.

CHAPTER 18: Brentt Williams Detects Things

At five months pregnant, Catherine was just putting out dinner for the family when the doorbell rang. Katie was in the living room watching television with John, who got up and answered the door. It swung open to reveal a six-foot-tall, middle-aged man that looked like he was straight out of a fireman's calendar, complete with a faux mustache and muscles everywhere.

"Hello, I'm detective Brentt Williams. I would like to talk to Catherine Jansen and the rest of the people that live here," he stated, flashing his badge.

"Come in officer. Katie honey, go upstairs and watch television in your room, okay. Let me get you the remote," said John, as he got the remote to Katie's TV from a high shelf.

"Mommy takes it away so I don't watch TV in the middle of the night when I'm supposed to be sleeping," she said as if Brentt needed an answer.

"It's just Catherine, Katie, and myself officer," replied John as he invited the detective in.

"I am investigating the attempted murder of Theo Steren Champlain and I believe you are his ex-wife, right?" asked Brentt Williams, getting down to business.

"Yes. We got divorced about three months ago. It was really quick and clean," replied Catherine.

The detective wrote in his standard-issue notepad. "What was the nature of your relationship with your ex-husband? Was he a violent man?"

"No, not at all. He was very kind and sweet and was not argumentative," replied Catherine.

"Why did you get divorced from him, was it monetary troubles or infidelity?"

"I cheated on my husband with John."

CHAPTER 18

"How did he find out? Did he get violent?"

"No. He came home early from work and found us together," she said looking at John.

"Did both of you get into a fight?" he turned to John.

"Surprisingly, he did not. He grabbed his things and left," said John.

"What do you think of his new girlfriend?" the detective asked Catherine.

"I think she's fake and might be using him for a quick buck. Let's be honest, she looks way out of his league. I was out of his league, but she is in another galaxy, out of his league."

"It did not seem that way when he got shot. She was a trooper. She was very worried about him. Do you know anyone else that had it in for Theo? Perhaps, any co-workers who disliked him?"

"I've been to his job. He's liked by all."

"The girlfriend said that the would-be killer waited for your ex-husband in his condo. That is a very serious issue."

"As far as I know, he does not have any enemies," said Catherine.

"What are your feelings on this matter Mr. Duboise?" asked the detective.

"Theo was once my friend, but as it is with all friendships, sometimes the love of a great woman comes between friends. To me, he's not worth the time and the bullet that it took to shoot him," said John coldly.

"I see. How tall are you?"

"I am six-foot, six," replied John.

"Do you own any boots with big thick soles?"

"No. I work in an office. My hiking boots aren't even thick-soled," replied John.

"Can I speak to your daughter?"

"I don't think she has anything to do with this," piped up John.

"It's okay John," Catherine soothed. "I'll get her. Katie, come down honey. The policeman would like to speak to you," called Catherine from downstairs.

CHAPTER 18

Katie came gingerly down the stairs, carrying the remote to the TV. She gave it to her mom. Catherine put a hand behind Katie's shoulder and smiled, "The policeman would like to ask you some questions about the booboo that daddy got."

"Okay."

"Do you love your daddy, um I mean...Theo?" asked Brentt.

"Yes."

"Do you know of anyone that does not love Theo?"

"No. Everyone loves him. Mommy, John, even that nice lady Asheley likes him. He buys everyone nice things. When we couldn't find the Ultimate Dolly Good Life Playset anywhere, he surprised me with it in my room," explained the child.

"Do you know if Theo spoke to any strangers?"

"No. I never see him speak to any people I don't know."

"Thank you all for your time. I would keep in touch just in case I have further questions," said the detective as he rose to go.

The door closed behind him as he stood for a moment on the front porch. He was lost in thought as he walked down the steps.

"My *extrasensory perception* is telling me that everyone is being truthful. I can find no one involved in this case, lying. The only one I cannot get a read on is Asheley and I don't know why. She seems very faux and I'm not sensing anything from her. I'll have to investigate further," Brentt said to himself as he drove home.

Brentt went through the front door of his house and saw that Agness was home. He quickly gave her a kiss on the cheek and said, "I need to borrow some of the Binky Animal Babies for a top-secret mission. I won't be long and they won't be in any danger. It's just some intelligence gathering."

"Sure, that sounds fine. Would you be home for dinner?" asked Agness with a soft hug.

"I'm not sure. I'll call if I'm late. How is Jenny doing? Is she getting enough rest and how about the situation with her jerk boyfriend?"

"That's a talk for after dinner. Go and concentrate on your case," she said with a light pat on the shoulder.

Brentt gave a quick smile and went to the animal common room in the basement.

CHAPTER 18

Most of the animals were crowded on the sofa watching a novella that was recorded on the cable box. MacGraw the macaw, was eating popcorn from a bowl and Squiggles the hamster, was downing a few as well. Boobie Woobie the cat, was drinking water from a water fountain.

"Hey guys, what's up?"

"Brentt!" they all exclaimed at the same time.

"Amigo, Brentt. Come have some popcorn and soda with us. You came at a good time. This novella that we are watching is getting good," said Squiggles.

"Really, what's going on?" Brentt asked.

"Right now, Ariella is married to Francisco. Fernando is the evil twin of Francisco, who is with Ariella, pretending to be Francisco. Maria Anna, who is Ariella's cousin, loves Francisco but doesn't know it's Fernando. Fernando is with Ariella for her money but really loves Juanita, the friend of Maria Anna. However, Maria Tia knows about the secret and is blackmailing Fernando about him pretending to be Francisco, who they think has drowned," explained Boberta, the guinea pig.

"That's too confusing for me. Listen guys, pause the show. I have a job for you."

Squiggles pushed the pause button and all of the animals gave Brentt their full attention.

"I need you guys to go on a stakeout. There's this woman that I need to find out more info on, but I cannot do it alone. She seems a little off, but I can't put my finger on it."

"You got it partner!" exclaimed MacGraw. "I'm in! It's going to be a rooting tooting time!"

"One question, amigo, does she eat hamsters? Also, can we get some veggie burritos to go?" asked Squiggles.

"No, I don't believe so. Yes, you will get food to go. I think that MacGraw should be on air support. Iigglloo, since you can blend in and camouflage yourself, you can be ground support, along with Boobie Woobie. Bunnie, you can be on scout duty," suggested Brentt.

"Aye boy, I can do dat just fine. I'm gonna rock back and watch de bacchanal," commented the iguana chameleon hybrid.

CHAPTER 18

"Squiggles and Boberta, I need you both to be on the inside. You need to find out anything suspicious about them, but more importantly, her," instructed Brentt.

"Amigo, have I ever let you down? Well except for that one time a long time ago when we stole, I mean borrowed, your car without you knowing. I'll do it. However, you have to provide me with food," demanded the little spy.

"Sure thing guys, anything you want. Go ahead and suit up," said Brentt, pressing an out of the way molding on the banister that opened up to a secret room.

The animals filed into the room and quickly started to gather their gear. There were animal sized headsets and microphones. Bulletproof vests tailored to fit the pint-sized spies hung low to the ground. Various grappling hooks and ropes blanketed the walls and had little ledges for the critters to access them. Bubble gum grenades and mini Taser guns were also available as well, just in case the occasion came up. Soon the excited Binky Animal Babies were ready for their big adventure.

CHAPTER 19: Detective Detrimentus

The God of Death walked along the balcony of his palace. He enjoyed the cool breeze that accompanied a radiant sunset. He looked out over the horizon at the planet he called home. It was filled with different landscapes and climates. There were desert wastelands, Rocky Mountains, green hills, swampy marshlands, and calm prairies. All were in the shadow of the palace of Death, located on the highest peak in this world. He looked out over the lush green valley far below, being cleaved with winding rivers of clear, refreshing water. A myriad of birds of all sizes, colors, and species, flocked together in the branches of towering trees that hung heavy with succulent fruits.

Animals great and small lumbered and scurried in the thick forests, supplied by the crystal clear waters of the rivers. Abundant fish swam in the rivers, pecking at whatever morsels they could glean. Some even became food themselves for other hungry animals. One would not think that the home of the God of Death would be so lively.

Detrimentus ran a muscled hand on the banisters made of the most colorful marble. They were intermittently topped with ornate bronze busts of tortured souls in their death throes. Some of the busts included Hitler, Niche, Socrates, and Pilate, among the many. The Mediterranean style of his palace had windows of the clearest crystal that allowed the most light possible into every room. The light could be seen from the loftiest pinnacle to the lowest depths of the dungeons.

Thousands of yards long curtains of the purest, strongest silk interwoven with gold and silver, hung from the windows. Rich paintings of flowers and idyllic landscapes of light hung on the ornately decorated golden walls. A slew of Caravaggio's masterpieces gave the walls life and the personality of the artist himself. Lifelike marble, bronze, and metal statues, forged by

Donatello, Michelangelo, and Da Vinci stood at every turn. It was as if they kept guard, adorned with their majestic armors, silks, and linens.

Pillars of embossed silver held up high ceilings. They were punctuated by what the casual observer might call mythological heroes and imagined goddesses in mid-action. The floors were of the purest granite tiles, each with different colorings, giving a rainbow effect as one walked upon the perfectly polished floors.

Not a speck of dust was to be found anywhere, thanks to a host of servants and attendants. His staff comprised of many alien beings from around the universe that were found worthy to be in the service of the God of Death. They scurried around cleaning and polishing his palace. Beings with six arms and two heads diligently cleaned the paintings. A fox-like humanoid race took over the task of cleaning the floor with their furry tail. A giraffe looking race took the helm at cleaning the lofty windows. A race of monkey people was busy polishing the pillars with special care. The race of spider people was busy pulling off the armors from the statues and polishing them. If need be, they would spin new linen and silks for them.

They all worked diligently for the pleasure of Detrimentus. He looked upon them as he walked, reading every one of their minds as he passed. There was some chatter of who was sleeping with whom and where they were going on their days off. Detrimentus treated his servants very good. Just because you were in the presence of the God of Death, didn't mean you had to be treated like you were going to die. They all bowed reverently as Detrimentus passed by them, awed at his powerful presence.

The God of Death teleported from his palace to a walkway that led to a giant, sun sized building. The temple planet itself was a trillion times larger than Earth's sun so the building looked small in comparison. Two giant doors were being cleaned and polished by some gray robots before him. The God of Technology suggested that things would be more efficient if the hired help were a blend of mechanics and flesh. He made the grays as a gift to the God of Death. Technon made tall and short gray robots, all without emotion. They had no feelings and no bias, just a duty to do.

CHAPTER 19

In fact, a few of the robots grew sentient and went off on their own to explore the universe. They attempted to be like the Gods, performing experiments on other lifeforms and used all manner of technology for mischief. The God of Technology made them too well. The novitiate sentient grays found the newly grown humans on earth. There they practiced their experiments and recombination techniques on the more primitive creatures. They attempted to make themselves more human. Technon made the next batch a lot better, more submissive and less rebellious.

As Detrimentus pushed at the double doors at the end of the walkway, it creaked and groaned. He stopped and turned around.

"Fellas, who is responsible for oiling the doors?" boomed Detrimentus, already knowing the answer.

"Me sir," said a tall gray.

"How come it is not oiled?"

"We didn't get the krakens to open the door yet sir. The Goddesses Cosmica and Galaxyia took the creatures along with a few others to planet Elystra."

"Work on it while I'm in here. Try not to be noisy."

The grays nodded and went their way to start on the task that the God of Death gave them.

Detrimentus used his God powers and looked in the past for his krakens. He confirmed what the greys said. Cosmica was always doing those sorts of things to Detrimentus. She thought he was so uptight and stoic all the time and she wanted to loosen him up.

Elystra was a planet that had an ocean so deep that it went to the core. The Goddesses were looking in on a royal family that had a dispute about something very meaningless. The issue divided the planet. The people of Elystra were good and friendly people that served each other with compassion and love. They were also very ardent worshipers of Cosmica and they did their duties to the Goddess well. Cosmica was surprisingly good friends with both of the ruling houses on that planet. They would pray to her when they needed advice on things. She looked after the planet as a mentor looks after their protégé.

CHAPTER 19

However, there was a situation that arose when the princess of the house Bhior got engaged to two princes of the house of Eira. Of course, the Goddess was implored to come and sort out the matter. She had heard the prayers of the planet when the Goddess Galaxyia was visiting her.

"Galaxyia, I see the futures of all the parties involved. Both princes of Eira treat the princess of Bhior well. There is a great golden age that follows after both of them marry her in alternate realities," surmised Cosmica, as she braided her knee-length hair without using her hands.

"Yes, that is the situation that I see. Both marriages will yield positive results. However, the princess does not truly love both. She will in time though but not now. Being the Goddess of love, I know that to love and be loved is very important for these people," replied Galaxyia.

Technon fashioned a viewing room that allowed Detrimentus to see anywhere in the multiverse at any point in time. It was aptly named the Death Dome. This contraption was actually helpful for his minions working there. This made it easier for the servants of the Gods to see what they needed to do and where they needed to go because they were infinitely less powerful than the Gods.

Detrimentus walked into a cacophony of dying shrieks and shrills that filled the air and assaulted his senses. Every single thing in the universe that had to die was viewed from here. He and Caddeussus shared a balance in the cosmos, just as the other Gods did. They looked after everything and exerted their influence on all. There comes a point in time when the line of life and death had to be crossed. With every life born, the God of Life got stronger and with every death, of course, the God of Death got stronger.

Detrimentus looked at the screen and floated up to the massive throne in the middle of the room. He looked down at his servants who were paying attention to all that was going on. All the Gods had Athlogoss Drone protégés to train and carry out their legacy and to keep the masses in check.

Detrimentus gave off the vibe to his fellow Gods that he loved to kill. In fact, he did not care one way or the other. He

CHAPTER 19

had to be unbiased because that was the law of the Gods, not to interfere and not to be biased. Laws that sometimes the other created Athlogoss Drones and protégés failed to adhere to. Zeus was a big lawbreaker, cavorting with experimental human women.

Right now, on the screen, an event was taking center stage. It was the clearest and most vivid aquamarine blue planet imaginable. It was in perfect orbit around its sun. It happened that today, this planet was to be a wasteland. Half of its creatures would die immediately and the other half would have to adapt to a new climate. That is because an asteroid was going to knock the planet closer to its sun. This was not a new concept to Death, but certainly very effective.

Elsewhere, the *Reptilians* and bird people of Avin were in a worldwide conflict thanks to the God of War. "Ahh there they are, that is very productive." Detrimentus felt the soul count rising inside him. He sensed when Life gave up control and threw them to Death.

He looked for Pel 6, a planet completely overrun by rainforests and an expansive river system that took the place of oceans. They were the marvel of their solar system by all who visited there. They were set to suffer an epidemic of deadly mosquitoes. However, the planet was not where it was supposed to be. He saw a curious thing. The planet Pel 6 was leaving its orbit as if it had a mind of its own. Without thinking, the God of Death teleported to the rogue planet to investigate.

Detrimentus saw the planet, Pel 6 moving in the distance. He had teleported himself from his palace billions of light-years away to this particular point in the blackness of space. He assumed a ten-mile tall stature and looked upon the planet with utter curiosity.

He moved closer to the planet that was floating in the cold, airless space. Being a God, none of these affected him. Suddenly, a smell hit him like a bug on a highway against a windscreen. The smell was the most horrible thing that he had ever come across.

CHAPTER 19

How Atomos could make a smell that was so putrid, was beyond the comprehension of Detrimentus. He wished he could go back in time and tell himself not to smell it, but that wouldn't make any difference.

The planet's movement stopped, but the smell did not. Detrimentus couldn't sense anything or anyone pulling the planet. This must be another God since their actions cannot be felt by him. He certainly couldn't sense any other Athlogoss Drones there. He flew around to the other side of the planet without caution because there was nothing for him to fear.

All the inhabitants of the planet looked at peace, oblivious to the impending predicament outside their planet. Even though the planet was out of orbit, it still behaved as if it was just a normal day around its dwarf star.

The God of Death saw who was pulling the planet. It was manipulated by an individual no more than twenty feet tall. Using his God vision which made it possible to look at objects at one end of the cosmos from the other, he saw that it was the God of War. He was clad in his armor.

"Brother Anthraxis, what is this god awful smell that pervades this place and why are you moving this planet?"

"Hhhheeeehhheeee!" said the armor, as the chortle came out full of phlegm and snorts. "I have no business with you Detrimentus."

"Why are you taking my planet? It is due to die and you are hampering the process," Detrimentus said sternly, trying not to inhale the stench coming off Anthraxis.

"Well, I'll just take this off your hands. You have finished with it anyways." He cackled and turned to go.

The God of Death teleported in front of the God of War and barred him from pulling the planet forward. He used his own powers to push the planet back but the opposing power of Anthraxis was incredible.

"Because of you and the whole destroying the galaxy situation, we got confined to our temple planets by Atomos. I did not think that Technon could have taken you but he surprised us all. I am very different than him. My hands are like foreverum. Do not test my patience."

CHAPTER 19

"I welcome the challenge. I was holding back with Technon, but I see that you feel you can take everything," surmised Anthraxis with a chortle.

"Are you seriously going to…" Detrimentus did not finish his sentence because he was put in a headlock from behind by another embodiment of Anthraxis.

The stench was even more putrid than he could have possibly imagined. Detrimentus quickly let off an embodiment to come to his aid, but it also was stopped by another embodiment of Anthraxis. He quickly teleported himself out of the headlock and took stock of the situation. Three Anthraxis embodiments versus two Detrimentus embodiments were squaring off against each other, not a fair fight. Detrimentus multiplied himself a hundredfold, bringing the total to one hundred and two Gods of Death to three Gods of War. Rushing at Anthraxis, he expected him to do the same. Instead, he had one of the embodiments put a shield around the planet and the other two merged together and readied for battle.

"I don't want anything happening to this planet. Now I'm sure I will get your spirit blood all over my armor. I'll just have my servants clean it off!" Anthraxis yelled. "Get over here so I can kick your ass!"

Detrimentus shrunk all of his embodiments to thirty feet tall and tried to dogpile Anthraxis. With superb precision and lightning speed, Anthraxis punched each of them while evading the barrages. Anthraxis teleported himself about a thousand miles away, having grown tired of the futile attempts of Detrimentus trying to bring him down. The God of Death pulled himself together and realized that he was getting in his own way every time he got close to Anthraxis.

"You're running away. I did not think it in you," he coaxed Anthraxis.

"I'll make you choke on your own words!" Anthraxis said as he teleported at Detrimentus with a big right hand.

The massive right hand would have taken Detrimentus' head off if he had not moved it back a few inches. He felt the wind from the punch on his nose, which was impressive in the cold vacuum of space. Detrimentus saw the south left hook coming and used his right hand to block it. However, he got a big head butt from Anthraxis. He'd have to be quicker than that to get a few in. Rallying himself after the head butt, he threw a big backward roundhouse kick with his left foot that missed the head of Anthraxis. He made up for it with a right cross as he came around the bend. This connected and just served to surprise the God of War.

Detrimentus shot a face full of lava from his hands in an effort to encase his fellow God. This slowed Anthraxis down as the lava cooled in cold depths of space. He then launched a barrage of punches at the midsection of War, as he beat the God back towards his doppelganger and the planet.

Anthraxis managed to get a left hand free and blocked a right from coming in. His grip was insane as he held the God of Death's wrist. Shaking the cooled lava free, Anthraxis countered with a knee to the stomach, followed by a nuclear blast from his right palm. This sent Detrimentus spinning out of control. Detrimentus produced an embodiment to help him stop and they both set their sights on Anthraxis.

A comet was passing by and the God of Death grabbed at it using his mind. He sent the other embodiment to attack the God of War. They exchanged blows, neither giving in to the other. Punch after punch landed and each felt the pain and sting of all. Detrimentus slipped past a left hook from War and he managed to get him in a grapple at the waist. The other embodiment of Detrimentus signaled and he sped off at the speed of light straight towards the comet.

Detrimentus let go of Anthraxis as he slammed into the comet that was barreling their way. The impact created a big bang that deafened the ears of both the Gods and their doppelgangers. Bits of rock, metal, ice, and dust spewed everywhere and flew through millions of miles of space. The God of Death, feeling that he knocked out that version of Anthraxis, turned to get his planet back from the other embodiment of the God of War.

"Not so fast," said an angry Anthraxis as he rose unharmed from the explosion that could have wiped out the dinosaurs.

The God of War stuck out his hand and pulled all the pieces of the comet back together. He then proceeded to condense them into a giant hammer. He was a million miles from the God of Death and looked ready to spring. Detrimentus braced himself for the attack and did not see 'the punch of punches' coming. Two embodiments of Anthraxis came out of nowhere. One held the Galaxy Cleaver that slashed down Detrimentus' back and the other, with a right hook a billion times the speed of light. Detrimentus, the God of Death was knocked into a planet that was in the same solar system as the planet he was trying to stop Anthraxis from taking.

His limp body broke through the atmosphere of the planet, instantly setting the whole sky on fire. Lifeforms were running for their lives in terror, as they had gone about their daily routines seconds before. He hit a mountain that happened to be in his way, causing an upheaval of the ground which liquefied upon his impact. Plants and animals were caught in the blast wave that liquefied their insides, shattered their bones, demolished their eardrums and destroyed anything that was left. This was all before the avalanche of liquefied earth buried them.

Down he went, melting stone, iron and other materials that were in his way. Soon he came to the core of the planet. Molten lava turned into vaporous gases from the momentum and friction of the God of Death. He flew past a race of beings that had made their home in the planet's core. He did not see them because he was still unconscious from the blow. Through he went and broke the mantle of the planet which held back the waters of a vast ocean. The seas flooded the inner planetary race and completely wiped them out before anything could be done.

Yet still, the limp body of Detrimentus plowed on. Up he came through the sea on the opposite side of the planet and a lone baby Korsol fish happened to get caught on his chest. His momentum pushed the hapless creature up from the depths of the seas to the sky. Detrimentus broke through the atmosphere once more.

The fish that hitched a ride with him died of suffocation in the coldness of space. Its innards crushed by the force at which they left the orbit of the planet. Behind could be seen the remains of a planet with a big hole in the middle. The lifeblood flowed and spilled out over the landscape. The planet convulsed and shuddered. It broke apart and finally perished. It exploded, sending bits and pieces of itself across the universe. The force of that explosion propelled the limp body of Detrimentus even further out into space, along with the dead Korsol on his chest.

The God of War smiled at the punch. He was working on that move for a while. He had to go back to his master. With a smile, he took the planet and teleported to where he needed to go, leaving a trail of destruction in his wake.

The darkness in that place was overwhelming. It was the kind of darkness that lies deep within one's soul and slowly seeps in and corrupts even the purest of hearts. It was a darkness so complete, that even your mind's eye could not penetrate it. It was deeper than the deepest depths of hell and more encompassing than being alone in the blackness of space. However, this entity and ninety-eight others made their home in that place of darkness. In addition to the impenetrable darkness, there was an impregnable stench that pervaded the whole area. The stench came from the individuals that resided in this unforgiving and hellish nightmare.

Wretch #1 stood looking at a great door, which was far beyond any door that had ever been dreamt about. He wanted to get through this door. The door spanned one light-year high and one light-year across. He and the ninety-eight others stood staring at that door. It had holes for keys in it, but whereas some doors had one or two, maybe even three keyholes, this door had thousands. They required not just any keys, but the ones you had to look for.

He was a being that sometimes had blurred features and a faceless head, but every so often, his looks shifted. He had no definitive body type. It just changed to suit what he needed it for. The other ninety-eight were the same but they had their individuality. They could grow big or get smaller. They could become heavy or light.

The others paced in front of the door that was too big to walk to the end of, but the end had been reached. They all were

CHAPTER 19

waiting for their comrade who had beaten up and possibly killed the God of Death. They all felt the fight and knew what was done. They felt all of the actions that had taken place and knew the actions that would have to be taken, in order to get behind the door.

The God of War appeared before the ninety-nine and with him was his prize, the planet Pel 6. The God of War twisted and turned in agony as he morphed into his true form, Wretch #100. The inhabitants of the planet had no idea where they were or what had transpired. All they knew was that it was another day to go to work, another day to tell your loved ones that you loved them, another day to shop and another day to exist.

The Wretch at the door, Wretch #1, grew to an immense size and took the planet in his hand. He turned it and watched it carefully, looking to see some minuscule detail. He rose to a particular hole in the universal door and waited. The hole was as large as the planet in question and he held the planet there at the cusp of the hole. He was waiting for something before he put the planet into the keyhole. It would bring him and the others one step closer to unlocking that doorway to the other side.

Down on the planet, where all were going about their daily lives, an ant walking along a tree branch stopped to bite off a piece of a leaf. He took a little time with it because he bit off more than he could chew. Eventually, he hoisted it on his back and began walking back to his nest where the others were.

Just then, the planet slid into the keyhole that was in the universal door. That moment was what Wretch #1 was waiting for. The planet groaned and creaked as the door felt the energies of every living thing upon the now doomed Pel 6. The locking mechanism clamped down on the planet and authenticated it as the correct key. In the process, the lifeblood of everything trickled down into the hole and the dying shrieks of the living fell upon deaf ears.

"One down but thousands more to go my brothers!" yelled Wretch #1, as he raised his hand triumphantly.

"We should split the work," said Wretch #2.

CHAPTER 19

"Yes, we should. I vote for the Unmade gathering the Gifts of the Nine, while we ourselves observe the keyholes and get the planets," recommended Wretch #33.

"The correct keys are vital and need to be researched. If it is not right, then the door will destroy the holder of the key. There are thousands of keys and only one hundred of us," reminded Wretch #71.

"Yes. I remember well that our numbers have dwindled since… I will summon the Unmade," said Wretch #1. With a shout he commanded, "Unmade come to your masters and do that which we command!"

Out of the darkness could be heard a deafening roar that was akin to the roar of the Leviathan and the Behemoth. The Unmade were fashioned after the great and terrible beasts that resided on the temple planet of Anthraxis. There was a Lawrellion of them shrieking in the darkness. They were fifteen feet tall, very agile and fast. However, they could grow as tall as fifty feet. Unlike their precursors on the temple planet of Anthraxis, these had unlimited brute strength and superior cognitive abilities, which made them deadlier. As if that was not enough, they could change shape and blend into any surrounding.

They had a captain that was as cunning and deliberate as the Wretches ever were. He served the Wretches with as much fervor as any could be found in the vastness of the universe. He was a seventy-foot tall fallen angel. He had six wings but a few of them were broken off. However, they had been repaired with Hycolium. He had vowed to settle the score with the angels that broke them off.

His right forearm had been severed in battle as well, but that too had been replaced. His six-fingered hand had claws as sharp as anything in the universe. Of course, no metallic hand is complete without the ability to turn into a 'handgun'. His arm turned into a weapon capable of destroying an entire planet in a fiery blast. He lovingly dubbed it 'the planet buster'.

His eyes were blood red. He fed off of the souls of the tormented and loved to dish out sorrow and destruction like it was Halloween candy. The name of this terrible creature that

CHAPTER 19

once knew the light but now was in the deepest depths of darkness is *Abaddon.*

He carried a wicked-looking one-sided blade that looked like an unholy union between an ax and a broadsword. The large curved ax head made up about a third of the blade, while the rest of it was a broadsword. It was thick on one side and it had an edge sharpened above perfection to the thickness of an electron. Studded with serrated teeth and an oversized blade guard, this wickedness was stocked with an even uglier and ungodly secret.

When in the heat of battle, the great sword opened and mini kamikaze Abaddons flew at his opponent, unleashing every elemental attack imaginable. This blade was presented to him when his new masters found him, beaten and broken. He called the blade The Abomination of Cain, a fitting title for one that would spill blood so easily. They patched him up better than he was before. His old blade, 'The Brimstone of Heaven' had been taken from him in the heat of battle during the war in heaven.

"Abaddon," said Wretch #1 with the voice of many monstrous voices, "take the Unmade and gather the Gifts of the Nine. We will stay here and examine the keyholes to ascertain the correct keys for them all."

"Serve us well and our master will give you your heart's desire," Wretch #7 spoke up.

"I have heard empty words from my previous masters. However, you have kept your word every step of the way. You have given me more than I could ever want. I shall gather all that there is to gather," he genuflected and said in a strong and raspy voice.

CHAPTER 20: Theo And Frank Lin Become Friends

Theo and Frank Lin Shao became unlikely friends in the hospital room. They would never have met, if not for a single act that brought them together. The other guy that was in the room with them was not much of a people person. He was asleep most of the time. Theo and Frank Lin talked about their childhoods and experiences in life. The kind of stuff you talk to someone about when you're in a hospital bed and had a near-death experience.

Theo had called work as soon as he was able and explained the situation. Benjamin Doyle was ok with it and told him to take as long as he needed, of course with the proper documentation.

During that time, he had been taken care of by an unseen hand in the form of great food left by his bedside. He could not figure out who was leaving the food, toiletries, and clothes for him. It was as if they knew him but did not want to be seen. The nurses and doctors did not know. Even Asheley did not know because she inexplicably fell into sleep mode and when she awoke, there was a food package right beside her. He'd have to make it his priority as soon as he got out.

He was feeling better, but for some reason, they did not discharge him from the hospital. It had been four weeks now and still no word from the doctors as to when he might be discharged. They said it was for observation, but the bullet wound had healed from the first day.

He was still trying to figure out how he had gotten that flaming sword scar. It had also been three days and no angel had come back to take him away. Maybe that was a very bad dream. It could have been a case of mind over matter, where if you think you have something then your body actually makes it happen. As far as Theo knew, he was not a budding hypochondriac. He did pass the days thinking and calming his mind.

CHAPTER 20

Theo had been practicing the meditation techniques the monk showed him. It was the day before Christmas Eve when the doctor came to discharge him from the hospital. He was happy and sad as well. Frank Lin had to stay in a few days more.

"Hey Theo, do you want to come over for Christmas? My parents and friends are having a welcome home party when I get out of the hospital. It is also a Christmas party," said the monk.

"It sounds good, but I have some things to take care of when I get home. Besides, I really need some time to think and figure out what to do now. I need time to be thankful for what I have and to reflect upon those things," said Theo thoughtfully.

"Okay, but you have to come to the gala at the Grand museum on New Year's Day. They will be unveiling the giant mace that was unearthed in China. I'll text you the details," the monk said as he shook Theo's hand.

"Thanks for everything, buddy. I hope you get better," Theo empathized.

"So do I. There are few girlfriends out there that I want to get under the mistletoe," laughed Frank Lin.

Asheley drove Theo to his condo about noon. He walked up the stairs and felt like a stranger going to the door of his own place. As he walked in, vague memories started flooding his head. 'This is where I could have really died', he thought to himself.

"Theo! I'm so glad to see you home. So this is what some people feel when their loved one is away and then they come back. Is there anything I can get for you?" Asheley asked excitedly not waiting for an answer. "You must be hungry and tired and just want to relax," she surmised.

"I'm okay. Just a little sore and confused, but I need a shower first," soothed Theo, as he headed for the bathroom.

The shower was very refreshing. Asheley kept him company. After the shower, he went into the kitchen to see if he could get something to eat. All the food in the fridge was old and moldy, so he decided to order some pizza.

While waiting for the two large vegetables with beef specials to arrive, he called work and updated them on his situation. His manager said to come in the day after New Year's. This was fine for Theo because it would give him time to get back in the habit of things. The pizza arrived and he tipped the pizza boy a generous twenty dollars. He looked surprised and trotted off. Theo hungrily dived into cheesy decadence and washed it down with the accompanying soda.

"I'm sorry but I neglected to ask you about your feelings, Asheley," said Theo.

"I was sad when you were in the hospital. I felt mad that someone tried to take you away from me. I felt what you would call jealousy when Catherine was holding your hand. I felt that she gave up the right to do so when she discarded you. I could not comprehend your feelings when you learned that Katie was not yours. I felt powerless to do anything when you started crying. I felt the urge to comfort you when you needed me.

I have never experienced anything like this before and it scares me. I feel like I cannot exist without you and that I would not exist without you. I have searched the databases of the entire world and I have come up with the conclusion that I love you. I love you and would never want anything to happen to you. She hurt you but I never will."

Theo sat awestruck for a minute and took in what the Artificially Intelligent Robotic Entity just said. "Thank you for expressing your feelings. I love you as well. Even though I cannot remember creating you, I am glad I did because you saved my life in many ways. Hey, I am taking you Christmas shopping and I'm going to get you some gifts!"

"Christmas is a holiday that signifies the birth of a person designated as the savior of mankind. That gave rise to Christianity or followers of Christ. Over the centuries there have been many points of contention about his teachings, which caused many splits and wars," said Asheley.

"Differing views of whom and what God is, are some of the reasons that people do not get along," reflected Theo.

"But I am not a believer in Christmas. In fact, I haven't really thought about a belief in anything," said Asheley.

"People have always had a need to worship anything that is greater than them. It is a yearning to worship the beings that created us as humans. It is a way to make sense and find purpose in our lives. A person's belief governs the way that they live and interact with people. Sometimes people are not tolerant of other religious beliefs, and that causes problems," explained Theo.

"How come different religions do not get along? They are practiced by people. Even different animals can get along and be friends such as a dog and a deer or a tiger and a grizzly bear," said Asheley, "I know everything that happened in history but, why?"

"It all came down to people straying from the truth. In any religious break or split, it is all about getting to the truth. In my opinion, everything is so convoluted now that I don't know if any one religion has all of the truth. Everyone believes that they have the truth and everyone else is wrong. However, during a natural disaster, all of the discord disappears and that's when humanity pulls together. It is a shame that it takes a catastrophe to bring out the best in us," surmised Theo.

"I, as an Artificially Intelligent Robotic Entity cannot disprove or prove the existence of a higher power other than yourself, Theo, because you made me. If anything, I believe in you. Should I worship you? Does that count?" asked Asheley innocently.

"Thanks for the confidence. Not quite what I was going for. Beliefs guide us through the struggles of life and I think that is why it is so ingrained in society.

Besides, it doesn't matter if you are a believer or not, most people are happy to receive gifts on Christmas. I am here to celebrate your first Christmas thanks to you. I am taking you shopping and we are going to celebrate Christmas together," said Theo jovially.

"You would do that for me?" asked Asheley.

"Christmas is a time for giving and generosity. It is a time for peace and love. Of course, I would!" explained Theo.

"What do you believe Theo?" asked Asheley curiously.

"I don't know what to believe anymore," sighed Theo.

"Well, believe that I love you and will always be with you," said Asheley.

Theo opened his arms for a big hug.

CHAPTER 20

Asheley looked straight out of a clothing catalog when she got out of the car in the department store parking lot. The lanes were busy with shoppers buying the last things for their holiday festivities. Theo grabbed a cart and made sure Asheley was okay with her instructions, stay close and don't wander off. The sights, sounds, and smells were exhilarating. Who knew that an ordinary trip to the grocery store would completely excite and bewilder this robotic entity, disguised as a human.

She processed and stored all the data that she collected from everyone that walked into the store. From what they bought, to what they wore, to the smells that surrounded them. All committed to memory without people knowing. A lady with two kids accidentally bumped into Asheley.

"Pardon me," the nondescript lady said as she moved away with her children. Asheley quickly retorted, "You are pardoned." The woman looked at her very oddly and carried on.

They started off by picking up some Christmas decorations and holiday goodies. While he and Asheley were in a very packed aisle, Theo spied Catherine and his little Katie moving through it farther down. Catherine looked just as beautiful as she always did and Katie looked just as adorable as she always did. He had mixed feelings for both of them, but he could not just turn it off. He looked down and the inevitable happened. Katie ran up and hugged him.

"Hi, Daddy! Umm I mean… I'm sorry I called you daddy," she said as she stepped back.

Theo knelt down and soothed her, "It's okay. People make mistakes. How are you? Did you have a good Thanksgiving?"

"I did. I ate a lot of turkey. I had a whole drummer sticks. Oh, and I had three kinds of ice cream!" Katie bragged.

Theo looked up at Catherine, who came right behind Katie. "Looks like mommy is feeding you very well! You look bigger than I last saw you. Did you make sure that you wrote your letter to Santa? Did you tell him what you want for Christmas?" asked Theo.

"I did. I told mommy too. I asked Santa to give me my mommy and daddy back," she smiled.

CHAPTER 20

"Theo? Oh gosh! Wow, you got out of the hospital!" Catherine smiled as Theo got off his knees.

"Hi, Catherine you look great. How are things?" he said as he faced his ex-wife. They gave each other a quick hug.

"Everything is okay. You know considering…" she trailed off.

"Hi, Katie!" chimed in Asheley, smiling broadly as she hugged the little girl.

Katie heartily hugged her back and beamed, "Hello, are you taking good care of my daddy?"

"She is taking good care of me," smiled Theo. Asheley nodded vigorously.

"Hello. Are you preparing for the Christmas feast?" Asheley said as she shook Catherine's hand.

"Yes. We are doing some last-minute shopping. You know how it is. You guys look like you're doing the same," chuckled Catherine.

"Yes, we are. Catherine, I must say it feels good to see you and Katie. After what happened, I thought I would feel more resentment towards you. However, the relaxation and meditation methods that my monk friend has been showing me, really is paying off," Theo exclaimed.

"I am glad to hear it. You do seem different. I am glad that you are keeping well," Catherine lied.

"What are your plans for Christmas and New Year's?" asked Theo.

"We'll be visiting John's mom and then my parents will be over on Boxing Day. For New Year's we are going to see the parade. Katie will be going to her grandparents because she said she doesn't want to be around lots of people," Catherine said smoothing the little girl's hair.

"Hey, I'm actually going to a gala at the Grand museum. They'll be unveiling some ancient stuff," explained Theo.

"How did you manage that?" asked Catherine, her interest piqued.

"The monk that I mentioned, he was sharing the same hospital room as me. He invited me," remarked Theo.

"We have to go. Our ride should be here in a few minutes," she said deliberately not to mention John's name.

CHAPTER 20

"Catherine, please don't be a stranger. If you need anything, let me know," Theo said with a hug and a wave.

They left and a still heartbroken Theo looked after them. Asheley observed him as he looked at them leave. She felt a little jealous of Catherine, but this time it was a little more pronounced than what she felt in the hospital. She did not know how to deal with the sudden rise in emotions.

She grabbed Theo's arm and happily said, "Let's go enjoy ourselves with some more shopping!"

"Here take this, one thousand, three hundred dollars. That way you can buy anything you want. Oh and If you want to buy me a gift that is good too but you don't have to," smiled Theo handing her the money. She looked at it and counted it, feeling the bills between her fingers. All her sensors were taking in the information that was on the money. Every line, every number, and every fingerprint that could be found upon it, Asheley knew it.

"I am an AIRE. I don't really need anything," stated Asheley as a matter of fact.

"You are wearing clothes aren't you? Do you need a new top or skirt? What about some new jeans?"

"You are right. People do shop for clothes and new outfits for the holidays. But what do you need? My multi-quantum processors are already calculating many things to get you. However I have to set the parameters such as the amount of money given and the cost of any new articles of clothing that I will buy," she calculated.

"Don't think too much about it. Just have fun. I will meet you back here in about an hour, okay?" he said.

"Sure. Locking in rendezvous coordinates now."

Theo headed towards the jewelry department, his mind on both Asheley and Catherine. Asheley looked all around her. She was storing all the information coming at her and determining the best course of action. She looked up and saw a sign that said 'Men's Department.' That's a good place to start as any.

She walked up to one of the sales associates and said, "Hi, I am looking for a Christmas present for a male about six-feet tall and weighs one hundred and eighty pounds. He has dark hair and a medium build. He got divorced about four months ago and he lives in a two-bedroom condominium. His place of employment is a department store similar to your own and he has a collection of comics and video games. He enjoys hiking and traveling. He was recently shot and is recovering from that wound. His driver's license number is."

"Hi, my name is Michelle. I believe that I can help you today. Is this person your boyfriend or husband?" the sales clerk asked quizzically.

"I love him very much. We are not married or engaged, so he is not my husband or fiancé. We have shared many moments of physical intimacy, so according to the social convention he is my boyfriend."

"Okay. We have a great men's cologne collection here. In addition, you get a free bag with the purchase. There is a great shirt and tie combo deal where you get two shirts and four ties with two handkerchiefs for a price. Here are a few samples for you," smiled the clerk wishing her shift was over now, but unfortunately she had seven more hours to go.

"I would like to buy something for myself as well. I am into everything. The total amount of money that I have is one thousand, three hundred dollars. Therefore the cost of the gift for Theo and the cost of the items for me must be equal to or less than that. I prefer closer to the total amount. Do you have any suggestions?"

"What are you looking for?"

"This is my first Christmas with Theo. I would like to obtain something that would commemorate that occasion."

"You love your boyfriend very much. Have you been together long?"

"About five months. He is my world."

"I think I might have just the thing for you. This is the special edition Christmas perfume set which comes with a free lotion of your choice from this section. This is going to be a great gift that is sure to please. I think this scent is going to be great for you."

"I will take it. May I see some more bottles of perfume?"

"Sure," Michelle said.

CHAPTER 20

Asheley held up the bottles and looked into them. Her eyes used macro lenses that saw down to the molecular level. She memorized the composition of each bottle and used her beautiful processing powers to determine which one was the ideal choice for her. She rated them on projected smell and the amount of time they lasted until dissipation. Eventually, she chose one and was a hundred percent happy with her choice.

"Thank you. You are very helpful. I will inform the manager of your great work performance," said Asheley happily.

"The cologne set for him has four full-size bottles of different fragrances. It does come with a free bag. You wanted the shirt and tie combo deal as well. I'll include some of his and her samples of other fragrances you might want to buy. I'll add in your perfume and lotion. The total is twelve hundred, forty dollars but let me see if I can do something about the forty dollars," she said as she scanned a card that reduced the price down to twelve hundred dollars.

Asheley handed over the money and the sales clerk put the items in a complimentary Christmas gift bag.

"Please fill out the online survey questionnaire so that way we can determine how our customer service was. You have a great holiday!"

"Thank you very much, Michelle. I hope you and your family have a great Christmas!" said Asheley as she looked at the receipt. Michelle did not know that Asheley had completed the online survey as she headed out the door to meet up with Theo.

When they got into the car, Theo sighed and leaned on the steering wheel. Asheley put a hand on his shoulder.

"Do you still love Catherine?" she asked very hesitantly.

"I do but that does not mean that I do not love you as well. Feelings cannot be turned off that easily," he said nodding his head. Theo's thoughts were racing and replayed the meeting with Catherine. He still loved her, despite the heartbreak.

CHAPTER 21: Cosmica And Galaxyia

C osmica and Galaxyia were coming back from their trip on Elystra, to return the krakens and the aliens they borrowed. They came to the Death Dome, where things were in full swing. They had been there a few times before but did not like the look and the feel of the place. They put the two great creatures back at their posts, overlooking the giant double doors, and walked inside. They did not see Detrimentus but noticed an outlandish scene on the massive monitors.

All of the alien workers were in shock at the events that unfolded before them. Detrimentus was getting beaten up by Anthraxis. They had just seen the God of War deliver a wicked punch to the face of the God of Death which knocked him into a planet. Anthraxis had disappeared, leaving his fellow God to his doom. The body of Detrimentus was plummeting out of control, into the far reaches of space.

Both Goddesses teleported across the infinite distance of the cosmos with ease and looked for their fellow God. They could see his blood splattered across the vast distances of space. It was a mix of energy and genetic materials that comprised the blood of the Gods. Cosmica quickly put her hand in the blood and called all of it back to her. Galaxyia scanned the horizon and found Detrimentus floating ten light-years from where they had originally landed. Both Goddesses hurried to him, but before leaving, they left some incarnations of themselves to collect the blood of the fallen God of Death.

The once chiseled and muscular body of Detrimentus, now floated broken and beaten, in the cold blackness of space. His enigmatic blood was gushing from a wound that almost sliced him in half. This reminded them of the fight between Technon and Anthraxis. They quickly gathered up the body of the God of Death and tried to reintroduce the blood back into him. They had to get him help, fast. The only problem was that no one knew what to do.

"He lost a lot of blood. I need a way to close the wounds up. Why would Anthraxis do this? Especially for a planet," commented Cosmica.

"Let me try to bind the wounds. I think that if we close them, Detrimentus will heal himself," suggested Galaxyia, doing exactly that.

Both women looked at their efforts and realized that this was making no difference. They had to get Atomos involved. However, that was going to be a problem since he had confined them to their temple planets. He would be wondering what they were doing there, in the first place, and what Detrimentus was doing there as well. Nonetheless, Atomos would have to take action against the God of War, which was way overdue.

Galaxyia and Cosmica took Detrimentus to the temple planet of Atomos. He was walking in the forest of his temple planet, enjoying the sights and sounds of an infinite amount of flowers and birds. He had stopped to admire a miniature rose bush. Its petals were of the clearest blue crystal and its scent inflamed the passion and desires of any that caught a whiff of it. The water and juices from the leaves of the bush cured any ailment whatsoever.

Atomos heard the sonic boom behind him. The two Goddesses put the limp Detrimentus on the ground and genuflected before Atomos.

"UKSCOGSM Atomos, we need your help. You have to know what happened," said Cosmica with tears in her eyes.

CHAPTER 22: The Library

The corridor was long, silent and surprisingly well lit. It was a strange place that even though unfamiliar, you wanted to go on and find the answers. He stepped towards massive, wooden double doors, which must have been five times his six-foot height. They were carved with reliefs of beings and symbols that he did not recognize. Perhaps, they were telling a story, giving a warning, or even a welcome to somewhere.

He passed his hands across the doors. The wood was unlike anything he'd ever seen. He worked in a department store that had hardware supplies and furniture, so he was pretty familiar with wood types. The doors were heavy but felt light on their hinges, as he tried them. The paint job and craftsmanship looked like they gave flesh to the figures embossed on them. There were no doorknobs or latches. In fact, any on the doors would have desecrated the artistry of the entryway to what lay ahead.

Suddenly, the figures on the door started to move in a slow, dramatic sequence. One figure of an old man stretched forth his arm and energy burst forth from his fingers. Another figure, this time of a woman, held upon her shoulders a glowing ball that seemed to grow with her. A third figure, one of an extremely chiseled man, had in his hand a giant ruby that collected something from the universe. Another figure of a giant man, tinkered with creatures that came to life right in the palm of his hand.

The next figure was of a beautiful woman, who walked among the stars. Right next to her was another woman, equally as radiant, who stood next to a black hole as it sucked away the stars. The next figure was of a dignified looking man dressed in warlike armor, who wielded a wicked looking weapon, cleaving the stars. Right next to that figure, was another man with flowers that flowed from his chest and spread into the other panels.

CHAPTER 22

Finally, the last panel showed another beautiful woman with a giant book clasped in her hands. The book opened and the pages fluttered.

He stood dumbfounded at what just occurred. The figures on the door had just acted out scenes and he had no idea what it all meant. These doors led to something amazing. Something that would change his life forever and he had no idea what to do. He was too afraid to go on, but too lost to go back, so he just closed his eyes and pushed.

"What's behind here?" he muttered to himself, as he leaned upon the massive doors. He expected a deafening creak when they started to open. However, the massive doors slowly swung open without any sound, as if answering his queries.

Beyond the doors, were illuminated rows of shelves, which contained books. He walked into the room which had no walls that he could see. The mysterious doors he had just come through, shut behind him.

He noticed that the floor was made up of unique tiles that reflected light as he walked. He knelt down to inspect them further and found that each tile was a complete diamond. He looked up to see where the light was coming from and realized that he could not see the ceiling.

The shelves of books rose into the sky and far beyond his vision, but the light continued to shine down upon him. He examined the nearest 'book' and found no identifying mark, number or anything that distinguished it from all the others. They couldn't be books. All of them were the same size, about a meter tall and half as thick. The color of the binding was a deep reddish-brown, like aged leather but felt nothing like it. He grabbed for one of the books expecting it to be heavy and cumbersome but it was as light as a comic book. He took a deep breath and started to read. The words were in a language that seemed to be foreign.

As he studied them intently, it seemed like a mist dissipated from his mind. This allowed him to understand fragments of this unknown language. The title page read 'Black Holes, the Definitive Guide: Rogue and Principal, Their Makeup, Purpose, and Destruction.' He thumbed through the book, still in amazement that the cryptic language was unraveling itself in his mind.

'It is made up of dark matter. This is the same that encompasses the universe and creates the foundation for it. Dark matter is similar to other matter in that it has an antimatter equivalent. However, the anti-dark matter cannot be pulled in by a black hole, even though it is well past the event horizon.'

He stopped reading. The subject was way too heavy at this point in time. He put the book back and decided to follow the shelves to the end, which he could not see. He started walking. The thud of his hiking boots upon the diamond tiles should have echoed through the rows of books. However, the only audible noises were his heartbeat and his breathing and even those seemed muffled by the acoustics of the place. He walked for hours but he was not fatigued, thirsty or famished, even though he should have been.

He saw a brightly lit sitting area up ahead. Beings moved about, apparently engaged in intellectual congress. He pressed forward almost hugging the shelves, trying to blend into them. He had been walking for hours and hadn't seen or heard another soul. Now he heard quiet talking as he stepped on black diamond tiles.

He stopped and listened to the quiet voices that spoke the language that he had just read. He was sure of it. He stepped back on to the clear diamond tiles and the voices disappeared. Looking at the tiles, it probably inhibited sounds in some way he surmised, but that was the least of his worries. As he moved closer, his hope was that the people there would be too engrossed in their conversation to pay him any attention.

He saw beings that were not fully human as he peeked from behind the shelves. They sat in comfortable lounge chairs talking in more alien languages. They didn't look wild or unruly, they looked academic and erudite. All of the aliens seemed at home in the library, no matter their appearance.

He didn't notice the alien woman coming around the shelf, to his right, until he saw her move in his peripheral vision. He turned casually as if he belonged, but knew that might have been the farthest thing from the truth as one could get.

CHAPTER 22

The alien woman was as softly colored as a pearl in the sunlight, fresh from the embrace of the ocean itself. Standing about ten-feet tall, she held a thick book to her chest. He looked into her shimmering eyes that gleamed like the insides of polished abalone shells. In the sweetest, most melodious voice, she spoke in the language that he did not understand. He stepped back, amazed at her beauty. She moved to where he had been standing and floated up about six-feet. She floated back down as light as a feather and looked down in his direction. She spoke in her melodious voice again, gave a smile, and walked away. He knew he understood what she said, but he could not quite put a finger on it.

"Don't be afraid, come and join us," said a luxuriant voice that both calmed him and terrified him at the same time. "Come and discover what you are looking for. Maybe, perhaps, you don't know what you need to find?"

It was hard to resist the voice calling him. He needed to see who or what this melodious voice was coming from. He was leaning against a shelf to steady himself as his heart raced with his brain in his chest. He thought about what could be done. With a big breath, Theo stepped forward into the lounge area of the fantastic library. As he did so, all eyes of the brainy aliens looked at him.

"Don't be shy." said the voice that was so sweet and delicious to his ears.

He cautiously walked forward knowing that they all knew that he was there but hoping that they weren't interested in him. In the midst of this erudite group of beings, there was a giant, magnificently plush lounge chair, upholstered with the brightest blue and richest purple imaginable. The chair back was turned to him but he could see a right elbow and some crossed legs, clad in a purple dress of otherworldly fabric. He smelled perfume, unlike anything he'd ever smelled before, intoxicatingly refreshing and pure.

Theo saw the lounge chair had four legs but as he got closer, the legs merged into one ball. This allowed the occupant of the chair to swivel and face him. He took a minute to process what happened. "What the heck is going on? Aliens, books, diamond tiles and weird chairs?" he muttered to himself.

The occupant of the chair would reside in his mind long after he left the library. She was that gorgeous. Not like a second look, gorgeous. Not like staring at her while she moved in slow motion, gorgeous. Not even like an Indian film break out in song and dance, gorgeous. She was way beyond the epitome of every man's imagination, gorgeous.

"I don't know you," said the woman, who must have been about twenty-feet tall sitting down.

She had on the most-purple dress, decked with all sorts of fine jewelry, which paled in comparison to her high cheeks and deep-set purple eyes. The dress hugged her more than ample curves that surprisingly showed nothing and left all to the imagination. Her long, thick river of deep-red hair rested over one shoulder and piled to the side of her lap like a fluffy sleeping puppy.

"Of course you don't, we've never met before," Theo squeaked.

"Hmm...Yes, that is right. We've never met, so you shouldn't know me. I don't know you and that is disconcerting. I know everything and yet I don't know you. Where do you come from? How are you here?" she asked in a delicious voice that sounded like strawberry syrup being drizzled over a vanilla sundae and topped with sprinkles.

"I'm from Earth. I was practicing some meditation techniques that a monk taught me. I stopped to watch television and now I am here Miss... Ma'am," he said timidly.

"Why are you here? Everyone who comes here comes to MY Library because they want to find something. Why do I not know you?" asked the woman heatedly.

"I don't know why I'm here. I know you are supposed to come with a purpose, but I got in."

"Are you telling me that you accidentally came here? I don't believe that's possible," she said.

"The last thing I remember is falling asleep during some doctor show that had the doctors falling in love with each other."

"None come here by accident. None come here by deception. All come because they want to. All come with their questions.

None leave without an answer. This is the way of the Library. *This is the way of my will.*"

"This Akashic Records Library has all the answers. I'm glad that I might get to find out a few things. The first is, why I got kicked out of heaven. It's not like I was very bad or anything," he said shaking his head in disbelief.

"You come here to beguile me with questions and I have no answers to them. First, you will answer me, mine: *How do I not know you, how is it possible?*" she said turning the sweet sundae voice of hers into full-on lemon juice.

The crowd of library-goers muttered between themselves at the sudden terseness in their Mistress' voice. In the back of them, a bearded older man and an older woman were pushing a cart full of books. The cart floated off the ground and it looked like they were putting books back on the shelves. They had stopped what they were doing to witness the entrance of this unwelcomed guest that had unintentionally upset their mistress. The lady put a hand to her mouth and looked in awe at the hapless Theo. The man put a hand on her shoulder and her demeanor changed to that of a nail on the wall, expressionless.

"Madame, I wish I knew why you don't know me. Couldn't the Library tell me that? After all, that's maybe why I'm here. They did not know me in heaven. Perhaps, I don't know what questions need asking. Most of my life, I always knew the answer to everything that anyone asked me, from A to Z. The biggest question of all was *what to do with my life* and I don't have an answer for that."

"That makes both of us that do not have answers now. I have never felt how it is to not know anything before, until this moment. I know nothing of you. This is a phrase I have never uttered before: what is your name?"

Just then, a buzzer sounded. Not an emergency buzzer or a fire alarm, but a time to wake up and enjoy the last day of the year, buzzer. His alarm was ringing. It was New Year's Eve.

CHAPTER 23: The Immortal Count

The one hundred thousand acre estate was larger than some countries on the planet. Situated in the Ortega Mountains of California, the owner had allowed a highway to be built through his lands. Of course, making sure that no motorists would wander upon his property, he insisted that most of the road be built with high rock walls on both sides. There were occasional scenic views to pacify anyone with wanderlust.

The estate was imposing to anyone not acquainted with the splendor and magnificence that radiated through it. Every meticulously planted topiary arrangement, every building and even the guest cottages situated upon this vast estate were tailored to the imagination of the owner.

The main mansion was so grandiloquent that there were golf carts to drive the guests, staff, and occupants to their desired location within the house itself. Its form and beauty surpassed the idyllic castles of Germany, the splendid chateaus of France and the magnificent palaces of Russia. Only the best and beyond perfect craftsmanship were allowed to be displayed on the walls, ceilings, floors and every other iota of the mansion. There were thousands of rooms that had a theme from every corner of the world. The attention to detail was so complete and encompassing, that any casual observer waking up in one of the rooms felt themselves in a particular country. Even the smells were replicated with precision.

A six-foot-tall man, that was a few pounds heavier than lean, walked through one of the great halls of the mansion. He was dressed in a purple suit, with a black shirt, accentuated with a white bow tie. He had a purple greatcoat that doubled as a cape if left open. It fluttered majestically behind him as he briskly walked through the perfectly embossed halls of the estate. He was not the owner, but he was there so often that his mail should have been sent there.

His gold, alligator skin shoes, complete with gel insoles, were impeccably shined and did not make a sound on the solid marble floors. He had ten ridiculously large rings on his hands. Each ring consisted of different stones and patterns. Thick gold, silver and platinum chains hung around his neck, which held numerous medallions and talismans. Some were so mysterious that no goldsmith or jeweler in the world had ever seen them.

On his right hand, he held a rugged timepiece that used to be a pocket watch, but he had it converted to a wristwatch. It looked out of place on him because the thing was so old and battered that it contrasted with every other shiny thing upon him. Nonetheless, he cherished it above everything else in his possession, including his friends. It was priceless to him and only he alone knew the value of the item that was always on his right hand.

He could have taken one of the ATVs or golf carts provided by his employer but he preferred the walk. It kept him in shape and he thought about everything as he continued through the vast halls of the mansion. He was soon at the door of his destination.

Two giant Sasquatches blocked the door that he needed to go through. They were fifteen feet of hair and teeth, with the vocabulary and intelligence of a thirteen-year-old. However, they had the strength of twenty of the world's strongest people. They were clad in dull, medieval iron armor specially outfitted for their unique physique. Each carried a spear that was as tall as they were and both had their visors up, looking down at the man trying to enter.

"Let me pass. The Master is expecting me. There will be thirteen others coming soon. Allow them passage as well. They have been summoned to meet with The Master."

The giant Sasquatch nodded in understanding and pushed an intercom button high up on the wall. He spoke in an ancient Native American language that the man with the gold shoes never had the time to learn. He made it a point to start tonight.

CHAPTER 23

The two giant guards unbarred the way through the great double doors.

Tris Megistus Tris Magnificus Nebuchadnezzar pushed open two great doors that were intricately carved and at least twenty feet high. The handles were of solid gold with a ruby in the center of the knob. The doors were made up of purple-heart wood that was embossed with gold, silver, and platinum. They were intricately carved by master craftsmen, long since dead and buried, with only their work on this door as a reminder that they ever existed. The "Thrice Magician" walked into a room that was equally and perhaps even more extravagant than the hallway and the door it took to get there. He looked down at his gold shoes and could see his reflection in the highly polished floor tiles.

In fact, the foyer to the room held the infamous amber panels of the *Amber Room*. The panels were as elusive as the air itself, with scores of treasure hunters looking for the priceless artifact. It was plundered from Catherine's castle in Russia during World War II by Nazi soldiers and was never seen again. Little did everyone know that it was in the possession of the owner of this "Palace of Palaces and Castle of Castles," as described by the owner of the property.

In the room, which contained things that were not for sale, were priceless books, ancient artifacts, weapons of antiquity, and archaeological discoveries that would remain a mystery to the outside world. However, to those privileged enough to see it, it was an everyday routine to keep this mysterious and intriguing place in hiding.

Next, he came into the office and chamber of Jacques Von Blutdruckt Gemacht, better known as *The Immortal Count*. Along the walls of his office and library ran shelves of books. They were intermittently interrupted by a skeleton of some unknown creature that scientists say doesn't exist. From the ceiling, hung the remains of a Loch Ness monster that The Count had confronted a century back when it crossed the road and dented his favorite car.

Off to the side, was a bedchamber that had a ridiculously large bed. It could hold about ten people. The bed was an intricately carved four-poster, whose thick columns rose ten feet high and were three feet in diameter. It was a carved relief that pictured nude angels standing over the occupants of the bed. The top was crowned with a stained-glass globe that did not resemble the topography of today's planet. It emitted a blue light when plugged in and created a very tranquil ambiance.

The head and footboard were padded with thousands of thread count silks, punctuated with pearl studs. The pillows were of the softest materials and covered with gold-threaded pillowcases, embossed with ancient writings and symbols. The bedsheets and the comforter were made from the same fabric and equally as ornate. The thickness of the comforter was unlike any that would be found on the market today. It could only be washed in a massive machine, which also might be custom-built.

There were eight occupants in the room. One was a seven-foot-tall female albino Sasquatch whose name was Dandelion. Another Sasquatch by the name of Sunflower was a golden blond seven-footer as well. The other occupants of the room were half a dozen seven-foot-tall robot women that held the brains of six former WW2 officers. Dandelion and Sunflower were exceptionally smart and showed amazing cognitive abilities. Their vocabulary was extensive and they were fast learners. They were also genetically modified, less than human but more than Sasquatch.

The six robot women were Nazi officers that made the mistake of trying to arrest The Immortal Count. That cost them their lives to some degree. The Count was in a good mood that day so he did not kill the officers, but instead, he transferred their brains to female robots of various shapes, sizes and ethnicities. They had been The Immortal Count's maids and now were watching the morning news while they tidied up. Meanwhile, the Count conducted his business in the adjoining office.

The Immortal Count quietly sat behind a magnificent desk made with a solid granite top, complete with limestone legs. The drawers of the desk were made of long-extinct Gopher wood. There was no need for secret compartments because the whole place was a secret. The front of his great desk measured thirty-three feet, three inches long and ten feet wide.

CHAPTER 23

On his desk, was a paperweight crafted out of a chunk of onyx. It was a hefty fifty pounds, which kept archaic scrolls and tomes from fluttering away. *The Devil's Bible* stood in one corner of the desk opened to God knows where, with notes scribbled on papers about God knows what. The Devil's Bible was a behemoth book, measuring a whopping three feet tall and just as thick. Several laptops dotted the gigantic desk, all opened to different websites depicting a myriad of things.

There was a pencil holder that held both mechanical and regular pencils. There were pencils that held .5 lead, .7 lead, .33 lead and the Count's customized favorite, .666 lead. There were pens present of different colors and each had its own niche on the expansive desk. The latest issues of various magazines were neatly stacked on a corner of his desk. Each was arranged alphabetically and lovingly put back in their wrappings. There were various sticky notes attached to a few of them with scribbles of some ancient languages.

Behind the desk sat a large chair. Actually, it was more of a throne. It was fashioned from a block that would have been used to create the capstone of the great pyramid. However, it was retrenched for another purpose. The throne was the fabled *Throne of Thoth*. Legend or fact, depending upon your point of view, said that it gave the person sitting on it, the power to manifest anything that they thought about. He had outfitted it with *The Black Box of Levitation* which allowed the sandstone throne to glide gracefully across the ultra-thick carpet.

The Immortal Count was not facing Tris Megistus but the rhythmic breathing indicated that the throne was occupied. Behind the massive desk was a wall of television screens that showed various places and things that the count was intently viewing. He was watching their outcome or in some cases, gathering the information that the media provided. The feed from someone's closed-circuit television, a news report, the front door of someone's house, a cartoon, and home movies of somebody else's family, were all viewed intently by The Count.

In one screen labeled twelve, an obviously hacked camera showed the footage of a man engaged in a heated make-out session with someone other than his wife. Tris Megistus knew that this information would be used at a future time when it was convenient for The Immortal Count.

"Welcome my magician," The Immortal Count said in a deep cadaverous voice that gave chills and commanded obedience at the same time. He did not turn around but addressed Tris Megistus as he was.

"Master, the task that you have assigned me is complete. The *Gang Crew Club Syndicate* is soon to arrive with the item that you requested them to steal," answered Tris Megistus reverently.

"Good. Though, I am still disappointed in you for losing the *Emerald Tablets* to detective Brentt Williams. However, if I dispose of everyone that disappoints me then there shall be no one left upon this Earth."

Momentarily allowing that statement to sink in, Tris Megistus replied, "Of course we are all grateful for your benevolence, Master."

"Speaking of the detective, you are keeping tabs on him are you not?" asked The Immortal Count somewhat amused.

"Yes. All his movements are tracked with precision and recorded," replied Tris Megistus. "Forgive the supposition, but why do you not rid yourself of the nuisance that is detective Brentt Williams? You are much more powerful than he," queried Tris Megistus with a cup of fear and a teaspoon of hesitation.

"Good question my magician. The detective is far stronger than you know. If I were to get him on my side as a subjugated ally to perform my will, then nothing would stand in the way of my plan."

"Pardon me, Master, he may not be so enthusiastic about aligning himself with you," offered Tris Megistus.

"You have come into my service. You carry out my will. You are strong in the arcane arts. I know and sense that you are spiritually formidable. If I got you to serve me, then I am above confident that the detective will serve my purpose," countered The Immortal Count, perturbed at the magician stating the obvious.

"Some people are born to lead and others are born to serve, Master. Both are a necessity for the other," said Megistus.

CHAPTER 23

"I find it irksome in distinguishing which you are," The Immortal Count stated flatly.

"I am in your service am I not?" replied Tris Megistus, shocked at the subtle meaning of the statement.

The intercom chimed and the gruff voice of the Sasquatch guard from outside could be heard speaking a Native American language. "Excellent, the henchmen are here to deliver the goods," Tris Megistus surmised. The Gang Crew Club Syndicate had never met the Count. He had relied upon the recommendations of the Thrice Magician to recruit the thieves to carry out the heist.

The posse that entered The Immortal Count's abode, the Palace of Palaces and Castle of Castles, looked genuinely out of place. The six-foot-six, dreadlocked, tanned and bejeweled leader of the group walked with the air of an alpha male at the head of his pack. He had on more bling than Tris Megistus and he wore an overly large, ultra-expensive fur coat. He was the son of two of the most powerful and richest crime families in the world. His overly expensive shades were halfway down his nose as he reached the side of the magician. His Gang Crew Club Syndicate was right behind him, decked out in their finest weapons and bulletproof vests.

Formerly born Melvin Poindexter Cleetus, the leader of the Gang Crew Club Syndicate changed his name to Reverend Gangsta Playa. He had gotten certified as a priest. It is circulated that if he was going to carry out an assassination, he would first perform the last rites on the individual before he killed them. He was a bad, no-nonsense kind of leader that preferred to be in the trenches with his men than to sit on the sidelines calling plays.

His companions consisted of four white supremacists that sung in an acapella group in their spare time. There were four Midnight Jaguar founders whose radical idealist group did not catch on. Lastly, there were four people from the Bloody 31's, a club in which the rules stated that only thirty-one people were allowed to join at any time. Two of the henchmen held a cart with the prize that The Immortal Count sought.

CHAPTER 23

"Sup my idiots. I got you your crap. Thanks to the stuff that you gave us, like the weapons and tech, it was easy pickings to get this," Playa said with a pompous air, looking at Tris Megistus.

"Thank you for your services Mister Reverend Gangsta Playa. If you could deposit the weapons and tech that we loaned you in the bin, I will give you the other half of your money. Then you are freed from your retention until your services are again needed. For your promptness I will throw in an extra fifty thousand," commented Tris Megistus.

"You see, we kind of like the threads and tech, so yeah. You might want to rethink that," Playa said squeamishly.

"That was not the accord. We loaned you the items and we get it back. You get the other half of the money. Do not ruin a great thing. The Count is not very forgiving," chided the magician.

The Immortal Count sat silently, still looking at the wall of televisions, whilst this unfolded. He did not care if the posse was aware of his presence or not, he would reveal himself when the time was right.

"I have some more bad news. I kind of like this big hunk of gold disc thingy. I know that I could get much more than what you guys are paying us. You know, it being a big hunk of gold and stuff," Playa said. He brandished his weapon in a non-threatening way, to show that he still had it.

"Do you want to appear to your underworld kingdom as someone who breaks their word?" queried Tris Megistus.

"Hey, politicians do it all the time and they're not really branded as bad guys," Playa said as he slapped the magician on the shoulder. He turned to leave and stopped short.

"The artifact that you have in your possession is called *The Death Toll of Hercules*. It was given to the demigod by the messenger of the gods, Hermes. Hercules used it to cross the river of the dead, the River Styx, in order to bring back the dead wife of a friend of his.

Normally, two coins would have worked but since the acts of Hercules were legendary and his murderous rampage so horrifying, the toll was much greater. It allowed passage to the underworld and then magically returned to the bearer's hand after crossing.

It permitted you to bring someone back from either Tartarus or the Elysian fields. Trust me, that one hundred pound, three-foot in diameter and ten-inch thick coin is not just a myth. The carvings depicted on both sides are of Olympus, in heaven and the Underworld, in hell. The craftsmanship of the coin is proof that people believed in such things," stated Tris Megistus.

Playa turned around and smiled, "Thanks for telling me this bra! Now I can charge ten times the amount I was going to ask for. You guys sure don't seem really good at hiring bad guys and loaning out good tech. You sure you been doing this a long time?"

"Keep your word now and you shall have no repercussions. I will attribute your insolence to whatever you ingested or inhaled before you and yours came here," said Tris Megistus authoritatively.

Reverend Playa stood up and puffed out his chest. His posse brandished their weapons and stood resolutely against Tris Megistus. The Immortal Count sat silently, still looking at the wall of screens.

"I'm the boss man here and I rule the two greatest crime families in the world. History has never seen anything like what my organization is. I take what I want and there's nothing you can do about it. Jeez man, did you not even think to take the weapons from us before you let us through the door?

I mean the guys on stilts in Big-Foot costumes. That's hilarious. And all these things in here, are they even real? You guys look like a bunch of circus freaks that mated with goths," laughed Playa and his Gang Crew Club Syndicate.

Tris Megistus went to raise his hand but at that moment, The Immortal Count interjected. His voice was so great, so terrible and so icy cold that it froze Playa and his posse in their tracks. "Silence you insubordinate fools!"

The air got thick and heavy with static electricity as the Count outstretched his right hand to the side of the throne. It seemed like the pressure in the air shot up from one atmosphere to a thousand. The Count's guests had trouble breathing as they buckled to the floor, feeling the twin onslaught of gravity and the atmosphere. They tried to raise their weapons but it was futile. The air just seemed too heavy to allow any movement. All thirteen of them were on their knees, looking towards the voice coming from the throne.

They focused on the Count's outstretched arm. It was muscled and sinewy with great veins, like highways of blood that coursed with anger at this intolerant behavior. Tris Megistus, unmoved by the change in the air and gravity, stood by quietly as the Count continued his spiritual and physical assault on the Gang Crew Club Syndicate. Dandelion, Sunflower, and the six robot women crowded at the door of the adjoining bedroom to see the ensuing show.

The Immortal Count slowly rose from the great throne made of stone. His giant eight-foot framed silhouette could be seen by all on their knees. He had the deepest, jet black hair which came to his shoulders. His powerful shoulders rippled with the energy of an earthquake, emanating across the landscape of his back and neck. He spoke with his back in the direction of the miscreants genuflecting before him.

"It is not by coincidence that you have come into my employ, but by my design. I knew of your character before sending my Thrice Magician out to retain your services. You are a brash and impatient leader of your gang. You are a wonton drunkard and a braggart. Your kingdom has been handed to you and all your henchmen serve you out of the love of money. You have not earned their trust but they have trusted your predecessors. They do you a kindness by following you. You neither lead with fear nor admiration.

That is the worst kind of leader because you have no idea where your followers stand. You are aimless in a directionless contrivance. You have criminal strength, but do not wield true power. Your mind is fragile. It is susceptible to all manner of suggestions and control.

The grandiloquence that you have seen on the way here has inflamed your senses. It has riddled your mind with greed and envy. Why do you think I had you come here in the first place? Every inch of this Palace Of Palaces and Castle of Castles was dedicated to me and has my imprint upon it. The embossed words and symbols have allowed me to access your innermost thoughts and desires.

I have used my surroundings to deconstruct your mind without you even being aware of it. I have been implanting my will upon your subconscious, even before you saw my face. All my followers do my will implicitly. Now, will you do the same?" dialogued The Immortal Count, focused on the immobilized henchmen.

"Who the heck are you? The whole world of criminals knows I'm here. If I don't come back, they'll storm your compound," said the leader of the Gang Crew Club Syndicate. He feebly tried to get up from the floor but he could not budge from his kneeling position.

"Even on your knees, you defy The Immortal Count. Master, do not trouble yourself with them. I shall call forth *Greek fire* from the heavens and incinerate them without damaging your pristine carpet. Undoubtedly, the carpet is worth more than their pathetic lives," interjected Tris Megistus.

"Gang Crew Club Syndicate, you have defiled my house with your mutinous actions today. I impose my will upon you and decree that you shall live till a century. Your lives shall be in service to my purpose. However, do not rejoice just yet, for your sentence will be passed down to your children and your children's children. It is my judgment that each here shall be reborn as your grandchildren upon your death. You shall know your purpose even from the womb.

Your houses shall worship me with unyielding vehemence, till I choose to release them from their servitude, with the slow torturous embrace of the death which I will deal." The Count spoke to the insubordinate men before him.

With that soliloquy, The Immortal Count turned around and allowed his new retainers to see whom they would be serving. His gaze rested upon each of them, analyzing and searching their souls. The search unearthed a myriad of crimes and delinquencies throughout their lives. Violence, evil and decadence came naturally to them. Under the tough-guy attitudes they fronted,

CHAPTER 23

were feeble minds. It was too easy for The Immortal Count to mold.

All thirteen of the Gang Crew Club Syndicate members started trembling violently and bowed even lower. The words of The Immortal Count ran through every fiber of their being and coursed through every molecule in their body. The Count's words burrowed deep into the minds and souls of the unfortunate hoodlums and sealed itself in their hearts. The will of the Count was bound to their very essence. Their futures were forfeit and in its place was complete and total servitude to The Immortal Count. He compelled them to carry out any order issued from him, even unto death.

Tris Megistus was in awe of the judgment that The Immortal Count pronounced upon the accused. Even he did not have any idea of the scope of The Immortal Count's power.

"Who are you?" one of the Gang Crew Club Syndicate members barely mumbled out of a seizure.

In a deeply controlled voice that radiated authority and demanded subservience and loyalty, The Immortal Count began:

"I am the shadow that you see from the corner of your eye. Your body knows me well because the hairs on your neck sense my presence. I am the dream you cannot remember but weighs heavily upon your soul, eating away at the very fabric of your mind. I am the gaze that makes you feel uneasy when no one is around, far-reaching even to the depths of your abyss. I am the raindrop that breaks the dam. My influence shall flood the world and drown all who oppose my will. I am the quarry that has thwarted the hunter, Death, which has given up his ardent and savage hunger for my being. I am much more than you can never know and far greater than you can possibly imagine. I am the Dreaded Lord and Sovereign Master. I am The Immortal Count."

Jacques Von Blutdruckt Gemacht sat down, disappointed at humanity and the filth that it bred. Disgraced that humanity did not have more of an iron will. Dejected that humanity could easily be subjugated and controlled. He was looking for an equal and did not find it. The only possibility of an equal lay in his nemesis, detective Brentt Williams.

CHAPTER 23

The Gang Crew Club Syndicate took a minute to let all that the Count had said enter their hearts. Their minds were influenced by his astounding spiritual power. The Immortal Count said to them, "Now your criminal kingdoms are mine to command. You are but a spec of sand in the desert of my master plan. However, a speck of dust in the eye can be bothersome. Carry out your operations as I allow you to, but heed me when I call. You will be an annoyance to detective Brentt Williams when I decide the time."

They rose and reverently took their leave of The Immortal Count, content with only doing his will.

"Master, it is truly a sight to behold. Your will power is awesome. You control the weak-minded with such ease. Please forgive me for letting this rudeness get to that degree," said Tris Megistus politely, waiting for a chiding from the Count.

"Thrice Magician, I have need of your services. The *Gadha of Gilgamesh* is on display at the Grand museum. It will be unveiled on New Year's Day. Get it for me."

"Forgive the boldness, Master. Why would one with such power as yourself, have need of a trinket from a bygone era?" Megistus asked meekly.

"I want to add it to my collection of great artifacts. Its power is unique and I shall use it to further my cause."

"I shall steal it in the dead of night, before it has a chance to be gazed upon by the unworthy masses, Master," chortled Tris Megistus.

"No. It must be looked upon by as many people as possible. The *quantum entanglement* of this object is such, that anyone just observing it is immediately trapped in its properties. When necessary, the user of this weapon draws power from all of those life forms that have looked upon it, whether alive or dead. That is the inter-connectedness of things. Send a band of four Reptilians and bring it to me. Make the attack at the parade."

"Master, the Reptilians are vile creatures that stink and their behavior is unruly. Surely the detective and his cohorts will be present to disrupt us. I believe some of his own are very powerful in positive magic, an anathema for the Reptilians," put forth Tris Megistus.

"Disguise them as homeless people. That will mask their stench and aberrant behavior. Use the Anti-Positive Energy Suits that research and development have available. You stay on the sidelines with six big foot soldiers. Be ready to act if the detective gets the upper hand," continued The Immortal Count.

"Master, it is your will and I shall carry it out with my life." The Thrice Magician bowed reverently and took his leave.

The Immortal Count continued looking at the screen, of the events unfolding in the world. The path to his ultimate plan was already unfolded in his mind.

CHAPTER 24: Heddonna's Problem

Heddonna sat on the throne in her temple planet with a towel wrapped around her. She had just finished soaking in a luxurious bath. It did not ease her mind one bit because she was still fully engrossed in contemplation.

Her temple took up the entire planet. It was situated in the center of the multiverse along with the other temple planets. Each of the Gods had their own unique style and décor. All of the temple planets were uniquely designed and perfectly constructed by Atomos.

Heddonna's planet was the most purple thing in the entire universe. In addition, the planet was so big that it could fit ten to the thirtieth (10^{30}) of earth's suns inside of it. The gravitational force on the planet was the equivalent of a few thousand black holes. However, for the nine Gods and Goddesses, that was nothing. From her seat in the temple, she saw the other eight temple planets.

Heddonna loved the color purple, all shades of them. The sky was not just purple, but different hues of the fabulous color. On land, it was the same story. The grass was every shade of greenish-purple you cannot imagine. The flowers that lived amongst the grass had the slightest traces of purple hues. Even the trees had brownish-purple bark. The orchids that grew on them also sported purple in some form or another. The river that wound through the valley was crystal clear, with a hint of purple.

Even her temple was purple. The solid gold walls had different shades of purple running through them. White, tan and silver tiles had purple tones in them. No craftsman, engineer, or construction crew could have made anything like this except for the King of the Gods. A myriad of purple shades flooded the walls, floors, and ceilings. Even the pictures of far-away planets had purple borders on them.

CHAPTER 24

Curtains, marble figurines, rugs, and crystal windows had some purple in them. All of Heddonna's servants wore purple uniforms of different shades. Some of the hues were so subtle, that the human eye could not comprehend it, except with the use of the most powerful spectrophotometer in the universe. Even then, it had its limitations when compared with the Gods.

Heddonna had an experience that she never had in her entire existence. It was all thanks to an individual she knew nothing about. Never before had that happened to her. The Goddess of Knowledge, who kept a record of everything in the multiverses, did not know about the man that was in her Akashic Records Library. She sat in her temple looking listless and pondered about the encounter. She had not seen his past or his future. She had not read his innermost desires or guessed his intentions. Nothing came to her mind about this individual.

A flood of collected anger flowed through her veins as she got up. She walked to the balcony in her temple. Her red hair flowed down her back and ended just past her rear. Her thick hair swayed as she leaned on the balcony. She surveyed the vast planet and knew all that there was to know. She knew every plant, animal, water droplet and molecule. She knew what atom was where and the destination for the rest of its existence. She could see the strands of DNA in the animals and plants. She looked up and saw the universes. She saw where everything was and where everything would be. Heddonna, the Goddess of Knowledge knew everything. Except about that Man!

Heddonna felt a hand on her right shoulder and saw slender fingers with dark purple nails trailing down her arm. She turned around to see herself dressed in a purple evening dress that was almost painted on. The ruffles of the gown barely skirted the floor as she spun around for herself to admire. The dress went from the top of her shoulders and revealed a plunging back. She had no shoes, but her toes had on celestial nail polish that turned different hues of purple.

"I look very beautiful today, don't I?" asked the clothed Heddonna.

"Yes you do," towel-clad Heddonna replied with a smile.

CHAPTER 24

"However, we cannot get that man out of our head," replied clothed Heddonna.

"Yes. I haven't thought about another male like this since Technon. He kicked Anthraxis' butt really bad. I must admit, the God of Technology looked really awesome doing it," recalled toweled Heddonna.

"You're thinking too hard about this. You need to relax a little and then resume your pondering," offered clothed Heddonna. She put a hand on toweled Heddonna's arm.

"I need... I need to go to heaven. They have the next best accounting and records in all of creation. It's impossible for me to make a mistake. Maybe there was a clerical error or something. No, they get their information from here," debated toweled Heddonna.

"Relax. Maybe we should tell Atomos. He could help," suggested clothed Heddonna.

"He's still pissed about us destroying the Milky Way Galaxy," answered toweled Heddonna.

"We searched everywhere in the library and did not come up with anything on this man," said clothed Heddonna.

"I must go to see Uriel. He's the keeper of the records for heaven. If anything is amiss, he'll know," commented toweled Heddonna as she materialized some clothes upon her body.

CHAPTER 25: Theo And Porast Dream

The whole universe was before him. He saw everything. He felt the life flowing through the universe. Every atom in the vastness of space moved before his eyes. When he took a breath, it was the deepest and most satisfying breath that anyone could have ever taken. He inhaled the scent of all that was.

The energy of the universe coursed through his veins. It strengthened him. It invigorated him. He felt like he knew all. He felt as if he was all. The past, present, and future were open to him. It was like reading a book on someone's life, except it was about all of the atoms that made up that person. He felt as if he could do anything or go anywhere. He felt as if he was in control of everything.

Looming behind him, there stood twenty-one dark figures. They watched him from the shadows. He could feel them. He should know them but couldn't remember who they were. However, there was an unmistakable connection to them. There was a cohesion to them that transcended time, space and universes. He had a feeling that they were part of him, but the forgotten part. That part of him needed to be unlocked. He tried to look through the haze. It was just too difficult to see the features of the silhouetted figures. They slipped away very slowly, one step at a time.

Then, he became aware of something more sinister than anything he had ever felt before. It was the embodiment of evil. It was not the evil that most people think of but an evil that held nothing. It had no boundaries. It had no beginning and no end. The evil came with overwhelming darkness, too thick to shake off. It was felt before it came into view. It was smelled before it came into view. It was heard before it came into view. He turned to look at the newfound terror with curiosity and fear. It spoke to him with the voice of many voices talking softly at once. He could not hear what it said and he certainly did not understand what it said.

The alarm sounded, signaling that it was time to get up. His heart still raced as he lay in bed for a few minutes and contemplated the dream. The darkness felt so tangible. He had to put that aside in his mind for now. Theo Steren Champlain had a morning gala to attend on New Year's Day.

Sister Angelina Porast sat up in her bed, sweating and out of breath. She had a terrible vision about the future, which usually meant it would come true. She rubbed her face with a shaky hand and a few strands of graying black hair fell around her face. She was three hundred and sixty-five years old but did not look a day over sixty-five.

Brentt oversaw her inculcation into the Legacy of the Ascended Knowledge of the Nine or LAKN9 for short. She showed so much promise and skill that they put her in charge of the Sisters of the Ascended Knowledge of Heddonna, a sub-branch of the LAKN9. She did not disappoint the organization. Her special ability to feel and foresee the future had helped many missions go according to plan. Most often, they thwarted The Immortal Count's diabolical machinations.

She saw the future and it looked very terrible. A soupy darkness veiled the outcome. It was a darkness that overpowered any light that tried to penetrate it. It stuck to her in the vision and threatened to engulf her. She hugged herself and pulled the covers close as she sat in the huge king-sized bed. It was in this very bed that she had shared a night of passion with Brentt Williams so long ago. He had a special place in her heart for as long she lived.

The soft covers gave her warmth, as the cold night cast its shadow across the land. She looked at the clock and saw it was three in the morning. Porast debated about calling Brentt because she did not want to wake him. She sat quietly in her thoughts when the phone rang at four. It was Brentt and he was getting ready to go to work at the museum.

CHAPTER 25

"Hello, Angel. How are you? I hope I did not wake you," he said flirtatiously.

"You're always welcome to wake me anytime. I was just dreaming about you," she said shyly.

"Really, a naughty dream or was it something else?"

"This was so dark and horrible that I wish it were a naughty one."

"Tell me about it, sweetie."

"I saw you fighting reptilians. It was a very heated battle."

"Reptilians, I thought they would send in the Animal Kingdoom? Reptilians are worse. They are far stronger and way meaner. I have fought a few, but it is not a fight that I relish. Everyone would have to give it all and more."

Porast continued, "Then I saw utter darkness amalgamating at the museum, waiting for that Gadha. I saw you and the others battle an enemy that will test your limits and take you beyond. The enemy had darkness so deep, that it threatened to engulf you. I saw your spirit breaking. You entered a transcendent state that broke the limitations of your body. Yet still, you did not win. I saw the carnage that was unlike anything that we have ever come across, but this was not a result of your battle."

"What do you mean? I break the limitations of my body? You mean I become my *higher self*? I become it in battle? Was someone else battling? Was it the Count?"

"I don't think it was the Count. I feel so. I don't know so. I can't describe what I feel. It is just so dark and scary that I can't stop shaking. I wish you didn't have to face it. Pray to the Gods. Brentt, pray for protection."

"You know I haven't willingly set foot in a church or temple since my parents died, much less pray. I look around and I don't see any indication of a God. I am a detective. Do you know what kind of monsters I come across on a daily basis? There are people who would kill for a pack of gum and the money in your wallet. There is evil everywhere and good deeds are disappearing," reflected Brentt.

"Prayers do get answered. There are stories of miracles every day," countered Porast.

CHAPTER 25

"What about all the other ones that go unanswered? What about me, when I prayed 'please don't let my parents die', or 'please give me the strength to fight'. I got no answer to that. I know I am the head of an organization that has knowledge of the Nine, but looking around, I don't believe they care anymore," stated Brentt, sounding dejected.

"*Every day that everyone is alive is a miracle.*"

"It is not the ones that are alive that I am interested in, but the ones who die needlessly."

"Brentt, I know where you are coming from. I see why. However, you have to know that there are things out there that we cannot understand. You have to be grateful for what you have and not be depressed about what you don't have."

Brentt was silent on the line and only the sound of his rhythmic breathing could be heard. "Continue."

"What happens after the darkness falls upon you is a blur. However, the next time I saw the vision, I could see a monk. The monk will be capable of great things. He just needs a chance to prove himself."

"That's heavy stuff. It sounds very ominous. Was it one of ours?"

"No, he was not one of ours. His name is Frank Lin."

"That is very interesting. I did hear him lecture Theo on going to the Akashic Records Library. Did you see anything about the Count, anything at all?"

"I saw Tris Megistus there, but he was not fighting. He was hesitant to get involved. The darkness kept even him away. This man has done many dark and evil things. He has sold his soul to the highest bidder hundreds of times and double-crossed twice that many in the process. If he won't come close, that means it is going to be one hell of a fight."

"Thanks for the heads up. I think I'll bring a little something extra to the party. What about Theo and Asheley?"

"I did not have any luck with them. I could not see anything for her. With Theo I got nothing. No past, present or future."

"What do you mean? You always find out about everyone. Well, except The Immortal Count."

CHAPTER 25

"I could not foresee their futures because there was nothing to read."

"In your case, a prognosis like that means they die."

"I don't know, Brentt. I am scared. I have never felt anything like this. This is unlike anything you will ever face. Just be careful. When you do come out of this, promise me another night like what we had long ago."

"You might have to nurse me back to health first if it is as bad as you say it is" he replied with a smile in his voice.

CHAPTER 26: Heddonna Goes To Heaven

The *River of Life* was the clearest and most majestic river that anyone cannot ever imagine. It flowed through the heart of heaven and passed the *Tree of Life*, which partook of its refreshing goodness. Animals drank and filled themselves from the river's cool bounty. Countless trees were fed on its banks.

The water was so mysterious that when you cupped it in your hands, it turned into edible, icy diamonds. When you were ready to eat the icy diamonds, just put one in your mouth and it tasted like you just drank a mouthful of the heavenly water. It had no shelf life and could be taken anywhere, retaining its diamond form. *The healing property of the water was unlike anything ever imagined, sustaining and nurturing the lives of everything it touched.*

The river flowed down a verdant valley in which houses of the saved were built. The empty homes waited for the inhabitants to come and claim their eternal prize. The tributaries of the river gently meandered through different fields and meadows. Even little garden fountains contained the hallowed waters, which retained the freshness of the main river itself.

As you followed the river, it cascaded into a mighty waterfall that had a seven hundred and seventy-seven-foot drop into the clearest pool imaginable. However, the force of the waterfall was like a light rain touching the pool. In fact, if anyone were to go over the falls the river would gently set you in the pool and let you be on your way.

Behind the waterfall was a secret grotto that only a few knew about. It was the back door into heaven. It was sealed with a solid gold door that was fashioned to look like smoothed rocks. The inside was filled with columns and beams that were a hundred and forty-four feet tall. There were five bed-chambers, a communal living area, a dining area and a kitchen with a giant tree. In addition, there was a great library that held exotic texts and books from different worlds, written in different languages. The occupants of these quarters were four angels and a Demangel.

The walls of the great halls were covered in the words of the Word, written in the language of the Nine. It was never seen by mortal men and certainly revered by those deemed worthy enough to look upon this fantastic place. The four angels were hand-picked to remain in this place and guard the back gates of heaven.

'Nobody came in and nobody went out.' That was the order that they were given and that was the order which they followed. They had shown their bravery in the battle of heaven when *The Morning Star* decided to rebel against the Creator. It was a terrible battle and there were casualties on both sides. Eventually, the bad guys were thrown out, but not utterly broken and destroyed.

The first of the angels chosen to reside here was Bastiel. He was a great and powerful, twelve-foot tall seraphim. His shoulder-length, brown hair was in a ponytail, tied back by the skin of the serpent that deceived Eve. He wielded a giant polearm with six ax heads and a spear on top. He had a massive rectangular Tower Shield of silver so pure, that it looked transparent. The *Ten Commandments* were emblazoned upon the front. His six wings were tough and leathery, with scars from battles that took place long ago. He was a staunch fighter with a brave heart and felled many opponents in the Great War. However, even with all his might, he was conquered by the beauty of Evriel.

His comrade and wife was Evriel. She was as tall as he and moved with the speed of lightning. She was also a Seraph. However, her wings were not leathery, but a soft, downy texture. Her weapon of choice was a giant two-handed sword that was blunt on one side but supremely sharp on the other. There was a dragon motif on the sword and the blade came out of its mouth. The dragon wings and body made up the grip and guard. A ruby adorned the very bottom of the sword's handle.

Her sister gave her the great weapon after she took it off Abaddon, a *Fallen Angel* commander. The sword's name was 'The Brimstone of Heaven.' It was a heated blade, in which fire from a

CHAPTER 26

hundred suns allowed it to burn through anything. She had gauntlets with mini shields that could stop anything that came her way. Flaming red hair, drawn back in a ponytail and deep red eyes matched her fiery and passionate disposition.

Loriel was Evriel's friend and older sister. She had stood with Evriel on the field of battle. She was an imposing fifteen-foot tall Seraphim as well, but she was missing two of the wings that covered her face. The unsightly stumps reminded her of what was and the price they had paid. Her wings were ripped off by Abaddon, a ruthless follower of the rebellion. He had cornered her sister Evriel and had broken her sword. Loriel came just in time before he was able to cut Evriel down. She valiantly fought the great angel and retaliated by cutting off his right hand with his own blade. However, the weapon was not her style and she gave it to her sister.

Loriel's weapon of choice was her twin Zanbato Nodachi hybrids. They were like giant scalpels a surgeon uses and could expertly slice her opponents open. In addition, her arsenal included two large *Chained Shields of Torment* that she would throw and control from a distance. They either sliced or hammered through any opponent. Her long and short-range fighting styles put any who came against her at a disadvantage. Well, any who dared challenge her, that is. The long tresses of her sunlight-blond hair were braided to make a crown on her head. She wore a tiara, studded with stars. The tiara was given to her by Moerdon, her soulmate, and her husband.

Moerdon was the leader of the little group. Actually, he was the General of the Fifth Company of the Host of Heaven. His friend, *Metatron,* leader of the Sixth Company of heaven and scribe, took over for him while he stayed here. He was a great leader that snatched victory from the lying mouth of the serpent. Moerdon stood fifteen-feet tall and had six wings, but he never used them. His dark hair was cut short and he had blue eyes that radiated a commanding presence about him. There was also a gentle side to this battle-hardened warrior as attested by his friends.

He had the cutest pet lamb that transformed into a monstrous seven-headed dragon named Revelation. He had rescued

CHAPTER 26

Revelation from the hatchery of *Shaol*, the headquarters of the fallen angels before they built Hell.

His weapon of choice was the bladed bow named 'The Full Measured Might of Heaven'. His bow rained down every kind of attack imaginable upon his foes. He also carried a sword called 'The Vengeful Covenant Breaker of the Heavens'. It was a weapon so powerful and so legendary, that it was forged before the war. It was made in anticipation of *doing what it needed to do at the right time*. Made from fifteen feet of the purest Hycolium possible, it was a magnificently balanced broad blade. It was not intricately carved or lavishly ornate but had the scenic simplicity of the sand and the seashore. It was also very deadly in the right hands. The sword was one of the 'Gifts of the Nine', which only the most worthy of owners wielded.

The only one alive that had ever seen him use it was his first wife Accordia, who was present when the planet Shaol was destroyed. He lost her that day. However, he got her back in a series of interesting events.

The last but certainly not the least interesting member of this party was the indomitable Accordia. She was the first wife of Moerdon and then she was resurrected as a Manticore Sphinx. She recognized the tattoo of her name on his shoulder and all her memories flooded back. She was fifteen-feet tall and one-hundred-feet long with very luxurious black hair. She had a woman's head and torso, demon's horns, and four arms. Her body was that of a lion, with two sets of eagle wings and four cobras for tails.

She recently obtained the ability to shapeshift. Her lion's body assumed the form of a beautiful woman and her tail and extra arms became tattoos on her back and stomach. This was her Demangel form. She was very strong and cunning and a great and fearless warrior. She loved Moerdon deeply and followed him anywhere. Accordia was one of the few that got into the good graces of heaven. She received a reward for her valor and was allowed to be with Moerdon. She carried no weapons because she was the weapon.

All five occupants of the chamber busied themselves reading the Word on the walls and looking at the old manuscripts that were contained there. There were reliefs that showed the universe long before they were created. Most of the language was so ancient that it took centuries to translate a few sentences. This kind of work actually relieved all of the occupants because they had been at war. It relaxed them to solve mysteries in old books. However, they did keep their skills honed by sparring every day.

Today was a day like any other. Moerdon had woken up and found that Accordia had crawled into his bed while he was asleep. Ever since he found out that his first wife had been reincarnated, that irked his second wife, Loriel. Of course, they had to do it Old Testament style and share, like *Lamech,* the father of Noah.

They ate breakfast at the table and said grace before the meal, as was their custom. The meal came from a special tree. When you picked the fruit, if you thought of something that you would like to eat for seven seconds, the fruit turned into what you wanted. It was the Tree of Gluttonous Desires. The crystal clear, almost gelatinous fruit always bloomed. You could cook a gourmet meal from it. You could eat your favorite ice cream, the most decadent cakes, or anything your heart desired. One time in jest, Bastiel thought about guano and handed the fruit to Moerdon, who innocently ate it.

The center of the great abode held a sight that was without equal in grandeur and design. It was the actual back gate into heaven. The ceiling dipped and it seemed that the whole place was held up by the rotunda which had nine doors, seventy-seven feet tall. Above each of the doors, were words in some ancient language that was similar to the ones on the walls. Each door told the story of The Contest of the Nine. The angels had never seen anything like it.

In fact, the carvings on the doors were exactly the same as found in the Akashic Records Library. The doors were made from a material that they had never seen before. The realism of the paint-job was unimaginable. Great metal rings, harder than the angels' weapons, made up the handles. Each of the Nine Gods had access to the back gate of heaven from their temple planets. It had been millions of years since any one of them stepped through those doors though. However, that was going to change.

All of the angels and the Demangel stood in awe of the great gate before they began their work. They searched the rotunda for any signs of breaches, but the result was always the same, all clear.

Suddenly, the figures on the doors started to move in a slow dramatic sequence. One figure that looked like an old man, stretched forth his arm and energy burst from his fingers. Another figure right next to the old man, this time of a woman, held upon her shoulders a glowing ball. There were other panels that moved with just as much life. Subsequently, the last panel showed another beautiful woman with a giant book clasped in her hands. The book opened and the pages turned and fluttered.

The fluttering grew louder as the wind generated from the book soon created hurricane-like gusts. This drove the now insanely curious angels and the half-angel back. Despite the gusts, none of the reading materials and sacred tomes moved from where they were. Nothing affected them. This was an important observation that Moerdon took note of. Unable to withstand the wind that pummeled them, they hastily grabbed their weapons, overturned two great gopher wood tables, and took cover behind them.

"What the heck is going on? It's never done that before," stated Moerdon.

"There's no time to read a book on it, honey. What do we do?" asked Loriel.

"We'll have to knock heads and ask questions after," recommended Bastiel.

"That might work if we knew what was happening," Evriel stated the obvious.

"Everyone, aim at the doorway. On my signal, open fire," ordered Moerdon as he readied himself behind the table.

"I'll stay in my Demangel form this time around," said Accordia.

'Damn! Revelation, where is he?' thought Moerdon, looking around for his pet lamb.

CHAPTER 26

The winds got even more violent and it seemed to chant. The wind spoke in the same language written on the walls and the doors of their abode. Moerdon readied his bow and made sure his comrades were prepared as well. Slowly the massive doors swung open and a giant figure filled the doorway. Energy and smoke crackled around the figure as it came through.

Heddonna stepped through the seventy-seven-foot tall gates that were the backway into heaven. The wind immediately died down and there was a deafening silence. Her imposing, seventy-foot tall frame took up the whole doorway. Her presence stopped the hearts of all the onlookers before her.

She was dressed in a purple bodysuit that hid all and left even more to the imagination. She wore calf-high boots, studded with purple gemstones, the likes of which the angels had never seen before. Her gloves were woven with gold and purple threads which ended with a bracelet of more purple stones. Her red hair was tied in a ponytail with a purple clip that had a light purple rose with magnificent petals and gold leaves.

She stepped down from the rotunda that held the gates. Her eyes scanned the area and that's when Revelation struck. He changed from a docile little lamb to a seven-headed dragon bent upon defending his friends. Seven super-hot flames tried to char and barbeque the omnipotent Goddess where she stood. This did little but to amuse her. Moerdon recognized the figure through the smoke and energy and prayed that Heddonna was in a good mood.

"We have to stop Revelation. He doesn't know who Goddess Heddonna is!" he yelled, as he sprang into action.

"Oh my word, the Goddess is here?" blurted out Loriel in shock.

He fired a few sticky arrows that gummed up Revelation's wings and he fell to the floor. His friends jumped from behind the tables and went to the dragon to try to calm him down.

Immediately Moerdon went to his knees, "I am so sorry for that, Goddess Heddonna. By the time I recognized you, my pet lamb attacked. Please forgive us," Moerdon pleaded.

"It is alright. You did your duty well. All of you are truly valiant warriors," she spoke calmly.

CHAPTER 26

The Goddess turned to the sticky, seven-headed dragon and looked him in the eyes. She then materialized seven embodiments and petted all of his heads. This seemed to ease the great beast as he nuzzled her. "There's a good boy!"

Heddonna amalgamated herself and spoke, "Everyone, do not be afraid. Come and see one of the nine originators of the language that you work so tirelessly to decode. Come and see one of the nine that lovingly crafted your great sword Moerdon, 'The Vengeful Covenant Breaker of the Heavens'. Come and see one of the nine that have come this day to the halls of Heaven." Her voice was smooth and rich as a warm triple chocolate cake with cold vanilla ice cream.

"Where did you get your interesting pet lamb?" she asked, knowing the answer already.

"We rescued him from the Shaol hatcheries," replied Moerdon.

"How can we help you, Goddess?" asked Evriel as she bowed gracefully and stretched out her wings.

"Where are you in decoding the texts?" asked the Goddess again, fully knowing the answer.

"We are maybe a quarter of the way done. However, we still have quite a way to go to translate the language of the nine into the language of the angels," said Loriel, bowing.

"Let me make it easy for you. I will give you the translation. All you have to do is read and understand," Heddonna said. She waved her hand and the inscriptions on the walls, in the books, scrolls, on the doors, and the ceiling, changed into the language of the angels. The five of them looked in wonder at the reading material. Instead of decoding the texts, they were finally at liberty to read them.

"All this reading material!" gasped Bastiel.

"One other thing, Loriel, let me restore your facial wings. I see that you lost them during a battle," smiled Heddonna. The stumps situated on Loriel's collar disappeared. In their place, were two of the most magnificent wings that an angel could have ever dreamt about. She felt, smelled, and stroked them to make sure that it was not a dream. They were actually there.

"Goddess, we can't thank you enough," stammered Moerdon.

CHAPTER 26

"Evriel, you are the fastest here. Can you summon Uriel? Tell him to bring the books of heaven. I need to look at them," ordered Heddonna.

"With all speed Goddess," said Evriel as she bowed and sped away.

"Would it not be more fitting for one such as yourself to be met with fanfare and a parade through the front gates, Goddess?" asked Bastiel.

"Mighty Bastiel, while I would not turn down such an opportunity, I want to keep a low profile. There were things that happened to limit my involvement with the Athlogoss Drones as decreed by Atomos. But that is beside the point. I need to be clandestine."

The cavalry arrived in minutes. Uriel and Evriel led the way, followed by sixteen burly looking Seraphim.

"By the Nine! Goddess Heddonna, it's really you!" Uriel gasped and genuflected before the Goddess. The others did the same.

"Uriel, I need your help. I need to know if you have knowledge of this man," she said. Heddonna conjured a likeness of the man in question, the man that was in her Library. "He came to my Library but I have no knowledge of him. There is no record of this man in the Library that holds all of the knowledge in the universe!"

"Goddess, I don't see how a being like me could help you. I will do my utmost. Come to think of it, I have seen him. He was here a few months ago," spoke Uriel.

"You have? I see the encounter happening, but you are speaking to no one. What came of the meeting?" asked Heddonna.

"We did not find him in any of the books. There was no trace of his soul print. I had to kick him out. We figured he got lost in some paperwork issues."

"Who took care of him?" asked Heddonna.

"Goddess, I remember this man," said a Seraph, as he bowed reverently. "I ran him through with my flaming sword. I sent him back to whence he came."

"I know he's from Earth. What time period did he come from?" asked the Goddess.

"I don't know. Earth's history is expansive. There are billions of years to cover," stated Uriel.

"You still have the sword. Give it to me, please. Somehow, anything related to this man I cannot see. I saw your encounter with someone, but it is as if no one is there. You, seraphim, I saw you running your sword through nothing. But you were behaving as if someone was there."

"Goddess, that is very frightening indeed. How is this possible?" asked Uriel, now a little worried.

"I know who would be able to help me. I'm taking your sword. I'll make sure and return it. I'll take the tablets as well. A diagnostic needs to be run to determine if there was an error. These warriors have fought very valiantly. They have a special recommendation from me."

Moerdon apologized once more, "Goddess, thank you for your grace once again."

"So that's where your sword originated from, Moerdon," whispered Bastiel.

"I thank you for your due diligence in guarding the back gate of heaven. Don't worry; I knew what was going to happen before I came here. I know everything. Well, except this thing that I came here for, but other than that, everything. I must go now. All that transpired here shall remain a secret until further notice. I hope there aren't any more of this being," she said. The Goddess disappeared with a sonic boom, leaving a room full of more questions than answers.

Archituria looked at the newest invention of Technon that was in orbit over his temple planet. It was a satellite that picked up radio waves and television signals from distant planets. He had already used it to stream cartoons, while he worked on various inventions for his fellow Gods. Archituria was having a nice time chatting with Technon as he tinkered with his creation.

She liked the way he paid attention to the details and not just called them into existence. He actually crafted them.

"This is the receiver that tunes in to the signals. It is like the receivers in the brain when it is stimulated by everything. This converter filters out the noise of the universe and keeps the signals of the radio and television broadcasts."

"Wow, Technon that is amazing! Can these signals be received from anywhere?"

"Yes. This gets signals from all multiverses. Because in one universe, a movie might end in a different way than in the next universe, so it is important to see all of them. This will sit in the orbit of my planet. I plan to have eight of them. You can come over and watch a movie anytime. That's if you want to?"

"That will be lovely. It will pass the time well until our penance is over. I foresee that radio, television and internet communications will be a key factor in the advancement and building of great civilizations. It will also cause their destruction because sometimes, some things are not suitable for everyone to know."

Heddonna arrived at the temple planet of Technon and a smile broke out on her face. She was looking for a reason to see him and had a damn good one. However, she would have never thought that this excuse was a necessity. She spied that he was talking with Archituria high above his planet. It seemed that they were tinkering with some contraption that he was always creating.

"Hello. How are you all doing?"

"Fine thanks, Heddonna. What is happening with you?" Technon replied as their eyes locked.

"I was out and about doing some examinations of the records in heaven."

"Oh that's great!" remarked Archituria.

"I hope I am not interrupting anything. I was wondering if you could spare a minute and assist me with something, Technon?" asked Heddonna, looking intently at him.

"Sure. That's no problem, anything for you. What is it?"

"I'll help too if you like!" chimed in Archituria.

CHAPTER 26

Heddonna gathered them up in a bubble to have the matter discussed in private. "I need both of you to keep this a secret from Atomos."

"A secret from Atomos, sure!" they both exclaimed in unison.

"A person came into my Akashic Records Library. However, there was no information about him, anywhere. I did not know who he was. Heaven did not know about him either."

"Wait. *You're saying that there is someone running around out there that the Gods have no knowledge about?*" exclaimed Technon.

"Yes, and everything related to this person is as though he does not exist. I looked at the interactions of the angels with him, but there was no presence there," explained Heddonna, greatly distraught.

"You have the tablets? I'll check them out," asked Technon, taking them from Heddonna. "Heddonna that outfit really suits you."

"Thanks. I just kind of threw this on," she said brushing an imaginary strand of hair from her face.

"Could it just be a mistake?" suggested Archituria.

"Not at all, here is the sword that the man was stabbed with. Go ahead and look at the past, present, and futures of it," Heddonna said, handing the blade over.

"I see the angel using the sword but there is no one at the other end. How is this possible?" remarked Archituria.

"The tablets are good. Do you have a picture or replica of the man that you are looking for?" inquired Technon.

"Yes, here he is. This is from the Library and this is from heaven," she said as she formed two life-sized mannequins.

"I am using the facial recognition features on the tablets. If they did not read the soul print of the individual correctly, maybe this could narrow down the search," suggested Technon as he programmed the tablets with the images.

"Let me examine the blade for any residue that could be on the sword itself," Archituria said as she used her macro vision to look at the molecular intricacies of the weapon.

"I am not getting any match on the physical features of this person. None of the tablets recognize his face. That is weird since physical features are often recycled during the reincarnation process. I am going to extend the parameters on the tablet and do an infinite universe sweep. What do you make of this Heddonna?" asked Technon.

"I am not sure. Do you think there might be one of him in a different multiverse? I don't think I saw any!"

"Different scenarios are presented in the universe in order to ascertain the spiritual capacity of an individual. This is applied to add a normative value to one's character with the change in the environment. Do the events make the man or do the man make the events? He should be in multiple universes according to the will of Atomos," explained Archituria, as she continued to examine the blade.

"Any luck on the blade Archituria?" asked Technon.

"I am seeing molecular residue from the stabbing, but I cannot see any past, present or future of any of the molecules. I am physically seeing them but I cannot gather any more information about them from what I see. I cannot look past them."

"Let me see if I can gather the atomic particles and run some tests on them. Is there anything else that we know about this guy?" asked Technon. He materialized some micro tweezers and started gathering the molecules to put into a test tube, which he also materialized.

"He comes from Earth. Which multiverse, I don't know," said Heddonna.

"That's a start. I will cross-reference the clothes that he is wearing to his approximate age and the hairstyle."

"Good luck with that. That's a tall order, Technon," said Archituria.

"I am seeing some molecules here that belong to the clothes he wore. Let's see if there are environmental markers in the fiber molecules to tell us where it is from. Please hold the tablets for me, they are taking a while to extrapolate the information," said Technon as he gave the good and the bad tablets to Heddonna and the other religions tablet to Archituria.

Technon looked closely at the fibers and mixed them with some solutions in test tubes that he quickly materialized from nowhere. They turned different colors as Heddonna and

CHAPTER 26

Archituria looked on. After a few minutes of mixing and looking and mixing again, he looked at them with a smile on his face. "I think we might get lucky."

"I believe the tablets are done extrapolating the data as well," remarked Heddonna as she looked at her tablet.

"Let's see, the tablets tell us that the period that this guy might have come from is between 1980 and 2020," Archituria said, as she read off the screen.

"The environmental factors that contributed to the chemical traces on this guy's clothes showed a sixty-five percent probability of him being in California, USA. Do you ladies want to go for a night on the town? That is most definitely without the knowledge of Atomos? Not to mention, capture a guy that does not exist?"

"I thought you'd never ask," smiled Heddonna.

CHAPTER 27: Attack At The Museum

John and Catherine finished making love a few minutes after midnight on New Year's Eve. It was a perfect start to the New Year except, Catherine called Theo's name instead of John's. He had continued despite that little distraction. She profusely apologized but he brushed it off like nothing. Catherine soon fell asleep but John remained awake. He contemplated this pesky occurrence and fell asleep with his mind still on it. He got up before the alarm and looked at himself in the bathroom mirror.

Theo. He kept Catherine for himself all those years. John snuck around like some burglar to be with the woman he loved, while Theo openly enjoyed her. He hated that Theo still had a grip on Catherine's heart. Even Katie called Theo daddy when she was not even his. Theo. Even now, when John took everything from him, Theo still remained a thorn in his side. Someone tried to kill Theo, but they were not very good at it.

John thought to himself, 'you had no idea how I hated you. I have everything that anyone could ever want. Money, power, every kind of luxury and good looks, but I lacked one thing. I have not attained the complete love of the woman that I would die for. Theo, what have you done? I have everything, but you still have a hold upon the last thing that I need. What do I do about it? I shall finish the job that some two-bit bungling thief could not. My New Year's resolution is to kill you. I'll not worry if I get caught. I won't worry, because I have the best lawyers money could buy. Besides, I have a family with dirt on numerous judges if need be.

Theo, enjoy your pathetic life while it lasts. Catherine was too good for you. What to do about your perfect bimbo girlfriend? I think when I'm finished with you, I'll see about seducing her. If anything, I know a good mystic that has very powerful love potions that get results.'

CHAPTER 27

Catherine walked into the bathroom as John was drying himself after a shower. He hugged her with a sweet, warm hug and kissed her on the forehead. "Let's get ready for a great day," he said with a big smile on his face.

Brentt and the security detail skimmed the perimeter of the museum. It was a well-organized building that housed some of the greatest works of art that the world had ever seen. Brentt himself was an avid collector that focused on European art. He loved to get lost in the halls of museums and art galleries. Often, he came across paintings by artists he was well acquainted with. The other museum-goers did not realize that it was his little secret. He visited this museum many times before, but not in the capacity as its guardian. He had the overlay of the museum memorized however, the crux of the plan involved keeping an eye on the giant Gadha of Gilgamesh.

It was an imposing piece that elicited awe from anyone fortunate enough to look at it. A specially designed pedestal held it at an angle as if it waited to be picked up by some giant. This heist would not be a challenge for the Count and his goons. However, you do not send just anyone to steal a fifty-ton relic. In Brentt's world, it did not only take a giant to lift the object but a powerful Thrice Magician.

The regular security detail screened the entrants as they made their way inside. Anyone of them could be an agent of the Count and he had to cover all bases. However, that's why he brought backup.

Jacob Ocaj and his wife Jezebelle Dorcas were two captains from LAKN9. The organization was made up of several branches that had specific disciplines. The Priests and the Rabbis were a part of that order. Brentt was the reluctant leader of the organization. A heavy burden placed upon him when his father died. He wished the world did not need the organization. However, there are things out there that common people just don't know about. He preserved the lives of the innocent and kept power away from the wrong hands.

CHAPTER 27

The crew he had assembled were a great bunch and very well-seasoned when it came to thwarting the efforts of the Count. The Warrior Rabbis included: Aleph Gimmel, a middle-eastern doctor of theology and history as well as an EMT: Baruch Obed, a general surgeon and the half-brother of Aleph by an Israeli woman: Hezekiah Habakkuk, a physicist: Zechariah Haggai, an archaeologist: Shalom Maccabbee, a doctor of philosophy at a prestigious university: and Sarah Ruth, the wife of Zechariah and doctor of Egyptian studies.

The lineup of Assassin Priests were equally as impressive: Ezekiel Daniel, a South African professor of Horticulture: Luke Timothy, a British native and doctor of biotechnology: Mark Jude, an Asian businessman with his own multi-million dollar robotics company: Joshua Samson, a professional bodybuilder and gym owner: Aarron Moses, a black belt karate instructor: and Mary Sheba, the fiancé to Joshua and a ninth level samurai with a doctorate in metallurgy.

Each of the team members mastered the arcane arts and the manipulation of their bioelectric fields. They projected the type of current that electric eels produce, only with a lot more kick. In addition to their bodily powers, each team member possessed gloves called the Weapon Warp Gauntlets. This allowed the person to warp a selected weapon to their destination during the heat of battle. Their weapons were contained in a personal storage facility. Each operative of the Legacy of the Ascended Knowledge of the Nine had the gauntlets as standard issue.

For good measure, Brentt brought a little something extra to the party. He would be ready to fight off the Animal Kingdoom if they were thrown his way. However, the intelligence from SAKH Porast suggested there might be more sinister entrants into the fray.

Brentt gathered the team around him for a final check-in and pep talk. "Okay guys and girls. We want this to go as smooth as possible. All of you have been briefed before we got here. We know the Count is going to strike. He wants this Gadha real bad. He might use the Animal Kingdoom or Reptilians to handle the weapon. We need to protect it, but we also need to keep these people safe.

Any sign of trouble, you get on it. Leave the officers to do their job, but the out of the way stuff is on us. There's a big crowd of people out there for the parade, so I need a protection wall put up in case there's fighting."

"I'll do it. I'll put up the wall. I have been practicing defensive arts," offered Aleph.

"Count my help too brother. I hoped we didn't have to use it, but you never know. I think it's time we showed off the move that we have been practicing together. It's called the Iron Fortress," suggested Baruch.

"That sounds great. I have been hearing a lot of good stuff about your bioelectric field defense from HQ," said Brentt.

"Make sure and use positive energy blasts. The Reptilians are very susceptible to those attacks," reaffirmed Jezebelle to the group.

"The Boss-man's right, we need that wall up. Aleph and Baruch, I'll have Mary watch your six. She's great at projectiles. Keep in mind, the Reptilians are very strong. I still don't know how the Count got a hold of such creatures, but they pack quite a punch. Your best bet is to be on the long-range attack. Watch out for their tails, it's like a third arm to them," warned Jacob.

"Everyone, go to your stations and stay on your radios!" said Brentt sternly, as they all headed to their respective areas.

"Hey Theo, glad you could make it!" exclaimed Frank Lin Shao. He came up to Theo and gave him a hearty hug.

"Hello, Frank Lin. It's good to see you on your feet. You remember Asheley, my girlfriend?" replied Theo.

"How could I forget? Theo, you hit the jackpot with her. It is very nice to see you again, young lady!"

"Thank you. I appreciate you inviting us to the gala. It is good to get out and socialize," Asheley cheerily said.

"We'll get checked in with security and then it's time to have a five-star breakfast with all the fixings!"

"That sounds great," said Theo getting in the line.

CHAPTER 27

Little did Theo know, that just beyond, detective Brentt Williams spotted him and Asheley through the giant glass windows. He fixed his gaze upon the six-foot tall, voluptuous, brown-haired beauty. Brentt's Binky Animal Babies had been doing some detective work. They gathered intelligence on her over the past few weeks. They had some very interesting stuff to say about her. Squiggles and Boberta reported their findings to Brentt before he came to the museum:

"Hola, amigo. We have good news and bad news. Oh, we also have some news that might be okay, if you are in a good mood," explained Squiggles.

"Okay, buddy. Pour it on," Brentt said as he sipped a cup of coffee in the animal common room.

"Well, we found out that Asheley does not eat things," explained Boberta.

"Does not eat things?" Brentt asked.

"She did not eat or drink anything during the time we watched her. Theo ate all of the time. He eats like a hungry *Chupacabra*," Squiggles continued.

"Was she on a diet?" asked Brentt.

"Nope, she was not on any diet. Not a scoop of expensive ice cream. Like the kind that Lynne was saving for her cheat day. But I did her a favor and ate it out so she would not cheat," stated Boberta.

"Yeah, I remember that. Did she seem to draw energy from Theo?" asked Brentt, now very interested.

"That's the funny part though; she did not get any energy from him. I used the thermal scanners and there was no energy transfer," explained Boberta.

"She was very kind and loving to Theo. She cooked him whatever he wanted. She seemed like a muy bueno senorita. She never ate any of the food," said Squiggles.

"Did she put any foreign substances in his food, like poison or other stuff?" asked Brentt.

"No, not at all. She seemed like a world-class cook," Boberta said.

CHAPTER 27

"Another thing is that every so often during the night, she would get up and laser beams would come out of her eyes and scan the room," explained Squiggles.

"What! Laser beams? Why didn't you start with that? Was she looking for something?" Brentt asked, shocked.

"Yes, she was. You see, after she finished scanning, she would say, 'no threats detected'. Then she went back to sleep, like immediately," explained Boberta.

"Did anyone try to hurt Theo during the night?" asked Brentt suspiciously.

"No. Heaven knows we took turns watching them all night. Nothing out of the ordinary happened. Well, except for her scanning the place. That part gave me the heebie-jeebies!" exclaimed Boberta.

"Amigo, do you think that someone will try to kill Theo again?" asked Squiggles.

"I don't know. I just can't shake this feeling about Asheley," said Brentt, worried. "What was the other news?"

"I got caught by Asheley. She saw me when I was crawling to the food to 'take a sample' for examination," said Squiggles. "Peanut butter and chocolate pancakes with bananas on top."

"What did she do? Did you talk to her or behave as a hamster would?" asked Brentt.

"She picked me up very gently and did that scanning thing. Then she spouted a lot of scientific jargon about my species, phylum, and domain. She had the whole thing memorized. Amigo, I don't even know that stuff! Then she let me go outside. Of course, bandito MacGraw made it look like he attacked me and carried me away," explained Squiggles.

"Hmm. So she does not eat. She gets up in the middle of the night. She has scanning beams in her eyes," repeated Brentt as he processed all of the info the little spies gave him. He reached into a cupboard, pulled out a few animal treats and gave both of them.

"Oh, I almost forgot, she did not have any smell on her," added Squiggles.

"No smell. Like, she had just showered?" asked Brentt perplexed.

CHAPTER 27

"No. She had no smell when I was in her hands. It is like when you stick your hand out for a dog to smell you. She had no smell on her," said Squiggles, munching on the treat.

Brentt snapped back to the present and looked through the large windows. 'What kind of woman are you? Even more importantly, what are you?' He'd have to keep a close eye on Asheley.

Elainney sat in the back of Theo's truck, enveloped in an invisibility bubble. She had hitched a ride with him to make sure that he was okay. For some reason, she had a premonition that things might get a little crazy. It was better to be safe than sorry. She made herself comfortable in the back of the truck, despite the chilly air outside. She saw the proceedings through the large glass windows of the museum. She saw Asheley and Theo enjoying the party with Frank Lin. She wished she could be there with him and enjoy those things too.

Suddenly, four homeless people strode through the parking lot of the museum and loitered around the front entrance. They were behaving very odd. The vibe that came off them felt very evil and very familiar.

After a while, most of the guests were inside except for a few stragglers. Brentt did a security sweep of the front door area. He noticed four homeless people wandering in the parking lot. They looked crazed and headed straight for the front door. Normally the museum personnel would not have bothered with them, but the four homeless guys demanded food. The odor which emanated from them was overpowering.

Brentt had officers quickly bring them several plates of food. They hungrily ate in front of the security detail. When they finished, one of the men nodded, "Thanks. This food was great but I prefer something a little more appealing."

The four homeless men shoved past several officers and rushed into the building. Their strength was phenomenal as the officers tried to grapple and cuff them. Unfortunately, the four homeless guys shook off the law enforcement agents like gnats. One of the officers broke out his Taser gun and fired at one of the incredibly strong homeless guys. He hoped to quell the situation, but this just fueled the fire.

Brentt had his team herd the patrons to a safe part of the building. They were away from the scuffle but he kept the agents in view of the Gadha. More officers came to aid the few that were dealing with the homeless men. Brentt held back his Assassin Priests and Warrior Rabbis just in case. He gave his men the signal to warp their weapons of choice from their gauntlets, but keep them hidden. Soon there was a barrage of officers that drew their guns and surrounded the four homeless men.

Seeing the scuffle, Theo grabbed Asheley and Frank Lin and drew them behind a giant sarcophagus. Several other patrons and guests that broke off from the herd, dove for cover behind anything they found. About a hundred guests looked on as the four homeless men were ordered to get on the ground. Instead, a bizarre thing happened that crawled straight out of a nightmare.

The homeless men twisted and contorted in agonizing poses that no normal human should be able to do. They got on the ground, howled and screamed terrifying shrieks that sent chills down the spines of everyone there. It seemed like they were possessed, but it was much worse. The flesh of the men peeled off from the inside as claws broke free of the bodies. The officers drew back in horror and some even fired at the four. Their skins dropped to the floor and blood dripped from torn bodies. In their place, arose four fifteen-foot tall Reptilians, carrying an assortment of spiked clubs and maces.

Their normally scaly green skin was covered by the transparent Anti-Positive Energy Suits. It was evidently provided for them by the Thrice Magician, in preparation for the ensuing battle. Every inch of skin other than their faces were covered. It gave the maximum amount of defense possible from their very formidable adversaries.

CHAPTER 27

Giant, six-fingered claws attached to powerful, sinewy arms flexed themselves in anticipation of ripping through human flesh and tearing other things apart. Beady eyes stared down the officers, all of whom were now frozen with fear. Forked tongues darted out and licked barely existent lips. This was a feast ripe for the taking because they fed on fear. *There was a lot to go around.* Four giant tails whipped to and fro, slowly and deliberately. All four of the cunning monsters showed their anticipation. Six-toed feet and jointed legs, brimming with muscles, readied themselves to spring into action.

"Oh no, it's Reptilians! Officers, get everyone out of here right now!" yelled Brentt as he fired a cold blaster at the Reptilians. "Jacob, Jezebelle, we have to hold them off till everyone is safe. Keep them here in the lobby," yelled Brentt over the screech of his cold blaster. "Whatever you do, don't let them near the Gadha!"

One of the Reptilians lunged at a few of the patrons of the museum hiding behind a statue. Fierce twin fire blasts from Aleph and Baruch quickly changed his mind. He focused on them instead, crashing through a replica of the Venus de Milo to get at them. The art was replaceable but the people were not. The Priests and Rabbis opened fire from all sides with the various weapons that they had warped in, halting the advance of the gigantic Reptilians.

"Damn, I would have taken the Animal Kingdoom over these guys any day!" grunted Jacob as he fired some ice blasts at the giants. Jezebelle was herding some bystanders out of the building.

Brentt noticed there was something off about the way the Reptilians were reacting to the assault. The Priests and Rabbis did not do as much damage as they should have against the monsters. One of them took a step back in the direction of Theo, Asheley and Frank Lin as he tried to evade the barrage. He whipped his strong tail and sent chunks of whatever the sarcophagus was made out of, flying.

Unfortunately, Theo, who saw the tail coming, pushed everyone out of the way and got hit. He went sprawling right into a glass case that broke open. A thirteen-foot long, very ornate, double-edged broad sword with a black and red blade almost fell on him. That was the opening that the Reptilians needed to switch on full berserker mode.

One of the four giants shouted orders in Chtultu, which is their native language, "Qi, Sen, Tza, split up and divide the enemy. I will go for the artifact."

"Yes, squad leader Zu. Long live the Unity!" shouted one of the others.

They split up and two of them drew the incoming barrage from the Rabbis and Priests towards the statuary. The third retreated to the front door, where Jacob and Jezebelle followed. Brentt was left with the leader and he did not back down an inch.

"You're not getting this. Go home empty-handed to the Count. What does he want with this anyways? It's some old relic of the past," small talked Brentt.

"The Immortal Count is very powerful and very generous. He gives us what we want and we give him what he wants," the scaly giant said in a surprisingly controlled and husky voice. He followed it up with a vicious left-hand cross that missed Brentt's head by inches. Brentt noticed that he did not strike with his spiked mace, which would have been the more logical thing to do.

Nonetheless, Brentt was surprised that they moved faster than the previous times he had fought them. Their initial assault had shown no indication of enhanced speed, but now they got down to business. He dodged ferocious left jabs and crosses, meanwhile blasting the giant with his cold blaster at every opening. Yet still, the giant did not swing the spiked mace.

The great beast turned and gathered up a statue with his long tail and hurled it at the detective, who expertly maneuvered out of the way. In the process, Brentt warped his Mortar Round Beast Cutter Giant Broad Blade to the scene. He was going to save it till the last minute, but it seemed like a good enough time now.

The total size of the weapon was eight feet long. It had an insanely sharp edge on one side that went all the way down and only halfway on the other side. This was because the handguard contained a mortar that fired five shots each of ice, lightning, Greek fire, smoke and 'cement'. The handgrip was eighteen inches long with a six-inch square weight at the bottom. This weight was equivalent to that of the whole sword, which balanced it during battle. There was also a secondary grip on the blunt side of the sword, which was used to steady the weapon when it fired.

The sword was crazy bad. Like it was stolen at knifepoint from a demon pawnshop, bad. Like it chopped the car in half that cut you off on the freeway, bad. Like, Reptilians pissed their pants when they see it, bad.

"There it is. The great blade which had many a Reptilian quake in their skin is now in front of me. I have been waiting for this. I have been practicing many months with worthy adversaries, all of whom fell before my might. When I got the word that we would be on this mission, I prayed for your presence here. I will peel the skin off your body. I will fillet you and dip you in barbeque sauce. Not the runny kind, but the really thick and mesquite tasting stuff."

"You talk too much," Brentt said as he launched an attack at the giant's legs.

He blocked the sword with his mace, which was electrically charged. Brentt felt the energy coursing through him, but it did not dull his wits. The scaly beast came in with a left jab but Brentt fired on the fist with his cold blaster, while he fended off the mace with his right hand. They broke the melee and the Reptilian ferociously brought the mace down on him with both hands. Brentt easily blocked the blow, but it sent him to his knees as the giant pressed the mace against his sword. He shrugged it off and continued to parry with the monster, both gaining and losing ground.

Priceless paintings and various antiques were collaterally damaged from the hits and misses that each combatant launched at each other. In his intercoms, Brentt heard the commotion from the others at various points around the museum complex. He quickly pocketed the blaster, gathered up a positive energy burst from his body and channeled it through his right hand.

"I like the threads, but too bad you'll have to clean your blood off it soon!" He fired into the midsection of the Reptilian.

CHAPTER 27

The blast should have severely injured the monster, but it had no effect. The giant went in for a tail swipe, which connected ferociously. It sent Brentt into a display of some ancient Egyptian stuff. The creature capitalized and was soon clawing at Brentt who was just barely able to dodge the razor claws. It ripped through a Caravaggio, tore through a Monet and decimated a Van Goh, to get to him. Brentt tried another frenzied burst of positive energy, right in the face. This one did the trick, but it was not the show stopper.

"Everyone, the suits are blocking our positive energy blasts. They are also faster and stronger than last time! Be careful!" he radioed to the rest of the team.

"We just figured that out a minute ago," a frenzied shout from Luke came over the radio.

"Aleph, Baruch, keep that wall up. The Reptilians are getting antsy here. We'll make sure you are safe!" Mary reassured the Rabbi Warriors.

The others were doing fine, for now, thought Brentt, as he raised his sword and readied for a frontal assault. He jumped a giant leap into the air and went to cut himself a big slice of Reptilian cake.

The dexterous tail of the creature caught him in mid-jump and Brentt's sword clattered to the ground. The creature's left hand found a steel beam that had fallen during the fight and picked it up. He glanced down at the legendary sword on the ground, and then menacingly looked at the detective with a big grin on his face.

"Looks like that sword will not drink any of my blood today! I will have to clear out space in my trophy room for it. I might even use it in battle if I deem it worthy," laughed the Reptilian.

Brentt looked down at his sword and then smiled back at the creature. The cold blaster that he had pocketed was now pointed straight down the throat of the giant lizard. It went off. The last dying gurgle of the Reptilian squad leader Zu, was flash-frozen in ice.

Hearing that bit of unpleasantness, Theo, Asheley and Frank Lin took this opportunity to get out of the way. Theo, for some reason, grabbed the sword that had almost sent him on another trip to heaven. They ran towards the parking lot, where Jacob and Jezebelle were having their own troubles. Seeing the giant beast, the trio hid behind a pedestal that had once displayed a replica of the statue of David, but it was now just his legs.

The great beast, Tza, threw high-end cars everywhere. Undoubtedly, most insurance companies did not have a 'got tossed around by giant Reptilians' policy in their plan. Jezebelle was under a shield made by Jacob as the giant beast brought down a large, ultra-high-end SUV. She knew the barrier would hold. She trusted her husband's bioelectric aura. She gathered all of the nearby broken glass and planned to give the giant a glass shower.

Brentt came up behind Theo just as Jezebelle rained down a ton of broken glass upon the beast. It ripped through his suit and skin, sending splatters of blood on vehicles that went unmolested during their fight. A big shard lodged itself in the eye of the reptilian. As he shrieked in agony, he flailed his spiked club around as if to stop the rain but there was no respite.

Theo pulled Asheley closer with his right hand to shield her from any debris that might fly toward her. The ridiculously large sword lay to his left. Finally, after a death scene worthy of an award, the lizard fell forward with a terrific thud upon a truck that happened to be Theo's.

"Awe man, I just waxed my truck. The insurance will not cover this!" he exclaimed.

"Yeah, my sports car is totaled too. It was a present from my parents. I was going to go out with a model tomorrow night and I planned to use that car!" Frank Lin said dejectedly.

"All right, you all need to get out of here. Go somewhere safe. Theo, I don't know why you grabbed that, but leave it here," said Brentt as he rushed to help the others.

Their battle cries were heard at the other end of the museum. Jacob and Jezebelle rushed past them and pointed in the direction that they should go. Frank Lin nodded as they ran off to join Brentt and the others. As the trio came out from behind the pedestal, they had to pass the body of the Reptilian. It was not a pretty sight. Asheley, Theo and Frank Lin stopped in front of the scaly beast and stared at the body. The glass had penetrated the

CHAPTER 27

suit and blood seeped from all of his wounds. He was huge. Never in his life did Theo think that such creatures existed before. Asheley stood there for a minute as she scanned the creature. She turned and shouted, "Get back, he's still alive!"

The terrible creature sprang up with such speed, that anyone else would not have had time to react. However, this was Asheley, an Artificially Intelligent Robotic Entity, who had insane reflexes. The Reptilian pounced upon her and rammed his giant spiked club down. She caught it with amazing strength and held the beast back for Theo and Frank Lin to escape. Theo gripped the big sword, which he had not yet put down and went forward to aid her. He sliced at the giant legs of the beast and it momentarily broke his attention from Asheley.

Frank Lin, seeing the danger, summoned all of his inner spiritual strength with some deep arm movements and chanted. His decades of training at the monastery readied him for this moment in life. He controlled his breath and forced all of his spiritual power into a wave that knocked back the great beast.

Theo moved with a speed that he never knew he had. The great sword which almost killed him became an extension of his hand. The creature came in for a second blow and was blocked by Theo wielding the blade effortlessly. Needless to say, all three were surprised at each other's newly found strengths.

The giant turned for a tail swipe but Theo cut through the suit and skin like a superheated knife through melted butter. The sword clanged upon the asphalt with such force, that it left an impact crater.

The angered Reptilian viciously swung the spiked club at Theo and would have connected, but he felt another spirit wave from Frank Lin. Asheley, seeing an opening, leaped up and sent a left uppercut home. She barely got back on the ground as the maddened lizard launched a frenzied haymaker. Tza swung the club wildly and Theo got in front of Asheley to parry the blow.

The lizard bent real close to Theo and whispered, "I am going to eat you first." Asheley pulled out an ax that apparently had been in the wide handle of the sword. She cut the lizard's left arm off without hesitation. The beast screamed in agony, but he did not let up as he came in for one final attack.

CHAPTER 27

The sword felt great in Theo's hands. It was as if he had been a samurai in a previous life or a great warrior. He held the weapon up to examine it more closely. The blade was broad, a lot broader than the blade of the detective and a lot longer too. It was thirteen feet long. In fact, it was so big that it had two hand grips, one at the bottom and one about four feet further up. It did have the space for the ax that Asheley had pulled out. Theo did not notice it, even though he carried the weapon. The carvings on the blade looked like some long-forgotten language. Now that he thought about it, they looked like the ones on the door of the Akashic Records Library. The blade guard was curved and it looked like it held four, three-foot-long daggers, two on each side.

The middle of the sword was thick and it tapered out to a fine edge as it went. The edge was out of this world. He studied the lines and the intricacies of the craftsmanship and saw that it had other hidden weapons inside it. There were two six-foot-long Nodachis on the top side of the blade. Apparently, the thick edge served as a sheath for the weapons.

In addition, there were four serrated, six-foot-long, one-sided broad swords that were magnetized to the main blade. Their handles were higher than where the secondary handle for the sword was. This made the smaller swords easier to detach. There was an insignia just before the secondary hand grip which contained nine stones. There was a diamond, an emerald, a ruby, an onyx, a sapphire, a purple amethyst, white quartz, yellow topaz, and light blue turquoise. At the bottom, was a twelve by twelve by eighteen-inch block that held the weight of the sword. It acted as a counterweight, to give the sword balance.

Who would design such a sword? For some reason, this 'black sword' felt familiar. It felt like it was connected to him. When he gripped it, the letters glowed. It reflected the passion that he felt. It seemed to magnify the passion he felt to protect Asheley and Frank Lin.

Theo mechanically sliced through the Reptilian, even before the beast knew what hit him. It was not an even slice down the middle, but it did the trick. Blood and guts spilled all over the place but none was on the sword. Theo swung the great sword around as if it were a baton from a marching band. He felt the connection to it. It felt good. It felt exhilarating to swing it. Frank Lin came towards Asheley and Theo.

"Asheley, that was incredible! How did you do that?" asked Frank Lin.

"I was just protecting Theo and you," she said with a smile.

"Theo, you just went up against a fifteen-foot tall Reptilian! How?" said Frank Lin, still shocked.

"I personally don't know how I did that," said Theo, looking intently at the sword.

"Theo? Are you serious? We all fought a monster!" said Frank Lin, stunned. He walked around in disbelief. "Oh man, this is a cool story to tell at parties, but no one would ever believe me!"

"Theo, how are you able to so easily wield a thirteen hundred pound sword?" asked Asheley puzzled.

"The sword does not feel that heavy. It just feels, like a part of my arm," said Theo raising the weapon. "Frank Lin, what was that? The thing you fired at the monster?"

"I used my monastic training to summon my spiritual energy. I wanted to save you both. They teach us that we have energy inside of ourselves. We can channel it for different uses," explained the monk. "I never thought I could do it before. I guess I needed to be in the right situation."

Elainney leaned against a tree amidst the chaos and invisible to the combatants. She had a big smile on her face. She had just witnessed Theo access some of his long lost powers. She was also impressed with the prowess of Asheley and Frank Lin. When it came time to explain to Theo about his past, maybe this might help reinforce the idea that he was a great warrior. After all, he was wielding the sword that belonged to him.

CHAPTER 28: John And The Museum Gets Turned To Nothing

There were people everywhere. Luckily, John and Catherine had a reserved booth, thanks to his no-good father. It was near the museum, which was a prime location to sit and see the parade. John's father was one of those parents that tried to mold his progeny into what his vision of a great child should entail. He had expectations too high for anyone to achieve, even his perfect kids. He was a philanderer, in which his one night stands laid waste to the countless hearts of women. Sometimes, his father was good for a favor, like borrowing money or getting out of legal trouble. Mostly, he was disappointed in his son. His father was disappointed that John threw his life away and did not get into the family business. Well, one thing is for sure, the booth that he provided was top notch.

There were parents here with their kids. There were people waiting in the streets from the night before and even before that. John never did any of this with his father. John's dad was too busy having him trained in martial arts and having him take college courses while he was still in high school. John's father pushed him to do things he did not want to do and in a direction, he did not want to go. John's mother had enough and left, but kept coming back for money.

Money, it's the thing that got you what you wanted. The more of it you have, the more it held power over you. His father had lots of money, but unlike most people, it did not control him. He used his money to control other people. John decided that he would not be like this to Katie or his other child. No, he would be different. He would be better. He would be better after he killed Theo, though.

CHAPTER 28

The water he drank made him want to use the toilet. He excused himself from Catherine and went to find it. He could not stop smiling all morning because of the resolution that he had made. The resolution stirred up hate in his heart. Hate for the man that he thought ruined his life, Theo.

The bathroom was quiet and he took to a stall. In mid-pee, he heard a noise that startled him. It sounded like four giant dudes dropped in from the ceiling. He saw the tops of their heads from the stall. They looked like goths and smelled horrible. They looked hungry. Their features were nondescript, even though he was looking right at them. They looked over the stall and John turned around and yelled, "Get out of here you perverts. I am peeing. You have never seen a big..."

That was as far as he got before one of the guys reached over the stall and grabbed him by the collar. He loosed his bowels in the air and peed on them as they held him up to face them. Their eyes were pitch-black and the four seemed unmoved by the pee that streamed on them. John had a very bad feeling about this, but he was already peeing himself.

"I feel the hate inside of you. I feel the seed of violence will sprout and grow into a strong and fertile tree of destruction. You love and hate at the same time. There cannot be room for both in this universe," said the person, who was about eight-feet tall, with a voice that was soft but with many voices.

"What are you talking about? How do you know what I hate?" said a scared John.

"When there is nothing, then there is nothing to hate and love. Where there is nothing there is no hate and love," said one of the others, picking up from where the first left off.

"What are you going to do to me? Put me down," replied a struggling John.

"Nothing is everything and everything is nothing. All is one and all are nothing. Come; get rid of your love and hate. Get rid of your life and death. Come, and be filled with nothing!" said one of the frighteningly tall guys as he put his forehead up to John's.

The frontal lobe of his head throbbed and a tingling sensation rushed through his brain. It was not really a headache, but it just

CHAPTER 28

pulsed. He felt his mind's eye open in his head, which multiplied his senses a hundredfold. His heart quickened and he could feel the blood rushing to all of his body. He felt every nerve, both inside and outside of his body. He felt each of the individual blood cells as they inched their way inside him. He could feel his heartbeat through his chest.

He was in darkness inside his head, a dreaded darkness that encompassed him and clothed him. It was dreadful at first, but the darkness just wrapped around him. Slowly, he started to fear it less and less. It warmed him, coddled him, and *infiltrated* him. His mind and body slowly accepted the darkness, as it made its way through his being. He could feel himself *exuding it like torrential rain.*

He could hear one of the Gothic dudes' voices in his mind, "Because you have hate and death in your heart, hate and death shall be a part of your body as well. You will feast on everything that is dead within your sight. It shall be a part of you. You shall take that energy as it were your own. It will nourish and sustain you. It will make you stronger. With that strength, you shall hate more until there is nothing."

He opened his eyes and saw Theo and Asheley about sixty feet away. They were among some destroyed cars. His rage suddenly flared at the man that still held the heart of the woman of his dreams. John had no idea how he ended up in the parking lot of the museum and did not really care. All he knew, was that he was hungrier to kill Theo than when he started the day. He hurried through the parking lot of the museum, towards his destiny. He saw the divided body of the Reptilian laying there on the pavement, its entrails still hot.

"John, what are you doing here? You need to go, it's too dangerous. Is Catherine with you? Is she safe?" inquired Theo.

"Catherine's fine. She's in a booth enjoying the parade. So this is what you're up to, huh?" John said nonchalantly.

"These things attacked us. We killed this one, but there are more. They are attacking the museum. We need to get out of here," Theo warned.

"No. This is perfect! This scenario is the most perfect way of me taking care of you and no one will ever know," John said with a devious smile.

"John, what are you talking about? I am getting a weird feeling from you," said Theo.

"I am getting a weird vibe from your buddy, Theo. He is giving off a massive amount of evil that is just freaking me out," remarked Frank Lin.

"You know, Catherine yelled your name while we were making love on New Year's Eve. I thought that she was through with you. I thought that knowing Katie was not yours would extinguish the love that she had for you. But it did not. Somehow, you still have her heart captive and I am going to set it free!" John vehemently yelled.

"John, I moved on. I have Asheley. I want to see you guys happy," he said as he moved towards Asheley and Frank Lin to shield them.

"I had to hide my love for her. I had to sneak around in the shadows, while you enjoyed her openly. Her parents loved you like their own son. They accepted you and I did not have that. I had to hide my feelings for Catherine and that burned me. I envied you for what you had. Even when I took everything away, she still would not let go of you!" John burned, pointing and emoting at Theo.

"Watch out Theo, he has foreign matter in his body," yelled Asheley.

Just then, John began convulsing and seizing. Suddenly, he put out both hands and the carcass of the dead Reptilian started moving towards John, by itself. John's hands grew larger and great gaping maws opened up in his palms. It sported razor-sharp teeth and a wicked-looking tongue. The giant lizard's feet were the first to be masticated by the monstrosity on John's palms.

Theo, Asheley, and Frank Lin heard the crunching of bones and the squelching of tissues. The sounds made them shudder and shrink back from the lover of Theo's ex-wife. John smiled and shuddered in delight as the second half of the body slid towards its destination. Soon, it too was pulverized and digested, suit and all, by the palms of John. He had a frenzied look in his

CHAPTER 28

eyes as he set his sights on Theo. The Reptilian's spiked club was on the ground and John picked it up with ease. The smile on John's face widened and he licked his lips with a forked tongue.

The battle heated up in the museum, as the Assassin Priests and the Warrior Rabbis held off the two remaining reptilians. Brentt, Jacob and Jezebelle came in to assist the group, who definitely held their own. Aleph and Baruch had done a great job in using their bioelectric energies to keep the wall up, which protected the parade-goers. Jezebelle and Jacob jumped in and assisted them, immediately strengthening the fortification and extending it out a little further.

Brentt went for the assist by firing a cold blast at one of the Reptilians. One wall of the museum had been broken down and the giant Gadha was in the eyesight of the valiant warriors. However, it was just out of reach of the giant lizards.

Brentt saw something out of the corner of his eye, as he aimed for another shot at the two remaining Reptilians. Four, eight-foot-tall, nondescript, gothic-looking dudes walked nonchalantly to the Gadha. He could not make out their features, even though his eyesight was spectacular, owing to his being hyper-human. He had a bad feeling about this. He felt his stomach churn as they got closer.

He radioed everyone else, "I am going to the Gadha. It looks like we have more company."

"Hey, boss-man you need back up?" Jacob asked.

"Yes, I have a bad feeling about this," he replied worriedly.

The closer that he and Jacob moved to the guys, the more the darkness and bad vibes overpowered them. It was as if you were walking in a cemetery on Halloween night, your cell phone battery died and you just heard shrieks in the darkness. The full moon that was out, went behind some clouds and you come across some blood splatters and intestines that feel squelchy under your shoes. They felt like that, except a thousand times worse.

CHAPTER 28

"Hello. You guys need to get out of here. It is dangerous. Go back outside," Brentt said authoritatively. However, he had a feeling that his words were futile.

All of the smelly Gothic looking men spoke in unison, the voice of four sounding like the voices of many, "Nothing is everything and everything is nothing. All is one and all are nothing."

"Who are you and why are you here?" asked Jacob.

"I existed before the light. For before the light there was darkness. I existed before the darkness. For before the darkness there was nothing."

"What the hell are you talking about? Get out of here now. I am not going to ask you again!" spoke Brentt sternly.

One of the eight-foot-tall Gothic looking men ignored the detective and kept walking to the Gadha. Brentt outstretched the giant sword in front of him to block the Goth's progress. He looked at the detective and suddenly, the detective flew across the floor as if someone punched him in the face. Luckily, Brentt had a big, hard chin because he really felt that one. He quickly got to his feet as the startled Jacob looked on.

"Shield it and look out!" yelled Brentt.

In a split second, Jacob put up a shield over the Gadha and in front himself, as he readied for anything that might come his way. Brentt swung the great sword in an arc that would have sliced the Goth from head to toe, but the enigmatic man, or whatever he was, blocked it with his mind.

Brentt's anger rose and so did his bioelectric field intensity. His body produced an aura that pulled and tugged on the heavens and the very earth under his feet. The atmosphere grew soupy and heavy with the weight of the world bearing down upon them. Gravity seemed to buckle and bear hug everyone within close proximity to Brentt.

Jacob, who fortified his shields even more, was surprised at the power of his comrade. The Reptilians, Warrior Rabbis, and the Assassin Priests felt the change in the atmosphere as they momentarily ceased their activities. They looked on in awe at the display of power by Brentt.

CHAPTER 28

Paintings, statues and other things crumpled with the twin onslaughts of the atmosphere and gravity. The super-expensive tiles cracked as they were broken by the intensity of Brentt's powerful bioelectric field.

The other three Goths walked away and turned to the Gadha as if nothing was happening. Brentt saw them and redoubled his efforts. Hundreds of tendrils made of electric energy wrapped around the Goths and stopped them in their tracks. The atmosphere and the earth continued to buckle and bend to the will of detective Brentt Williams.

Theo, Frank Lin, and Asheley had their own problems in the form of a supercharged and super-evil John. He continued to attack them with vicious ferocity. He intended to pummel them with the spiked club that he picked up from the ingested Reptilian.

"You won't get out of this alive, Theo. Catherine will forget you. Katie will forget you. Surprisingly, I will remember you because I will relish how I killed you," cackled John as he picked up Theo's totaled truck and pelted it at him. Theo easily dodged it.

Theo raised the great sword and came in for an attack. John blocked it with the mace and sneered, a bubbling, saliva-filled smile. He pushed Theo back. Frank Lin fired a spirit wave that pushed John back. Asheley supported it with a right cross, then a few left jabs, followed by a right hook, then a left uppercut. It was a barrage that was worthy of a prizefighter. This drove John back and maddened him at the same time. He seemed unaffected by the attacks of the trio and came at them more vehemently.

"Asheley, Frank Lin and I will hold him off. I need you to scan him and see if there are any weaknesses at all. We need to neutralize him," stated Theo.

"What do you mean scan?" asked Frank Lin.

"I'll explain later," Theo answered. He blocked the incoming John and proceeded to battle him anew.

CHAPTER 28

"Oh my God, what the hell is that? I feel like there is something very wrong!" Frank Lin said to Asheley.

"There is a rise in the atmospheric pressure coming from inside the museum. In addition, there is a gravitational distortion which is actually increasing the force of gravity on objects," she surmised as she looked toward the museum. Frank Lin noticed that her eyes focused and changed color. He drew back and wondered what was going on.

"Who or what is doing that?" asked an awed Frank Lin.

"The distortion is caused by Brentt Williams. His bioelectric aura is so powerful that it is warping the atmosphere and gravity. He is using that mechanism to assist him in defeating the four Gothic looking entities inside. They have some of the same properties that are present in John. There are materials found inside them that I cannot place, nor could I find anything like it in the *Secret Periodic Table*," said Asheley to a dumbfounded Frank Lin.

"How are you doing this?" asked the bewildered monk.

"Don't tell anyone, but I am an Artificially Intelligent Robotic Entity built by Theo."

"That explains a lot," mused Frank Lin. "How do we help Theo?"

"I need to create a gravity encasement that will slow John down. A fifty-foot radius should suffice. I was examining how detective Brentt Williams is manipulating his bioelectric field and I will duplicate it.

I also managed to scan the weapon that Theo is using. The sword has a lightning emitter inside. Theo must activate it by pressing the quartz and aiming the sword at John. This will immobilize him while he is under the strain of gravity. Theo has to lure John here and fire the lightning. Other than that, I do not have any more information to stop him," explained Asheley.

"I hope that works. He looks like he needs our help. I'll move out the way and let you do your thing. Are you going to be okay?"

"I will be okay Frank Lin. Because I am the one creating the field," said Asheley.

CHAPTER 28

Frank Lin moved out of the way and turned to go help his friend, Theo. He took one last look back and felt the earth and sky bending to the will of Asheley.

CHAPTER 29: The Thrice Magician Pulls A Disappearing Act

T he sun shone hot but the air was chilly as Tris Megistus and six Big-Foot soldiers sat on the rooftop of the building abreast of the museum. They were five stories up and had a bird's-eye view of the parade below. Megistus created a cloaking bubble, which hid their presence from the unwashed masses. They were here since before dawn.

They arrived on an antique Persian flying carpet, courtesy of Megistus. It was fifty feet wide and a hundred feet long, very similar to Solomon's, except this was faster. He lovingly took great care of his rides. However, he felt that after this mission, he might have to vacuum out Big-Foot soldier hairs and give the carpet a good washing.

The soldiers busied themselves playing cards and gambling away their various snacks and drinks. Megistus knew how antsy they got and had packed food for them in readiness for a long day.

"Hey, you are cheating! You have a card in your trunks!" yelled a greenish-brown, fur-covered Big-Foot soldier named Avocado.

"That's why it is called Bad Man's poker, idiot! You are allowed one card to cheat with!" answered a small, greenish, furry Sasquatch called Cucumber.

"Then why don't we know about it?" asked a red-brown colored one, aptly called Redwood.

"Because you are not supposed to let people know that you are cheating. If you do, then it isn't cheating. It's just plain wrong," lectured Cucumber.

CHAPTER 29

Redwood broke open and gulped down a can of soda that he had placed on the poker bet. He carelessly threw the can off the roof.

"Hey! Be careful where you are throwing those things, you imbecile! We need to keep a low profile," yelled Megistus at the Big-Foot soldiers.

They looked at him and grumbled something in a Native American language. Then in unison, they nodded their heads.

Megistus had a decent line up of soldiers today. There was the big, red-brown Redwood, who was the alpha male of the group. Baobab, a fifteen-foot tall, brown Sasquatch, was the beta male. Cypress was also fifteen-feet tall with black and brown mottled fur. He loved playing in fountains, puddles and anything water-related in general.

There was Mango, who stood ten-feet tall but sported an attitude that made him think he was fifty-feet tall. His fur was an orange-green color, like that of a half-ripe mango. His brother, Avocado, had a greenish tint to his fur as well. He liked candy and it always made him hyper.

Cucumber was the last on the squad and sometimes he could be a real cucumber-head. However, he was the smartest of the group, albeit the smallest, coming in at nine feet and eleven inches, which he made up with thick-soled hiking boots.

After gambling their hearts out, they sat quietly and enjoyed the parade, but Megistus knew that they were patiently waiting to throw it down with the Assassin Priests and the Warrior Rabbis.

The parade was actually not that bad. Some of the concepts of the floats were great and the craftsmanship, excellent. However, the parade was not why he was there. It was the Gadha of Gilgamesh. Gilgamesh used the weapon to fend off all of the beings that tried to board his ark during *one of the great floods*. It was given to him because he was a just person in a wicked world. Unfortunately, things like that did not happen anymore. The good and law-abiding citizens are given nothing and what they have, are taken away by crooked people. *However, sometimes without the right knowledge, most people do not know that they are being fooled.* Megistus pushed that thought from his mind.

CHAPTER 29

He had been in the service of The Immortal Count for close to four thousand years. He had never come across anyone like him. He was a vastly superior being in physique, intelligence, and spiritual prowess.

Yet still, after thousands of years, he could not fathom the Count's master plan. The Count thought that detective Brentt Williams might be a worthy nemesis and ultimately, an ally to him. However, when Megistus faced Brentt in the past, he did not get that feeling. He admitted that Brentt's wit was quick and his battle prowess very impressive, but Megistus did not know how he was beaten last time.

That would not happen again, because everyone will know the power of the Thrice Magician. He looked at his staff, which he had with him. His great gilded staff, that stood eight-feet tall, was embossed with ancient inscriptions and magical spells. The top had the biggest rainbow diamond that one could fit on a staff. The stone was one of a kind, mined from the deepest parts of hell by an unwilling slave of his. He lovingly called it 'The Might of Megistus'. This will surely bring that pathetic detective and his self-righteous band of misfits to their knees. This encounter was payback for him having lost the emerald tablets.

He saw when the four Reptilians entered the building and when they morphed into their original forms. It was a great battle indeed. They divided Brentt and his cohorts just like he had planned. The suits the Reptilians got from research and development really did deflect most of the damages from their foes. He saw the destruction of the building and the havoc that they created. One of the Reptilians outside played dead and three people he did not recognize managed to kill him. That was disappointing because Megistus personally oversaw the gene-editing process that was supposed to have made them stronger. He'll have to fix that when he went back to The Immortal Count's Palace of Palaces and Castle of Castles.

Suddenly, Megistus felt an overwhelming sense of dread and doom. He had never felt anything like this in his existence. It was a dread that sought to consume and overpower you. He dealt with dark entities before, but none of them gave off the vibe that he felt now. He looked around to see and feel where the

CHAPTER 29

sensation came from. It made him sick to his stomach and beyond, as he searched for the origin.

He noticed that the spectators of the parade had gotten the feeling as well. They were jumpy and fidgeted, as they unknowingly felt pure evil. They looked around and readied themselves, as if for a violent outburst. He observed the Big-Foot soldiers as they paced the rooftop, growling and grunting. They were trying to force the evil feeling away.

Finally, he saw four, eight-foot-tall Gothic dudes as they walked to the front door of the museum. A fifth guy strode to the three in the parking lot. The fifth guy looked out of place and the evil that surrounded him was not as strong as that of the other four. Megistus would have to pay close attention to this new development. The aura that the Goths gave off was phenomenally evil. It was a wave of darkness he had never felt before. For the first time in his life, he felt terrified. Megistus saw them walk into the museum and in a few minutes, it seemed like the gates of hell broke open.

He felt a wave of power come over him. A power which he had not felt since The Immortal Count subjugated the Gang Crew Club Syndicate. It was amazing. It felt awesome and terrible at the same time. He did not believe his six senses. This was coming from the vicinity of the detective and his cohorts. Megistus felt the earth and sky as it buckled to the will of the detective. He sensed that it mixed with the evil auras from the Goths and wondered who would win.

He turned his attentions to the activity in the parking lot and wondered who the two men and the woman were. He had not encountered them before. He saw that the man with the bad vibes ingested the remnants of the Reptilian, including the suit, as if it were a bowl of ice cream on a hot day.

The gaping maws, which sprouted from John's hands, reminded him of some of the entities that he had done business with in the past. Tris Megistus looked on in amazement as he proceeded to fight the others after some ridiculous pre-fight banter. It was an intense, hate-filled battle that needed to end in bloodshed.

CHAPTER 29

Presently, he felt the power coming from the woman as she used her bioelectric field to manipulate the air and gravity around her. He quickly turned to his squad of Big-Foot soldiers.

"Big-Foot soldiers, go get the Gadha! Kill anyone in your way! Do as much destruction as you want. I just want that weapon!" Tris Megistus yelled.

All six Big-Foot soldiers jumped from the rooftop and landed with a terrific thud upon the ground below. All six of them had yellowed, toothy smiles that turned into bloodlust growls as they sprinted to their prize. They crashed through what was left of the giant windows and barreled over any art pieces that stood in their way. They saw the four gothic-looking dudes with the bad vibes and funky smell coming off of them. All six raced towards them with rabid savagery and overzealous joy. They seemed more excited about the fight than for their mission.

Suddenly, they were hit by the seemingly invisible wall of atmosphere and gravity, courtesy of Brentt Williams. The powerful bioelectric field greatly slowed their advance but they still inched their way towards the Gadha and the four Goths.

Brentt watched as the Big-Foot soldiers entered the area and pounced upon the four Gothic guys. They pummeled them and clawed at their non-descript faces and bodies. The four Goths did nothing to deter the Sasquatches but continued to plow on to the Gadha. Fortunately, it was encased in a shield created by Jacob. An almost ten-foot-tall, furry foot soldier spied Brentt and menacingly lunged for him. He was overtaken by a tendril of bioelectric power that sprouted from Brentt.

The Warrior Rabbis and Assassin Priests realized that Brentt and Jacob needed help on the double. They tried to quickly dispatch the two remaining Reptilians, Qi and Sen.

"Looks like your buddies came to your rescue," taunted Mark, the businessman with his own robotics company. He fired a few rounds of his laser blaster, which the creature avoided with ease.

"We do not know them but, I fear they are here for our prize," replied Qi in English.

"Leave them be. Let us get what we came for and then get out of here. Tza and Zu are dead. Their leader is in trouble. They will no doubt, go to help him. In addition, the Thrice Magician has

CHAPTER 29

sent Big-Foot soldiers to help. I feel that these new Goths will take care of our problem," said Sen to his teammate.

Both turned tail and leaped away from the Priests and Rabbis. They were hell-bent on getting their prize before things got worse. Brentt's friends followed and tried to fathom what their leader had gotten himself into.

The three other Gothic guys, that had Sasquatches on their backs, soon made their way to Jacob's shield. They threw a punch in unison, which echoed through the museum and was heard by the crowds of people outside. The shield barely held.

Gothic guy #2 grabbed two handfuls of hair from Redwood, who had sunk his claws into his back and brought him down with a loud thud. Brentt's tendrils strained to keep the Goths immobilized. Gothic guy #2 crushed the windpipe of the furry soldier with ease and threw the dead weight through the wall of the museum. It broke through the defensive shield put up by Aleph, Baruch and Jezebelle. The body landed on a very colorful float that showed cartoon characters from a very popular show dancing in harmony. Screams of disgust and terror were heard as thousands of people looked on and some started to flee. A good majority of people took out their cell phones and recorded the terrifying event.

"Oh no, they have broken through the wall!" Mary yelled. She struggled to help the others bring it back up with her own bioelectric field. They spoke too soon, as the body of another Sasquatch burst through the wall, this time, of Mango. His body was bent and distorted into an unnatural state, courtesy of Gothic guy #3.

"Aleph, Baruch, Mary, forget the wall. We got to get to Brentt and Jacob!" yelled Joshua as he ran by.

Meanwhile, Gothic guy #1, who had used his mind to stop Brentt from bringing his blade down, reached out with a right hand and got Brentt in a vice grip around his head. He gripped the giant sword in his left hand and stopped it from swinging wildly. Brentt mustered all of his energy into a blast which had no effect upon this curious foe. The heaviness of the gravity and the atmosphere alleviated a little, as the grip on Brentt's head tightened. He was losing consciousness and soon he was going to die.

Brentt escaped into his mind, which was surprisingly calm and peaceful. He was on a beach and sipped a soda with lots of ice under a cabana. He watched himself rise up out of the ocean. Fresh beads of clear seawater gleamed all over his skin. 'I do not remember myself being this ripped and chiseled', Brentt thought to himself. The Brentt from the ocean strode to the Brentt that was sitting in the cabana. There was a cola with an iceberg that waited for the wet Brentt. They sat in silence, each enjoying the sights, sounds, and smells of the ocean. The Brentt that came out of the ocean broke the silence first.

"You and I both know that these bad guys are nothing like you have ever faced before. You have to call upon the power of the Nine to help you reach your ascended form," said the Brentt from the ocean.

"I don't believe in them."

"I don't think that it matters if you do or you don't. They will still exist even if you don't exist. But there is nothing to stop you from using the power of the universe around you. From dipping into their power that resides in everything that was ever created. Everyone needs you."

"How do I do so?" Brentt asked, reluctantly.

"I call upon the power that binds everything in the universe together. The power that was present from the beginning. The power of the One from which all comes. My free will is in peril and I willingly receive this power from everything around me to become my higher self. I will ascend to a more perfect state. I want to ascend to a higher density and be one step closer to a perfect union with the universe. I call upon the power of the Nine which binds the universe together. Lend me your power so that which was established before the beginning will be."

CHAPTER 29

Jacob saw the two Reptilians coming at him from the corner of his eye and tried his best to fortify the shields. The punch by the three Goths took a lot of energy to deflect and he was not sure if he could hold out much longer.

The Goths ripped apart the Big-Foot soldiers and threw their pieces into the street. Baobab and Cypress saw their limbs hit the parade floats before their bodies. A giant, furry, right leg landed on a family of three, killing them instantly. Soon the Big-Foot soldiers' heads followed and landed among a field of roses displayed on a passing float. Their eyes admired the delicate petals and the intricate craftsmanship that went into creating the float for about seven seconds. Their nostrils were filled with the scent of lovely perfumed flowers as they died.

Jacob's teammates arrived and immediately started blasting anything that moved. The two Reptilians scrambling for the Gadha were not in the least way spared. Jezebelle helped Jacob strengthen the shield around the weapon.

The others fired on the four Gothic dudes and Sasquatches without distinction. Avocado had his head burnt to a crisp by the twin fire blasts from Aleph and Baruch. He fell to the floor and was quickly chewed up by the blasts from several other Rabbis. Cucumber, who was now free from the tendrils of Brentt, let out a giant-sized roar and went after the still unconscious detective.

He stopped short as he felt something in the middle of his chest. It was a small hole that grew bigger and bigger as he saw what the inside of his chest looked like. Zechariah, Hezekiah, and Shalom decided that they needed to make a wall to section off the Big-Foot's head and torso from the rest of his body. Soon, the furry soldier was cut in three.

He lay there dying and watched a revitalized and renewed Brentt Williams punch through the arm of the Gothic dude that was crushing his head.

CHAPTER 29

Tris Megistus levitated to the ground with his great staff in hand and quietly watched the proceedings from a good vantage point. He was hidden from the view of the others by a spell of unseeing. His Big-Foot soldiers were decimated and there were two Reptilians left. However, there were four Gothic dudes and a bunch of good guys in his way of getting the Gadha. Not to mention, there was a lady that tore up gravity and three other guys that fought in the parking lot. He stood there and contemplated for a minute about what to do.

He watched the renewed conflict between the Assassin Priests and Warrior Rabbis versus the Goths and Reptilians. He saw the powerful punch that Brentt had landed upon the non-descript face of the Gothic guy. Brentt overpowered them and thrashed them good. He doled out lefts, rights, and kicks that sent the Goths into shock. He picked up his legendary blade and fired a few cement mortar rounds at one of the Goths. The shot encased the creature in a block of cement-like substance. He ran the sword through another and shot a Greek fire round while the blade was still inside the Goth. The flames flared and burned the creature. The smell of burning whatever mingled with the putrid scent of the creatures. Megistus felt the power that emanated from Brentt.

Now he knew why The Immortal Count had said Brentt was a worthy adversary and why he gave him his respect. The Thrice Magician looked on as the battle heated up. He felt the earth and sky convulse again under duress from the detective. The success rate of his mission decreased by the second and he had to work quickly.

The four Goths were bombarded by the blasts from the LAKN9 operatives and they barely moved with Brentt's gravity impeding them. The Reptilians hammered on the shield over the Gadha but an angry Jezebelle put a stop to them. She entrapped them in a bioelectric bubble that shrank. Sarah and Aarron took point on this one and put the two remaining scaly giants out of their misery. They used a rocket launcher, which they had weapon warped, and fired missiles into the bubble. The bubble clouded over with misted blood and guts, which were unceremoniously dumped upon two of the sluggish Goths.

CHAPTER 29

That was the catalyst that turned the tide. The four Goths stopped what they were doing and hummed in unison. They chanted as monks did. They sounded like many monstrous voices humming softly in unison. The fighters stepped back and readied their shields.

They continued to hum and they grew larger and bulkier. Their shapes changed into something which none of the fighters had ever seen in their lives. They had morphed into two Leviathans and two Behemoths right before the bewildered eyes of the LAKN9 operatives. All four of the fifty-foot tall monsters looked upon the Assassin Priests, Warrior Rabbis, Jezebelle, Jacob, and Brentt with a great and terrible expectation. They were going to die and be turned into nothing.

Asheley had the earth's atmosphere and gravity bent to her will and patiently waited for Theo to lure John into the trap. She saw what went on in the museum and saw the transformation of the four Gothic individuals. She wondered what they were and unbeknownst to them, took a deep scan. She analyzed their composition but got no new data. She had access to all of the data in the world but had no idea what they were dealing with. *She remembered that Theo had gone to the Akashic Records Library. She wondered if she was able to go there as well.*

One of the massive heads of the Leviathan turned its attention from Brentt Williams and his team and focused on the proceedings of Asheley, Theo, and Frank Lin. A toothy smile spread across his barely-there lips as he breathed, "Ah, some of our own, here!" Asheley saw him and heard the exclamation. She looked defiantly into one of his ten red eyes. Theo, Frank Lin, and John were too engrossed in their battle to notice.

Asheley tossed a glance at Theo as he parried and blocked the onslaughts of John. John did not let up one bit. With every blow, John felt the hate inside grow. It fueled him. Theo knew he had to get John over to Asheley, fast. Theo bounded towards Asheley and landed at the edge of the gravity trap. John was right on him and they locked in a melee.

CHAPTER 29

"I am going to kill you and then after the parade, I am going to make sweet and passionate love to Catherine. I might even do it during the parade. I haven't decided yet!" John snarled.

"Theo, watch out!" Frank Lin said as he fired a spirit wave.

Theo dove out of the way as the wave hit John and pushed him into the gravity trap. John was caught in the trap and struggled to get free but he could barely move. He held the spiked club in his hand but it sat outside of the gravity radius.

"John, I am sorry. What happened to you? How would Catherine and Katie feel if they saw you like this? I don't know how to help you," apologized Theo.

"You could help me by dying, so that way I can eat your rotten and putrid corpse. That way there is nothing for Catherine to remember you by," John said, icily.

"Theo, use the quartz in the sword. It fires lightning. It would immobilize John and hopefully stop him," shouted Ashely from the middle of the ring of bent and distorted gravity.

Theo sadly nodded and held up the great sword. He gripped the secondary handle and put his finger on the huge quartz on the insignia in the middle of the sword. He readied to fire and that's when they heard the bone-chilling roar of the Leviathans and the Behemoths. Theo's and Frank Lin's attentions were momentarily disrupted by the roar.

In a last-ditch attempt, John mustered some unknown strength, swung the spiked mace and drove it into the side of Theo. Theo felt the pain and saw the spiked club stuck in his side. He reeled from the blow and stepped back. Asheley jumped from the middle of the circle and landed on the arm of John, breaking it instantly. She grabbed Theo as he fell back, barely conscious and moved him out of harm's way. Frank Lin arrived at Theo's side a few seconds later.

"Theo, no, don't die. I can heal you. We have to get somewhere safe. The gravity trap won't hold for much longer. Frank Lin, hold on to Theo, we are leaving now," said Asheley.

"What about the others, in there?" asked Frank Lin.

"We are barely surviving here with John. Detective Brentt Williams and the others look like they face this stuff all the time."

CHAPTER 29

Asheley and Frank Lin looked back at the battle that went on inside the museum. They saw the four monsters. They felt the power that came from them and knew there was going to be a lot of destruction that followed. Asheley was sorry she had to leave Brentt and the others. "Hold on, we're going to be teleported to your house!" Asheley, Theo, Frank Lin, and the over-sized sword, were teleported very far away.

Megistus saw the transformation of the four Gothic dudes and it shook him to his core. He held his head and lamented this development. The prize slipped away from his hands and there was nothing that could be done about it.

He looked upon John as he lay in the middle of the gravity disruption which slowly dissipated. Maybe he would take him to The Immortal Count and use him as an explanation for why the Gadha was not obtained.

"The battle is lost and I need something to take back as proof of my efforts," the Thrice Magician said out loud to himself. He slowly and deliberately walked up to John.

"Get out of my way, old man, before I kill you and eat you for a snack!" John snarled as he tried to get up.

"You dare threaten me, boy! Just because I haven't spilled any blood today does not mean that I will hesitate to shed yours!" spat Megistus. He rounded up John in an impregnable shield that was tried and tested over a few millennia.

Suddenly, from the skies above, came the most deafening sonic boom that anyone had ever heard. It was so loud, that it was heard by everyone across the globe. The earth convulsed and the sky opened, as three heavenly beings, seventy feet tall, landed upon planet Earth. Heddonna, Archituria, and Technon landed in the middle of a scattered New Year's Day parade, amidst a crumbling museum and a myriad of people that fled for their lives.

Megistus looked in disbelief at the new players in this game to capture the Gadha. They were beyond the epitome of perfection. The power of the universe itself crackled around them. His heart instantly leaped out his chest and danced for joy at seeing two of the most beautiful and mesmerizing women that ever existed. Megistus stood there and lecherously lusted after the full-bodied, red-haired goddess as she moved. He gawked at her as she spoke to her equally stunning cohort.

The Thrice Magician stood oblivious to the impending doom that would befall them all. He quickly snapped back out of the moment and whisked himself and the captured John Duboise, back to The Immortal Count. As he left, he had a yearning in his non-existent heart, something that he had felt only once before.

Elainney, still invisible, saw the transformations of the four Gothic dudes. She was awestruck by their power. She saw when Asheley carried Theo and Frank Lin away from the carnage that was to come. What were the Unmade doing here? Were they looking for Theo? She also saw when the Gods arrived. That was the Goddess of Knowledge with the red hair. She might have been looking for Theo. *After all, he proved that she did not know everything. That probably pissed her off.*

CHAPTER 30: Prisoners And Problems

Anthraxis surveyed his courtesans that were clad in their various armors. He excitedly and immediately multiplied himself a billion-fold. The revelry and celebrations had occurred for billions of years and it never got old. Time slipped thru unnoticed by the inhabitants of his temple planet. They did the deeds which they loved with the deity that they worshiped. Nothing else mattered to the courtesans because they lived in their paradise.

The giant Anthraxis, who sat upon his throne, raised his left hand and spoke in a thunderous voice, "I shall hunt and slay the *Leviathan* and the *Behemoth*. Then, we shall barbeque their flesh with specially blended barbeque sauce. I have a special treat for all of you, my faithful subjects.

For dessert, we shall eat warm and delectable German chocolate cake, topped with the smoothest whipped cream and sprinkles. It shall be joined with ice cream wrought with chunks of white chocolate. This treat was fashioned by the finest chefs the universe had ever birthed, the Cocoans. We will feast until the moon is at its zenith!"

Both the Leviathan and Behemoth were resurrected more times than one could count. The great beasts rose as one and it was an awesome sight that the inhabitants of the planet beheld. However, today was different. Joined with the two great beasts, were three more powerful opponents which the God of War had not intended to face.

All looked stunned as Cosmica, Galaxyia, and Atomos rose from the pit with the monsters. All eyes were upon them. All mouths stopped cheering and dropped in awe of the three Gods. Every heartbeat raced. In some instances, there were beings with multiple hearts and they too, raced at the sight of the Gods.

CHAPTER 30

Everyone immediately fell to their knees and genuflected before the King of the Gods and the God of the Gods. All of the Anthraxis' showed consternation on their faces and wondered what this was about.

Soon, he noticed that the three of them had multiplied themselves to match the number of Anthraxis' embodiments, which were scattered across his temple planet. The normally happy and carefree face of Galaxyia displayed hate and anger. Even the ever stoic Atomos, had downright displeasure in graffiti over his majestic features.

"Courtesans and followers of Anthraxis, I will remand you all to a planet that is just as sufficient to live on, whilst we three have an audience with the God of War. Go, enjoy yourselves and do as you would. Rejoice, for now instead of one God overseeing your festivities, you have four," said the mighty Atomos in an even and authoritative tone. Everyone disappeared as Atomos waved his mighty hand. He did as he had said and carried them safely to another planet.

"What the hell did you do to Detrimentus," spat Cosmica. All of her embodiments walked up to all of the Anthraxis' and slapped him hard.

"Atomos, did you see that? There was no provocation and I got assaulted by her!" stated a maddened Anthraxis.

"We are here because there was a provocation. You were seen trying to destroy Detrimentus and you stole a planet. Cosmica and Galaxyia not only saw you but a whole sun-sized room of Athlogoss Drones and servants. Your actions were captured on surveillance videos. I am here to lock you up and get an explanation out of you!" said Atomos as he lost his composure a little.

"What do you mean? Harm Detrimentus? I did not do such a thing. I am here enjoying the fruits of your creation. I have exerted my influence upon the universe. I have not interfered with any planet. I have learned from the past," defended Anthraxis.

"I have witnesses at my beck and call, including two Goddesses. Come quietly or there will be destruction. *I am the*

CHAPTER 30

creator of the universe, but I will not hesitate to tear it down to get to you," pronounced Atomos.

"I want to see the proof. I want to see what I am accused of. Show me the thing that you say that I have done!" challenged Anthraxis.

"That is acceptable. We will go to the death dome," spoke Atomos. Before he took another breath, one each of their embodiments materialized in the sun-sized viewing room amongst the servants of Detrimentus. Atomos waved his giant hand and the footage in question was replayed on the screen.

Anthraxis stood silent as he viewed the events in question. He saw the fight and the punishment doled out to the God of Death, Detrimentus.

"Do you need more? Why don't we go to the scene of the crime?" Cosmica sarcastically said.

"Yes, let us do that. I want to feel it, where it happened," prodded Anthraxis.

Atomos made it happen again. The next instant they appeared in the middle of a destroyed star system. Planets were misaligned and no doubt all of the inhabitants were on the brink of death. All four Gods looked into the past of the molecules in the area and saw that there had been a great battle that had taken place between Anthraxis and Detrimentus. Surprisingly, only the Pel 6 from a specific multiverse was missing, the other multiverses' planets were intact.

"I felt the power coming from your Contest of the Nine while you battled Death. No one else would wear that armor but you. It has your essence inside of it. You feel it as we all do. Do you deny this?" asked Cosmica.

Anthraxis shook his head and stood quietly. "I felt my armor's power," he whispered.

"Even though Gods cannot foretell the actions and know the minds of other Gods, this does not mean that they cannot feel the power that each possesses. This doing has your power smeared all over it," explained Galaxyia in anger.

"The whole universe is a witness against me and my supposed actions. The power of my Contest of the Nine has given me up for trial. However, I did not do this!" shouted Anthraxis as lightning flared from his eyes.

Atomos grew larger for an anticipated conflict. Cosmica clenched her fists and stood her ground. Galaxyia braced herself for anything that was aimed her way.

"Atomos, you have to believe me. I did not do this. I did not attack Detrimentus. Yes, that is my armor and essence, but that was not me. I will go quietly, even though it is not in my nature to do so," submitted Anthraxis.

"Let it be so," Atomos said. He summoned two more giant Atomos' to take Anthraxis into custody. "I have a remnant from a long time ago. I think it might be useful. This gravity box is like the one Technon used on you, except it is the size of a mountain. I have added a few upgrades. Each of the six walls is exerting the same gravity. You will be confined on my temple planet until I am able to sort this out."

"Is this it? A holiday in a hole, you can't be serious," cried Cosmica.

"Calm down. It is a prison. He won't be able to do anything. Besides, Atomos will sort him out. We have to look after Detrimentus. He needs us," soothed Galaxyia.

"Before I go, let me right the destruction that has been done here. I will fix this solar system and its surroundings to its natural course," spoke Atomos. He waved his hands. In an instant, everything went back to before the fight between Anthraxis and Detrimentus.

Atomos, Galaxyia, and Cosmica looked at the imprisoned Anthraxis and wondered what to do next.

The day was nice for a parade, very sunny, not too hot but not too chilly. It was perfect weather to witness numerous floats that showcased the artistic craftsmanship of thousands of people. Unfortunately, it was in disarray by the time Technon, Archituria, and Heddonna arrived. Thousands of people fled for their lives as the sky cracked open and the three Gods touched down with a sonic boom. They landed upon planet Earth, in the middle of the New Year's Day parade.

"Do you see your little man, Heddonna?" asked Technon.

She closed her eyes and ran through the whole history of this area. She looked for the man but did not find him. She used her God powers and searched the adjacent areas as well. She searched for the elusive man which had made his way into her library but came up empty. "No, I don't, but I am seeing something else that I don't have any knowledge about."

"Are you sure that you are the Goddess of Knowledge?" kidded Archituria.

Heddonna rolled her eyes and moved towards the commotion. Technon saw what made everyone run, besides them, and it was not good. The Gods foresaw everything that was to ever happen or exist in the entire universe, except this. They were not ready for the sight of two monstrous Leviathans and two giant Behemoths which awaited them.

"Now do you see what it feels like to have something in front of you and not know what will happen next?" Heddonna said as she bumped Technon's arm in jest.

"I do. I don't see anything past them. There is no past or future. I can't tell what they are going to do next. I am powerless to do anything about it," replied the awed Technon.

Off to the side, Heddonna saw a weird-looking man, who ogled her. He had captured someone in a force shield, who also gawked at the God and Goddesses. 'Megistus and John are up to no good', thought the Goddess to herself. She turned her attention to the great beasts and put John and Megistus out of her mind.

"Hey, that's the Gadha of Gilgamesh. The Athlogoss Drone said he misplaced it. However, it's located right here," pointed out Archituria.

"Looks like these things are after it. If they get a hold of that power, there's no telling what they will do!" observed Technon. "We need to contain these things and figure out what they are."

The seventy-foot tall Gods strode with a purpose to the Leviathans and Behemoths. The courageous Rabbis and Priests, along with Brentt, Jacob and Jezebelle, thought a new threat was headed their way. Each of them silently prayed for a miracle. The four great beasts bent on acquiring the weapon, now turned their attentions to the incoming Gods.

"Hey you, who are you and where do you come from?" asked Archituria in an authoritative tone. The overpowering stench from the monsters caused her to choke on her words as she neared the beasts. "Oh my Atomos, what the hell is that smell? It is killing me just by inhaling it alone!"

"Nothing is everything and everything is nothing. All is one and all are nothing. I existed before the light. For before the light there was darkness. I existed before the darkness. For before the darkness, there was nothing," spoke the four creatures in unison, with the voice of many soft voices.

"What does that mean? You need to come with us. We are the God and Goddesses of Technology, Knowledge, and Civilizations. Obey, and come with us peacefully. You cannot win," stated Technon, also taken aback by the smell.

Both Leviathans reared their total of sixteen heads and let out a great and terrible scream that shook the earth. The two Behemoths flexed their powerful muscles and shrieked as well. That action magnified the aromatic stench that they gave off.

"This will get really ugly. There will be a lot of destruction. These pesky humans are in our way. I am going to stop time and see if that will have any effect on the monsters. If they are immobilized, then they will be easier to capture," said Technon, as he did exactly that.

Birds in mid-flight stopped the beating of their wings and hearts. Bees, which busied themselves collecting nectar from flowers, stopped buzzing. People, who fled from the terrible sights, stopped in their tracks. Their blood froze in their bodies, as cells stopped making energy. Water, which ran from broken mains, stopped cascading. The whole world stopped moving, like in the moments before Atomos had breathed life into the universe. The four creatures stood still, apparently frozen in time.

Heddonna observed the people gathered around the monsters and saw their past, present, and future. They were a good bunch of people that protected the world from bad guys. Technon examined the frozen Behemoths and Leviathans. He marveled at their powerful physique. He tried not to breathe in too deeply, but it did not work. Their smell still found its way into his nose. He looked over at Heddonna and said, "Looks like that worked!" However, it did not work.

At the moment he looked away, an eight-headed Leviathan decided to munch on some God pie. He violently bit into the hand of Technon. The four tails of the other Leviathan lashed out and stung Technon with a mighty crack. Technon reeled back and tried to shake off the toothy kisses of the beast, but to no avail. He started punching the monster's heads, in no particular order, but they held on. The other Leviathan circled around him and wrapped a tail around his feet, in an effort to trip him.

Heddonna tried to come to his rescue, but she was blocked by a very stout and burly Behemoth. He swung a heavy-handed right that connected with her midsection. The blow sent her to her knees. She would have to do better. He went in for a knee to the face but she blocked it and retaliated with a head butt to his rock hard abs. That did little to the monster. However, it left a mark on her face, her beautifully sculpted and impeccably perfect face.

She rushed up and speared him into a building, which only a few hours before, had been the lookout for Tris Megistus and his goons. She rolled off the creature and shook her head. 'That was a lot harder than it looked', she thought to herself. She kicked the creature for good measure and he did not like that one bit.

Archituria was shocked at the power with which the beasts challenged the Gods. The other Behemoth had his eyes fixed on her as his dance partner. She backed away and stepped on a dog, which immediately squished underfoot. Archituria paid it no attention as the Behemoth rushed her and knocked her onto a float. It pummeled her mercilessly, as she screamed in bewilderment and pain. She tried to put her hands to guard her face, as she closed her eyes and hoped for a miracle.

Technon was her miracle. He sent another of his embodiments to her rescue. His seventy-foot tall frame pulled the fifty-foot tall Behemoth off the scared Goddess and punched him in the face. He then proceeded to unleash a barrage of blows that rocked the beast.

CHAPTER 30

Technon had some experience in fighting brutes and was somewhat of a pro. He summoned another embodiment behind the Leviathan that tried to trip him. Technon caught the eight heads in a chokehold and proceeded to strangle the beast.

This freed up the first Technon, who continued punching the heads of the Leviathan that initially tried to eat his arm. Finally, a kick to the midsection did the trick and the monster let go of his arm. Technon grabbed one of the heads and flipped the creature over. The monster screeched in pain as Technon straddled it and raised his hands to fire a face full of lava. Its tails stopped the blow as they wrapped around his arms and neck. Soon the tides changed for the worse.

The Technon that saved Archituria was contending with a Behemoth. He pummeled the monster, but suddenly felt a tail wrap around his neck. The tail belonged to the Leviathan that the other Technon had in a headlock. He had to give the creature some credit, it had very good proprioception. The creature used his mighty tail and pulled Technon off the Behemoth and freed his fellow monster. The next thing he knew the Behemoth gave him a hard right fist to the face. Technon reeled with the tail around his throat.

Heddonna violently attacked the downed beast but it struggled to get up amongst her kicks and punches. He threw a big right hand that barely missed her jaw but connected with her left shoulder. She winced as it throbbed with pain and retreated slightly.

"Damn, we're getting our buts whooped here. These guys won't stay down. They seem just as strong as us," said Technon with the tail still wrapped around his throat.

"Yeah, I noticed. Any bright ideas tough guy?" replied Heddonna, favoring her shoulder.

"We have to take things to the next level," said the other Technon, his hands tied down with tails.

Yet another embodiment of Technon appeared, but this time, he had a huge building in his hands. He brought it down upon the heads of the Leviathan with a thud. It immediately loosened its tails and freed the hands of one of the Technons.

CHAPTER 30

Another Technon appeared again and landed a blow with a cement truck to the back of the head of the Behemoth that was after Heddonna. He let up the attack and sunk to the ground. The leftovers of the building and the truck were then force-fed to the other monsters via an angered Technon. They unenthusiastically relinquished their holds and this allowed the three Gods to regroup.

"Archituria, you have to get involved. You have to fight. We need you. I know, deep down, you have courage inside you. In the beginning, you were the first one that shared your creation. You know the rise and fall of empires, but your sun shines on. This is just like that," prompted Technon.

"Are you kidding me? These guys are powerful!" she exclaimed.

"If we work together, we can overcome them," reassured Heddonna.

"I know we're probably going to mash up the planet. I know we are going to incur the wrath of Atomos. However, you see them for yourself; these things are not known to any of us. That is not good for anyone," explained Technon.

A bewildered Archituria stared at the imposing creatures, which started to regain their composure. She did not know the outcome and that was new for her as a Goddess. It was a new feeling, to not know. *'So this is what every being in the universe felt, every day of their lives, to not know'*, she thought to herself.

"Ladies, I have a gift for both of you. While we were fighting those monsters, I put together a little something," Technon said, smiling.

He gave Heddonna a spear that had a large pointy tip at one end and a rounded, spiked ball at the other. It was as tall as she was, with a balanced feel to it. It was forged out of parts of buildings, cars, and even people. At the moment, it did not matter what the weapon was made of, just that it evened the field. He also gave Archituria a short sword and a mid-sized shield. On the shield was a caricature of herself. It was hastily thrown together, but the thought counted.

"Give them everything we have!" Technon rallied, as he stared into the eyes of both Goddesses.

CHAPTER 30

Heddonna was thoroughly impressed with the God of Technology and made up her mind to tell him how she felt, after the free for all. The five Technons that were present merged into one and armed himself with a mini God Breaker Cannon that was attached to a giant sword. He led the charge and the two Goddesses followed.

Heddonna passionately thrust the spear into the Behemoth as he ran to her. The tip hit above the abdomen and came out the other side. She threw punches upon punches at the monster and even summoned three embodiments to attack from behind. The spiked balls found their mark, upon the body of the Behemoth. Heddonna had the Behemoth on the ropes as he let out an agonizing scream of pain.

Archituria held out her shield and caught an incoming blow from her Behemoth dance partner. She quickly stabbed it with the short sword as he had his attention on the shield. The monster drew back in terror, as three more embodiments of her appeared and impaled him from all sides. She had the beast trapped, as she rained down blows with her shield.

Technon gave a crooked smile as he faced off against the two Leviathans with a total of one hundred and sixty eyes, sixteen heads, twelve wings, eight tails, and eight legs. He raised his sword which contained a mini God Breaker Cannon and looked through the crosshairs. Each of the heads was in it. He fired and rockets crashed into the heads. A blinding flash of light charred the putrid flesh of the beasts and rendered them unconscious.

"Archituria, Heddonna, move away from the Behemoths. I'm going to blast them!" Technon yelled.

The Goddesses simultaneously dove out of the way, as the God of Technology fired his weapon at the beasts. There was a terrific explosion as both creatures were downed by the awesome blast. The stench that came from them was magnified by the fire that seared their bodies. When the dust and smoke cleared, the monsters lay motionless on the ground. Down but not out, they still posed a threat to the Gods.

"I need you to look after them. I have to fashion a holding trap for them. It will be a minute," asked Technon, as he started to work.

CHAPTER 30

He fashioned a cell out of the very earth itself, carefully tuning the molecules and forging the links of each atom. As he worked, more of the earth eroded and filtered into the prison. Whole cities were used as the building blocks for the containment unit. Sides of mountains were gouged out and roadways were torn up. Anything and everything within reach were used.

He was halfway done in a few minutes. The attentions of the Goddesses wandered to Technon as he worked and they let their guard down. He moved with newfound purpose and his every action seemed intriguing. He crafted things instead of calling them forth. It was a little more time consuming, but they had all the time in the universe and beyond.

A Leviathan slowly moved one of his tails, unbeknownst to the Goddesses. He slyly snaked his tail around the handle of the Gadha, which was strewn amidst the carcasses of buildings. A few of his eighty eyes settled upon Archituria as he made his move. He was in mid-strike with the weapon as Technon saw what was about to happen and teleported in front of the Goddess.

The blast from the Gift of the Nine dealt a vicious blow to the God of Technology. He was no stranger to vicious blows and fortunately, had remedied that beforehand. He reeled back from the blast and cradled his face. He was badly injured and materialized another few embodiments, which quickly finished the prison trap. The Leviathans and Behemoths rose with new hope and faced off against the Gods one more time.

The Technons activated the prison and a Leviathan and a Behemoth were instantly captured. The other two had managed to get behind the weapon and used its shield against the Gods. Archituria leaped for the Gadha, but in an instant, the two remaining monstrous thieves disappeared.

Heddonna came up to his left side and put Technon's arm around her shoulders. He sagged heavily upon her and sighed. He felt the Nanobots inside him already rebuilding his injured body parts.

"They're gone. They took the weapon with them. That Gadha had the power of the Gods in it. The Gifts of the Nine have the power that we gave our Athlogoss Drones. Now things that we don't know, have it. Things we don't know have the power of the Gods," he said dejectedly.

"Well, at least we have this prison and two prisoners. We have to find Atomos and tell him about this," stated Archituria. She came up to Technon and touched his face. "I am so sorry you got hurt. I am sorry that I was not strong enough."

"No. You were fine. We all did great today. Don't beat yourself up. None of us knew," he consoled the others.

"Let's get you somewhere relaxing. Chances are, we will have to put all of this back together. Well, because you are using a piece of the Earth as the prison," said Heddonna.

The three battle-scarred Gods gathered their prisoners and teleported to the temple planet of Atomos. They left a broken Earth in their wake.

CHAPTER 31: Back To The Drawing Board

B efore the beginning, the Gods had convened to decide who would be King of them all. Subsequently, they assembled to discuss matters concerning the welfare of the universe. Now, they held a council to discuss recent actions and the consequences associated with them.

"Greetings to you, my fellow Gods. In the beginning, there were nine of us, who sat upon marvelous thrones. Now there are seven of us. Seven Gods, who sit upon mighty thrones that I have built. Seven Gods, over the temple planets I have given you. Seven Gods, in the shadow of The Contest of the Nine. Detrimentus is on his temple planet, recuperating from injuries sustained as he fought Anthraxis. Anthraxis was remanded to a prison cell, awaiting our judgment for his actions. We have witnesses to the events. The Goddesses Cosmica and Galaxyia also felt the energies during the attack. Detrimentus said it was Anthraxis. We shall deliberate upon the punishment for this heinous act.

However, it has come to my attention that there are other matters just as pressing, which need to be deliberated on," spoke the mighty Atomos to his fellow Gods and Goddesses. "Heddonna, I give you the audience of the Gods."

"Thank you, UKSCOGSM Atomos. Hello everyone, I have an urgent matter to be presented before you. Technon, Archituria and I were investigating the whereabouts of this man that appeared in my library. I had no knowledge of him, nor could any record be found in the Akashic Records Library," said Heddonna, as she conjured up a likeness of the man in question.

"He had also appeared in Heaven a few months before. They could not identify him either. It was as if he never existed. I did not see anything about him and even the actions which surrounded him proved futile. The people and beings he interacted with did the actions that they were supposed to, but it was as if they acted with no one there," she spoke as she made a second likeness of the man that went to Heaven.

A murmur went through the ranks of the Gods as they took in the gravity of the situation. They looked at each other in bewilderment. Heddonna raised her hand and continued.

"My fellow Gods, things get worse. In our investigations, we went to California and discovered that these things were present in the vicinity of our search. They have no past, present or future. No multiverse versions of them were seen. We could not gather any information from them," she continued, as she revealed the prison in which the Leviathan and the Behemoth were kept. "There were two others like them, but they got away with the Gadha of Gilgamesh. They were very strong and cunning. Now, they could be even stronger with the power from the Gift of the Nine."

"Those things were on the planet of Anthraxis!" shouted Cosmica as she pointed to the prison that held the two great beasts. She got up and continued to point at the caged monsters.

"Yes, they may look the same. These, however, were not made by my hand," replied Atomos.

"What are they? Where are they from? What do they want with the Gift of the Nine?" asked Caddeussus, as he sat and looked at the beasts in their cage.

"None of us know. I tried doing experiments on them to determine their origin, but I come up empty-handed at every turn. I could get nothing out of them," stated Technon.

"Let us not forget about the man that was in my library and in heaven. Where does he fit in? How could we not know about this?" reminded Heddonna.

"They smell very bad. I mean horrible. I have never smelled anything like that before," mumbled Technon to himself.

"Did you say smell? Detrimentus was mumbling about some smells when we found him," recalled Galaxyia. "Are they secured in there? Will the prison hold them?" she asked, concerned.

"They are very secure. Atomos, about that, I had to use a piece of the Earth to make the prison. I am sure that we might want to fix it back. To keep everything going," recommended Technon.

"That is a good idea. I will rebuild Earth and put everything back to how it is supposed to be. Looking at the situation, a battle brewed in the area. The Rabbi Warriors and Assassin Priests fought Reptilians and Big-Foot soldiers. However, the creatures interrupted the battle. I will allow it to be as if they were not there.

In addition, I shall put something else in the Gadha's place, perhaps a statue. The confrontation with the four beasts will be like it never happened. Let it be, that the actions of these creatures and the actions of the Gods will not affect the multiverse lives of the planet Earth," commanded Atomos, the God of the Gods.

He waved his mighty hand and all of the actions that had taken place after the arrival of the four creatures and the Gods were now erased.

"What do we do with these guys?" asked Technon, pointing to the prisoners. "We also have two very dangerous creatures on the loose."

"We shall send the word out to all of our Athlogoss Drones. They should be careful and be watchful about any suspicious activity. They should not hesitate to call on us," replied Atomos.

The Nine had begun with the problem of trying to decide who would be King of the Gods and lead them in creation. This time, they had a new problem. Who created these beings and what to do about it?

CHAPTER 32: Theo And
The Ladies

In the back of some shelves, located in the non-fiction section of the Akashic Records Library, was an old man. He effortlessly pushed a cart full of books, which hovered above the ground. His job was to put the books back on their respective shelves. He stopped what he was doing and muttered to himself, "The Mistress went off to find the guy in the Library. The man, she did not know. She went to heaven. We have books on heaven. We have books on everything except him. After that, she visited Technon, since he built the Tablets in heaven. She obtained information on Earth. We have books on Earth. We have knowledge of everything that exists, except that man that showed up here."

A nerdy alien named Niff, who also worked in the Library, passed by with three thick books in his hands. He came up to the floating cart and deposited them on it. "Here is a Theory on Things Unseen by Mga Ji, The Civilizations of the Hycolites by Dju Durd and this is my personal favorite, The Art of Seducing a Zyster Female by Qui Qu." The old man was lost in his thoughts, as Niff rattled off the names of the books.

The old man continued talking to himself, "The Gods knew everything, but who this guy was. He was here. I am the master of this Library and I should have seen it. I should have stopped him from coming to the Goddess, but I did not. The Goddess saw him. This was my fault."

"You still worked up about that stranger that came here? It might be a clerical error. But I have to say, if the Goddess really doesn't know him, that is a bad place to be. They are going to beat it out of him for real," Niff said, as he shook his head.

"Even heaven did not know him. They think he is on Earth. Many things are on Earth. The Gods brought back two unknown things from the Earth. *The Unmade*. I don't have books on them.

CHAPTER 32

There are so many more questions and no books or information on them."

"Earthlings, man, they are really messed up. Look, Bibtoran, you are the chief librarian here, but you are just the hired help. How could you have known about this dude? You don't have to beat yourself up. Stop talking to yourself too. It freaks everyone out," chided Niff.

"I converse with myself because I understand myself."

"Okay, whatever. You're like a half a million years old, so I'll let you have that. See you around," the nerdy alien said, as he walked away.

"I have to be careful. We all have to be careful because things we do not know could hurt us. The Gods were in a council meeting. It was in the minutes for them. All of the minutes are kept from all of the meetings. The minutes are being kept right now. That is the way. We have to be careful because things are about to happen. Things that have happened were reversed to make them not happen. How far back, it is unclear." He moved past a bookcase shaking his head.

Soon, he was in a different part of the Library, doing what he did for the past five hundred thousand years. The spot that he vacated looked like the heat that rose up from the road on a hot day. A camouflaged something moved and looked in his direction. It materialized into the form of Raechellee. She quickly teleported back to Earth and met up with her friends. They gathered in their spacious living room.

"Father spoke to me. I have good news and bad news," she announced.

"Well, don't be a daisy downer, what is it?" asked Aerica impatiently.

"The good news is that Theo got to the Akashic Records Library. He was supposed to go where the Goddess was not. The bad news is that Heddonna saw him and did not know about him. She mounted a search in heaven, however, she could not find anything about him there either.

We knew that already. Then she and some other Gods came to Earth to look for him. They stumbled across other beings. There were Unmade at the museum," explained Raechellee.

"How come there were Unmade there? Theo was at the museum with Frank Lin and the mysterious Asheley!" exclaimed Alexyia.

"I saw the fight. I was there," Elainney disclosed.

"What! Where were you? Why did you not come to his aid?" voiced Aerica.

"I suspected that I should keep an eye on Theo. When I saw the commotion at the museum, I got ready to jump in, but Asheley did it for me. She looked very powerful and I did not want a confrontation in the middle of all of that. There were Reptilians and Big-Foot soldiers and four Gothic guys that grew into Unmade creatures. Looks like they can shapeshift as well. Not to mention, Theo fought some other guy too.

Luckily, the three of them got out of there before the Gods arrived. Heddonna was among them. I figured she was looking for Theo. He barely escaped. Two Unmades were taken captive, but two escaped with the weapon," explained Elainney.

"That's the least of our worries. In light of the discovery of the Unmade, the Gods changed the events that occurred at the museum. We don't know if he was affected by the time shift on planet Earth. Maybe he won't remember us," surmised Raechellee.

"He doesn't remember who we are now. Besides, they probably won't change what they don't know. We have to keep him safe, at any cost," said Alexyia.

"The Gods are looking for him. Do you think he knows?" Aerica sighed.

"I don't know. Asheley could have teleported him anywhere. In any case, it looks like his new friends can take care of themselves," reassured Elainney.

Theo regained consciousness, in a very plush and cozy bed. It was one of the guest rooms at Frank Lin's house, in Tibet. His shirt was off and where a few big holes in his body should have been, there was now really good-looking skin. Asheley leaned over him as he turned his head. She smiled and gave him a good morning kiss on the cheek.

The covers were soft and he did not want to get out of bed. Theo just laid there for a few more minutes. His eyes lazily scanned the huge room. Leaning in the corner, he spied the giant sword which had been teleported with them yesterday. The blinds were pulled partially open revealing snow-capped mountains that looked like they were in Frank Lin's backyard. There was fresh powdered snow on the ground but the sun shone in all of its radiant warmth.

The room was lavishly furnished for the home of a monk. The walls were decorated with intricate artworks and designs that took ages to do. Different sized statues of Buddha and other deities were sprinkled on shelves around the room. There sat a complete living room set, a little ways off to the side. A high-end flat-screen television hung solidly on the wall. There was even a satellite cable box underneath.

An ornately frosted glass desk sat in one corner of the room. Next to the desk, was a modest, personal library that contained venerated books. It was only a part of the grand library, situated in the other wing of the mansion.

The bed in which Theo rested, was an ornate four-poster with dark wood finishing. The grand bed was definitely handcuff-compatible, owing to a fuzzy handcuff still on one of the posts.

"Where are we?" he asked, as he realized that the dream he had about New Year's Day was real.

"We are in Tibet, at one of the mansions of Frank Lin," smiled Asheley as she moved on the bed. "The windows of this bedroom open out to great views of Mount Everest."

"You teleported us here?" asked Theo, unsure about what to make of it.

"Yes, I did, yesterday. In fact, during our battle at the museum, I learned a lot of new things. I have accumulated an exponential amount of data about the things around me. I can mimic the powers of the Reptilians, the four Gothic guys, the Big-Foot soldiers and the abilities of Brentt and his crew."

"That's incredible! I feel very useless now. Speaking of..." Theo trailed off. "Listen, Asheley, I want to thank you for saving me and Frank Lin. I don't know how to repay you," he solemnly said.

"Just be in love with me forever and don't leave me, then we will call it even!" she cheerily said.

"Okay. How is Frank Lin? I wonder what he thinks about all of this?"

"He will be finished making breakfast in about ten minutes," winked Asheley.

Asheley moved in for a good, long hug and he enjoyed every second of it. He opened his eyes and smelled her hair, which smelled of apples. Just then, the room faded away and came back into focus. A nagging sensation traveled through Theo's body. Asheley noticed it too because she looked at Theo and then looked around. Soon everything came back to normal and Frank Lin walked in with a cart full of breakfast items.

"Morning you two love birds, how are things?" he chirped, as he uncovered a large platter.

"Great!" answered Theo. "Did you happen to see the room fade and then come back in?"

"No, I did not. Why?"

"I know you noticed it too, right Asheley?" asked Theo.

"I think time was disrupted because the inner workings of my mechanics are registering two different scenarios that transpired at the museum," explained Asheley.

"What do you mean?" asked Frank Lin, as he seated himself on the arm of a sofa.

"Frank Lin, what do you remember about the museum?" asked Asheley.

"We were there and then some homeless guys came in. They turned into Reptilians. Then the security blasted them with space lasers. Next thing we knew, Big-Foot soldiers ran around the place. Brentt and his guys killed them. Oh, and by the way, your ex-wife's boyfriend hated you. He tried to kill you with some sort of hand mouth thing."

"Is that all the bad guys? Do you know what they were after?" Asheley prodded.

"That's all the bad guys I know. They went after some old broken up statue of some dude named Giggle Mesh or something. You remember, I told you we found it under the Great Wall," Frank Lin recalled.

"There were no Gothic guys that happened to be there?" asked Theo, making sure.

"No. No eighties Gothic dudes that I was aware of."

"He does not know about the Gothic guys. Theo, they were made of matter that could not be found. Perhaps, they might have changed time? How come we weren't affected? Was John affected? He had the same matter in his body," surmised Asheley.

"I don't know. Why do we remember the change? Those guys are still out there and John still wants my blood. We have to try to stop him or at least cure him. I don't want to take away Katie's dad. Besides, he has an unborn baby on the way. He may have ruined my life but I cannot take him away from his family," contemplated Theo.

"May I ask you something Frank Lin?" asked Asheley.

"Sure. I am still trying to wrap my head around what is going on."

"I need you to show me how to get to the Akashic Records Library."

CHAPTER 33: The Immortal Count And Brentt, One Step Closer

It was the day after the showdown at the museum and Brentt was dead tired. After the four Gothic dudes changed into great beasts, he thought that was the end for him and his team.

Then, there appeared three beings that crackled with energy and power. They were beyond the epitome of perfection. His recollection of the beauty of the two female beings did not do them justice. One of them gouged out half of a mountain without a second thought. The surrounding cities were felled in an instant, torn apart like it was nothing. The beings tossed around whole buildings as if it were pieces of trash. They were in multiple places at once, battling the creatures. Who were they and what were they doing there?

The news channels covered the carnage extensively. The military had quarantined the area and was just as clueless as the LAKN9 operatives. First responders looked after the injured and police kept the remaining crowds at bay. Brentt and his team assisted anyone that needed help. Scientists surveyed the area for any signs of what might have done this.

Families and friends looked for their loved ones among the wreckage but did not find them. Tears gushed from watery eyes and unanswered questions flowed from everyone. The LAKN9 were used to dealing with the fallout from things like these, but this was different. How do you explain what happened to multiple cities?

Brentt sat in the driver's seat of his awesome muscle car. He needed a cup of 'wake the dead' coffee. He half-heartedly listened to the traffic report on the radio without really paying attention to it. He was headed back to the precinct and dreaded the mountains of paperwork as per usual after some big thing goes down. His mind wandered to the fight as he drove. What the heck did he see?

He stopped at a traffic light, which took way longer to change than it should have. He stared at the light and it faded away and then came back into focus. He stared around at the other cars and they shuffled back into view as well. He dismissed the experience as too much stress and carried on to work. The three giant beings took on the monsters as if it were just a workout. What did it all mean?

At the precinct, he immediately high tailed it to Maxx Chief's office. "Hey Chief, how are things? Is everything that bad from the museum?" he instinctively asked.

"I am buried under a mountain of paperwork. I got the Chinese government on my neck about returning their Gilgamesh statue," he said. He took a big gulp of super black coffee with two sugars and some cinnamon.

"What do you mean their statue? It was a Gadha, a weapon that The Immortal Count tried to steal."

"No Brentt. I think you are mistaken. The Reptilians and the Big-Foot soldiers tried to steal a statue from the museum. You and your men did a terrific job and stopped them. Nobody was hurt and no one noticed anything. You probably bashed your head a little too hard buddy," he said, as he tapped himself on the head.

"What about the four Gothic dudes that turned into monsters?" asked Brentt.

"Everyone on your team gave me a report except you. They did not mention anything like that. You sure you don't need a few days?"

"I saw it on the news. I was there. My team was there. Lots of people died and buildings were reduced to rubble. There were whole mountains torn apart and the surrounding cities decimated!" Brentt vehemently demanded as he flipped on the television.

The place that was supposedly ruined was not destroyed. Everything was back to normal. The buildings were placed back in their spots. The people that he saw killed, walked around like nothing happened. The news covered the success of the parade and the failed battle. He looked at Maxx Chief in disbelief and then looked back at the television, stunned.

"I think I'll take the few days. I need to sort some stuff out," acquiesced Brentt.

"Brentt, sometimes this line of work really does a number on your head. Don't push yourself too hard. Come back when you are well-rested," the Chief said sympathetically.

Brentt nodded and left. He knew it was a Gadha and not a statue. He knew there were monsters and not just the parade. Something was not right and he had to get to the bottom of it.

Tris Megistus stood at the door to The Immortal Count's office. He was too petrified to go in. He feared the reaction from his master for his failed attempt to complete the mission. If today was his last day among the living, he was absolutely gladdened that he gazed upon the two most beautiful beings in all of creation before he died. He tried to dispel the vision of the tall red-headed woman out of his head, but he failed. Megistus marveled at her beauty, even though his recollection had not done her justice. He quietly walked in and glided over to the Count's desk. He readied himself for his punishment.

Before his desk, the Count set up a six-person dinner table made of the finest teak and inlaid with intricate carvings. On the table, a crystal ball, so clear that it almost looked as if there was nothing there, resided. An inch square piece of cloth was placed over the ball.

The medium, Mademoiselles Cordova, dressed in a simple white dress which hugged her ample curves, sat at the table. Her light red hair was tied in a bun to one side. She remained in deep concentration. She held the hands of five other henchmen, which the Count had allowed into his chambers. He himself stayed seated at his great and mighty desk. His back was to the proceedings, but he was fully aware of what went on.

It did not surprise Megistus if the Count already knew about the pandemonium at the museum. More importantly, that he had failed in the retrieval of the mighty Gadha.

CHAPTER 33

"Come to us and be with us. Come here to this place and show yourself, that we may see you. Use the energies presented here and manifest your presence. Yes. This cloth was something dear to you. Reach out and feel it. Remember the memories you have attached to it," spoke the medium in a clear and dramatic voice.

Megistus watched as an apparition slowly materialized over the table. She had shoulder-length blond hair and was dressed in fifteenth-century clothing. Her face and features were elegant and smart.

One of the henchmen opened his eyes but quickly closed them, as if he could not believe it. The medium looked at the apparition and then looked in The Immortal Count's direction. He turned the Throne of Thoth, which served as his desk chair and faced the medium and her specially summoned guest.

"Jacques. How good to see you, my love," said the apparition sweetly.

The massive hands of The Immortal Count moved upon the desk. He put his chin in the crux of the thumb and pointer finger of his left hand. The giant pinky on his right hand held a ring that was too small to fit his whole finger. It encircled his fingernail and pad. It was a plain ring, which had no distinguishing features or markings. It was out of place in the palatial atmosphere with which The Immortal Count was accustomed. He studied the apparition and her words, as she spoke to him again.

"You look like you carry the weight of the world on your shoulders," she smiled, as she floated closer to him. She was still over the table.

The Count did not wince but sat steadfast, as he examined his guest, staring right through her soul.

"You are not whom I seek," he spoke in an even and cadaverous voice, that demanded the utmost respect.

The apparition was taken aback by the accusation. She did not speak for a minute but floated in silence. "Jacques what are you saying? I am your long lost love!" she defended.

"Do you know what this ring is?"

"Yes, I know it," she replied.

CHAPTER 33

"It is the *Ring of Solomon*. Any demon or spirit has to obey the wearer of this ring. I am wearing it right now."

"Yes. I know the rules."

"Tell me your real name. Show me your true form."

The apparition slowly changed into an old, deformed demoness. She quietly hovered over the table, before the frightened eyes of the medium and henchmen. Her skin was leathery and parched, like the oldest mummies, plucked from the sands of Egypt. Her hair was scraggly and graying, with strands of black. Her deformed nose was bent, as if it had been broken a few times but never set right. She wore a simple tunic made from sackcloth.

"My name is Medini," she submissively said.

"Why did you deceive me? What have you to gain?" asked the Count.

"Your soul is very tortured and dark. It is very attractive to me and my kind. I wanted to overtake you and possess you," she explained, truthfully.

"You will find that impossible, but I applaud your tenacity for trying," complimented the Count. It was the first nice thing he had said in five decades.

"You mock me! Jacques, The Immortal Count. I tell you, the day you take off the ring, I will come for your soul!" she screamed.

"All I want is the truth. I am very hospitable to my guests. Let me not have you wait too long," said the Count. He flicked the ring, which was barely on his giant pinky, onto the table below the apparition.

She quickly dove towards The Immortal Count, but then stopped in her tracks, inches from his face. She shuddered violently and her eyes widened. She did not fathom what happened and fearfully gazed into the Count's eyes.

"Don't worry, you are not trapped or bound by any spells. You are under my spiritual power. Can you feel it? Do you feel my power as it encompasses and permeates your nonexistent body?"

"What are you doing to me?" she screamed, as her now corpulent body became heavy and sluggish. She slowly sank onto the desk and fell to the floor. She struggled and gasped in agonizing pain. "How is this possible? I am feeling pain and fear. I have a body?"

"I have a place for you to reside until your services are needed. It is very cozy, with lots of amenities. Actually, it is a pocket dimension prison I specially designed for just such an occasion. There are other guests who have their own suites as well."

The Count opened a very technical-looking box, about six inches on each edge and trapped the shocked and overwhelmed Medini inside. Her screams were a mixture of excitement, fear, and surprise. The medium and the henchmen, who had witnessed the drama in silent bewilderment, sat at the table, unsure about how to proceed. They were too scared to get up, even though they wanted to be out of there as soon as possible.

"If I ever hear a word about this breathed out loud or uttered in your thoughts, I shall cause all of you to suffer the same fate as this being and the rest of her kind," spoke the Count in and even and cadaverous voice.

He typed in a description on his label maker, situated on his desk. He printed out the label and stuck it on the box. He put the box next to the Devil's Bible on his perfectly groomed desk.

"Everyone leave. Megistus and I have to speak," the Count said, as he turned to face the wall of television screens that showed different things.

"Master, I am listening," said Megistus, timidly.

"What news do you have about my Gadha?"

"I do not have it. There were complications," spoke Megistus, terrified.

"If you mean to tell me that you died and your apparition came back to tell of your failure, then that is acceptable."

"No. The detective was too mighty. The Rabbis and Priests were trained beyond our expectations. Also, there were more evil forces than ourselves to contend with. There were four unknown, Gothic looking entities, equally as interested in acquiring the object. They just ripped apart my men." Megistus hoped the explanation was enough. However, deep down, he knew it was not.

CHAPTER 33

"So you failed, oh mightiest of all magicians."

"I failed to recover the Gadha because I learned that there are some forces greater than myself," said Megistus.

"I know. I felt everything. I saw even more. If you had gone into battle, I would have troubled myself to find another Thrice Magician. My Artificially Intelligent *Black Knight Satellites* serve me well, even from space. Ashamedly, the same cannot be said for you, my vicar."

"The four Gothic men turned into terrible beasts. They were the essence of evil," defended Megistus.

"What about the giant man and two women?" asked the Count, disinterested.

"I do not know about them. They seemed very powerful indeed. It was as if the power of the universe surrounded them."

"I saw and I felt."

"I have some more news, master. *It is about John Duboise, your son.* He fought two men and a woman. All of them had extraordinary abilities."

"I have sired many sons and daughters. All of them are supremely unworthy of their genetic inheritance. They are much less deserved of the monetary wealth that I possess. Better were I to have spawned children by Sunflower and Dandelion than to have wasted any time on my fruitless progeny.

They lack an indomitable will and an unbreakable fortitude. Their spirits are weak and easily broken. They cannot do what my legacy demands of them. However, a legacy implies that the originator has long since died. I am much more alive than you can imagine."

"Your son is now more than you knew him to be. He has abilities inside him derived from matter that is unbeknownst to the planet," put forth Megistus.

"Alien or supernatural?" the Count asked, only imperceptibly interested.

"I have used deep and dark divinations and gained no morsel of information. I have congressed with the darkest of beings and found that even they are clueless as to the origin of this material. The darkness that inhabits your son pales in comparison to any that I have dealt with before. I have a video feed to the cell in which he is being held. Screen two will do," said Megistus.

The Thrice Magician pulled out a phone and called the warden of the prison department in the Palace of Palaces and Castle of Castles. He ushered in a shackled young hominid, which had been an experiment from the Research and Development department. John Duboise was burdened with chains as he sat quietly in a chair. John looked at the creature and rolled his eyes in defiance.

The Count watched the screen as the warden slit the throat of the experiment gone wrong and then stepped out of the cage. The lifeblood seeped out of the body of the hominid, as it quickly died. Suddenly, two great, gaping mouths emerged from the palms of John and pulled the carcass of the creature towards him. The extra appendages loudly munched on the bones and flesh of the creature as John shuddered in delight. Forked tongues licked the blood off the floor so that the janitor had as little work to do as possible.

The Immortal Count sat back in his throne and stroked his chin. The wheels of his incomprehensible mind turned in a symphony of elaborate machinations. As he looked at the screen, the room darkened and everything faded out of view. He felt something wrong, like a nagging at the back of his mind, wrong. He was surprised to hear the people that he had just dismissed, back in the room. He turned and saw that the séance was in full swing again. This was déjà vu, except that he was aware of the change in venue.

"Come to us and be with us. Come here to this place and show yourself, that we may see you. Use the energies presented here and manifest your presence. Yes. This cloth was something dear to you. Reach out and feel it. Remember the memories you have attached to it," spoke the medium in a clear and dramatic voice.

"Fools, did I not dismiss you? Shall I throw you out of this world as well?" the Count vehemently said as he slapped his hand upon the desk. A pound would have meant certain death.

"But Immortal Count, we just began a few minutes ago. You summoned us here," soothed Mademoiselle Cordova.

CHAPTER 33

Megistus watched as an apparition slowly materialized over the table. She had shoulder-length blond hair and was dressed in fifteenth-century clothing. Her face and features were elegant and smart. One of the henchmen opened his eyes but quickly closed them, as if he could not believe it. The medium looked at the apparition and then looked in The Immortal Count's direction. He turned the Throne of Thoth, which served as his desk chair and faced the medium and her specially summoned guest.

"Jacques. How good to see you, my love," said the apparition, sweetly.

"You mock me Medini. For I know that is who you are," said the Count, as he pulled off the ring of Solomon and flicked it on the table.

"Jacques what are you saying? I am your long lost love!" she defended.

Suddenly, her ethereal body convulsed and shook, as the power of the Count took hold of her nonexistent personage. The air turned heavy, as the sky and ground crushed the energies of the being and she sunk to the table in futile resistance. The medium and henchmen died in seconds. It was an agonizing death caused by their fragile bodies being crushed by The Immortal Count as he manipulated the earth and sky. The apparition looked fearfully around and then stared into the Count's eyes.

"What are you doing to me?" she screamed, as her corpulent body became heavy and sluggish. "How is this possible? I am feeling pain and fear. I have a body?"

"I have a place for you to reside until your services are needed. It is very cozy with lots of amenities. Actually, it is a pocket dimension prison which I specially designed for just such an occasion. There are other guests confined to their own suites as well."

The Count opened a very technical-looking box, about six inches on each edge and trapped the shocked and overwhelmed Medini inside. Her screams were a mixture of excitement, fear, and surprise. He printed out a label and stuck it on the box. He placed it next to the Devil's Bible on his perfectly groomed desk.

"Megistus."

CHAPTER 33

"Master, I am listening," said Megistus timidly.

"What news do you have about my Gadha?"

"You sent me for a statue, Master. I know of no such mission to retrieve a Gadha. I regret that I have not acquired it. There were complications."

"A statue? I sent you to get me the Gadha of Gilgamesh!" said the Count, as he raised his voice a little.

"Here is a museum pamphlet on your desk that told about the statue. It is this that you desired us to obtain. We did not acquire it due to some unfortunate circumstances," spoke Megistus.

"If you mean to tell me that you died and your apparition came back to tell of your failure, then that is acceptable."

"No. The detective was too mighty. The Rabbis and Priests were trained beyond our expectations."

"What about the four Gothic men and their transformation?" inquired the Count.

"What are you speaking about? We fought detective Brentt Williams and his friends."

"I know. I felt everything. I saw even more. My *Black Knight Satellites* with AI serve me well, even from space. I saw the giant monsters. I saw what you did not see," said the Count, as a light went on in his already illuminated head. "You don't know because something has changed. What about the giant man and the two women?" asked the Count, now showing interest.

"I do not know about them, but there were two men and a woman that fought your son," defended the Magician. "All of them had extraordinary abilities. I know the disdain you have for your children. However, your son is now more than you knew him to be. He has abilities inside him derived from matter that is unbeknownst to the planet."

"Unchanged," murmured the Count.

"I have used deep and dark divinations and gained no morsel of information. I have congressed with the darkest of beings and found that even they are clueless as to the origin of this material. The darkness that inhabits your son, pales in comparison to any that I have dealt with before. I have a video feed to the cell in which he is held. Screen two will do."

CHAPTER 33

"No. I will allow him an audience," the Count stated. Both of them went to the prison wing to see John Duboise.

The eight-foot-tall, powerfully built, Immortal Count looked with disgust upon his chained and shackled son that sat in a chair. John did not look up but sat silently and stared at the floor. The warden ushered in a shackled young hominid, which had been a failed experiment from the Research and Development department. John looked at the creature and rolled his eyes in defiance. The Count's giant right hand grabbed the hominid by the neck and squeezed. The life sped out of the creature's body, as it quickly died. The Count stepped back and waited.

Suddenly, two great, gaping mouths emerged from the palms of John and pulled the carcass of the creature towards him. The extra appendages loudly munched on the bones and flesh of the creature as John shuddered in delight.

The Count had seen this happen before. The actions of Megistus and the others changed slightly, but the turn of events related to his son remained the same.

"I will be in my office. Leave me to my thoughts," the Count commented. He turned from the disturbing sight and made his way to his chambers. He reflected upon the recent events. As he sat and contemplated, a very faint, one-sided smile grew on the side of his lips. Something his face had not seen in centuries.

CHAPTER 34: Technon Visits Anthraxis

Anthraxis stood alone in the prison cell Atomos had specially designed for him. He heard, felt, and smelled the life that flourished upon the King of the Gods temple planet. He sighed and sat down, dejected and sullen.

"Anthraxis. Hello. Can you hear me?" Technon's voice drowned out the trickling streams and the chirping birds, as he called.

"What do you want? Have you come to gloat about my predicament?" spat the God of War.

"I came to ascertain the viability of your innocence or guilt. Did you attack Detrimentus? Did you take his planet?"

"I may be a ruffian and a brute. I instigated a fight with you. I used my Contest of the Nine to destroy a galaxy. But, I did not attack Detrimentus. He gave me no reason. And, I certainly did not take his planet."

"Cosmica said that Detrimentus spoke of a smell which pervaded the area," stated Technon.

"I do not know of any smell."

"They saw the armor and the sword. They felt your power," pressed Technon.

"Even though the power was mine, it was not me. I did not attack him."

"For some reason, I believe you. You are a brute and bullied me, but I do believe that you are innocent," surmised Technon.

"Why do you care about my business? I would think that you are the last one to come to my aid?" queried Anthraxis.

"Let's just say, my adventures with Heddonna and Archituria had some similarities with what happened to Detrimentus," spoke Technon, as he walked back to the council of the Gods.

CHAPTER 34

Cosmica fumed and burned at the sight of Technon talking with Anthraxis. She wished she had defied the will of Atomos and kicked the God of War's tail across the universe, just as he did to Detrimentus. Technon walked back to the meeting and voiced his opinion that Anthraxis was not guilty.

"We saw him and even Detrimentus said it was him," demanded Galaxyia.

"Is Detrimentus able to speak before us?" asked Caddeussus.

"I am!" said a voice, that rang through the ears of the council and reverberated off The Contest of the Nine.

The other Gods looked at the God of Death as he materialized upon his mighty throne which was overlooked by his contribution to The Contest of the Nine. His countenance seemed much better, thanks to the love and care of the Goddesses, Cosmica and Galaxyia.

Technon remembered when he was beaten up. Heddonna saw to him and her company took away the pain. After that time, he vowed to be ready for any battle. Therefore, he introduced Nanobots into his body, which kept him in tip-top condition and even more beyond perfection.

"Speak Detrimentus, God of Death. Let your side of this matter be heard," adjudicated Atomos.

"Anthraxis wore his armor. I noticed him as he moved the planet and I followed him. He stunk so bad that I wanted to barf. He acted more brutish than normal. Anthraxis seemed stronger than me. He fought very well and used underhanded moves. He did not behave and sound as he normally did. I don't know if it was an act to throw me off. But for what purpose?"

"Detrimentus, you said there was a stench. Did it smell like the one coming from those creatures over there?" asked Technon.

Detrimentus inhaled a deep breath. He took in the smell which emanated from the creatures in the cage. Each of the molecules entered his body and made their way to the receptors in his nose. His omnipotent mind recognized the scent immediately, out of quadrillions he was already familiar with. He nodded his head, in recognition that it was the same scent. He shook his head as he tried to force the smell out of his nose, but it was already carved into his mind.

"There is the problem of not knowing about these things. They have no past, present or future. Did you see anything of your assailant, Detrimentus?" asked Heddonna.

"No, I did not. That is what made it so difficult," replied Detrimentus.

"Do you think that the captured creatures are related to the being that took the planet and attacked Death?" asked Archituria, looking at Technon.

"They share two features that are quite peculiar. The smell is a big point, but it can be duplicated. However, not knowing anything about them, it was not something that should be possible," explained Technon. "Heddonna, the guy you did not know in your library, were there any other distinguishable features?"

"No, not at all," she replied.

"I feel all of them have something in common. Perhaps they were a different version of the same creature. Maybe they originated in the same manner," surmised Technon.

"Are you saying that all of them could be from one?" asked Cosmica.

"I think that is right on the money. I agree with Technon," piped up Archituria.

"Didn't you find it strange that the two captive creatures resembled the ones on the temple planet of Anthraxis?" interjected Caddeussus, still implicating Anthraxis

"Is that so?" asked Archituria.

"Yes. What are the chances of that?" chimed in Galaxyia.

"Technon, do you think we should examine the creatures on the temple planet of Anthraxis and compare them with the ones we captured?" asked Heddonna, turning to Technon.

"That is a very good idea. We should question those monsters of his," supported Technon.

"*Atomos, you made them. Do you think they have a tendency to rebel against their master?* Even more so, to have beaten up one of our own?" asked Caddeussus, with a raised eyebrow.

CHAPTER 34

"I made them, yes. However, all of their movements are known to us. They have a past, present and future. We can see that, if we questioned them, what their answers will be," defended Atomos.

"Atomos, I think they should be examined by our embodiments, just for us to be placated," put forth Technon.

"I feel that we should follow the recommendations of the Goddess of Knowledge and God of Technology. Perhaps one might see, what another did not," surmised Atomos.

Each God teleported an embodiment to the temple planet of Anthraxis, in order to examine the creatures. Since Atomos created them, he took point and called them forth. The Leviathan and the Behemoth knelt before the council of the Gods.

"Rise creatures. We have come to do some preliminary investigations about you and your master, Anthraxis. Do not be afraid," reassured Atomos.

"Has Anthraxis ever asked you to attack a planet or any one of us?" questioned Technon.

The eight heads of the Leviathan answered in unison, with a great and thunderous voice, "No. We were not ordered by our master to do such a thing."

The mighty Behemoth also answered, "No. I was not ordered to do such a thing."

"Please, stand still," ordered Heddonna.

She and the other Gods looked at everything which made up both creatures. All of the molecules and the energies of the monsters were tracked by their minds. They looked into the past, present, and future of the great beasts. All of the multiverse versions of the creatures were observed as well. The Gods saw the journeys of each particle as they were ingested by the courtesans and servants of Anthraxis. Nothing indicated any clues as to the similarities of these creatures with the two held in captivity, on the temple planet of Atomos.

"Okay everyone, looks like we are done here," spoke Atomos, as all the embodiments of the Gods went back from whence they came.

Back at the temple planet of Atomos, all of the Gods walked up to the cleverly fashioned cage which held the two monsters.

CHAPTER 34

As the Gods had their attentions on the front, Technon went around to the back of the cage. He quickly caught hold of one of the mighty tails of the Leviathan. It struggled and screamed, as its giant tail whipped around. Heddonna saw that Technon was having difficulties, so she rushed to his aid. They both held down the mighty tail and marveled at the power of the beast.

"Atomos, see if there is anything that you can tell from this. The creature is very strong!" grunted Heddonna.

Atomos came closer and placed his massive hands on the tail of the beast. He carefully avoided the sharp metallic spikes. He sensed the power flowing in every cell of the creature. He felt the life that flowed in the vast networks of veins and arteries. He did not feel where the creature originated from and he could not feel where the future of this creature resided. He felt the darkness that lurked inside and permeated throughout the beast. *It was something he had not felt in a very long time. Atomos had not created this monster. Suddenly, he felt very afraid.*

CHAPTER 35: Asheley In The Library

A sheley, Theo and Frank Lin looked in awe as the great doors to the Akashic Records Library came alive and presented its story. Frank Lin had been there many times before, but it did not diminish the experience as he stepped through the entrance.

This was Asheley's first time at the Library and she memorized every detail, which was stored in her advanced, computerized brain. Over the past few days, her knowledge had exponentially skyrocketed and she did things that she could have never done before. She had copied the powers of Brentt Williams and expounded upon them. Theo entered last and he placed a gloved hand on the door. He felt the wood and the texture of it, just like last time.

"Asheley, these gloves feel like there is nothing on my hands. It is hard to believe that you created weapon warp gauntlets that are so thin and form-fitting," exclaimed Theo softly.

"I just wanted you to be prepared for anything. I extrapolated that since we were attacked by Reptilians, having had no prior contact with them, they might perceive us as part of detective Williams' group. In addition, John has powers that we do not fully comprehend. We must be vigilant at all costs," explained Asheley.

"Okay, guys. So, go over the plan again, please," said Frank Lin.

"We need to find out what's wrong with John. Next, we have to find a way to help him. Then, we ought to see where he is located, to give him that help," explained Theo, as Asheley looked at him. "In addition, I would like to find out some information on Asheley, to see what the future has in store for her. Lastly, I would like to get some information on my trip to

CHAPTER 35

heaven. Why was I not recorded in the tablets? Why did that lady not know me?"

"That is very succinct and pointed, Theo. We should have no problems staying on track," chimed in Asheley. "Frank Lin, where do you normally get your questions answered?"

"A kiosk is a good place to start. Hold on to me guys," Frank Lin said, as he touched the shelf. "Can I go to a Kiosk please?"

Before they knew it, they found themselves in front of a rotunda. It was a hundred feet in diameter and lined with fifty tall pillars. The material itself was a shimmery, clear marble, unlike anything Earth offered. There was a pedestal located in the very center of the rotunda, where the entity known as the Kiosk, stood.

The Kiosk was linked to everything in the Library and served as a guide. It spoke every language imaginable in the universe and it greeted everyone in a warm and inviting manner. It assumed any form but usually took on the likeness of the being that asked the question. There were trillions of Kiosks located in the Library, each willing to help out those who sought knowledge.

Frank Lin stepped onto the clear marble and left Theo and Asheley behind. The pillars scanned Frank Lin with an electric blue, wide-angled beam as he stood in front of the pedestal. It deeply scanned his brain and soul and identified him to the great expanse of the universe. The scan read his memories and saw the contextual origins of his questions which he asked of the Library. The silhouette of a human materialized before him and waited to be greeted.

"Hello. I am looking to heal John Duboise from his ailment," Frank Lin asked.

"Hello, Frank Lin Shao. John Duboise was the human that attacked you at the museum. I have found no ailment within him. You will find that encounter in Multiverse number 369258147, Galaxy number 741852963, Solar System number 147258369, Planet number 3, Year number 2019 and Soul Print number 963852741," remarked the silhouetted Kiosk, in a warm voice.

"What do I do? It didn't find anything wrong with him?" Frank Lin asked his friends.

"Try: Is there any foreign matter in John Duboise? Maybe that will elicit an answer," suggested Asheley.

"Is there any foreign matter in John Duboise?" asked Frank Lin of the Kiosk silhouette.

"Yes. There is foreign matter present in his body that has not coincided with any known materials relevant to the human race," answered the Kiosk, frankly.

Frank Lin looked at Theo and Asheley and continued.

"Is the foreign matter alien? And if so, what is it?" prompted Frank Lin.

"Frank Lin, I do not know the chemical makeup of the substance found within him. I do not have any record of such matter in the multiple universes. Perhaps, there is an error in your question. Suggestions include: Does John do drugs? or Does John have a substance abuse problem?" suggested the Kiosk.

"It doesn't know. Asheley, didn't you say that you didn't know what it was either?" asked Frank Lin.

"I did not recognize the substance in John based on my knowledge of everything in the world. In addition, it shared some of the same properties that were found in the four Gothic dudes. I reasoned that the Akashic Records Library, with all of the accumulated knowledge in the universe, would have data on it. I noticed that it scanned your mind and body. Perhaps it drew upon some references to him, from your recollections," surmised Asheley.

"Let me try. I knew John a lot longer than you do," Theo said, as he stepped on the rotunda and walked to the pedestal. *He and Frank Lin were on the rotunda at the same time.*

The pillars deeply scanned Theo. The scan lasted a few more seconds longer than it did for Frank Lin. It stopped and Theo expected to address the Kiosk, but the scan started back up again. This time, it scanned much longer. The silhouette of the Kiosk looked perplexed as if it were possible for a silhouette to do that. It scanned the surprised Theo again, yet a third time. Asheley and Frank Lin gave each other a worried look.

"There is an error in the scan. I have detected matter which I do not recognize. There is no soul print that identifies the originator of the query. That was two incidents in a row in which

I do not have information on the subject matter. An internal diagnostic will commence in one minute," the Kiosk stated.

"Theo, get off the rotunda, quickly!" yelled Asheley, as she floated up, over the clear marble and grabbed his hands. She floated back down as he hugged her in relief.

Frank Lin quickly stepped towards the pedestal and asked the Kiosk, "Hello. I am looking for the location of John Duboise. Can you assist me with that?"

The scans began on Frank Lin and there seemed to be a sense of normalcy as the silhouette of the Kiosk answered him.

"Frank Lin. John Duboise is located at The Immortal Count's residence in the Ortega Mountains of California. The address is 666 Ortega Mountain Road, room 777 in the prisoners' wing of the estate. A map of the property and the surrounding area is available for use. It is located in Multiverse number 369258147, Galaxy number 741852963, Solar System number 147258369, Planet number 3, Year number 2019 and Soul Print number 963852741. The same as your previous inquiry," the Kiosk reiterated.

"Ask: Is there any way that the unknown matter could be separated from John's body without hurting him," recommended Theo.

Frank Lin nodded his head and continued, "Is there any way that the unknown matter could be separated from John's body without hurting or killing him?"

"Yes. There is a way for matter to be separated. It requires the Quantum Matter Trans-Substantiating Extraction Machine. A blueprint of it could be found in Multiverse number 152487963, Galaxy number 325698147, Solar System number 124875963, Planet number 12, Year number 568924 and Soul Print number 956847312."

"Could you pull up the blueprints, so we can see it, please?" asked Frank Lin.

"That is possible," the Kiosk stated. There appeared a blueprint of the machine, in a larger than life three-dimensional model. It was completed with notes and inscriptions in a language that none of them knew.

CHAPTER 35

"Oh great, what are we going to do about this? Does anyone know how to read alien?" lamented Frank Lin.

"I have finished memorizing it. Frank Lin, you can step off now. Let me see. The Kiosk has not identified Theo because he had no soul print. The material in John was not identified as well. I wonder what would happen if I stepped forward and asked a question?" theorized Asheley.

"Asheley, wait till Frank Lin gets off the rotunda, then try. Be careful. We don't want to mess around with the Library that has all the records in the universe," cautioned Theo.

Asheley took off her light hiking boots and socks and stepped onto the rotunda. The pillars scanned her as she stood in the middle of the beams. Unbeknownst to the Kiosk, she scanned back. The Kiosk stopped and started a second scan, this time it lasted a few minutes longer. She tried to establish a digital connection with the Kiosk, which took the entire length of the second scan. She rose a few feet off of the rotunda and contemplated for a minute.

"It has not read me either. First, I will have to hack into the Akashic Records Library to steal and impersonate a soul print. After I have finished, I will have to alter my mind and body to become the person. After gaining uninterrupted access, I will reconfigure my brain and body in order to amalgamate all of the information that we need. Hopefully, in the process, become more advanced," explained Asheley.

"I don't believe this. You guys aren't even on file in the Akashic Records Library. To top that, you are hacking into it!" gasped Frank Lin.

Asheley's eyes closed. Theo looked on in amazement and horror as Asheley winced and grunted as she sifted through all of the information that flowed within her. Her resolve inspired Theo and Frank Lin.

"I will be fine gentlemen. This may take a few minutes. Don't worry," she reassured.

"We should do a perimeter sweep. Just in case there are any prying eyes. I did not think that this would take so long. We'll meet back here in ten minutes," suggested Theo.

"That sounds good. I'll take over here," said Frank Lin.

CHAPTER 35

After they looked around the perimeter of the rotunda, both Theo and Frank Lin met back at the designated point.

"I have succeeded. I used the soul print of Catherine. Theo, I hope I have not offended you by doing so," she said, as she came back down on the rotunda. The scan resumed for yet a third time. Her skin rippled and moved as if it were alive. The Nanobots inside of her burst out and covered her body, reshaping it. Her skin took on a new texture, as she reorganized the molecules in her body to become more fleshly and biological. She had a confident smile on her face as the electric blue beams of light stopped scanning her and the silhouette of the Kiosk appeared.

"Oh great, universal identity theft, that's just what we needed!" exclaimed Frank Lin.

"It's okay. Just be careful," soothed Theo.

"I have upgraded my brainpower a Lawrellion-fold," Asheley said, smiling.

"That means that she will definitely beat me at any kind of board game," joked Theo.

"That statement was a billion percent accurate, Theo," she smiled back. "According to the Kiosk, I could not be sensed in my previous form. I reasoned that since I am not a biological entity, I would not have a soul print. I mimicked Catherine's soul print to have unrestricted access. There is some information here that does allow for Artificial Intelligences to access the Akashic Records Library, however, that is of secondary importance."

"I am very interested to know why Asheley and I are not in the Library. However, we need to help John first. There's no telling what he could be capable of, with this power inside of him," recommended Theo.

"These are the things that we needed information about: the extended blueprint of the Quantum Matter Trans-Substantiating Extraction Machine, information on The Immortal Count, details of his residence, how come Theo and I haven't shown up on any records in the Library, why he was not in the books or tablets of heaven, and why were there similarities between the matter in John and the four Gothic dudes," Asheley said as she turned to Theo and Frank Lin.

"That seems about right. Anything else, Frank Lin?" asked Theo.

"I wanted to know if I will die of brain cancer," said Frank Lin solemnly.

"Frank, I thought they cured that?" said Theo, empathetically.

"No, they could not, Theo. I didn't want to tell you because you had your own things that needed to be dealt with. Besides, I have something to tell you."

"Okay, Frank Lin, what's going on?"

"I was at the Akashic Records Library a few times before I met you. I asked for an answer to the same question that I'm asking now. This was the answer I got:

'Find the one who is not found. The found must first be lost. Be unable to put your hands on what is mislaid. The unwritten must be read. The unthinkable must be conceived. The unknown must be acknowledged. The impossible must come to pass.

I have trans-versed many dimensions. I have defeated immortals in combat. I have been to the edge of the universe and beyond. I am a man among men, a man among kings, and a man among the Gods...'

I feel that I was meant to bring you here, Theo. It is no coincidence that you are not in the records. I realize that now. Why that is, I don't know," explained Frank Lin.

"I had no idea. After everything we have been through, I could not have gotten here without you. Frank, it's not your fight with John. If you want to leave before we go after him, I will understand," said Theo, putting a hand on Frank Lin's shoulder.

"Frank Lin, I have *wirelessly* accessed information on how to cure your cancer from the Akashic Records Library. Perhaps, before we go to get John, I will give you a clean bill of health," said Asheley with a smile.

"Theo, your robot girlfriend is truly amazing!" exclaimed Frank Lin.

"She is. Asheley, how is it coming with the info that we need?"

"The extended blueprint of the Quantum Matter Trans-Substantiating Extraction Machine: got it. The information on

The Immortal Count and details of his residence: got it. I am having trouble with finding the other pieces of information."

"Okay. I don't know where to go from there," sighed Theo. Asheley continued her search for answers.

"Everything in the entire universe is recorded in this library. *I did a cross-reference of your biological constitution, my biochemical makeup, the makeup of the four Goths and the signature of the foreign matter in John. All four of us entities have the same composition. All of us are unknown in the infinite universes,*" stated Asheley.

"Are you kidding me?" exclaimed Theo, as he sat down with his back against a bookcase.

"Okay. Theo. I don't know how this is possible. Maybe, look at who made the Library. Maybe, they left out a part. Maybe, they haven't finished entering the data," suggested Frank Lin.

"The Library was made by the Goddess of Knowledge, Heddonna. The Kiosk entity was worked on by the God of Technology, Technon. I shall pull up a picture of them for your consideration," said Asheley, doing just that.

"*Oh my God, I know that woman. She was the lady from when I first got to the Akashic Records Library! She was the one that said she did not know me,*" exclaimed Theo.

Bibtoran sat quietly as he watched the shenanigans of the trio on the security cameras of the Records Library. The deep furrows on his face slowly vanished, as he saw the one that his charges tried to find. He had taken care of them for hundreds of millennia and they never gave up hope on finding this individual.

He pushed a strand of graying hair out of his face and stroked the very luxurious beard that grew on his squared jaw. He had seen the one called Theo in the Library when he had caught the attention of Goddess Heddonna.

He leaned back in his ultra-plush chair, crafted of materials from out of this world and sighed. Theo came back to find out more. It was a bold move. Maybe he did not realize that the Goddess was looking for him. He did not realize that 'they' were looking for him as well. He had to get the word out to them, the

CHAPTER 35

four that he loved like daughters. Raechellee, Elainney, Alexyia, and Aerica were going to finally get to see Theo.

CHAPTER 36: Does Brentt Become A Believer?

Brentt hurried through the front door of the Williams' house and went into the kitchen. He felt severely agitated. He found Agness there with a tray of freshly baked white and dark chocolate chip cookies. He ravenously ate a few as Agness looked on, amused. When Brentt calmed down, she spoke to him.

"I saw that you guys did a neat job at the museum."

"It was a nightmare and a miracle rolled into one," Brentt said, as he seated himself on the kitchen stool.

"How so? The news said that you stopped some people from carrying out a heist. I am assuming that was not the case?"

"No. There were Reptilians and Big-Foot soldiers. There were four Gothic dudes as well. They changed into monsters. Then, three powerful beings came down from the sky and fought the monsters. They tore up the place and cities were destroyed. My team and I saw it. Something happened on the way to the precinct this morning. When I arrived at work, the events which had occurred at the museum were as if they had not taken place," explained Brentt, exasperated.

"I haven't heard any of that on the news," answered Agness.

"I believe that everyone was affected. Why I wasn't, I don't know," theorized Brentt.

"Brentt, I know there are some weird things out there. Like our neighbors for one. But I trust everything that you tell me. On the news, there are no destroyed cities. If you say that it happened, then I believe you."

"The giant beings were beyond perfection. I felt the power that emanated from them. Who or what were they? I need to find out who they are and why they were there. I have to find out who the monsters are. I have to find out what happened. I have to go to the Akashic Records Library," said Brentt resolutely, as he ate a few more cookies.

CHAPTER 36

Brentt looked at the clear diamond tiles on the floor of the Akashic Records Library. He had already passed the great looking door. He wished that his dad had hired the architect that fashioned the Library door. He could have constructed the door to their castle-looking mansion. However, he and his dad painstakingly carved, varnished and polished their door. The door which held an embossment of a being, that no one could identify. The sentimental value was priceless, even if the design was a little muddled. He looked at the unmarked 'books', a meter tall and about half as thick and wondered whose story they contained.

He had to find the answers and a Kiosk seemed a good way to point him in the right direction. Luckily, he knew where one was. However, someone was in the process of utilizing it. He crept along the shelves that led up to the Kiosk. He saw two giant images of the powerful beings that fought at the museum.

"Welcome, to the Akashic Records Library, detective Brentt Williams. Last time we saw each other, four beasts tore up the place. Good to see that you emerged from that battle, unharmed," said Asheley, out of nowhere. She was still gathering information from the Library's database.

Theo and Frank Lin turned and saw the stunned Brentt as he emerged from the shadows of the shelves. He looked at the images and then looked to the trio that was in the midst of the commotion. He shook his head as he came closer.

"Asheley, I knew you were a lot more than I originally figured. I don't know what happened to you guys after Jezebelle and Jacob killed the Reptilian. I was kind of busy with the end of the world stuff."

"Actually, it jumped back up and attacked us. We killed it good though. Theo cut it in half," replied Frank Lin.

"I see. Asheley, you accessed the Library. These beings were at the museum. You saw them too?" asked the detective, nodding towards the images.

CHAPTER 36

"I did not observe them at the museum. I arrived at this point through a series of queries that were concurrently made," she explained.

"They made the Library," replied Theo. "She is the Goddess of Knowledge and he is the God of Technology."

"What were Gods doing at the museum?" Frank Lin asked.

"This can't be. These were Gods at the museum? They fought the four monsters on Earth!" exclaimed Brentt.

"What are you talking about? Those guys were at the museum and they fought monsters?" queried Frank Lin

"Oh boy, this might get a little crazy. I think everyone needs to straighten their end of the story. How about you go first, detective Williams?" suggested Theo.

"I assume that you are Frank Lin?" Brentt asked. Frank Lin nodded.

Brentt told them about the battle and the events which occurred at the museum. He also informed them about the change in events. Everyone around him was affected by the change except him. He detailed his mission to get to the bottom of things and how he thought he might find the answers here.

Theo then told his side of the story. He expounded upon the events that took place at the museum. He covered the battle with John. He also had an experience similar to Brentt, in which he felt events had changed. He filled in the details of their escapades at the Library. Theo debated about whether to tell Brentt about his and Asheley's relation to the monsters.

In the end, he told the detective because he seemed to have had knowledge of this type of subject. Frank Lin did not remember some of what happened because he was affected by the change in events.

"You are kidding me! You are made up of the same stuff as the monsters and the thing in your friend?" asked Brentt.

"Apparently so," sighed Theo.

"This was the same person that you saw, the first time that you were here? That said she did not know you?" inquired Brentt, pointing to the image of Heddonna.

"Yes. But why would she come to Earth?" queried Theo.

CHAPTER 36

"Theo, it is possible, that since she had no knowledge of you, she wanted to investigate why that was the case," suggested Asheley.

"That could be. It leaves a big question. What was she going to do with you? Why did she fight those monsters? Did the Count send those monsters? If so, then where did he get them?" puzzled Brentt.

"Asheley, are you okay? You have been on the rotunda for a while now," asked Theo, concerned.

"I am fine. Actually, Theo, I have completely changed my composition. I have become more than a robot. During the last few minutes, I have updated myself with the most advanced technology available. I can do things that are, to human beings and some aliens, impossible. In addition, I have found the strongest metal in the universe, which I have infused into my body. I used the energy that flowed through the Library and manufactured foreverum," explained Asheley.

"Does this mean that you will be all metal and clammy?" asked Theo.

"No. I am as human as you or Brentt, but indestructible," she said, as she stepped off the rotunda.

In her hand, she materialized a Quantum Matter Trans-Substantiating Extraction Machine. It looked larger than a red, handheld vacuum. The theory was, that it scanned John and separated the foreign matter from his body by teleporting it from inside him into the containment chamber. The machine used a quantum computer, which calculated the positions of the matter so that none of the molecules of John ended up somewhere else.

"Okay, looks like we are set," said Theo. "Detective Williams, we are going to get our friend, John, from The Immortal Count's house."

"That's the tyrant that sent the Reptilians and the Big-Foot soldiers to the museum. He's very dangerous and is responsible for the deaths of lots of people, whether directly or by henchmen that followed his orders. I don't think you are up to it. I need to come with you," warned Brentt.

"Yes, it will be very treacherous indeed. I have seen the information that the Akashic Records Library has on him. He has been alive for ten million years and has lived through multiple catastrophic events. He is extremely powerful and could have easily taken on the four Gothic dudes.

The Library says that there was a fifty percent chance that he would have been evenly matched against the Leviathans and Behemoths. *Because of his unique physical makeup, the Library can calculate his future actions and assigns probabilities of them occurring.* This is unlike looking at the future actions of other lifeforms in the Library, which is completely accurate and telling of their actions. His life is a series of probabilistic occurrences," explained Asheley.

"Oh my God, are you telling me that he is that powerful!" exclaimed Brentt.

"Yes. However, I have some ideas that will help us. Theo, I would like to relay some information that I have gathered to you and Frank Lin before you go. Brentt, this would give you some time to access information about the Count," said Asheley.

"Sure. That sounds good. I'd like to see what we are up against," he said as he stepped onto the rotunda. The pillars scanned Brentt and in a few seconds, the silhouette of the Kiosk appeared.

"Frank Lin, I noticed that when you fire your spirit blast, you have to charge up for a minute or two. I have accessed information that will allow you to unlock your full potential and use your energies efficiently. In addition, this will give you the potential to use three different types of auras. The green aura will be used to heal anything within a hundred-foot sphere around you. The blue will be used to stun anyone in the same area. Lastly, the red aura will be used to kill anything in the prescribed sphere as well. I will have to relay that information via the Nanobot infusion. Do you agree for me to do this?" explained Asheley.

"Have little robots in my head? Okay, sure. I definitely want a fighting chance. It sounds like this Count guy is tough."

Asheley placed her hands to Frank Lin's ears and a stream of unseen, supercharged Nanobots, little copies of Asheley herself, climbed into his ears and entered his brain. They opened up the neural pathways, which allowed him to control this incredible power.

In addition, they programmed the muscle memory of the aura control, without Frank Lin ever having done the moves. He felt a tingling sensation all about his body, as new superhighways of information were constructed into his physique. His nerves were multiplied, in order to allow him to control the density of the blast.

The cancer in his brain dwindled as the Nano Asheleys broke the disease apart and repaired the damaged tissue. The Nano Asheleys eliminated harmful substances that had accumulated over the years, from his entire body. When she finished, Asheley moved away and scanned Frank Lin.

"I feel the same but, I feel more of everything. It is as if I am taking in more information," he gasped.

"Everything is as it should be. You are free from cancer. You are in one hundred percent good health," smiled Asheley. Frank Lin was speechless. He hugged Asheley, who gently hugged him back. When the hug was over, she turned to Theo.

"It's your turn baby. I have a special surprise for you. Since you might have a Goddess after you, there are some things we need to accomplish. I will transfer all of the information I have garnered from the Library, into your brain via Nano me's," she said with a smile. She gently put her hands on Theo's ears as she hugged him.

Brentt Williams paid no attention to the trio outside the rotunda. He was focused on getting information about The Immortal Count. The Kiosk provided that information, albeit most of it was in the fifty percent or below probability range of it being accurate. However, it was still better than nothing. He then requested information on the so-called Gods that he saw on Earth.

"Why did they come to Earth?"

"The God of Technology and the Goddess of Knowledge searched for an individual that could not be identified. They captured two creatures that could not be identified as well. The information is on…"

"Okay stop. I don't need it. Are they part of the nine that the organization, the Legacy of the Ascended Knowledge of the Nine, is based upon?"

"Yes," the Kiosk replied.

"Oh my God, they are real. And I just ended up helping a man on their most wanted list!" Brentt exclaimed as he rubbed his hand over his face. Graying stubble grew on the square of his jaw.

"How do I become stronger, to unlock my higher self, right now?"

"That is easy…" the Kiosk said, "Let me show you."

A few minutes later, Brentt Williams stepped off the rotunda a new man. Energy crackled around his body, as sinews and muscles moved in unison. He created an aura that was unlike anything he could have possibly imagined before. He felt that he could do anything and go anywhere. 'So this is what The Immortal Count feels', he thought to himself. He spied Asheley and the others as they wrapped up their enhancements.

"You guys ready?" Brentt cheerily asked.

"Sure. We are good to go," said Theo, ready for an adventure.

Asheley watched Brentt Williams with a slight glimmer in her eyes. She knew that there was something odd about him. She had seen Brentt's story in the Akashic Records Library and came across an interesting revelation. Brentt also had a unique physical make up, in which the Library had calculated his future actions and assigned probabilities of them occurring. *Just like The Immortal Count.* She decided that she had better keep this little tidbit of information to herself, for the time being.

Aerica woke up from her trance as her friends crowded around her. She was on the plush, tanned sofa in the den. She sighed and looked into Raechellee's blue eyes.

"Our father contacted me with the information that Theo's in the Library! He's with our neighbor and two others, Frank Lin and Asheley. We have to go now if we are to catch him," reported Aerica.

"Oh my, that is the break we were waiting for!" exclaimed Elainney.

"He also said that the Gods examined two beasts that they captured," continued Aerica.

"If they are preoccupied with that, then we can get below their radar," suggested Alexyia.

"What are we waiting for? Let's Go!" exclaimed Raechellee.

They all teleported to the Library, excited and hopeful, that they would finally meet up with the person that they had long been searching for.

CHAPTER 37: The Unmade

The Leviathan and Behemoth presented the Gadha of Gilgamesh to Wretch #1 as they bowed in reverence to their master. Wretch #1 took the weapon and excitedly examined it. He turned it over in his hands, as he savored this minor victory.

Even though the place was blacker than the darkest reaches of space, they saw as if it were noonday with two suns. The other Wretches worked at various points in the universal door, as they examined the keyholes.

Luckily the hole, into which the Gadha fitted, was nearby. He slid the weapon into the keyhole and the locking mechanism hungrily clamped down upon it, soaking up the energy within.

Since Wretch #1 had ordered the Unmade to obtain the Gifts of the Nine, only two teams had returned. These guys brought the Gadha and another team came with the *Legs of Anansi*, another Gift of the Nine. Eight mighty Leviathan heads spoke in unison while it genuflected.

"Master, two of our kind were captured by the Gods. What shall we do about this?" It was more of a demand than a question. All of the other Wretches stopped what they were doing and crowded around the two monsters that spoke.

"Really, who were the Gods?" asked Wretch #1, with a voice that spoke softly with many voices.

"Heddonna, Technon, and Archituria," the Behemoth replied.

"That was a complication that we did not intend. How could they know of our plans? They do not know of our existence," contemplated Wretch #1, as he turned from his servants.

"There is something else. I saw Him," stated the eight Leviathan heads, shakily.

"What! What do you mean? He's alive? Are you sure?" Wretch #1 exclaimed in consternation, as he turned around.

"Yes, I am very sure. He was fighting one that we infected. And he created another," the eight heads added.

CHAPTER 37

While the Leviathan and the Behemoth dished out bad news, Wretch #100, who stood next to Wretch #1, spoke. He had more bad news to report.

"The collection of the Gifts of the Nine is taking too long. There are an infinite amount of universes that need to be searched and only a finite number of us," reminded Wretch #100.

"Hush you idiot. Two of our Unmade got captured by the Gods. Did you not also hear that He may have survived," hissed Wretch #1.

"No. That is not possible. We would have felt him," exclaimed Wretch #100.

"In any case, we must speed up the process of collecting the Gifts of the Nine. The Gods now know of our existence. We must also retrieve the two captured Unmade. I feel they might have been taken to the temple planet of Atomos," surmised Wretch #1.

"That might be true, but it is in the heart of the multiverse," warned Wretch #71.

"Wretch #100, do you think you can handle the Gods?" asked Wretch #1.

"I have beaten Anthraxis. I will retrieve the Unmade. Give me four Leviathans and four Behemoths and we're good," Wretch #100 said with a smile.

Moerdon and his friends devoured a delicious, five-star breakfast that consisted of chicken tikka masala with seasoned paneer, brown basmati fried rice with vegetables, and roasted garlic potatoes. Afterward, they turned their attention to reading the newly deciphered inscriptions on the walls of their abode.

The Goddess Heddonna saved them a lot of time by her kindness and they leisurely read to their hearts' desire. Moerdon thought it was strange that she came through the back gate and not through the front. However, it was a nice detour from the daily grind. He looked over at the rotunda with the nine intricately carved doors and smiled. He did not think that it would have ever been opened in his lifetime.

Suddenly, a great thud echoed in the halls of the back gate of heaven. Moerdon looked up from his reading material as did everyone else. Revelation cocked his head as he was awoken from a nap and bleated. A second thud, much more violent than the first, resounded through the abode. The sound originated from one of the nine doors. Quickly, the angels and Demangel overturned two great gopher wood tables and took cover behind them.

"Doesn't this seem familiar honey?" Accordia jokingly asked Moerdon.

"Something's on its way. I can feel it," stated Moerdon.

"No kidding, Sherlock sweetie. What do we do?" asked Loriel.

"We could bash it and then ask questions later," recommended Bastiel.

"We don't know what it is," Evriel stated the obvious.

"I am sure it is not the Goddess. This thing is trying to break down the door. I'll construct an ice wall around the rotunda with my ice arrows. Loriel, Accordia, and I will do a long-range assault on whatever is coming through. While we have their attention, Bastiel and Evriel will spring from the back and strike. But only on my signal," said Moerdon, as he planned the battle strategy.

"That sounds fine with me," said Accordia, as she changed from her Demangel form to her Manticore Sphinx form.

"That freaks me out every time she does that," Bastiel shuddered.

Moerdon worked quickly and generously shot ice arrows around the gate, which immediately formed an ice wall. He then fired some sticky arrow traps on the ground, just for good measure. His teammates moved into place as he carried out his part.

The doors shook even more violently as whatever wanted to come through, tried to rip the door-jam apart. He ascended the ice wall, looked over it, and made sure his comrades were positioned properly.

The pounding grew louder and more intense. With a loud crash, the massive doors gave way as the lock broke. One of the doors was almost off its hinges and it was unceremoniously ripped off and thrown aside. A giant silhouette filled the entrance. Energy and smoke crackled around the figure as it stepped through the massive doorway.

During the pre-emptive actions, Moerdon remembered his pet lamb, Revelation. "Revelation, damn where is he?" said Moerdon, as he looked frantically for his pet. He spied Revelation as he meekly moaned on the very top of a bookshelf.

Abaddon stepped through the seventy-seven-foot tall gates that were the backway into heaven. There was a deafened silence as his imposing seventy-foot tall frame took up the whole doorway. The sight stopped the hearts of all the onlookers before him. The great ice wall, erected by Moerdon, barred his way and that perturbed him. His six new hycolium wings shone in the light of the abode, as he outstretched them menacingly. His severed right hand, which now brimmed with lethal claws, pushed the other door that he had come through, off its hinges. It fell into the ice wall that had been set up as a deterrent.

Abaddon's blood-red eyes scanned the room. His left hand held a blade that looked like an unholy union between an ax and a broadsword. His weapon, the Abomination of Cain, was thirsty for blood.

"Abaddon. He's still alive!" gasped Moerdon, as he peered over the wall.

"I want to kill that piece of rotten fruit!" exclaimed Loriel, putting a hand where two of her wings had been ripped off, then restored by Goddess Heddonna.

"Hello, is anyone here? I know that these ice walls could only be the work of one person, Moerdon. Don't tell me that you have left your post?" prodded Abaddon.

"Abaddon, what rock in hell did you crawl out from under!" answered Moerdon loudly.

"I do not reside in hell anymore. I have become more powerful than even *Lucifer* can fathom," Abaddon answered, with a sly smile. "Is your wench wife, Accordia, still with you? Last time I checked, she died saving your sorry hide."

CHAPTER 37

"Sorry to disappoint you, buddy, she is very much alive. I have two wives now. Both of them could thrash you real good," shot back Moerdon.

"I remember you quite well, Abaddon. I assure you, that I am not the same since we last saw each other," Accordia yelled. She would have attacked if Moerdon had not signaled her to stand down.

"You blew up my planet and nearly killed me. Not to mention, that harlot, Loriel, cut my hand off with my own weapon," Abaddon vehemently spat.

"Good. That should have kept you away. Do you want me to take the other one too?" Loriel rebuffed.

"I am shopping for a few things. I want my Brimstone of Heaven. I want payback for my hand. I want vengeance for my planet. I want that sword of yours, The Vengeful Covenant Breaker of the Heavens. I will take it and your lives as well!" Abaddon said with a laugh.

Abaddon stepped down from the pedestal and right into the sticky traps that Moerdon had set up. He felt his new battle boots stick to the rotunda and that bothered him even more.

"Looks like somebody supercharged you," said Moerdon, as he showed himself to Abaddon. That got Abaddon's attention.

His eyes locked on to Moerdon and that's when Revelation struck. He had changed from a docile little lamb to a seven-headed dragon, hell-bent upon defending his friends. Seven superhot flames tried to char and barbeque the new and improved Abaddon where he stood.

Moerdon fired or rather, rained down a myriad of elemental attacks from his mighty bow, 'The Full Measured Might of Heaven.' Lightning bolts, water torrents, ice shards, wind walls, firebombs, and boulders, were fired with greater than true aim. Loriel used her long Chained Shields and rained blows upon the intruder with all her angelic might.

Accordia, who was transformed, used her four cobra tails and spat poison upon Abaddon. She fired crackling blue lightning from two of her four hands. Her other two hands fired a stream of ice that encased Abaddon's massive feet and secured them to the already sticky ground. For good measure, she blew a few fireballs at him from her sharp-toothed mouth.

Revelation was on air support, as the group of angelic warriors closed in on the intruding Abaddon. They unmercifully assaulted the intruder.

Abaddon staggered under the attack, as he used his wings and tried to block the onslaught of the defending angels. Moerdon finally gave the word and the other two warriors, lying in wait, pounced upon their prey.

Evriel moved like lightning and immediately tried to gouge out a piece of Abaddon's left arm, with her 'The Brimstone of Heaven', but to no avail. She was caught in mid-air and slammed down into the sticky trap laid by Moerdon. Abaddon raised his mighty weapon and would have brought it down upon Evriel, but he was interrupted.

"I'm going for his legs. That should cut this intruder down to size!" yelled Bastiel, as he jumped off the wall and landed upon the pedestal.

With a mighty swing, his six-headed polearm ax connected with the armored calf of Abaddon. Three of the six ax heads sunk deep into the left leg of the intruder and he screamed with pain.

"Accordia, get Evriel out of there," Moerdon said, as he fired a nullifier arrow to void his sticky traps by Evriel.

He ran along the top of the wall as he shot a barrage of arrows, laying down cover fire for her. Accordia went in for an extraction.

"Grab my tail! I'll keep him occupied," Accordia shouted, as she shot a face full of lightning at Abaddon.

Accordia used her four cobra tails and helped Evriel up. She then launched Evriel, with a mighty swing, in the direction of the intruder. The powerful Brimstone of Heaven ignited with the intensity of a hundred suns as it came down with a thud upon one of the hycolium wings of Abaddon. It burned and hissed as the sword seared the metal of his wings.

Bastiel pushed his weapon deeper into Abaddon's calf, which elicited more screams of pain. Accordia, joining the fray, decided to use her long poisonous tail to wrap Abaddon in a chokehold from behind. Her cobras hissed and spat excitedly as they repeatedly bit their prey.

Abaddon tried to use his right hand to swat her away, but Moerdon blasted him with an ice block arrow that encased his arm in ice. Loriel swooped in as she pummeled him with barrages from her twin Chained Shields. The weapons had a buzz-saw effect, which tore at his abdomen.

Revelation landed and decided that it was time for a snack and he wanted some deep-fried angel drumsticks. All seven heads hungrily bit into the right leg of Abaddon.

Moerdon released a few more nullifier arrows to void the sticky traps that were unused. He jumped down and loaded his bow with three earth arrows, to launch a boulder barrage at Abaddon. He ran towards him, rolled under one of his wings and released the arrows. Three huge boulders appeared out of thin air with the velocity of a comet and crashed into the face of the intruding Abaddon. The attack rocked Abaddon as Moerdon loaded up even more arrows.

Abaddon had been powerful before he had an upgrade and knew that his opponents were strong as well. However, this was ridiculous. They just pummeled him stupid! *Their combined attacks were ruthless and well organized. It was a tribute to their leader, Moerdon.* He would have to come up with something to stop this. He needed to divide them. He would unleash the Abomination of Cain.

The left hand of Abaddon moved with surprising speed as he seemed to slice thin air and bring the sword to the ground. The others thought that it was a futile attack, but Moerdon noticed it. He turned to the blade and saw it open. Mini Abaddons flew out of the back of the sword and they went in for the kill.

"Everyone, go take cover!" Moerdon yelled, as he frantically shot an ice arrow at the Abomination of Cain to stem the tide of mini Abaddons. However, a million got through.

The courageous angels and Demangel quickly got out of the way and started swatting the mini Abaddons. The five-foot-tall monster angels packed a punch with every elemental attack imaginable. They came in with a kamikaze attack that sacrificed themselves to blow up their opponents. A few hundred launched an ice attack that rocked Revelation. Accordia tried her best to outmaneuver them, but a few hundred exploded in a massive fire blast that threw her into a bookcase. They swarmed everywhere and tried to overwhelm the defending angels.

Big Abaddon managed to break his right hand free from the block of ice that it was encased in. He freed his legs with a swipe of his powerful sword. He was ready to rock and roll.

He saw an opening to slice at Moerdon and he took it. The blow was blocked by Bastiel and his massive Tower Shield with the Ten Commandments engraved on it. A loud clang was heard through the abode as metal clashed against metal.

A few mini Abaddons flew into the back of Bastiel and exploded with lightning, which rocked the burly seraphim. He went to his knees, while the heavy sword of Abaddon pushed upon his shield. Moerdon shot a barrage of arrows to stem the other mini Abaddons that came in for the kill. Those guys exploded with a fiery pop. He rushed over to Bastiel and pushed the sword away with his bow.

Above them, Accordia and Revelation had a hard time fending off a swarm of Abaddons. Revelation wished he had seven times seventy heads, to burn them with his super hot flames. Accordia used every appendage at her disposal and warded off the incoming menaces, but it did little except make room for more. She spied that Loriel and Evriel were in some difficulty and decided to come in with air support.

"Revelation, heel," she shouted to the dragon. He followed her to their friends.

Evriel slashed and cut her way through a wall of mini Abaddons. Her sister's Chained Shields chopped down countless foes but, to Evriel, it did not make a dent. They were back to back and there seemed no end in sight to the mini Abaddons that raced their way.

Suddenly, a burst of flames and lightning tore through the enemy. The figures of Accordia and Revelation swooped in and formed upon them.

"Where's my husband?" asked Accordia.

"You mean *our husband*. He's over there, trying to figure out a way to kick this supercharged donkey's butt," remarked Loriel.

CHAPTER 37

"Bastiel is with him," chimed in Evriel.

Abaddon swung with a huge right hand full of claws, which was surprisingly quick. Moerdon blocked it with his bow, sidestepped and fired a barrage of fire rounds. He then quickly followed it up with massive subzero ice shots. Bastiel was not fully recovered from the swarm ambush. Moerdon wanted to shut this thing down and fast. He decided to do something that would be a long shot, but it just might work.

"Get in Delta formation! Use the rotunda with the eight doors to your back. Do it without me. Loriel, use your Chained Shields as my substitute. Going to launch the Omega arrow!" he yelled at his team.

He fired some exploding arrows and cleared a path for Bastiel to reach the others. "I have to get Abaddon's attention. If he is facing me then it will be as a shield to you. He'll get most of the blast."

Delta formation was when Bastiel, Evriel, and Loriel used their shields and surrounded Revelation, Accordia and Moerdon. The three long-range specialists blasted whatever came at them. This time, the formation was missing Moerdon, who had to get up close and personal with his enemy.

"No, get over here! Don't do it!" yelled Loriel to her husband.

Her Chained Shields flew in the air as they mixed with Revelation's seven-headed flames and the ice, lightning, and fire from Accordia's attacks. Together, they created a cocktail that was hot and as hard to swallow as anything a very bad bartender served up. The mini Abaddons that went in for the kill, were mercilessly toasted. Their charred remains dropped to the ground and exploded. The giant shield of Bastiel and the gauntlets of Evriel stopped anything from coming through, as they backed into the rotunda that had eight of the nine doors still intact.

Moerdon shot a dozen protection arrows at the doorway of the rotunda that had been broken open by Abaddon. He felt good knowing his friends and wives were now secured. All of the mini Abaddons stopped their assault and stood in place. They looked at the resolute angelic soldier with the insane bow and the weapon that he had not even taken out yet.

CHAPTER 37

"Well done, Moerdon. You and your little band of merry heroes have managed to kill eight hundred thousand of my mini Abaddons. Are you able to take out the others by yourself? I assure you, that there are a Lawrellion more waiting to kill you," Abaddon said, with a sly smile.

"I just have to take you out," Moerdon said, as he looked at his friends and wives that frantically pounded on the shield. He did not hear a word of what they were saying.

"When I kill you, I will kill them, slowly and deliberately. I will bring upon them every kind of torture imaginable. Then I will heal them, to get them ready for the next round of unimaginable agony," hissed Abaddon.

While Abaddon talked bad guy banter, Moerdon loosed the scabbard that held, The Vengeful Covenant Breaker of the Heavens and turned it so that the sword was to his front. He then loaded a hundred arrows, the maximum he could fire, into his mighty bow, The Full Measured Might of Heaven.

"Moerdon, give me the sword and I shall give you and your friends a quick death," Abaddon said in a raspy voice.

"Why do you want this sword?"

"My new masters have need of it. It is all part of the plan."

"Who are your new masters? What plan?" asked Moerdon.

"They are far beyond the reach of anyone. No one knows them. They are even hidden from the Gods themselves. Their plan is larger than anyone can imagine," laughed Abaddon.

"What do you mean, hidden from the Gods themselves?" asked Moerdon.

"You need not concern yourself with it," chided Abaddon.

"Take this back to your masters!" Moerdon yelled as he fired a barrage of arrows that were mixes of fire, ice, earth, lightning, sticky traps and explosions. Abaddon managed to catch a few of them in both of his hands. He looked pleased with the result.

"Is that all you have? Where is the arrow to end it?" Abaddon scoffed at the last-ditch attempt of Moerdon.

Unbeknownst to him, Moerdon used a sticky arrow to attach the Omega arrow to Abaddon's damaged calf.

"Get your rear end back to hell!" yelled Moerdon, as he had a detonator in his hand.

CHAPTER 37

With lightning-quick reflexes, he placed the scabbard of the sword in front of him as he pressed the button. Abaddon did not know what happened before it was too late.

The blinding explosion rocked the cozy abode that the battle-worn angels, half-angel, and dragon-lamb had called home. It was not only one explosion but a series of explosions, which ripped apart Abaddon. First one leg, then the other leg and then his wings, were all blown apart by the blast. The wings were not destroyed but just torn off his body, because they were made of hycolium. Both his hands landed in two separate directions. The metallic claws of his right hand were embedded in the door to the outside, which lay behind the waterfall of the River of Life. Big rocks and boulders that had newly translated texts upon them, crumbled from the walls and the ceiling.

Everything came crashing down upon shelves and the manuscripts they contained. Old books and tomes burned and were vaporized, as all of that knowledge disappeared in a firestorm of chaos.

A hole to the outside opened and water rushed in. It mixed with blood and debris from the clandestine battle that took place. The torso of Abaddon was still intact, as the last dregs of life slowly slipped from his pitiful existence.

The twelve shield arrows that Moerdon had placed over the doorway to protect his friends, had now expired. They rushed out of the rotunda into destruction. Flying was impossible because of all of the debris that fell, so all of them waded through the Water of Life to find their friend.

He was buried underneath a boulder that Bastiel and Revelation moved out of the way. The sheath of his sword had absorbed most of the blast and saved his life. He and his friends looked at the huge body parts of Abaddon that floated down the river. The Tree of Gluttonous Desires, whose branches still burned, was violently eaten up by the roaring torrent.

The six warriors took one last look at their home and decided it was time to go. Quickly they scurried out of the grotto that had been their home for countless millennia and emerged beaten and battered upon the banks of the river.

CHAPTER 37

"I am really going to miss this place," Loriel said with tears in her eyes, as she hugged her husband.

"I will too. But I am glad that we still have each other," sighed Accordia, as she assumed her Demangel form and also hugged Moerdon, her husband.

"Come here Bastiel, I need a hug," said Evriel, as she choked down tears. Bastiel just hugged her with a wordless hug. That was all of comfort she needed.

Suddenly, the reverie was broken with a big splash as a reconfigured Abaddon rose from the depths of the River of Life. He was renewed with a power that flowed through heaven and he wanted blood. The six valiant warriors looked on in terror as the seventy-foot tall Abaddon moved towards them. He menacingly brandished his sword-ax hybrid, The Abomination of Cain.

The dam broke inside Moerdon as he finally pulled out The Vengeful Covenant Breaker of the Heavens from its plain and unassuming sheath. The purest silver hycolium blade imaginable glimmered in the sunlight as he pointed it at Abaddon. Accordia shuddered at the sight of the plain, giant blade. She was at the same time, relieved that a weapon of its caliber was in the hands of a mighty and righteous warrior.

She, Abaddon and Moerdon were the only ones who had ever seen this weapon unsheathed. She used it to save Moerdon's life and to destroy a planet full of bad guys. She gave her life for him that day and she would do it again if necessary.

"Everyone, be on guard. He might release those mini things again," Moerdon said, as he moved towards his enemy.

"It's the River of Life. We have to keep him far away from it," warned Loriel.

"I am going in for a close attack. You guys stay on the perimeter. Revelation, you are on air support. Use fire tornado if necessary," Moerdon said, as he patted the dragon on one of his seven heads. "Everyone else, stick to the ground. Don't get out of the river. Keep everything out of the water," he ordered.

"Got it, Moerdon, will do," grunted Bastiel.

"What are you going to do?" asked Loriel, worried.

CHAPTER 37

"I am going to end this. Accordia, I need you to shoot lightning into the sky. Like a signal flare. Hopefully, the heavenly guards will see it and bring backup," Moerdon said, as he kissed the Demangel on her cheek.

Moerdon spread all six of his wings and in an instant, was on top of Abaddon with the fury of a thousand hurricanes. Moerdon's hycolium blade fell upon Abaddon's hycolium wings. The fallen angel barely had time to get his weapon up before Moerdon had unleashed a thousand slices with his sword. The sonic boom from his speed, echoed through the plains of heaven, like thunder on a mountain top.

While they were locked in a melee, Abaddon unleashed his mini Abaddons into the air. The other warriors sprang into action and started picking them off.

Evriel was the first to be hit by a few kamikaze Abaddons that exploded into ice blasts. Luckily, her gauntlets shielded her and she mowed down a couple thousand or so with a coronal mass ejection from her Brimstone of Heaven sword. Big Abaddon saw the attack from the corner of his eye and was thankful that it was not aimed at him.

Bastiel, his Tower Shield in his right hand, bashed his way through a wall of mini Abaddons. He used his left hand to wildly swing his polearm ax in a tornado, which kept the rest at bay.

Loriel decided to use her Zanbato Nodachis as a deterrent for the mini Abaddons by slicing and dicing her way through a wall of them. They retaliated by exploding and created an earthen wall that separated her from her friends. However, her Chained Shields shot that idea down hard, when she broke through with a Chained Hurricane. She generated hurricane-force winds with her wings and used the force to propel her weapons in a vortex that penetrated any obstacle.

Accordia, as per Moerdon's instructions, shot a few streams of lightning in the air every few minutes as a signal beacon. She threw everything at the mini Abaddons, from any appendage she found. The hate that she had for Abaddon, coupled with the love that she carried for Moerdon, fueled her will to live and overcome this foe.

CHAPTER 37

Revelation was in top form, as he used all of his seven heads and tail to swat, barbeque and eat his way through hundreds of mini enemies. He enjoyed himself a delicious meal.

Abaddon had his hands full with Moerdon and his crazy sword. He lost ground big time as he was pushed back by the ferocity of the attacks. 'This guy's speed is insane', thought Abaddon to himself, as he got one foot out of the river. He used his indestructible left wings to stop an attack from Moerdon. At the same time, he went for a metallic right hook. That did the trick and caught Moerdon off guard, in the stomach. The momentary reprieve was all it took for Abaddon to follow up with a wing slice to the chest.

Moerdon fell back into the water and Abaddon took a breath. In seconds, the wound healed and Moerdon shot back with a lightning bolt barrage that emanated from his sword. Abaddon blocked the bolt with his right hand and then quickly transformed it into 'the planet buster' gun. He fired at Moerdon as he came in for close combat, but the angel was too quick and deflected the blast into a wall of mini Abaddons. They disappeared in a puff of smoke.

Abaddon needed more time to charge the weapon if he were to be successful. He would have to fight one-handed and keep the cannon out of reach of the warriors. He blocked and parried the blows that came from the relentless Moerdon, as he bided his time.

Finally, Moerdon came into the home stretch as he redoubled his efforts to bring down Abaddon. He landed a big lightning-filled slash on his right shoulder wing. A torrent of electricity flowed through the conductive metal wings and rocked the seemingly unstoppable Abaddon. Abaddon's sword dropped as bolts of electricity ripped through his body. He feebly grabbed at the wings of Moerdon with a left hand. Finally, he found a handful with which he brought the warrior down. With split-second thinking, Abaddon managed to bring down Moerdon on the bank of the River of Life rather than in it.

The savage, sought-after blade was between both of them. That was the upper hand Abaddon needed and he took full advantage. Abaddon used his wings as a shield and put all of his body weight on the fallen warrior. He excitedly pulled out Moerdon's right side wings. Moerdon screamed in pain as bones, sinews, and muscles were torn apart. His grip tightened around his sword as he tried to shove the giant Abaddon off with a burst of lightning for good measure. But it did not do as much damage as he had hoped.

The cannon was primed and ready. Abaddon had a shot that he could not miss. However, the blast was going to put a crater right through the center of heaven. Not Abaddon's problem anymore, because he did not live there any longer. Abaddon put his right hand close to his opponent and the heated cannon seared the face of Moerdon. The stench of burning flesh mingled with those of the dead mini Abaddons as it permeated the air.

"I am going to enjoy this. In fact, I wish I had a time machine so I could go back in time and do it again," Abaddon whispered in a raspy voice.

He raised his right hand to fire upon Moerdon, but it fell limp on the ground beside him. The stump of his shoulder had been cauterized by the heated blade, The Brimstone of Heaven, which had once been his. The cut was so clean and so quick that it had taken a few seconds for the pain to register a scream.

"I want the other one sister!" screamed Loriel, as she drove her twin Zanbato Nodachis into the shoulder of Abaddon and severed his other arm.

"Get off him, now!" Evriel yelled as she shoved the armless Abaddon over and out of the way of the bleeding Moerdon.

"You okay, baby?" Loriel said as she looked at Moerdon. "Get him to the river and check on the others. I'll take care of this one," Loriel told her younger sister. Chained Shields started battering the body of Abaddon, as Loriel unleashed her angelic anger upon him.

"Moerdon, you have to lay off the sweets man," Evriel kidded, as she hoisted him up and moved him to the River of Life that seemed miles away.

Just then, Accordia flew in and gently wrapped her tails around the wounded Moerdon. She gently carried him to the river. He was face to face with one of the cobras in transit and it smiled at him and kissed him. She set him in the middle of the watery oasis and he sank down to the bottom. Accordia then joined Evriel and they looked back at Bastiel and Revelation to see how they were doing against the mini Abaddons. They were doing fine.

"Evriel, go and fight with them. I'll help Loriel. Moerdon's going to be okay," Accordia said, as one of her arms patted the shoulder of her friend.

"You will never defeat me. You never have. Even if you succeed, you have no idea what is coming. Pray, but it will be useless. My new masters will win. The best part is, that no one will know when they are coming," rebuffed Abaddon, as he somehow managed to block a few of the Chained Shields with his hycolium wings.

"You monster! Everything was good until you and your friends brought evil into our heavenly home. Then you come and ruin our lives. I don't know what is coming, but I do know I'll make sure you don't live to see it!" Loriel hissed, as she vehemently went after Abaddon.

He surprisingly blocked her slashes and thrusts with his six wings. Loriel had a hard time penetrating his defense. He menacingly locked wings with shields, as he leered at her with deep, red eyes full of hate and determination.

Just then, Accordia swooped in behind Abaddon and planted a fist full of claws in both of his shoulder blades with her four hands. She then ripped out his two main wings with a deafening crack followed by the tearing of sinews, muscles, and cartilage. Even though his wings were hycolium, the rest of his body was not. Abaddon yelled in pain, however, his day was about to get a lot worse.

"Everyone out of the way!" yelled Moerdon, as he rose out of the water, fully reconstituted and a hundred percent mad.

His bow, The Full Measured Might of Heaven was loaded with The Vengeful Covenant Breaker of the Heavens sword.

Both weapons brimmed with so much energy, that it warped the very river, the nearby banks and the surrounding plains. The clouds above the fighters swirled and darkened as the bow, glowed a wicked electric blue and the sword shone red in the waning light. The wind kicked up and howled and the ground beneath them heaved and trembled in fear. The mini Abaddons flew back into their master's sword because they did not want to be in the front row for this show. Before Abaddon could block himself from the attack, Moerdon fired without a word of banter or conversation.

The sword penetrated the chest of their foe in a blaze of apocalyptic glory. The mountains were scorched for miles as the heat from the blast melted the ground and ignited the sky. Clouds vaporized and vanished as the heat rose and disintegrated a part of the atmosphere. The blast wave broke apart everything in its path. Houses were destroyed and people were trapped inside the rubble.

When the dust cleared and all of the valiant friends found each other in the ashes and debris that littered the landscape, they saw that the marred body of Abaddon still stood in the distance. The ground belched magma all around him as half of his body bubbled and dribbled super-heated skin and flesh. In some places, there were bones that had turned to ash and were as tough as burnt toast. The few of his hycolium wings which remained had shielded parts of his body from the blast. However, they had grown super-hot and caught fire at the joining of the metal wings and flesh.

Moerdon and his group came over to inspect their enemy and to retrieve the sword from his chest. They were a few feet away when Abaddon smiled with a charred and deathly grin from an unrecognizable face.

"Thank you!" he mouthed. The Vengeful Covenant Breaker of Heavens sword had melted the insides of his body and fire burned inside him. *Abaddon, The Abomination of Cain and the Gift of the Nine, disappeared with a sonic boom.*

Uriel came with squads of Seraphim in tow. Like always, sometimes the cavalry arrives too late.

"What happened here?" asked Uriel in astonishment.

"It was Abaddon. He came through the back gate of heaven. He was after the Gift of the Nine, my sword."

"You stopped him?"

"We thought we did, but he got away with the sword in his chest," Moerdon answered.

CHAPTER 37

"The Gifts of the Nine have fallen into wrong hands before."

"Not like this. He looked supercharged. He said that his new masters are far beyond the reach of anyone. No one knows them. They are even hidden from the Gods themselves. Their plan is larger than anyone can imagine."

"Oh my God! I wonder if it had anything to do with the Goddess coming to heaven and looking for that man."

"Uriel, I don't know. He left behind a few wings and this handgun contraption. We should examine it more closely."

"Agreed. The Gods warned the Athlogoss Drones to look out for anything suspicious. This has to be reported at once. Good work guys. Even though you destroyed half the planet, you stumbled across something very important."

"I could not have done it without these guys," said Moerdon, as he motioned to his friends.

"Let's get a statement from everyone and we'll begin to clean up. The Gods must know about this," Uriel told a captain angel, as he surveyed the ruins of the heavenly plain.

CHAPTER 38: Brentt, Asheley, Theo, And Frank Lin Finally Encounter The Immortal Count

The three friends and one detective teleported, courtesy of Asheley, right into a room filled with Big-Foot soldiers and henchmen. Everyone looked shocked at the sudden appearance of the intruders into the Palace of Palaces and Castle of Castles. The energy that crackled around the four comrades was overwhelming and everyone was too awestruck to move.

All four had just been overhauled by their explorations in the Akashic Records Library and they felt ready for anything.

Theo looked over to his left and spied room 777. In that cell, he saw a chained and tortured John. He also saw a man that accompanied him. An eight-foot-tall and very powerfully built man, that had black hair and the most ridiculous aura possible.

Brentt Williams saw him and felt him. That man had sent henchmen to kill his parents, all those years ago.

"I got this, guys," Frank Lin said, as he used a blue aural burst to stun everyone in the room, except his friends. The Big-Foot soldiers and henchmen were easily felled by Frank Lin's newfound powers.

"Good job," Theo said automatically, as he turned to the door.

"The Thrice Magician is in there as well," said Brentt nonchalantly.

"Frank and I will get John. Brentt, you get your Count. Asheley, do you mind keeping Tris Megistus entertained?" asked Theo.

"No, not at all. I want to throw a party when we get home, Theo. I think it would be very nice," she cheerily said.

CHAPTER 38

"We'll do it. Have a nice, big party. We will invite everyone," smiled Theo, at Asheley's optimistic attitude.

"Stay sharp, everyone, I think The Immortal Count has come to greet his guests," warned Brentt.

The piercing eyes of the Count never faltered from his callers as he easily opened the heavy door with the viewing panel. His midnight blue retinas were a sight to behold as he focused with unwavering intent upon the visitors. His eight-foot-tall frame filled the doorway, as the form of Megistus was just barely seen beyond him.

He walked out in a tight, black shirt. It fought to hide bulging abs, biceps, triceps, and whatever other muscle groups that were not usually found on any other person. Long, black khaki pants barely kept his thigh muscles concealed. Thick, ankle-high, shiny, black boots barely made a sound as he moved toward them. The reflections of his visitants could be seen in his boots, if only he had looked down.

He sported a belt buckle which contained the reddest ruby imaginable. It was probably worth more than Theo could make in his life, including pension. His terribly ripped arms, which overflowed with Amazon-River-like veins, hung loosely at his sides as he studied his unwanted guests.

A gold and platinum watch, that must have weighed a hundred pounds, resided on his giant left wrist. There was a shadow of stubble on his square jaw that outlined high cheekbones and a blunted, but beaked nose. The blackest of jet black hair went to his muscular shoulders that rippled with the energy of a mountain range.

Usually, when people met The Immortal Count for the first time, they showed fear and reverence. However, these four intruders indicated none of that. They exuded pure power and confidence, both in their abilities and in their chances of survival.

"Welcome. I am Jacques Von Blutdruckt Gemacht also known as The Immortal Count. I hope that you had no trouble finding the place?" he cordially said.

"We had no trouble at all. In fact, I see you have more henchmen coming to attend to our needs," kidded Brentt

CHAPTER 38

Williams, as more Big-Foot soldiers and other henchmen filed into the room.

They stepped over the stunned bodies of their comrades and in some cases, piled them up on the other side of the room. In total, there were two hundred of the Count's henchmen and only four of the guests.

"It cannot be said of me that I am not hospitable to my guests, whether they are enemies or friends of mine. Which you are, is yet to be determined," smiled the Count, a tight-lipped but smug smile.

"I don't think we're going to be your BFF's. If you don't know by now, I am Brentt Williams. I know we have not formally met, you know, with the whole you sending guys to kill my parents, thing," spoke Brentt, tersely.

"I know you well detective Brentt Williams, even better than you know yourself. I have often wondered about you and looked forward to our meeting. You and I have much to discuss. We have more things in common than you can possibly imagine," said the Count, in an even and cadaverous tone that commanded respect and reverence. "Let me introduce my Thrice Magician. I believe you know him on a professional level."

The Thrice Magician stepped forward, dressed like a ringleader of a circus, full of gold chains and rings. He held his staff and battered fob, turned watch. His ensemble was completed with a greatcoat that doubled as a cape and shiny gold shoes. Beyond them was John, bloodied and hooked up to some machinery that seemed unpleasant to be around.

"I am his humble servant, Tris Megistus Tris Magnificus Nebuchadnezzar, his Thrice Magician," he said, as he bowed to the guests.

"We have volleyed back and forth for significant items over the years," said Brentt to his friends. "I whooped you really good for the emerald tablets. I looked forward to seeing you at the museum, but we missed each other," he told the Magician.

"I assure you, that my absence at the museum was not by choice. There were some unforeseen circumstances that hindered my entrance into the fray. I will not allow myself that folly again," said Megistus resolutely.

CHAPTER 38

"Well, let's get this started. Theo, Frank Lin, and Asheley are here to pick up John Duboise. I am going to arrest you for crimes against humanity. And of course, all of us are shutting your operation down," explained Brentt, with a hint of anxiousness in his voice.

"Before we begin, detective Williams, tell me of what happened at the museum on New Year's Day," pressed the Count. "My Thrice Magician maintains a different scenario than I," he spoke, as he focused on Brentt.

Brentt, Theo, and Asheley looked at each other in bewilderment. Did the Count have the same experience as they did? About something else that happened, but nobody else remembered? What were the implications of that? How was the change in venue even possible? Was there a deeper connection between all of them?

"You sent goons to get the Gadha of Gilgamesh," said Brentt cautiously.

"I did send him for the Gadha of Gilgamesh, but my Thrice Magician knew it as a statue. Which he failed to obtain in either case," chided The Immortal Count, as he looked down on Megistus.

"There were four Gothic guys that transformed into beasts. I have never felt so much power before," Brentt said, as he shook his head.

"I felt that power all the way here. I feel that power now as it flows through my distasteful son. I took out the best parts of my genetic material and gave him the rest," said the Count, as if uttering the word 'son' was bitter to him.

"Excuse me, did your son tell you of how he got the foreign material inside of him?" interrupted Asheley.

A surprised Count looked in intrigue at Asheley, who showed no hint of fear. "Yes, he did. We had to get it out of him by unpleasant means, though. He had contact with the four creatures. However, I am perplexed that the foreign matter in his body gave him special abilities. No doubt, you three have witnessed it firsthand," the Count said.

"We faced him and saw what he could do. He was very powerful," stated Asheley.

CHAPTER 38

"I want to know who or what those creatures were. I already know about the three Gods that came down and fought. I have found probabilistic information on you, detective Williams, the same as myself. Frank Lin Shao, your life is of little significance to me. I will allow you safe passage from here. But, the day that I see your face again, it will promptly be ripped from your skull."

"I am not leaving my friends. I will help them to the end," voiced Frank Lin, stubbornly.

"The end shall it be then," the Count sighed. "You two, I did not find anything on what you are, Asheley, or you, Theo Steren Champlain," the Count stated, as he looked intently at his guests. "Why that is, I need to find out. I cannot allow you to leave without the truth being uncovered."

Brentt, Theo, Asheley, and Frank Lin were surprised for the second time in a few minutes by The Immortal Count. Did he know of their coming too?

"How did you find out about this information?" queried Brentt.

"Did you not think that in all my millennia alive, I did not have access to the Akashic Records Library," The Immortal Count spoke, as he focused on Theo, his gaze penetrating and invasive.

"Damn, they let anybody into the Library. I am done playing twenty questions. Your plan to rule the world ends now!" Brentt exclaimed with emotion, as he readied himself for an attack.

"Rule the world? I am not some cookie-cutter despot that seeks to impose my idealistic views upon all that I look upon. Do not be so narrow-minded, detective Williams. My machinations are far more elaborate than such frivolous notions," said the Count, as he stepped over the bodies of his henchmen and came closer to his guests.

"It's all the same. A madman that tries to subjugate people," said Brentt succinctly.

"Not subjugate, control. And not people. You control people yourself. You have used your aura to influence people and deterred them from committing frivolous infringements of the law. I seek to do the same but on a wider scale. You and I are the same. We are reserved about our beliefs in a higher power. Belief, that things are not the way they should be.

Do you want to know why your record had the same probabilistic occurrences as my own? Do you want to know why there was a fifty percent chance that you were born to Henry and Flora Williams? Don't you want to know why they were killed? Do you want to know who you really are?" the Count persisted.

Brentt glared at the Count with a vengeful look. He had unresolved issues with his parents' death for hundreds of years. He wondered why his prayers were not answered that night. He doubted the existence of the Gods ever since that day. Now, he found out that they existed. But is it true or were they just beings that were more advanced than humans? He had encountered entities with lots of power. The Count, Megistus, the four Gothic dudes and even the three beings. That did not mean they were real Gods.

The Count saw the hesitation in Brentt and took advantage of it. "Brentt, would you like me to show you something that you have not seen in a long time? Follow me and I can give you all the answers the Library cannot," the Count said, welcomingly.

"Guys, I have to find out one way or the other. Save your friend, John. I got this," said Brentt.

"Megistus, Big-Foot soldiers, and henchmen, please keep our guests here and do not let them escape with John. They must be alive and able to talk. In what condition other than that, I care not," ordered the Count, as he led Brentt away from his friends and towards *his* Library.

Everyone in the prison wing watched the door close and all eyes turned upon Asheley, Theo, and Frank Lin. All of the henchmen had big smiles on their faces as they inched closer to the trio.

"You guys look like you had a hard day. Take five!" Frank Lin shouted as he fired an aural stun blast that knocked everyone in the room unconscious. Megistus still remained standing with his staff in hand.

"That was very impressive, monk. I too am very skilled in aural manipulation. However, I do not like to get my hands dirty. I would like you to meet one of the Count's friends, *Azmodial.*

Today, he will be fighting on my behalf," Megistus smiled, as he waved his hands over a massive medallion that hung around his neck.

Before the trio, there appeared one of the scariest looking demons that Megistus had in his arsenal. Azmodial was at least fifteen feet tall with four huge wings, covered in reddish-brown leathery skin. He sported four large horns, of which two were curved upwards and two downwards. There were spikes that ran along his back and ended in a two-pronged tail, which had four spikes on each of them. His six-fingered hands were massive and brimmed with steel-tipped claws and metal-plated knuckles that looked like they were cauterized on.

He had a giant mallet that still had the bloodstains from his previous encounters. His face was pleasant to look at once, but now, it was battle-scarred and misshapen. No doubt, from countless fights that he had engaged in. An iron crown, that burned the flesh on his head, was studded with twelve different stones, each as big as Theo's fist. That was the circlet of the King of the Demons. Very tough, cracked and gristly skin, completed the hellish ensemble. He looked transparent and it was as if he phased in and out of reality.

"Oh boy! This guy is huge!" Frank Lin said in a panic.

"Asheley, you drove us here, Frank Lin, you did crowd control, so I'll do the heavy lifting with this one," Theo said, as he stuck his hand out and weapon warped his sword to the starting line. The giant, thirteen-foot long sword felt good in his hands, as he pointed it towards the enemy.

"Wait. Theo. Let me get these sleeping beauties out of here," said Asheley. She raised her hands and blue static electricity formed around her. All of the unconscious henchmen rose up from the ground while Asheley concentrated. Megistus and Azmodial looked on in amazement as all of the henchmen disappeared through the wall. "I have placed them in the gardens and tied them up. The weather is forecasted to be a nice, cool day, so there is no chance of sunburn."

Azmodial looked over at Megistus and before he knew it, Theo had moved forward two steps and swung the first slice. Unfortunately, the giant blade hit air. Theo stumbled forward from the momentum and he was at a loss of what to do. Before he recovered, Azmodial waved his bloodied mallet and caught Theo in the back. He crashed into a wall, with his sword in hand.

"Oh no!" yelled Frank Lin.

"I am okay. I can take a hit. You can hit me but I cannot hit you," he said, as he looked at Azmodial. The demon just stared back and a smile crossed his face.

"Theo honey, remember what we learned. He is probably in a different *spiritual density* than both of us. You have to raise your *vibrations* in order to match his. Then you will succeed in fighting him," reminded Asheley.

"Okay, let's go. Frank Lin, can you check on John? Asheley, see that the Magician does not invite any other bad guys to the party, please," said Theo, as he slowed his breathing. He tried to find the right frequency.

Asheley stuck her hands out and Megistus moved through the air. He shot a fire blast from his staff at his assailant, but she swatted it aside as if it were a cobweb. He grabbed the summoning medallion around his neck and in an instant, a captured *Jinn* was before them.

He was eight feet tall with fiery red eyes and a dark-as-night, powerfully built body. Cothar looked at the person that imprisoned him in that nightmare of a place. The Count had especially built that place to house his menagerie of creatures.

"Attack them and I will free you from my servitude," Megistus hissed, as his hands became useless under the power of Asheley.

Cothar turned to Asheley, who just stood there. Behind Cothar, she saw Theo and the King of the Demons as they fought. He found the right frequency and battled toe to toe with the entity. Frank Lin tried to find a way past the fray and crawled along the walls.

"Your fight is with me, woman. The others cannot save you from death by my hands," Cothar grunted, as he advanced.

"I will send you and the demon back to your plane of existence. We only want John Duboise. Nothing else," Asheley smiled, as she closed her eyes.

CHAPTER 38

When she opened her eyes again, a white light emanated from them. Using her mind, she pulled the summoning medallion off Megistus and levitated it to her hand. She scanned the artifact and saw that it contained hundreds of thousands of trapped spiritual entities inside. Immediately, she opened a one-way portal to the Jinn's realm and looked at the entity. She spoke through white glowing eyes.

"I do not want to fight you. I know that you have been trapped for millennia in service to the Count. Go through the portal and have your freedom. I will also go through and let out these entities trapped inside the medallion. They will not be able to return to this plane of existence anymore, to harm or be harmed," explained Asheley. The portal opened in a shimmer of air that braided itself and folded back space, like that of a bedsheet.

"Why are you doing this? I don't know you," the puzzled Jinn asked.

"*You don't have to know someone, to be kind to them.* Theo is trying to save John even though he tried to kill him," smiled Asheley, as she nodded to Theo.

"I have never said this to any human before, but thank you," Cothar said, as he turned and entered the portal.

Asheley was half in and half out of the portal, when she opened the medallion and let the trapped ones out. She came back in a jiffy and resumed her dealings with the situation at hand. Megistus looked in horror and awe at the display of power that emanated from Asheley.

The Immortal Count had taken a long time to collect those beings that resided in the medallion. He had loaned it to Megistus and the Thrice Magician had added his own set of creatures to it. The Immortal Count was going to be pissed.

"Theo, use the power that you have. Drive the King of Demons back to his plane of existence. I know you can do it. Remember what we learned at the Library," said Asheley supportively.

"Ok, Frank Lin, go!" Theo said as he weapon-warped his sword back into his hand.

CHAPTER 38

The demon king laughed as he came in for a huge swing with his mallet. It stopped just above Theo's head and did not budge. Azmodial grunted and huffed but he could not move it. Theo used his mind and mentally picked up the great demon. He sent him through the portal to another plane of existence. Asheley quickly closed the portal and focused on Megistus.

"I am going to take all of these things from you," said Asheley. She took all of the rings and medallions and other things from Megistus' person. "They are very dangerous for anyone to have around. I will take all this stuff and reorganize its composition into a special cage for you."

"Not the watch, please. It has special meaning to me," begged Megistus.

"Why?" asked Asheley.

"It has my wife in it. I sold her soul for power. To make sure that she did not die, I used the watch and created a place that has no time. She will never die," said Megistus solemnly.

"Did you ever love your wife?" asked Asheley.

"I did, but I loved power more," he said dejectedly.

"Why did you do it?" asked Theo, as he came to the mixer.

"I did it to rule the world and have her by my side, but The Immortal Count had other plans," said Megistus, who feigned remorse.

"You monster! How could you?" gasped Theo.

"I will let you keep the watch. Find a way to free her. Make sure and tell the LAKN9 about it. Sometimes, there are more important things than power. You are going into a special cage and then the LAKN9 are going to take custody of you when they get here," Asheley cheerily said, as she waved her hands and the Magician disappeared.

The trio went into the room in which John was held captive. Good thing he was unconscious as Frank Lin took out needles, electrodes, hooks and other things that definitely should not be in the human body.

Theo used the healing techniques that he had garnered from the Library and began to heal John. Asheley materialized the Quantum Matter Trans-Substantiating Extraction Machine in her hand. It turned on just like a handheld vacuum. Its powerful computer extracted the foreign matter from John.

"What the hell are you doing here you sorry excuse for a human being?" hissed John from bloodied lips, as he regained consciousness.

"We are trying to save you and get you back to your family, meathead. Just give us a few," said Theo sternly. He firmly held John and tried to finish heal him. "Don't bite me. I am not your enemy."

"Looks like the machine is almost done, guys," Asheley stated.

"Why are you doing this? I tried to kill you and you are now helping me?" queried John, as he tried to sit up from his ordeal.

"I don't want to tell Katie that her dad left her. I don't want to tell Catherine that you're not coming back. You have a kid on the way. I don't want them to grow up without a dad," assured Theo.

"I love Catherine very much. I hated seeing her in your arms. We should have not let it gone on for that long. It was terrible on all of us," said John, remorsefully.

"I have moved on with Asheley," said Theo, as he smiled at Asheley. She smiled back.

"You guys should not have come. My father is a very treacherous and devious man. He is very powerful and even his enemies are in his pocket. He will not let this go lightly. You are all in great danger," warned John.

"Brentt's got him. I feel his power flowing. He can take him. He will shut down the Count's operation," said Theo.

"Let's go find him," Frank Lin said, taking the Quantum Matter Trans-Substantiating Extraction Machine from Asheley.

She and Theo helped John to his feet. John shook Theo's hand and nodded his gratitude. That was probably about as good an apology he was going to get from John.

Brentt and the Count made their way to his Library which was filled to the brim with mysterious artifacts that had never seen the light of day. Brentt looked in awe at the collection of oddities that dotted the room. 'The LAKN9 would have a field day with this', he thought to himself.

The Count went to his massive desk and pulled out a ten-foot-long drawer on the right side. He motioned for Brentt to come over. He looked at the Count and then at the desk, then he scanned the room for any other occupants. There was another door that was closed.

Brentt cautiously walked around the desk and looked in the drawer. He drew back in horror as he eyed the Count and then the contents of the drawer. His anger boiled as he started to bend earth and sky with his power.

"Explain yourself!" shouted Brentt.

"Calm yourself, detective Williams. This is the body of the person that raised you, but not the one that gave birth to you," said the Count.

"It is the same to me. She raised me. You have no regard for life!" shouted Brentt. "You even harm your own son to get power. No wonder you are alone."

In the drawer, lay the body of Brentt's mother, who had died all those years ago. She looked peaceful and serene like if you spoke too hard or whispered in her ears, she would wake up. She wore a white dress with blue trim that looked very elegant and grand. Her shoulder-length blond hair rested on one shoulder. She had a blue rose behind one ear that accentuated her perfect features. There was a glass over the drawer that kept her body in pristine condition. Why did the Count have her in his drawer? Why could she not rest in peace?

"In the universe, there are things called soul prints that identify an entity to the cosmos. No doubt, you had to identify yourself to the Akashic Records Library in this manner. The soul is reborn into different bodies upon death. Lifetimes before, I found my soulmate. A woman of such grace, fortitude, vitality, and passion, that our lives became entwined until even after death. I am immortal and she was not, but that never stopped us from finding each other countless times before.

I tracked her soul to the body of your mother and sought to reignite her memories of passion for me. She died when my henchmen apprehended her. The henchmen from that night are still alive. However, they have experienced different kinds of pain every day since then, until I see fit to release them from their torment."

"So, are you my father?" queried Brentt, as his head churned with ideas.

"You are more what I would like my son to be, than my own progeny. You are strong-willed, independent, and powerful," praised the Count.

"Who are my parents, since according to you, Henry and Flora were not?" asked Brentt.

"Unfortunately, the Gods made their conceptions too good. They have broken their own rule and had relations with their creations. I have come to learn that you are a product of such a union. Your mother was a mortal and your father was a God.

In my case, both my parents were half-mortal and half-divine. I, therefore, have inherited the genes and traits from the more dominant God genes, a whole created when two God halves are put together. However, some mundane intricacies are present in my genetic code, more of a nuisance than anything. My trusted servant Megistus does not even know the true extent of my lineage," explained the Count.

"What are you saying? What does that mean? Is that why there is a probabilistic occurrence present in every single action of ours in the Records Library?" asked Brentt, trying to put two and two together.

"The Gods made the Library and their actions are not part of the order of things, but their creations are. That is why there is a conflict between the divine and mundane sides of us. I only seek to obtain the rightful inheritance of ours," continued the Count.

"No, this can't be! How is this possible?" Brentt managed to choke out the question, as he dropped to his knees.

"Detective Williams, the very Gods that you have disdain for, the very Gods that have not answered your prayers, the very Gods that allowed evil to run rampant upon this world: it is their blood that flows through our veins.

Join me and I will show you the answers that we both seek. Join me and we will confront the bane of our existence. You have already seen three of the Gods that descended from their lofty perches, high above the pestilence that they created for humanity and the universe. I seek to find out the reason why we are bombarded with turmoil and hardship," pushed the Count, as he stretched out his right hand to the kneeling Brentt.

Theo, Asheley, Frank Lin, and John walked the halls of the magnificent Palace of Palaces and Castle of Castles, awed by the splendor around them. At times, they forgot that they were searching for Brentt Williams.

They encountered lots of henchmen on the way, but they were quickly dispatched by either Theo or Asheley. There were hundreds, if not thousands of Big-Foot soldiers and henchmen that tried to bar the way of the trio, but they ended up restrained on the lawn of the estate. Tied up henchmen looked up and saw new captives pop out of nowhere and safely lowered to the ground by some unknown force, careful enough to not have them land upon each other. It was a veritable garden of goons as seen from the air.

The whole construction, design, and architecture of the estate were dedicated to the power and might of The Immortal Count. His power crackled around it and the walls seemed to be held up by his power. There were inscribed magical words and incantations everywhere. In addition, *sacred geometry* fortified the spiritual integrity of the unique building. There were glyphs that had unknown meanings, but you could bet that they were bad.

Asheley made a mental note to research these when she got home. Now that she had hacked the Akashic Records Library, she accessed it at any time and from anywhere, no questions asked. She would make sure she shared that information with Theo as well.

The use of his newfound power did not come as easily to Theo as it did to her, but when it manifested, his power was truly incredible. The stint in the Library had been worthwhile because they were prepared for anything.

The series of events that led them here caused Asheley to believe that the Gods were looking for Theo. However, they may not know about her. That gave her the advantage if they tried to harm him.

She still did not know about the four beasts. Maybe they had the same origins, which was the most likely answer. She did not know about her own origin other than the fact that Theo had created her. *To Asheley, that was enough. Theo was her life and she worshiped the ground that he walked on.*

The search for Brentt led them to the Count's library, which contained things that they had never seen before. However, all of that was secondary to them finding their friend. They came upon them as Brentt knelt in front of the Count and grasped his hand. The Count looked up at the trio and his son with a smile on his face.

The smile quickly evaporated as the great sword of Brentt Williams, the Mortar Round Beast Cutter Giant Broad Blade, cut through the giant hand of the Count. The giant sword sawed its way through his crotch and out the other end of The Immortal Count's body. Brentt moved the blade up in a quick motion that sliced the perfectly muscled eight-foot build of The Immortal Count, in two. Brentt got up from his knees and launched his Greek fire rounds at the pieces of the Count's corpse, setting them ablaze. The four were still in shock from what they had just witnessed.

"He won't be able to harm anyone again. I can't believe you did it! The world is safe thanks to you," said John, through tearful eyes. He shook his head and looked down. Tears of joy rolled off his cheeks.

"Thanks for the distraction. You guys get out of here. I am going to bring this hell hole down," said Brentt.

"Detective, are you going to be okay?" asked Theo.

"I'll be fine. This sicko had my mom in his desk drawer. He deserved it," Brentt said, as he began to warp the earth and sky to his will. "It's been an adventure, guys. I'll see you on the flip side. I have a feeling we're not out of the woods yet."

"Theo, my darling, would you do the honors and take us to Catherine's house?" asked Asheley.

"I would love to, sweetheart," said Theo, as he teleported them to the porch of Theo's former residence.

The earth shook and the sky trembled as the walls of the great Palace of Palaces and Castles of Castles came crashing down.

CHAPTER 38

Gravity hugged the foundations and embraced the roof of the estate. The sky weighed in with its might as it crushed everything that Brentt told it to destroy. Not even two stones were upon each other when Brentt finished destroying the place. There was one thing he saved though.

Brentt saved the drawer that held the body of Flora Williams, his mother or according to the Count, the woman who took care of him. He walked among the rubble and surveyed the scene. Finally, this part of his life was over. He needed a respite for a little while so he could lay his mother to rest.

He looked at the thousands of henchmen that were tied up in the garden. The LAKN9 would deal with them. The cavalry had arrived and was doing the things that needed to be done. Brentt walked over to the cage that held Megistus and looked at him, as an onlooker observed a caged tiger. The Thrice Magician stared blankly at the detective. No words passed between them. Brentt Williams' job was done for the day.

CHAPTER 39: The Gods Are In For A Fight

The seventy-foot tall Wretch #100, four Leviathans and four Behemoths landed on the temple planet of Atomos with several loud sonic booms. They arrived in a grove that contained lots of trees and nesting birds. Everything was destroyed at the advent of the uninvited visitors.

The Gods were assembled around the cages that held the captured Leviathan and the Behemoth. When they heard the commotion behind them, all of the Gods stood in disbelief at their unexpected guests. The two prisoners rejoiced at the show-stopping arrival of their friends. They issued a loud roar as their saviors faced the mighty Gods.

Technon and Heddonna, who were still behind the cage, released the tail of the Leviathan. They discreetly looked at the nine interesting guests. Technon grabbed Heddonna's hand and enveloped both of them in an invisibility bubble.

"Quick, send out an embodiment so that the creatures don't realize what is happening. I'll do the same," said Technon.

In a split second, it was done and a Technon and Heddonna came out from behind the cage and stood with the other Gods.

"What are we going to do? These guys are powerful. There are nine of them and eight of us," remarked the Heddonna, which was in the bubble.

"They probably came for their friends. They'll make a play for the cage," said Technon. He furrowed his brows, as he thought hard.

"What if we set a trap next to the cage?" suggested Heddonna.

"That sounds like a plan, maybe a couple of cannons?" Technon put forth.

"We should get started on them," she prompted with a smile.

"Let's do this," he said. They shared a knowing look and quickly set to work on a plan they hoped would work.

CHAPTER 39

"Surprise!" yelled Wretch #100, as he saw that the mighty Gods stood in disbelief at their arrival. A great redwood tree was in his way, so he uprooted it and threw it at the feet of the Gods. All nine intruders stomped forward, as energy and power crackled around them. The surrounding flora and fauna of the temple planet of Atomos were disregarded by the monsters.

"Give us our guys and you will not have any of your guys beaten down. Four of you have already seen our might. Do not make light of this situation," warned Wretch #100.

"Whom might we have the pleasure of addressing?" asked Atomos.

"I am Wretch," he said, as he gave no further information.

"Nothing is everything and everything is nothing. All is one and all are nothing," chanted the Leviathans and the Behemoths, both in the cage and outside.

"What do you want? Why did you attack some of our own?" asked Atomos above the chanting.

"We were there on business. None of yours though," spoke Wretch, as he spied the cage in which Anthraxis was incarcerated.

"You dare speak to the King of the Gods in that manner?" chided Galaxyia.

"I speak how I want to whom I want," Wretch flatly said.

"I am assuming you are here to get your friends?" asked Detrimentus, as he stepped forward.

"That is a very good assumption. Looks like there was some sense knocked into you from last time," smirked Wretch.

"I assure you, that it will not be as easily done this time around!" Cosmica said stoically, as she laid a hand on Detrimentus' shoulder.

"I am afraid we cannot allow you to get to them. Tell us what we want to know or else there will be a lot of violence," answered Technon.

"I am okay with that," Wretch #100 smiled, as he flexed his arms and solidified himself. His pitch-black body bristled with powerful sinews and boldly cut muscles. "I call dibs on the King of the Gods," he said, as he teleported next to Atomos and launched a big right hand.

CHAPTER 39

Atomos shot a face full of lightning at the same time Wretch connected with the punch. It rocked Atomos, but the lightning did little to slow the entity, as he barreled on and tackled the King of the Gods. It was a good way to get the party started.

The planet heaved and buckled as it felt the power of Atomos, the Gods and their opponents. It cringed in anticipation of the ensuing conflict but could do little to stop the Armageddon that had already started.

Detrimentus spied a Leviathan that moved close to him and sent a meteor in its direction. It knocked three of the heads, but there were still five more he needed to contend with. The meteor landed in a field filled with idyllic sceneries and the most fragrant flowers unimaginable. However, in an instant, that tranquil picture, fit for a postcard, disappeared. In its place was an aftermath of death and destruction. Detrimentus quickly followed his attack with some punches and kicks that seemed to go nowhere, fast.

Cosmica chose a Behemoth as her dance partner and went in for a high kick, which connected. She continued with a barrage of punches and knees to the hardened abs of the monster. Her anger fueled her resolve as she continued to hammer at her opponent.

Galaxyia saw a Behemoth as he snuck up to his comrades' cage and stopped him in his tracks with a wave of lightning and ice. The ice tore up the grassy ground. The lightning set fire to the green forest and surrounding area. She produced a petrified stone club and started to beat down the monster. Sounds of stone hitting flesh scared animals from their home among the Gods.

Archituria learned from last time and materialized a shield and a short sword in her hand, like the one that Technon gave her on Earth. She looked into the eyes of the oncoming threat and pushed forward. She blocked a big right hand from her Behemoth opponent with her shield and slashed at him with her blade. She followed it up with a torrential barrage of thrusts that took her opponent aback.

Caddeussus took to a Leviathan. He teleported behind him and kneed the giant in the back. He used his powers to create a giant chain, which he wrapped around the great creature's heads. However, Caddeussus' idea was short-lived as a Behemoth came from behind and punched him in the back of the head.

The Behemoth that nailed Caddeussus, turned around and saw Technon with a Leviathan. He went to its aid because, it just so happened, that they were the same two that fought with Technon previously. The Behemoth went in for a double team but received a surprise instead. Technon had calculated his move and teleported an embodiment that dropped from the sky and landed on him. Technon shot a face full of lava that momentarily blinded the mighty Behemoth.

Heddonna was stuck with a Leviathan. All eight heads wanted to give her toothed kisses on the cheek and a razor-sharp, claw-filled hug. She denied him that honor as she picked up a nearby throne and bashed the beast over a few of its heads. She continued her torrential barrage as it retreated a few paces. Soon, the beast and the Goddess found themselves in a lake that had a myriad of aquatic creatures. They tried to crawl, swim, and run away from the action, but lots of them died in the process.

One of the heads of the Leviathan whipped at her legs, but she sidestepped it and managed to get a knee over it. The feisty Goddess submerged it in the water and held it there, trying to drown the head. One of the huge Leviathan's tails swatted her and disabled that idea.

Anthraxis looked antsy in his cell as he saw what was happening. The pristine temple planet of Atomos, which had all the life in the entire universe, was being destroyed. However, the foreverum foundations of the planet held amidst the worsening chaos.

Wretch #100, the Leviathans and the Behemoths went toe to toe with the Gods. Punches and kicks were traded like baseball cards and everyone received a fair deal. A Behemoth managed to sneak away from the fray and made its way to the cage that held Anthraxis. He opened it discreetly and bounded away, back to pummeling the God of Technology. Anthraxis did not know what to think about this new development and hesitated to exit the cell.

CHAPTER 39

Atomos noticed the action and was momentarily distracted. Wretch managed to kick him in the abdomen a few times. The King of the Gods fell to his knees in pain before Wretch #100.

"That's right. On your knees before me," snickered Wretch.

He jumped back and from his hands, produced a powerful ball of energy and blasted the King of the Gods. The blast sent Atomos flying into his throne and momentarily distracted the other Gods.

Wretch then teleported to the cage, which held his underlings and pried the locking mechanism open. The two creatures freely walked out of their prison cell and their roars of joy resounded on the temple planet of Atomos.

Just then, a veil dropped and eleven God Breaker Cannons appeared out of nowhere, with the unwanted visitors in their crosshairs. They were a hundred feet long and thirty feet tall with bullets the size of trucks. There was the standard God Breaker Cannon logo spray-painted on the side of the weapons.

"Gods, get out of the way!" Technon and Heddonna yelled in unison, as they fired the great cannons.

A volley of supercharged energy balls burst forth from the cannons as they honed in on their targets. A couple of the monsters sidestepped the blast, but they did not realize that it was life-seeking. The blast struck a home run on the return trip. All of the intruders were enveloped in a blinding flash that rocked the planet. It also destroyed any little life that had managed to survive the desecration of Atomos' temple planet.

When the dust settled and the stench of burning flesh subsided a little, the bodies of five Leviathans and five Behemoths were knocked down, but they still posed a threat. Technon looked at the beasts and wondered how they could have survived such a powerful blast. Wretch, on the other hand, survived and was ready to kick real hard.

All of the Gods looked at each other in amazement as Technon and Heddonna amalgamated themselves. The Gods' might was challenged on their home court. Everyone needed to step up their game. They ran the universe together, but everyone would have to work together in order to succeed.

CHAPTER 39

Thinking fast, Technon erected a barrier over Wretch and the beasts. He knew that it would not hold, but gave them enough time to formulate a plan.

"Everyone, we need to work as a team," rallied Technon. "These guys are getting the upper hand on us."

"You just blasted them and they are still coming!" voiced Caddeussus.

"Atomos, I have an idea, but it will take time," said Technon.

Atomos paused for a minute and took a look around his temple planet. His world was crumbling before his eyes. He hated the fact that he did not know what needed to be done.

"What is your plan?" he said reluctantly.

"Cosmica, make a black hole. Galaxyia and Archituria, make your galaxy and sun, but condense them down. Make them about the size of a comet. Caddeussus, you help Galaxyia, Cosmica, and Archituria condense their creations. Detrimentus, since you were in a fight with Wretch, you know how he moves. You will be the bait to lure him to the black hole. Anthraxis, I know they unlocked the cage for you. Come out and fight with us," said Technon, as he turned to Anthraxis.

He lazily came out, "I don't know why they did that."

"I don't care at this point," Technon paused and looked at the shield on which the creatures pounded. It could not hold out much longer against their might. "I need you to fight alongside Detrimentus, against the Leviathans and the Behemoths."

"Not going to happen," Detrimentus said stubbornly. "I still think he is in league with the creatures. Why else would they let him out?"

"I am not in league with them. I don't know why they did that," said Anthraxis.

"This is not open for discussion. Do it," said Atomos. "Carry on, Technon."

"I'll need to make some modifications to the cannons. Atomos, I need you to give them more juice. Heddonna, great job last time, but I need your help again. We are not going to blast the creatures, but this time, we are going to paralyze them so that the others can blast them."

CHAPTER 39

"I see, they would think to block this attack, but it would really come from the others," surmised Heddonna.

"Sounds good to me, let's get started," voiced Caddeussus.

"Better get to it, the barrier cannot hold out much longer!" exclaimed Technon.

The shield burst and out rushed eleven of the Gods' worst nightmares.

Detrimentus and Anthraxis multiplied themselves twenty-two-fold and set their sights on the incoming threats. Caddeussus, Cosmica, Archituria, and Galaxyia worked on creating their part of the plan. Atomos stood nearby the cannons that Heddonna and Technon tinkered with and fueled them with extra power from his mighty hands.

Anthraxis had managed to procure his Galaxy Cleaver Blade from the pedestal and now swung it at whomsoever he willed. It connected with one of the sides of a Behemoth and elicited a deafening scream of pain. One of the heads of a Leviathan, who saw his comrade in trouble, managed a very perceptive bite on the neck of Anthraxis. The other seven heads busied themselves as they tried to chew on Detrimentus.

The odds were four embodiments of the Gods to one intruder, but it was not even a fair fight. The Leviathans and Behemoths kept getting hammered and retaliated with three times the ferocity.

Technon looked over from his vantage point and saw the battle. Overhead, he noticed that the others were not done yet. He had to get in there and do something. He quickly formed the weapon with which he had faced the Leviathans and the Behemoths on Earth and armed himself with it. 'This should even things up' he thought, as he entered the brawl.

In the midst of the fight, eleven Technons armed with eleven swords, teleported into the fracas and carved up the invaders with surgical precision. None of the combatants expected this interjection.

Anthraxis and Detrimentus rallied themselves and redoubled their efforts to take the creatures down. Anthraxis swung his huge cleaver and sawed a hapless Behemoth in half while the others looked on in amazement for a millisecond. This created the opening needed for the other Gods to penetrate the defense of the monsters. Technon, in a flurry of slices and dices, had ripped apart most of the intruders with the combined help of Detrimentus and Anthraxis.

Wretch saw what happened and jammed a knee into the midsection of Detrimentus, whom he fought. Wretch #100 immediately concocted a super hurricane, made of lightning and fire, and ferociously drove back the defending Gods. Body parts of Leviathans and Behemoths littered the landscape. Unfortunately, Wretch #100, battered and bloodied, still stood. He looked at the parts of his teammates and laughed a giant, joy-filled laugh.

"Now we have a real fight! Before, I only toyed with you. You all shall see my true power," he bragged, as he stuck out his hands.

Two great, gaping jaws formed in his hands and stuck out wicked-looking, forked tongues. They gathered up the scattered body parts. His eyes rolled back in his head and his body convulsed in delight, as he digested the corpses of his dead underlings. He acquired a more foreboding appearance which caused the Gods to step back in horror. He sprouted two more beefy arms for a total of four. Instead of one head, he sprouted seven more, on metal-plated stalks with rows of spikes that trailed down his neck. Six wings sprung from his back and flapped with the power of millions of hurricanes and cyclones.

Wretch #100 took on the build of the Behemoth and the appendages of the Leviathan. It was a very unpleasant union and it got even worse. The four tails that sprouted from his back was the amalgamation of all the tails of his fallen comrades, five times as thick, five times as spikey, and five times as powerful. The bad news kept coming as his body size increased from seventy feet to two hundred feet tall.

All the Gods looked in unison from their respective areas at this improved threat and wondered how this was going to play out.

Eight big smiles crossed the eight super-ugly faces of the new and enhanced Wretch, who grinned with razor-sharp teeth at the Gods. All of a sudden, a shadow crossed Wretch #100's face, as

CHAPTER 39

a giant-sized Anthraxis entered the fray, wielding a giant-sized Galaxy Cleaver Blade. He had amalgamated himself and he looked enraged.

Anthraxis lunged at the eight-headed beast. He sought to skewer Wretch #100, but two of the mighty arms caught hold of the sword with lightning speed. Two of the Leviathan heads forcefully rammed into the chest of Anthraxis and knocked him back. The beast almost pulled the sword from Anthraxis' hands, but his grip held. Atomos, who saw that things were about to get worse, leaped into the mix and landed a big right hand on one of the heads of the beast. Soon, all the Gods but Technon and Caddeussus had entered the free for all.

'Damn, they are not sticking to the plan', thought Technon as he followed suit. He grabbed a throne and smashed it over one of the heads. He then teleported over to the cannons, which he and Heddonna had set up and primed all of them. "This would have to do," said Technon.

Detrimentus, Cosmica, Galaxyia, Archituria, Heddonna, Atomos, and Anthraxis all took a head and unleashed their anger upon the seemingly unstoppable Wretch #100. Only Caddeussus was left as he condensed the black hole, the sun, and the galaxy. He multiplied himself by three and concentrated on his work. Wretch's eighty eyes looked on, as the Gods unmercifully pummeled him from every direction, but he also dished out big hits with his goliath tails and razor claws.

Anthraxis did not get the chance for a kill shot with his sword because someone or the other was in his way. Surprisingly, Wretch maneuvered himself with unbelievable proprioception during the confrontation. Sometimes he even shielded himself with another God. Anthraxis was the only one that had grabbed his Contest of the Nine.

Atomos looked over in the direction of Technon, who checked on the canons, but it seemed like they were not done yet. Lightning flared around Atomos and his planet trembled under the duress as he redoubled his efforts to eliminate the threat.

"Get out of the way, now!" yelled Technon, as he was ready to press the trigger.

CHAPTER 39

Wretch turned two of his heads, just as eleven cannons fired at him from the direction of the God of Technology. He tried to block the assault, but it froze all of his appendages, immobilizing him. Now, he was at the mercy of the Gods. He saw the destruction that this battle had wreaked on this planet and seethed that there was not more. He wanted to get his two captives and teach the Gods a lesson, but that went down the drain now.

Caddeussus launched the black hole which landed at the feet of the frozen creature. He felt it, as the hole hungrily tried to gobble him up. The molecules in his outer extremities compressed and warped within this energy grinding mechanism. He groaned in pain as Caddeussus, above, launched the other two creations that sealed his fate.

The compressed sun landed first and seared already burned skin. It filled the nostrils of everyone there with the disgusting odor, including Wretch #100. The compressed sun enveloped him and boiled his blood. There was nothing the creature could do but endure this horror, immobilized.

The weight of the created galaxy crushed him and added to the already overbearing weight that pushed him further into the black hole. Both the sun and the galaxy were gobbled up with the supercharged Wretch in a trembling, violent shudder that quaked and rocked the temple planet of Atomos. *He vanished in a flash of oblivion, gone from the presence of the Nine Gods.*

Everyone breathed sighs of relief, as they looked at each other in stupor and wonderment. It never crossed their minds that they would have faced a foe that tested their mettle and pushed them on their home court.

"My fellow Gods, the foes were vanquished, thanks to the combined efforts of everyone here! Like in the care and the running of the universe, we have worked together and gotten past this problem," said Atomos, as he raised a mighty hand.

"Today is a day of celebration and I will mark it with a new creation! We shall make a new temple planet even more grandiose and fortified, than it was before. It shall teem with life beyond measure and it shall be a beacon in the darkness. It will showcase The Contest of the Nine in all of their splendors. The

~ 382 ~

mighty thrones that we sat upon shall be even more majestic than they ever were. It was all because of your actions today."

"Yes, UKSCOGSM Atomos. I think we all did very well today. I, myself was a little unnerved at the attack on your temple planet. However, knowing that we worked together, gave me hope," explained Heddonna, as she put her hand on Technon's shoulder.

"So much life was lost in the battle though," said Galaxyia, tearfully.

"It's okay. We can rebuild. I did not think that I would have created a black hole to destroy a solitary individual, but it happened," expressed Cosmica.

"I think a lot has happened that we did not plan on. Knowing that, scares me. It shows us our limitations in a universe that we helped create and preside over," Archituria wisely said.

"Yes, we have to find out who or what was behind this. Furthermore, we have to know if there are more of those things out there," voiced Heddonna.

"I vote we rebuild first. Then we find out more about these things. Rebuild, to give the Athlogoss Drones and the universe some hope. They cannot see us like this," offered Caddeussus.

"Well said. You are right. They cannot see the makers of the universe in disarray. It will dampen their morale," said Atomos, as he concurred.

All of the Gods put their hands together in a great circle and concentrated on one thing, to rebuild the temple planet of Atomos, bigger and better than it was before. The landscape began to form hills, valleys, lakes, streams, deserts, and forests. Animals and plants sprang forth from the circle of the Gods, like a torrent of life. Every kind of alien materialized exactly in the environment they inhabited. Anyone and anything that was, or ever will be created, took shape and formed upon the temple planet of Atomos. The temple itself got an upgrade, with the walls built thicker and more splendid. The lush gardens and hallways were more adorned with precious stones, metals, and works of art.

There was a new throne room added to accommodate the powerfully built thrones and The Contest of the Nine, which were displayed behind them. The temple planets of the others were seen from the overhead crystal clear ceiling that viewed the entire universe. When the Gods finished, they marveled at what their combined efforts had done. In addition, they removed the memory of the attack of the creatures, so that it did not mar the tranquility of the place. They saw that everything was very good.

"Detrimentus, you were brave out there," smiled Cosmica.

"It was a hard-fought battle, but I needed retribution for what happened. I felt like I got it. However, I still think that he had a hand in this," voiced Detrimentus as he pointed at Anthraxis.

"I told you all, I don't know why they did that. I don't know who that was," said Anthraxis defensively.

"Everyone, take to your thrones. Let us discuss the ideas that we have to offer on the events that occurred," spoke Atomos. Everyone did as he said.

"These guys were tough. They stood toe to toe with us. I think that we have nothing to fear from them again. That combined blast should have erased them from existence," put forth Caddeussus.

"What were they to begin with?" asked Galaxyia innocently. "They were not Athlogoss Drones for sure."

"The darkness inside of them was very great. Being the Goddess of Chaos, I was perturbed at the amount of disorder in them," remarked Cosmica.

"They seemed very organized and gutsy to launch an assault on the King of the Gods. I still haven't figured out why they would want my planet though," remarked Detrimentus.

"Maybe they used it for raw minerals. There are some races that use up entire planets for minerals and resources. Part of the throne, on my temple planet, is made up of one of the crafts that did that," said Anthraxis.

"That is true. Did you see how the main guy, Wretch, ate up the others?" reminded Archituria.

"The main thing is that they were defeated. I am glad of that. I am glad we did it together," reinforced Caddeussus.

"I still could see no past, present or future for them while I examined them. You saw nothing too, did you not Atomos?" asked Technon.

CHAPTER 39

"I did not see anything," replied Atomos distractedly.

"We are still left with the guy in my Library. Where does he fit in?" asked Heddonna, puzzled.

"Do you think that one of the creatures was the guy from the Library? Maybe he tried to find out information?" asked Caddeussus.

"I don't know. I have never seen these things before. Well, besides when we went to Earth. I found no indication that the Library guy was one of those things. But there is no way for me to know," Heddonna said, as she shrugged her shoulders.

"Atomos, you look like you have something on your mind. Do you have an idea?" asked Technon

"My fellow Gods, I believe I saw something like this before. Let me tell you about the time I encountered The Void," said Atomos.

CHAPTER 40: The End And The Beginning

Abaddon teleported himself to the wall, but he was in no shape to speak. He barely survived the battle with Moerdon and his team. He hoped that his masters would have mercy on him and patch him up a second time. They would have to, since he had brought them what they wanted, in his body.

The stench of putrid, burning flesh alerted his masters to his presence. A surprised Wretch #1 looked at the battered and mutilated body of his underling and smiled a coldly wicked smile. He placed his foot on the body of Abaddon and pulled out the object of his desire. Abaddon shuddered as the sword was ripped from his chest and a moan of agony issued from his lips. He floated listlessly in space as he awaited the kindnesses of any of the Wretches. Wretch #1 barely paid any attention to his underling, as he eagerly jammed the sword into the correct keyhole. The locking mechanism clamped down on it ferociously, as it signaled another lock opened.

"Wretch, numbers thirty through thirty-nine, can you please come and clean this guy up? He looks as though he got his butt kicked as he tried to obtain one of the Gifts of the Nine," yelled Wretch #1 to his partners.

Wretch #33 reluctantly came and picked up Abaddon, shaking his head as he did so. "We have to stop meeting like this, man. It is getting old. We gave you hycolium wings and a planet buster cannon and this is what happened?"

"They were very strong," mumbled Abaddon, as he slipped into unconsciousness.

"Make him more powerful. Upgrade his sword too. We'll need all the help we can get," said Wretch #1 as he turned back and examined the wall, with all of its special locks. "The Legs of Anansi, the Gadha of Gilgamesh, Pel 6 and now, The Vengeful Covenant Breaker of the Heavens sword. Four down and lots more to go. This is going to take a while," he said out loud, as he looked at the wall.

Wretch #2 came up to Wretch #1 and excitedly broke him away from his reverie. "We found something that might be useful. Have a look at it." Wretch #2 put the object in Wretch #1's hand.

Wretch #1's day got a lot better as he looked at the object in his hand. It was very shiny and made of Foreverum, the metal of the Gods. It had a piece of an inscription, 'UKSCOGSM:'. Wretch #1 knew exactly what it was. It was a piece of Atomos' diadem of Godhood. The energy it contained was phenomenal. It held part of the powers of the other Gods as well. *It must have broken off during the confrontation with his master. Looks like his fortune was about to change.*

The spirit of Jacques Von Blutdruckt Gemacht, also known as The Immortal Count, walked among the destroyed ruins of his Palace of Palaces and Castle of Castles. He saw when the detective had set fire to his corpse. He saw when Brentt's friends teleported out of the way before Brentt had brought the house down. He saw when Brentt took the embalmed remains of his 'mother'. He saw when he encountered the caged Megistus.

The LAKN9 had taken the captives away and the Count had immediately started to do what he needed. It was all part of his plan. *His spirit had thrown off the chains of his body and now, he fully tapped into the power of the universe.* He would rebuild everything better than ever. He had started to rebuild his body, better than ever. He would get the answers to the questions that he had. Who were Theo and Asheley? Why were they not in the Akashic Records Library? What was in John?

The Count saw a rabbit that lurked around the rubble and he was curious as to its intentions. The rabbit was no ordinary rabbit, it was a disguised Megistus. He had quickly switched bodies with one of the henchmen and turned himself into a rabbit and avoided detection from everyone. Now, he searched for something. Megistus transformed back to his original human form and scavenged around the rubble.

Megistus was still aghast at the power displayed by Brentt and his friends. Brentt seemingly killed the Count. Asheley just humiliated Megistus in front of his opponents. She threw him around like a rag doll and took away his toys. Not to mention, Theo fought the King of the Demons like it was nothing. He could not believe that they sent his creature collection back to their plane of existence. His only lead on more power was to get a sample of the black sludge, which he had managed to hide away from the eyes of everyone.

"It should be here somewhere," mumbled Megistus to himself, as he sifted through the rubble with his powers.

He used his telekinetic abilities and moved some large stones. He finally found the small vial of the sludge that was extracted from John. It was a piece that Theo and the others did not get. The dream of ultimate power was in his hands, as he lovingly gazed at the unknown substance. The thing that gave John power and not even known to the spirits, was his. The Count was out of the way, courtesy of Brentt Williams. Jacques should have killed Brentt when he had the chance and he paid for his mistake with his life.

Megistus would learn from the Count's mistakes and build upon them. Ultimately, he would have to bring down the detective and the others. *One goal at a time is all it takes.* Soon, he would take his rightful place among the most powerful men on earth.

"Tris Megistus Tris Magnificus Nebuchadnezzar, I knew that my faith in your failure and treachery were not misplaced. Again, you have managed to bring me more disdain and regret of my employing your person into my service. Your ineptitude knows no bounds and equally as irrefutable, is your penchant for impertinence," the voice of the Count chided, from seemingly thin air.

"Master, is that you?" asked Megistus scared, as he looked all about him.

"It cannot be anyone else!" the Count said, as he produced a shadowy figure that appeared in front of Megistus.

CHAPTER 40

"How is it that you are present? I thought detective Williams killed you. I heard him talking about your death with other operatives," offered Megistus.

"I cannot be stopped or curtailed that easily. My powers are beyond the comprehension of most, save for the few Gods that rule the universe."

"This destruction must be avenged. I will have his head on a silver and gold platter studded with precious stones. It will be submitted as an offering to you," said Megistus as he tried to convince himself.

"While that is an appealing and somewhat hollow expression of your worthiness, I will not have it. The detective must think that we are defeated, so that we may yet work from the shadows," the Count said, as he appeared more solidly, but still as an apparition in front of Megistus.

"What shall we do?" asked Megistus timidly.

The Count's spirit moved over to where he lived his last moments. He moved the rubble that covered his newly formed body. He had worked incessantly day and night since the LAKN9 operatives left. His new body was beyond the epitome of perfection, beyond anything any mortal had ever seen. It was the body worthy of a God.

He had formed it from the remains of his corpse and his estate. His bones were crafted out of the strongest hycolium possible. Muscles, sinews, and ligaments abounded, as they were covered with heat resistant skin. Skin cells had cellular walls sprinkled with bits of hycolium. His body was fed with veins and arteries that were as voluminous as the Nile and Amazon rivers. *Sacred Geometric* symbols were emblazoned upon every cell in his new body and even built into the very fabric of his existence. The Count used all of the enigmatic and arcane knowledge in his Library, which had never seen the light of day and constructed his new body.

Megistus looked on in fascination as the spirit of the Count took hold of his new body and pulled in his first breath with a great heave of his mighty chest. The Immortal Count had resurrected himself.

CHAPTER 40

The power crackled and emanated from the Count as he rose from the grave and stood before Megistus. He was alive and in better form than he had been before. The Thrice Magician quaked with terror as the Count stood before him.

Megistus bowed submissively before the Count and offered the last bit of sludge to him. Megistus' dreams of ultimate power had eluded him once again. Suddenly, a small voice as of many people mumbling, spoke in the stillness.

"Follow me and I will give you more power than the Gods themselves."

"More power than the Gods themselves? That is quite a claim," asked The Immortal Count, with no hesitation.

"I was present before the beginning. For before the beginning, there was nothing," spoke the sludge in a calm and even voice that spoke with many voices.

"That claim means nothing to me. Both my parents were demigods. Just talk from some imprisoned entity that wants to be released. I have heard grandiloquent speeches from beings that grant power and glory, but in the end, their actions were hollow and frivolous. Just how will you deliver upon it? Who might I say is willing to grant me that power? What is the price for such an offer?" asked the Count of the vial of sludge.

"I am the Void. I was before the beginning. I saw the creation of the beginning. Everything was created out of me. Even the Gods fear me. I can give you power that even the Gods cannot match," spoke the sludge with the voices of many people mumbling.

"Now we are getting somewhere," smiled The Immortal Count as he looked at Megistus. Even though the Count had just come back from the dead, he had a big smile on his face.

Catherine had called John when he failed to come back from the restroom, at the New Year's Day parade. It went straight to voicemail. A few hours later, she got a frantic call from him. He said that he had received word from his dad about an emergency. His dad sent his chauffeur and picked him up and that she could go home without him. He also told her, that he would keep in touch as soon as he got more information. Some hours passed by and she had not heard back from him, so she decided to call Theo to see if he had any news on John. It did not make sense for her to do that, but it was worth a try. She had no luck with Theo as well because her calls went straight to voicemail.

Consequently, she received text messages from John about his father being sick and that he needed emergency surgery. However, no actual conversation was had, because they played phone tag. A day passed with messages back and forth but no concrete direction in which Catherine could pinpoint John.

Katie had just been tucked in and was fast asleep. Catherine sat on the sofa in her living room and watched the news about some robbery that was thwarted by detective Brentt Williams and his team.

Catherine noticed that it was the same detective who had spoken to her about the Theo incident. She wondered what was going on when, all of a sudden, there was a quiet knock on the front door. Catherine sprinted fifteen feet to the door and pulled it open. There stood John, Theo, and Asheley. Catherine hugged John so hard that he felt his back crack.

"It's so good to see you guys! I was worried sick. I could not get a hold of you after the initial phone call, John. How come you did not call me back?" Catherine asked, worried.

"There was some trouble at the museum and we got sidetracked," said Theo, as he skirted around the issue.

"I was kidnapped by my dad. Theo, Asheley, and Frank Lin saw what happened and helped me escape. They called in detective Williams and he helped us out. The phone call was not from me," explained John.

"That's horrible, John. How did it happen? Why?" asked a worried Catherine.

"It happened during the attempted heist at the museum. My father wanted power in his own twisted way. Luckily, Theo and his friends came to save me," said John, as he nodded a thank you.

"He won't be hurting anyone anymore," voiced Theo.

CHAPTER 40

"Does this mean that things are cool between you guys?" asked Catherine innocently.

"It is okay for now. How is Katie?" asked Theo.

"She is fine, I just put her to bed," said Catherine. "She was asking when John would come home. She thought that he went to find Theo so that we could all have ice cream together."

Theo smiled generously at the kindness of his little girl. "Maybe someday. Maybe someday it will happen. Now is too soon, though. We have to be thankful for what we have right now. All of us have been through an ordeal. Take a five and then we'll go from there."

"Yes. We have to think about planning that party we talked about," said Asheley cheerily, as they turned to go.

They walked outside and as Catherine closed the door behind them, Theo and Asheley teleported home. They took a much-needed shower and felt very relaxed after a hard and interesting time. He wanted to order pizza, but Asheley stopped him.

"We don't need to. We should make homemade pizzas," she suggested.

"Asheley, can you eat stuff now? I know that you did not before," asked Theo.

"Since our adventures in the Library, I can do many things. I can eat now and I am partially biological in a sense," she cheerily said. "You can do many things as well. We will do them together."

"I didn't really think that eating was really high on your to-do list when you upgraded yourself," remarked Theo.

"I know that you love to cook. I would love to enjoy food with you and be able to taste all of the wonderful things that you make. Whenever I prepared food, it was from a recipe but, I was never able to ingest it," she stated.

"I don't think we have the ingredients to do that. We might have to go to the store. Besides, it takes a long time to make," offered Theo.

"Not the way that we will do it," Asheley said, as she raised her hands and concentrated.

Soon, a light mist surrounded her as the molecules and atoms in the air clumped together. The elements present in the air, formed the building blocks for life as they were bent and twisted into the ingredients which made up the pizza.

"Join me Theo, and let us make love in the kitchen. The outcome would be pizza," Asheley laughed.

"You got it," smiled Theo. He concentrated and moved the ingredients around to form a perfectly round and exceptional looking pizza.

"Let us heat it up with the power of our minds," prompted Asheley, as they both concentrated. Soon, the smell of hot, freshly baked pizza filled the air without the oven being turned on.

They delightedly bit into the pizza's warm, gooey goodness. It satisfied their pallets and appetite. Asheley had the biggest smile on her face as she enjoyed every bite. The melted cheese ran from her beautiful lips to the delicious slice, as she tried to herd it into her mouth. When the whole pizza was finished, there were no dishes to do. Theo could get used to this, stuff being pulled out of thin air.

"Theo, I love you very much. I cannot literally imagine life without you," said Asheley with a smile.

"I love you too, honey. I don't know how you entered my life. However, I am glad that you did," returned Theo. His arms encircled Asheley, as he went in for a huge squeezing hug and wet kisses, which she happily returned.

Suddenly, the television turned on to the evening news in the living room. Four distinct voices were heard as they conversed with each other. Theo and Asheley looked at each other and peeked around the corner. They saw four ladies that made themselves quite at home in the living room. They took no notice of the lovebirds in the kitchen.

"Let's turn invisible and see what's up," whispered Theo into Asheley's ear.

"That sounds good," she said and did exactly that.

They walked softly into the living room to observe their uninvited guests. Theo thought that it was a congregation of the most beautiful group of women he had ever seen, since Asheley and Catherine. He wondered why they were here.

CHAPTER 40

"Hey Theo, we could smell that cologne of yours. If you are doing invisibility, do no smell too," remarked a buxom blond who sat on the love seat, as she looked at the news.

"That cologne does smell great, but she is right," offered a brown-haired beauty, who sat on the sofa.

Theo and Asheley uncloaked and looked at their seated guests. They all stood up and stared back at them. Tears welled up and streamed down their eyes, as all four tried to keep their composure.

"Who are you guys? Why are you here?" asked Theo, as Asheley got into an attack stance.

"Hey take it easy. If we wanted to hurt you, we would have. Let's introduce ourselves. I am Aerica. She is Elainney. The blond is Raechellee and that is Alexyia," said a red-haired woman.

"First, I wanted to apologize for shooting you," said the blond Raechellee timidly.

"You shot me? Why? Did you come to rob me?" asked Theo.

"No. I had to make sure that you were the person that we were searching for," explained Raechellee.

"You could have just asked," said Theo.

"Okay. Why were you looking for Theo?" asked Asheley tensely.

"We are here because we knew him a long time ago. Not like 'went to high school' know him, but a way longer time than that," explained Elainney.

"I hope the toiletries were okay? How did you like the food that we prepared for you?" asked Raechellee, still with the pleasantries.

"I actually enjoyed it. Thank you. How did you get past Asheley?" asked Theo.

"Sorry, Asheley. I had to put you to sleep so that we could do what needed to be done," Raechellee apologized.

"I assure you that it will not happen anymore," said Asheley sternly.

"Did you furnish my condo too?" pressed Theo.

"No, we did not do that. You probably did that yourself," stated Alexyia with a starry smile. She sat back down on the sofa.

"You mean I had the potential to make stuff out of thin air?" said Theo, quizzically.

"Theo, we just made pizza out of thin air and that is after we supercharged you at the Library. It is not so far-fetched to think that you had some innate ability to perform those actions before," suggested Asheley.

"Oh my God! The furniture, the playset, and Asheley, I made all of them unknowingly!" exclaimed Theo.

"Wait you made Asheley? Seriously, you made your girlfriend?" exclaimed Alexyia.

"Theo did make me. I am an Artificially Intelligent Robotic Entity. Well, I was. Now, I don't really know what I am anymore," explained Asheley.

"Asheley, no matter what you are made of, I will still love you," reassured Theo. The four ladies looked a little jealous of Asheley.

"Thanks," Asheley said.

"I can't believe I had those powers," Theo shook his head in disbelief.

"You wielded the sword at the museum, before going to the Library. Doesn't that say something about you?" said Elainney, as she sat on the arm of the sofa.

"You were very powerful and very special. Just like the rest of us," said Aerica. She sat down on the recliner and crossed her legs.

"You do have the power to be in multiple places at once. Perhaps while you were asleep, the other you made those things," suggested Elainney.

"We know that you have been to the Akashic Records Library. Did it turn out the way you intended? Did you find anything on yourself, Theo?" asked Alexyia.

"How did you know I was there?" asked Theo.

"Our adoptive father told us that you were there. He said that you were looking up stuff on The Immortal Count. We just missed you at the Library," said Elainney.

"The others wanted to track you to the Count, but I had a better idea," said Raechellee with a smug smile.

CHAPTER 40

"How come you did not seek us out at the Count's residence?" asked Asheley.

"Because you were busy saving your friend and stuff. You know, there were too many people around. I didn't want everyone knowing your business. Besides, where do people go when they finished what they had to do? They go home," Raechellee casually said. "So, did you find anything interesting?"

"No. I did not find anything on me. They did not have a file on me in Heaven as well. I still don't know why that is," said Theo, his curiosity piqued.

"Your story will not be found in any of the records in any of the multiverses," stated Raechellee.

"How come?" asked Theo, puzzled.

"You were once a great warrior that commanded a vast army. We were part of that army. In fact, there are a few more of us that made up an elite force of twenty-one loyal soldiers, followers, zealots, acolytes, whatever you want to call us. More importantly, we five, were friends," explained Raechellee.

Aerica sighed, "All of us are the same. We found each other and at last, we found you. We have searched beyond time and space for you. It seemed like forever. We are here to tell you that you were not created in any universe. *You were created outside of the multiverses.*

Message From The Author

Hello there,

Thank you for taking the time to read my book. I hope you were thoroughly entertained as you joined my characters on their thrilling adventures. I definitely enjoyed bringing their world into yours.

If you did, please leave a review on the purchase site. I would greatly appreciate it.

Be sure to look out for my next book in the series, where this exciting world continues to be unraveled.

Sincerely,

L.W. Cipriani Jr.

Author

www.ingramcontent.com/pod-product-compliance
Lightning Source LLC
Chambersburg PA
CBHW020637020726
47494CB00001B/236